## *Lee Library Association*
## **BOOK MARKS**

If you wish to keep a record that you have
read this book, you may use the spaces below
to mark a private code. Please do not mark
the book in any other way.

| | | | | | | |
|---|---|---|---|---|---|---|
| | | | | | | |
| | | | | | | |
| | | | | | | |
| | | | | | | |

D1399328

# ROASTBEEF'S PROMISE

Published by Smack Books.com
P.O. Box 10232
Fullerton, CA 92835

*JeROME*
*00036 9254*

Distributed by Emerald Book Company

For ordering information or special discounts for bulk purchases, please contact Emerald Book Company at 4005-B Banister Lane, Three Park Place, Austin, TX 78704, (512) 891-6100.

Design and composition by Greenleaf Book Group LLC
Cover design by Greenleaf Book Group LLC

Publisher's Cataloging-In-Publication Data
(Prepared by The Donohue Group, Inc.)

Jerome, David, 1965-
    Roastbeef's promise : a novel / David Jerome. -- 1st ed.

    p. : maps ; cm.

    ISBN-13: 978-0-9815459-1-2
    ISBN-10: 0-9815459-1-2

    1. Fathers and sons--Fiction.   2. Voyages and travels--Fiction.   3. Cremation--Fiction.   4. Funeral rites and ceremonies--Fiction.   I. Title.

PS3610.E766  R6  2009
813/.6                                        2008909003

Part of the TreeNeutral™ program that offsets the number of trees consumed in printing this book by taking proactive steps such as planting trees in direct proportion to the number of trees used. www.treeneutral.com

TreeNeutral

Printed in the United States of America on acid-free paper

11 10 09 08   10 9 8 7 6 5 4 3 2 1

First Edition

10-21-10 23.95

Ingram

# ROASTBEEF'S PROMISE

### A NOVEL

DAVID JEROME

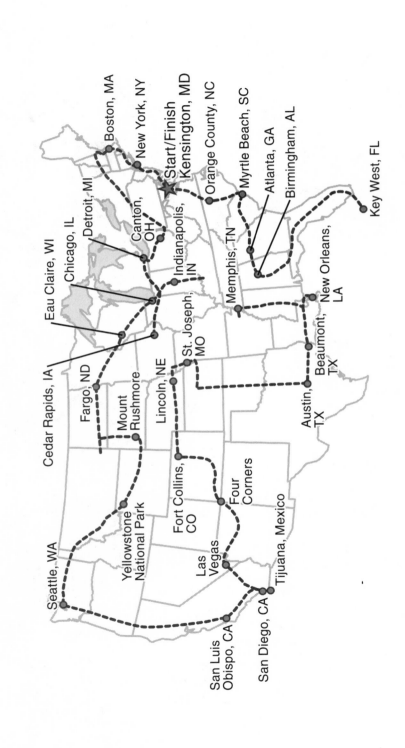

*Dedicated to Dapper Don, Jackie J., and JoJo*
*All three of whom have taught me about the*
*love between a father and son.*

# CHAPTER

# 1

"A CHICKEN IN EVERY POT!" Dad screamed out to no one in particular from his slightly inclined hospital bed. A young hospital volunteer battling a severe case of acne looked at him quizzically as she set down his dinner tray and then began to tiptoe out of the room, anticipating another outburst.

"The only thing we have to fear is fear itself," he blurted out in a louder, more assertive voice. The teenage girl, dressed in a red-and-white striped dress and looking like a gangly barber pole, paused a moment. She seemed obviously confused with my father's ramblings and answered tentatively, "Well, enjoy your dinner," as she left the room.

"Shut up, Mr. President!" a gruff voice stated from behind the curtain of the shared, semiprivate room. "I'm trying to listen to the TV."

"If my legs were not riddled with polio, my good man, I'd get out of this bed right now and kick your ass from here to Hyde Park!" said Dad, as he adjusted the invisible glasses in front of his cloudy and distant eyes.

It was hurtful to see what had become of my father. He had had a good build at one time, but now age and disease had taken their toll on him. He had been diagnosed with Alzheimer's disease a few months before by his doctor, who called Dad's condition the most aggressive case he had ever seen. My father had gone from slight forgetfulness to drifting in and out of reality, and then he'd deteriorated to the point where this lifelong Republican now believed he was Franklin D. Roosevelt.

My dad's name was Charles Lindbergh Hume. He was born on May 21, 1927, the same day "Lucky Lindy" touched down outside of Paris after completing the first-ever solo trans-Atlantic flight. His parents, convinced they were having a baby girl, never even considered a single boy's name, so with the newspapers full of the exploits of Charles Lindbergh, my dad was given the heroic aviator's name instead of the previously decided upon Peggy Lynn.

Years later while serving in the army, he had made the unfortunate mistake of telling this story to his army buddies, who, from that day on, always referred to him as Peggy Lynn. Sadly now, his name and the story that accompanied it had become a distant memory. His life memories had been lost.

As a seventeen-year-old, he had been sent to fight in Northern Africa and Europe during World War II, where he was among the liberating forces in Berlin in 1945. After the war, he returned to the states and attended the University of Minnesota on the GI bill. He remembered his university days as some of the happiest of his life. He used to say, "I was just happy to be someplace where they weren't shootin' at me."

Dad met his future wife on a blind date during his sophomore year, but tragedy soon followed when he learned that both his parents had been killed in a car crash. His mother had fallen asleep at the wheel and steered their '38 Ford into a pine tree, leaving Dad to raise his four teen-age siblings.

After dating for just six weeks, my parents were married in the St. Paul county recorder's office by a justice of the peace. They dropped out of college and moved to North Carolina to rear their instant family. After a few years of "flying by the seat of their pants" and "pickin' shit with the chickens," as he used to say, Dad's siblings were old enough to go out on their own. Mom and Dad then had two sets of twins ten years apart, starting with Paul and Minnie, who were named after Minnesota's twin cities, and then Mark and Karen, named after no cities at all. You'd think that raising two sets of twins a decade apart would be enough parenting for anyone, but years later they adopted me as the empty-nest syndrome set in.

"Time to check your blood pressure," a Filipino nurse said, walking into the room as if she owned the hospital.

"Never a moment's peace!" Dad retorted. "This is a day which will live in infamy!"

"Is this your son, Mr. Hume? He's good-looking, just like you," the nurse asked as she began to roll up the sleeve of his pajamas.

If he had been in control of all of his faculties he would have said something like, "It sure is. The acorn doesn't fall far from the tree, you know." Instead, he introduced me as his Secretary of the Interior, Harold Ickes.

All the years I knew him, he never told people that I was adopted, though it was obvious because we looked nothing alike. Dad was a short, stocky man with a full, round face and deep-set eyes. His thick, black eyebrows were so bushy they should have been named a national forest. He had olive-colored skin and a dimple in the middle of his chin that would have made Kirk Douglas envious. And he always looked like he needed a shave, even if he had just had one. I, on the other hand, am lanky with a fair complexion and sandy brown hair, and I shave about once every two weeks whether I need to or not, just to stay in practice. But he always introduced me either as "my boy" or his "number-three son." It might not sound like much, but for somebody who was passed around with the regularity of a flu bug, it always seemed to give me a strong feeling of security and inclusion.

I only lived with Mom and Dad together for about three years before Mom died in a freak accident at the nut plant. Dad had been a very successful businessman, owning a nut-packing plant outside of Winston-Salem, North Carolina. One day, while counting the inventory, Mom slipped on a catwalk and fell into a large storage vat of Brazil nuts. Investigators said she must have landed in an air pocket and sunk below the surface level. The more she struggled to get out, the deeper she sank. By the time the fire rescue crew got there, she had fallen ten feet below the surface and died of asphyxiation.

This was another tragedy for a man who had suffered so many losses in his life. We all took her death hard, but after forty-three years of marriage, Dad was devastated. He said he never wanted to see another Brazil nut as long as he lived. He immediately ordered the plant manager to change the recipe of the mixed nuts to exclude Brazil nuts and dispose of every Brazil nut in the plant.

A couple years passed and he couldn't shed the memories of my mother's death, so he sold the plant and our house and we moved to Kensington, Maryland, a suburb of Washington, D.C. I was thirteen at the time we moved and in my last year of middle school, and transferring to a new school was tough. I only made a few friends that year and, due to the school district's boundaries, I was assigned to a different high school than most of the other kids so the next year I was the new kid again. The whole experience was reminiscent of my early years, when I bounced around multiple foster homes, always starting over again and again.

A few years ago I asked about my birth parents and was told they were hippie-types who discovered that a love child interfered with their love-ins and peace rallies, so they placed me in state care. Some adopted kids obsess about trying to establish contact with their birth parents, and for them that's fine, but I never had the yearning.

My last foster home happened to be next door to the Hume's. My name is Jim, and as an eight-year-old I smelled their roast beef dinner cooking, knocked on the door, and basically invited myself to join the meal. I ate so much roast beef that night they started calling me Roast-beef. Over the years, the nickname stuck with me (what the heck, it beats Butch or Chip or Rusty). By the time I was ten years old, I was the newest and youngest member of the Hume family.

"I want to be cremated!" my father blurted out loud enough to echo all the way down the hospital corridor.

"Oh, Dad, don't talk like that. You'll be okay. You just get some rest."

"Listen," my father said in a stern voice. "I want to be cremated and I want you to sprinkle my ashes in all forty-eight contiguous states of the country I loved and served so well."

I tried to change the subject, but the president wouldn't have it.

"When the President gives you an order, you say, 'Yes, Mr. President.' Now do you understand?"

"Yeah, I understand."

He looked at me coldly with a snarl on his face.

"I mean, yes, Mr. President," I said formalizing my previous answer.

"I want you to promise me you'll fulfill my wish."

"Okay," I said, followed by a half-hearted, "I promise."

"Now let's talk about something else," I said with disgust in my voice.

I bent down to hug him good-bye. He didn't sit up so I couldn't get my arms around him, but when I pulled myself in, he pulled away. This was the saddest part of all. He would have never done that before. He hugged everybody: family, friends, employees, even acquaintances in town. A hug to him was like a handshake to most people. Fighting back the tears, I told him I'd see him again tomorrow. As I was leaving the room, another nurse entered. I heard Dad say, "Ah, the First Lady. Eleanor, you'll be the belle of the ball."

I visited Dad every day for two weeks, and he'd remind me of my promise. This man couldn't remember his name or what he'd had for breakfast, but he continued to remind me of my promise to sprinkle his ashes in each state. On one visit he said, "Don't sprinkle too much of me in Vermont. In four elections, I never carried that damn state." I went home and looked up presidential elections in the almanac and found he was correct. FDR never carried Vermont, but how could Dad in his condition possibly know that? The Alzheimer's disease had miraculously opened up something in his brain, making him some kind of FDR savant.

It was two weeks later in the middle of March 1996 (a fairly uneventful time after the O.J. murder trial but before the Clinton sex scandal), and the East Coast was basking in an early spring warming trend. It was the second semester of my sophomore year of college. I had suffered through two subpar semesters and was again struggling to get a C average to stay off the dean's shit list. Late one night I was reading *Daisy Miller* for an Introduction to Literature test the next day, when a friend stopped by, and the study session quickly turned into beer drinking and *Letterman* watching.

The telephone rang at 1:15 AM with the inevitable news I had been dreading. The nurse started in with her death spiel that sounded like she was reading from a card. "It pains me very much that I should have to be the one to inform you that your father, Mr. Hume, passed away at 12:35 this morning. If you would like to come to the hospital, we have grief counselors that you can speak with." She went on to give me condolences and blah, blah, blah. After a while it sounded like Charlie Brown's parents.

I hung up the phone, a bit stunned. I knew the news was coming, but there's something different between knowing that death is imminent and the cold, hard, smack-in-the-face reality of it. I sat down and sipped from my beer. My friend offered a bit of condolence.

"Sorry, man," he said. "You okay?"

"Yeah, I'm okay. I just think I'd rather be alone."

"That's cool," he said, grabbing the remainder of the twelve-pack and carrying it out the door like a football under his left arm. "I know how it is, dude. When we put my dog to sleep, I didn't want to talk to anyone for, like, a week."

I sat idle for a moment, unable to cry or feel much of any emotion. Everywhere I looked sparked memories of him. I went to the hall closet where our family kept our voluminous collection of photo albums. I grabbed a few and carried them back to the sofa, where I stayed up most of the night looking at pictures of family vacations, holidays, and parties and feeling a tremendous sense of loss not only about Dad, but also about the times captured in those photographs that were gone forever.

Around dawn, I fell asleep and woke up at noon. I hurried off to school for my one o'clock class. I knew I was ill-prepared for the test but hoped somehow to weasel my way into a passing grade. While I should have been taking the test, through tear-filled eyes I began developing a plan to honor dad's wishes by sprinkling his ashes in each state. As I worked on my travel plans, one-by-one the other students finished their tests, took them up to the professor's desk, and exited the classroom. Eventually I was the last student in the classroom, and the professor asked me for my paper. I had drawn a picture of the United States and devised a plan to quickly and efficiently visit all of the contiguous 48 states. I had figured how much it would cost me to make the trip but hadn't mentioned a word about ol' Daisy Miller.

Things weren't going any better in my accounting class, where I was crediting the debits and debiting the credits, quickly on the fast track to a career in the fast-food industry. My plan had been to wait until the end of the semester to take the trip, but due to my lackluster academic efforts, I decided to take withdrawals in all my classes (even the two I was somehow pulling passing grades in), and without further delay get on the road. The price tag of the cross-country ash-dropping trip was considerably larger than the available balance in my savings account. I decided I would scrimp here and there, sleep in the car as much as possible, and make it work.

My brothers and sisters flew in for the funeral, and we discovered that Dad had prearranged his cremation and funeral long before his diagnosis of Alzheimer's disease. It showed he either had great insight or that the former Eagle Scout had continued to live by the Boy Scout oath. He had decided on everything: white gardenia flowers, a silver-plated urn that looked like a tea kettle without the spout, a mix of religious and patriotic music, and a buffet table set up with Krispy Kreme glazed donuts. He even left a handwritten note to the mortician saying, "Anyone caught crying at the funeral should be asked to leave." He wanted a happy gathering of friends and family celebrating a life well lived.

Since Dad had done all the arrangements for us, the five days between his death and the funeral were spent relaxing with family and thanking friends and neighbors for their support. We received dozens of sympathy cards from every genre: religious, nature scenes, and cartoon characters. It's hard to believe people would send a cartoon character sympathy card, but we got several. My family had a good laugh at a crying Snoopy sitting atop his dog house mourning a fallen Woodstock.

We also received countless numbers of the worst-tasting casseroles imaginable. I now believe the only thing worse than the loss of a loved one is being one of the surviving relatives who has to eat all the sympathy tuna casseroles and three-bean salads. The tradition of making food for the grieving might have been appropriate years ago, but nowadays with restaurants on every corner, home pizza delivery, and convenience stores open twenty-four hours a day, this is a tradition that must also die; the mourners have suffered enough.

One day I mustered up enough courage to tell my brothers and sisters my plan of fulfilling Dad's wish. I knew that some, if not all of them, would think it was a stupid idea and was pleasantly surprised when two out of four liked the idea. Minnie and Mark thought Dad's ashes should be placed in Mom's crypt at the mausoleum. Minnie tried to filibuster the whole discussion with a long emotional rant, and when I couldn't change their minds with any of my high-school debate techniques, we agreed to split Dad's ashes. Mark's and Minnie's shares of the ashes would go to the mausoleum, and Paul's, Karen's, and my shares would go on the road.

The day before the funeral, Dad's obituary appeared in the local section of *The Washington Post*. It was a bit disheartening to read that a man who had given so much to his country, community, friends, employees, and family was given only three lines of tiny print wedged in between the obituaries of Gerald Hamsteil and Rodney Ivansauer and next to an ad for discounted mufflers. To add insult to injury, Dad's obituary contained a major typographical error.

---

Charles L. Hume, 68, a retarded nutpacker, died of complications from Alzheimer's disease. He is survived by three sons, two daughters, and six grandchildren. Funeral services pending.

---

The people at the newspaper agreed to reprint Dad's obituary stating that he was a "retired chief executive officer of a nut-packing company," but by the time it reran it seemed pointless. Dad was so unpretentious anyway that I think he probably would have gotten a kick out of being called a retarded nutpacker.

The funeral was on a perfect spring day. The air was cool and crisp with clear sunny skies. Occasionally a soft breeze would bring the faint sweet smell of cherry blossoms blooming down the road in our nation's capital. People arrived and we brothers and sisters had to lie about how much we loved their gruel-like casseroles. Dad's long-time minister, Pastor Emory Haden, eulogized him and then opened up the floor to whomever cared to speak. Several people stood and told stories about what a good man Dad was. Others shared tales of jokes and pranks he had played on people over the years. The laughter would occasionally turn to tears, but no one was ejected. Terrance Tyler, an army buddy who Dad called "T," told the story of Dad's experience during basic training in 1944.

"Peggy Lynn couldn't remember to call his rifle a rifle. He was always calling it a gun. The drill instructor, a real SOB, got tired of correcting Peggy Lynn and made him march bare-ass naked around our barracks. Peggy Lynn had his rifle in one hand and his penis in the other, screaming at the top of his lungs, 'This is my rifle, this is my gun, this is for fighting, this is for fun, Ol' Peggy Lynn never called his rifle his gun no more.'"

At the reception following the service, Mrs. Pringle, our neighbor whose breath always smelled like she'd just eaten a tuna fish sandwich, asked me where Dad would be buried. I told her "the Plan," which she thought was just awful. "Everybody needs a final resting place," she said. "Being scattered around the country like garbage is not a proper burial for a lovely man like your father." A few other people chimed in with their disapproval.

Nancy Jergen, Dad's holy-rollin' cousin from Macon, Georgia, was horrified that the word *penis* had come up during the funeral service and gave me a severe tongue-lashing for "letting those filthy army men speak." You can't please everybody, and I remember in other situations Dad telling me to "go with your gut feeling." My gut feeling was telling me to honor my father's wish.

The night before I left on the trip, my high-school lacrosse buddies threw me a going-away party. They bought a keg of beer and we played numerous drinking games on the kitchen table. Mildly hungover the next morning, I loaded up the Hyundai that Dad had purchased for me two years earlier in Washington at an embassy surplus sale. The car had previously been owned by the African nation of Chad and driven by their diplomat's errand boy. The car still had diplomatic license plates, which allowed me to park anywhere I damn well pleased. I strapped Dad's urn containing three-fifths of his remains into the front passenger seat. Before I pulled out of the driveway, I took a spoonful of the ashes and sprinkled them on the front lawn of the house I had shared with Dad for eight years.

"One down, forty-seven to go," I said to myself, as I shaded in the state of Maryland on the map I carried to show the trip's progress.

Looking back now it's hard to believe just how primitive this trip was. I got onto Interstate 95 heading north toward Baltimore with no cell phone, no access to the Internet, not even a AAA card—but as they say, ignorance is bliss—and crossed my first state line into Delaware within the first two hours. Rolling along the Delaware Turnpike, I scooped up more of Dad's ashes and threw them out the window. The heavy wind coming through the window blew the ashes into the backseat. I pulled over and sprinkled another scoop of ashes under a road sign that gave the mileage to Wilmington, Philadelphia, and New York City.

A few miles up the highway, I steered the diplomatic Hyundai across a bridge that spanned the Delaware River and came down into the Garden State of New Jersey. Soon thereafter I noticed the turn off for the Atlantic City Expressway. It took me a couple of hours to cross the green fields of south Jersey and arrive in the neglected slum neighborhoods of Atlantic City. I followed the street signs to the world-famous boardwalk, checking several times to make sure that my car's doors and windows were locked. I parked the diplomatic Hyundai in the giant concrete monolith known as the Taj Mahal parking structure, noticing there were cars with license plates representing nearly every state in the Union.

I thought about giving each driver a small clump of Dad's ashes and asking them to sprinkle them in their home states. It was just a passing thought, but I was growing tired of that half-assed, cut-every-corner attitude I had adopted during my college career. I decided right then that there would be no shortcuts on this trip.

I grabbed Dad's urn and carried it into the casino. I was instantly greeted by the incessant ringing, buzzing, and generally annoying presence of endless rows of slot machines. I wondered how cocktail waitresses could tolerate eight hours a day in here schlepping watered-down booze to blue-haired old ladies and chain-smoking twerps from Philadelphia.

I exited the casino and walked on the boardwalk where I'd walked with Dad several times before on summer vacations to the Jersey shore. An elderly woman carrying a plastic change bucket filled with nickels approached me on the boardwalk.

"Excuse me, sir, where'd you get that change bucket?"

"What are you talking about?" I asked the woman, figuring she must be confused.

"Your silver-plated change bucket. Which casino did you get that in?"

"It's my dad's . . . ," I began to answer truthfully, but then I figured, what's the point? "I mean, it's my dad's change bucket. He hit the jackpot at the Taj Mahal. In fact, Donald Trump gave him the bucket personally."

"Really?" The old woman's eyes sparkled through her bifocals.

"Sure," I said, "The Donald is a helluva nice guy. He's just giving money away down there."

"Thanks, kid," she said. She turned and screamed, "Myrtle! He got it at the Ta-a-a-j!" The woman's friend, who had been sitting on a bench massaging her feet, quickly stood up. The two elderly women waddled down the boardwalk arm-in-arm toward the Taj Mahal casino to claim their own jackpot and silver-plated change buckets.

I took the stairs that led from the boardwalk down to the sandy beach. I walked to the shoreline, took off my shoes, and walked in the water. The beach was crowded with teenagers trying to look grown-up. They were smoking and blasting their radios with no regard for the families sitting under large multicolored umbrellas right next to them.

After a fifteen-minute walk, I stopped and sprinkled some of Dad's ashes on the wet sand in front of me. I sat and watched the boats anchored just off the shoreline bobbing up and down with the ocean's current. Soon a jogger came by and his enormous foot made an imprint in the sand right where I had sprinkled the ashes. I wondered if Dad's ashes had been smashed down into the sand or if they were now on the sole of the jogger's feet. I briefly considered sprinkling more ashes on the sand. Instead, I thought of the jogger's feet as a free service spreading

Dad's ashes all over the Jersey shoreline like a bee spreading pollen around a garden.

As I strolled along the boardwalk back toward my car, I was stopped by a Green Party volunteer who asked me to sign a petition to protect the marshland by stopping the growth of casinos along the boardwalk. I signed the petition with one of my alias names, Serge Vienna.

"Vote Green," the guy said to me as I returned the clipboard. I just nodded and began looking for the hotel that was offering the best all-you-can-eat buffet.

"$4.99 All-You-Can-Eat Lunch Buffet" one sign flashed, while the others on the boardwalk tempted gamblers with similar offers. I ate at Golden Nugget's. After stuffing myself on prime rib, I slipped a few apples and rolls into my pocket and left.

Returning to the Taj Mahal to get my parking ticket validated, I found a large mob of people huddled around a slot machine. As I peered through the crowd, I saw the very same lady I had talked to on the boardwalk having her picture taken with a large, cardboard, publicity-sized check for $4,500.

I pushed my way through the crowd, saying the woman was my grandmother, a trick I had used successfully as a kid at Disney World to move through ride lines faster. When I got to the front, I asked the elderly woman what happened. She immediately recognized me.

"Oh, you're the young man from the boardwalk. I wouldn't have won this if it hadn't been for you."

"What did you win?" I asked.

"I won $4,500 playing Quartermania!"

"Congratulations!" I said with enthusiasm.

"I'm going to give you a reward. You sent us down here to the Ta-a-a-j, which made this all possible."

"That's okay. I'm just happy you won."

"No, no, I won't hear of it," she said, reaching into her purse and ripping a ticket out of her coupon book. "Here, this is for a complimentary breakfast tomorrow morning."

I worked up a half smile, trying hard not to show my disappointment. "Does this include coffee?" I asked sarcastically.

"You betcha, the works."

I took the coupon, shook the woman's hand, thanked her, and made my way to the parking garage. On the boardwalk, I put the coupon into the open guitar case of a down-and-out street musician playing and singing "Bad, Bad Leroy Brown."

I drove north on the Garden State Parkway, headed for the bright lights of the city so nice they named it twice. My greeting from Gotham, however, was delivered in stop-and-go traffic at the entrance to the Lincoln Tunnel by a swarthy man in the car next to mine. I didn't let him cut in front of me, so he flipped me off and yelled, "Nice tin can, ass face."

After my official NYC welcome, I drove through the tunnel, crossing the New Jersey/New York state line halfway underneath the Hudson River. I emerged on the island of Manhattan near the thugs, riffraff, and hustlers around the Port Authority bus terminal. At red lights, my car was swarmed over by squeegee men and homeless guys selling *The Street News.*

I crisscrossed my way through honking horns and jaywalking pedestrians, heading toward my friend Jeff's apartment on the Upper West Side. Jeff had moved to the city two years earlier to pursue his dream of writing, but so far all he had written were IOUs back to his parents.

Jeff was living in a five-story walk-up apartment building on the corner of 95th and Amsterdam over a convenience store and an Indian-food restaurant that caused the whole area to smell of curry. I found the apartment building easily enough but then spent the next hour and a half trying to find a parking space. I eventually parked ten blocks away on 106th and Broadway in front of a movie theater featuring current releases dubbed into Spanish. I grabbed my bed roll, Dad's urn, and my duffel bag.

The sidewalks were packed with pedestrians walking hurriedly in both directions, but they parted like the Red Sea as a lunatic wearing an unbuttoned long-sleeve plaid shirt and stained and tattered slacks approached, performing the umpire duties for a baseball game he was apparently watching in his mind. He lifted his right arm, made a fist, and screamed, "You're outta here!" When he passed me, like many other people, I turned to watch. The man stopped and swiped at his knees with a cupped hand, "Clipping #42 on the receiving team. Ten yards from the sight of the infraction."

"What a seamless transition between sports!" I muttered to myself.

I reached Jeff's apartment building and spotted his name on the mailbox, but there was no doorman, no intercom, and no way of entering the building without a key. "Jeff!" I screamed from the middle of 95th street, looking up at the open windows in the building. After I had screamed his name a dozen or more times, an elderly Hispanic woman came to her window, looked down at me angrily, and, without saying a word, shut her window.

*I guess I should have brought his phone number with me,* I thought. *That was stupid. What was I thinking?*

I decided to wait by the door until somebody came in or went out and then sneak in. I quickly learned that New Yorkers know this trick, and they don't take kindly to people sneaking into their buildings. I walked a few feet up to the corner and began looking around, trying to spot a public phone. A young black woman walked up, wearing a lime-green halter top that wasn't nearly big enough to support her large breasts. She asked, "You lookin' for a date?"

"No, not right now. Thank you," I said politely and walked away. I was able to find a pay phone down the block and across the street. There was a small steel cable with frayed ends dangling several inches below the base of the phone, where I assumed a phone book had once hung. I called the operator for assistance, but Jeff wasn't listed.

I decided to try again to sneak into the building, but this time I'd figured out a better scheme. I found an old pizza box in the trash and, pretending to be a pizza man, was able to finagle my way into the building. I climbed the stairs and found apartment 503W. Although it was nearly sunset, at 7:15 Jeff was just getting up.

"What's up?" Jeff said answering the door, still very sleepy. "I thought you were going to be here at six."

"Yeah, it really looks like you've been on pins and needles waiting for me."

"Well, at least you're here on a good night. A friend of a friend of a friend is having a party."

"And you're invited?" I asked.

"Sure, that's the way things work around here. So, did you bring any beer with you?"

"No. I'm the guest. You should be buying the beer."

"Man, I'm broke. My parents cut me off again."

"Well, my travel budget is about twenty bucks a day, so don't expect me to be buyin' all night."

"Don't worry, we'll get by. I always do. Get some beer at the Red Apple while I grab a shower down the hall."

"You don't even have your own bathroom?" I asked with amazement.

"Welcome to New York City, my friend."

I walked to the market and bought a twelve-pack of Black Label, the cheapest beer the store had. While standing in the checkout line, I noticed what looked to be a homeless man stuffing aluminum cans one by one into what looked like a vending machine in front of the store.

"You can only turn in ten," the manager yelled at him. "And don't come back here tomorrow."

The homeless man took his money from the recycling machine, walked over to the beer cooler, pulled out one sixteen-ounce can of Colt 45 and got in line behind me.

"Colt 45, the beer of me and Billy Dee," the man said. No one else said anything or even turned their head to acknowledge the man. It was as if no one else had heard the comment.

New Yorkers are good at ignoring weirdos, I realized.

On the walk back to Jeff's place I learned the importance of carrying beer in a paper bag.

"Hey, man, can you spare one of them beers for a Vietnam vet?" a man sitting on an apartment stoop asked.

Another man further up the block said, "How 'bout me lightening your load by one can, my man?" I liked the rhyme, but I'm not the beer Santa of street beggars, so I kept on walking with the twelve-pack intact.

I had brought Jeff's key with me, so I was able to open the front door without incident. I climbed the stairs to the fifth floor, which after two trips was already getting old, and wondered how the residents of the fifth floor could do this every day. I arrived out of breath and saw Jeff looking out the slightly ajar bathroom door.

"I forgot my goddamn towel, and you locked me out, you son of a bitch!" Jeff said in a playfully angry sort of way. I opened the apartment door, and he scurried through the hallway looking like he'd been caught in a thunderstorm at a nudist colony.

While Jeff got dressed, we drank beers and listened to a scratchy vinyl record of Sam and Dave. Jeff was tall and skinny with dark brown hair, and he wore eyeglasses with circular frames. One day in high school he made the mistake of wearing a red-and-white striped shirt, and a few football players started calling him Waldo. The combination of his hatred for the nickname and his volatile personality led to several fistfights during his high-school years.

"So where'd you get this crazy idea about droppin' acid in every state?" Jeff asked.

"Ashes," I stated clearly. "I'm dropping my dad's ashes in every state."

"His ashes?! What's up with that?"

"Hey, it was his dying wish, what can I say? You actually thought I was going to drop acid in every state?!"

"Oh yeah, my bad," Jeff sneered. "Dropping acid, that's really crazy. Dropping ashes . . . yeah, that's real normal. Happens every day."

We segued into a discussion of my travel plans and Jeff's writing career, but since both were still in their infancy, we reverted to talk of high-school days. We finished the twelve-pack and were comfortably numb enough to venture out into the Manhattan night by ten thirty. Before we left, I put a spoonful of Dad's ashes in a plastic sandwich bag and tucked it down into my pocket. We road the number one subway train down to the Financial District and mistakenly got off one stop too soon at Rector Street. We walked east for a few blocks, headed toward Wall Street. I had no preconceived ash-dropping locations for anywhere else on the trip, but I was adamant about dropping some of Dad's ashes on Wall Street. For decades he was a subscriber to *The Wall Street Journal* and read it religiously every day. He used to say, "I buy it for the pictures," the way a *Playboy* reader says that they buy the magazine for the articles. I thought dropping ashes on Wall Street would be a fitting tribute. Between the subway station and our walk to Wall Street we stopped at a small tavern called Clancy's Pub. There was no room at the bar so we sat at a nearby table for two.

Since we were headed for Wall Street, I told Jeff the story of Dad's reaction to Black Monday. On Tuesday morning, October 20, 1987, I came into the kitchen and he was reading *The Wall Street Journal*. I asked him how his stocks had done in the crash yesterday. He looked up and said, "My stocks went so far into the toilet that I'd have to call a plumber to look at my portfolio."

While gesturing at the end of the story, I accidentally knocked over the table's small globe candle, and some of the hot wax spilled out onto the table. When it had cooled, I peeled the wax from the table and rolled it into a ball with the palms of my hands. We finished our beer and continued walking for a few more blocks until we came to the corner of Broadway and Wall Street. It was now past midnight and America's financial Main Street was dark and forlorn. We walked down the street and saw a gigantic building with numerous support columns in front of it and the words New York Stock Exchange etched into the granite. In front of me was a large statue of George Washington. The plaque on the base of the statue stated that George Washington had been inaugurated on this sight in 1789. I decided this would be a good place to sprinkle Dad's ashes. I asked Jeff to hold the marble-size ball of wax I was still manipulating so I could retrieve the small plastic bag of Dad's ashes from my pocket.

"I don't want to hold this," Jeff said, turning up his lip at the ball of wax. "It looks like a disgusting ball of snot. Just throw it away. Hey, better yet, why don't you stick it on ol' George here."

"Why not?" I thought. I began mixing some of Dad's ashes into the wax. With a boost from Jeff and a stabilizing hold on the leg of the father of our country, I was standing on the base of the statue. I only came up to Washington's belt buckle. Jeff told me to make the wax into some crazy teeth or a stream of snot coming out of Washington's nose. I told him to keep a lookout for anyone wandering by, mainly the police, and I settled on forming the wax and ash mix into a quarter-sized fingernail for the index finger of Washington's right hand. The look and fit of the fingernail was so perfect that Madame Tussaud would have been impressed with my work. I jumped off the statue and we scurried off undetected.

We took the R train uptown toward Greenwich Village and got off at the Prince Street station. We walked around looking for the party Jeff claimed to know about, but nothing was going on. We ended up in Washington Square Park where college-aged kids were gathered in groups playing guitar and singing. Others were playing hacky sack, while a few drug dealers roamed the park, attempting to generate business by whispering, "coke, speed, cess" to people they passed.

The weather that night was humid and thunderclouds had begun rolling in. "We've got about five minutes 'til it's going to start pouring," Jeff said. We began looking for a bar, coffeehouse, or anywhere to get out of the storm. We could no longer be picky as the sky opened up, pouring rain on us. Jeff ran up some stairs into the doorway of a business building. I ran a distant second due to a slip on the wet street and was pretty well soaked from head to toe.

We joined three black men in their thirties who were standing in the doorway waiting out the storm by passing around a forty-ounce bottle of Olde English 800 in a scrunched-up paper sack.

"Man, that was a nasty spill. You okay?" one man asked me.

"Yeah, I'm okay."

"Here, have a hit of the eight ball," he said.

"No, that's okay. Thanks anyway."

"So what are you guys doin' up here?" Jeff asked.

"Just drinkin' and singin' and keepin' dry."

"I hear that," Jeff said, trying to fit in with their vernacular. "What were you singin'?"

"The Four Tops, The Temptations."

"Cool, I love Motown!" Jeff said, then started singing the first bars to "My Girl"—"I've got sunshine on a cloudy day . . . " Everybody joined in.

When we finished the song, they passed the bottle and this time both of us drank with them. Our newly formed a cappella group sang about five songs, and when the weather started to clear and the beer bottle was nearing its end, one of the men said, "Hey, how 'bout you fellas go buy us another bottle. We got lots more songs on the playlist."

"Okay," Jeff said, "we'll be right back."

We walked like we were going to the store and then took off running down a street of Brownstones.

"I know a bar nearby that has late-night happy hour food," Jeff said, because by then the munchies had set in. We walked into The Cadillac Bar, a bar and restaurant whose gimmick was allowing customers to write on their walls. The happy hour food turned out to be a basket of tortilla chips and a small cup of salsa. We devoured the basket like we'd never seen food before and then subtly swiped the basket of chips from the people sitting next to us at the bar.

"Hey," the bartender screamed. "Those chips are supposed to be a snack, not your dinner!"

We finished our beers and went to catch a subway. By now it was pushing three o'clock, and the trains were running infrequently on a late-night schedule. I slept on the floor at Jeff's apartment, but it felt as soft as a feather bed.

The next morning when I returned to my car, I found the backseat side window on the driver's side shattered, with tiny bits of broken glass in the street and scattered throughout the car's inside. I looked inside; several multicolored wires were hanging out of a hole in the dashboard where the car stereo had previously been mounted.

"Great, this is just great," I said with disgust. I picked up my things and placed them in the car, then patched the window using a piece of cardboard and some duct tape. Just then I noticed two policeman strolling down the street. They had stopped in the middle of the block to peek inside a topless bar. I walked over.

"Excuse me, but my car has been broken into," I said.

"What?" one of the officers said, still peering around the long black velvet curtain hanging in the doorway.

"Someone stole the radio out of my car."

"Did you see the person?"

"No."

"Did you have a 'No Radio in Car' sticker in your window?"

"No."

"Well then, what do you expect us to do about it?"

I just shook my head and walked back to the car.

It would be at a time like this that my mother would say, "This is wrong. Somebody needs to write a letter about this."

Battered but not beaten by the Big Apple, the diplomatic Hyundai and I got back on the road.

I CROSSED THE GEORGE WASHINGTON BRIDGE, taking the free tollway toward New Jersey. I drove northeast through Connecticut and Rhode Island. Dad's Connecticut drop was in a park in New Haven, where a yappy little dog in a red-and-black checkered sweater loudly registered its disapproval of me and my mission. Back on the Connecticut Turnpike, headed for our nation's tiniest state, I decided to do some reading from my Fodor's USA travel guide. I found the Rhode Island chapter (if you can call one page of information and three pages of stretching and embellishments a chapter) and propped the book up against the steering wheel as I drove. I'd discovered from recent trips that reading and driving is a good way to raise your insurance rates.

I decided to spend the night in Providence. For my first night's sleep in the Hyundai Hotel, I found a quiet residential street near Brown University. There was a large, overgrown tree, its drooping branches hanging down into the street, so I pulled into the middle of the branches thinking that they would afford me some privacy from my new neighbors.

I was walking around the Ivy League campus and the small business district searching for a place to scatter some of Dad's ashes, when I came across every ash sprinkler's dream, the holy grail of ash dropping: freshly poured cement. A twenty-foot strip of sidewalk had been replaced and was cordoned off with bright yellow caution tape. The edges of the cement had solidified to the dense consistency of year-old unwanted fruitcake, yet the center of the new sidewalk was still wet and pliable. I found a twig and scratched Dad's initials into the cement, sprinkled some ashes, and then prodded them into the cement mix. I celebrated another successful dropping with a beer at a local bar.

Around midnight, I headed back to the car and rearranged my things to maximize sleeping space in the Hyundai's cramped backseat. I fell asleep quickly, but soon awoke a bit worried that I would be discovered by the homeowners. I eventually went back to sleep, but my fear of being discovered by angry citizens stayed in the back of my mind all night. I woke at dawn to the noise of an occasional "tap tap" on the roof of my car. The frequency and loudness of the noise grew. I wiped the sleep from my eyes and tried to figure out what was happening. I wondered if I'd been spotted by homeowners who were now pelting my car with rocks to get the transient out of their neighborhood. As the rat-a-tat-tat continued, I brought my head above the window level to look for an angry lynch mob hell-bent on ridding their community of riffraff. I looked around the neighborhood, which was quiet. I got out of the car and looked on the car's roof to discover bits of berries and twigs that had fallen from the tree as the early birds had their breakfast.

I joined them by picking up some McDonald's and was finishing my last bite of Egg McMuffin by the time I arrived at the first tollbooth of the Massachusetts Turnpike. I pulled into the toll plaza. A woman of substantial size dressed in an official-looking uniform sat in the kiosk. Let's just say she got in line several times when God was giving out chins. She appeared expressionless, in a tollbooth trance that comes from breathing engine exhaust eight hours a day. The only sign of life she possessed—which kept her from being hauled off to the morgue—was that as each car rolled through the toll plaza, her left arm reached out to accept the driver's toll.

"Is this Massachusetts?" I asked.

"Yeah. Three bucks," the woman responded mechanically.

I handed over three dollars and then sprinkled some ashes out the window onto the road.

"Don't empty your goddamn ashtray here," she hollered, almost like a real person.

"I'm not. That's my dad," I said matter-of-factly, then drove away. I was heading for Boston where I had planned on spending the night. I stopped at a Howard Johnson's on the outer limits of the city to discreetly use their restroom and yellow pages. I looked up motels within the city, but decided on a youth hostel in the Alston section of town. I rented a bed for eighteen dollars a night in a room with two sets of bunk beds. The room smelled like dirty socks and was empty except for two backpacks on two of the beds. I set my stuff down on the lower bed of the vacant bunk, then seized the opportunity to read the name tags on the backpacks to find out where my rotten-feet roommates were from. One of the backpacks had souvenir patches sewn onto it from many of America's top attractions and a thin, tightly rolled, aqua-colored sleeping mat attached. The name on the tag was Matthew something or other—I couldn't make out the last name—but whoever he was, he hailed from some little sauerkraut village in Germany that I'd never heard of. The other backpack belonged to Ethan Owens from London, England.

I sat down on the bed and started my trip journal. In just a few days I had enough information to fill up several spiral-ring notebook pages. I wrote about the past two days and how I'd already dropped Dad's ashes in seven states with the stolen car stereo as the trip's only setback.

I laid down to take a rest before going out to explore Beantown. I had just about fallen asleep when my two roommates returned. I sat up and we all introduced ourselves, and although I felt groggy, I talked for a half an hour with them. They had spent the afternoon walking the Freedom Trail, seeing the Old North Church, Bunker Hill, and Paul Revere's house, and now they wanted me, the American, to fill them in on the Revolutionary history of the things they had just seen.

"You know," I said, looking at Ethan. "All I know about that war was that your guys wore bright red coats and marched in a straight line and our guys made 'em pay for it."

"Ah, we didn't want this dodgy little country anyway," Ethan replied with a smirk on his face.

Ethan was a business man in his late twenties. He had sold his part of a printing business in Britain and was spending six months touring the States. Matthew was twenty and was taking a year off from his university studies to travel until his money ran out. So far he had been to Australia and New Zealand and had spent nearly four months in the United States. The two of them had met through a flyer on the ride board at a youth hostel near Disneyland, and although they had significant communication problems, they had been traveling together for two months sharing driving time and expenses.

Neither had a car, but they had discovered car-transportation services. People don't want to drive their car to their new business or residence in another state, so they hire a car-transportation service, which in turn lures drivers with free transportation to the city where the car needs to go.

"We've crisscrossed the country in everything from a Winnebago to a Ford Fiero," said Ethan.

I told them I was going to dinner and they were welcome to come along. We road the streetcar, or the "T" as the locals call it, down to the Back Bay area, where we ate out on the patio of a coffeehouse that was featuring an open-mike night.

A steady flow of college students got up on stage and one-by-one read their poetry. Most of it was self-indulgent, whiny crap by upper-middle-class white kids who were feeling angst because they had to type their own term papers.

We all ordered a beer from the young, nubile waitress with a bare midriff and countless belly-button piercings. She asked to see identification from Matthew and me. I showed her mine and Matthew changed his order to a coke.

"I can't believe you have to be twenty-one to drink beer in this country," Matthew grumbled with amazement. "I've been drinking beer since I was fifteen years old."

"Well, I think they're pretty strict here because it's a college town."

After dinner, we walked back to the hostel up Commonwealth Avenue past Copley Square and the Prudential Tower and into Kenmore Square, where over the buildings you could see the light standards of Fenway Park, home to the Boston Red Sox. I briefly attempted to explain the basics of baseball to them to no avail. In fact, I had actually done better explaining my myopic view of the American Revolution.

When we returned to our room, another traveler had been assigned there. He was on the top bunk fast asleep completely in the nude. The room was hot and stuffy due to the unseasonably warm New England night, and it now featured a slight body-odor scent added to the dirty-socks smell. Ethan opened the window and door to air the place out. Nature Boy woke up just long enough to say what sounded like hostile words in some language that none of us could immediately identify. We tried to sleep, but with the window open the street noise was too loud, and with the window closed the heat and smell were unbearable. I tossed and turned all night in the noisy sweatbox, all the time thinking that a smelly, naked foreigner was sleeping on top of me. Something like that you don't factor into your trip when you set out. Around six o'clock, when complete exhaustion set in, I was able to finally fall asleep. Soon after that, the mysterious, stinky roommate got up, put his clothes back on, slammed the door on the way out, and preceded to rev the engine of his car for the next fifteen minutes until he finally drove away.

At 8:30, I went down to breakfast, which consisted of juice, coffee, breads, and jams. The hostel's dining room was filled with an eclectic group of travelers dressed in everything from pajamas to a suit and tie. I was greeted by an elderly gentleman with a "Good Morning My Name Is Percy" happy-face name badge attached to the lapel of his tweed blazer. He was dressed immaculately if you're willing to overlook the fact that the left arm of his coat and shirt had been cut off just below the shoulder to accommodate his broken left arm, entombed in a thick plaster cast.

"What would you like?" he asked me.

"A bagel, orange juice, and coffee."

While he single-handedly performed each task, I noticed many signatures in a variety of colors on his cast. "You've got a lot of friends," I said, pointing to his cast.

"Oh, they're all people from other countries who have stayed here. Thirty-three and counting," he said proudly, then added, "and I've only had it on for five weeks."

"How much longer do you have to have it on?"

"A couple weeks more. So where are you from?"

I started to say Maryland, then paused and tentatively answered, "Chad."

"Chad. Really?" he said curiously.

"Yes, I'm from the great African nation of Chad."

I figured at this point he'd whip out a pen and ask me to sign his cast, but he hit me with a follow-up question that left me standing there like a deer in the headlights.

"What part of Chad?"

"Are you familiar with Chad?" I asked, while hurriedly thinking to myself, "Please say no, please say no."

"Not too much, but I am a bit of a geography buff."

"Is the orange juice fresh squeezed or from concentrate?" I asked, attempting to distract him.

"Concentrate. Where did you say you were from?" he asked again as he reached for his handy world atlas.

"I come from the central area. It's a tiny village, I'm sure it won't be on the map."

"What city are you near?"

*Damn, he's got me*, I thought to myself. *Why did I say Chad? I don't know even one city in the whole country.*

"Concentrate, huh?" I said, as he searched through the atlas. "It's good. It could definitely pass for fresh squeezed."

"What city is your village near?"

"Uh, well," I paused, grasping for African straws. "We're not too far from Chad City." He had turned to the northeastern Africa page of the atlas and asked me to point out my hometown on the map. I was spared an immediate answer when two backpackers approached the serving table inquiring about herbal tea. Percy talked to them just long enough for me to study the map of Chad only to discover that there was no Chad City. There was a Lake Chad, so I planned to build my story around that.

"Now whereabouts is your home?"

"It's just east of Lake Chad," I stated, confidently pointing to the map. "We go water-skiing there all the time," I added, not leaving well enough alone.

"Well, isn't that somethin'? Here," he said, handing me a red Sharpie pen, "Would you sign my cast?"

"Dear Percy," I wrote. "When you get your cast off, let's ski Lake Chad. Your friend, Jim 'Roastbeef' Hume."

I felt a little guilty but rationalized the situation because I was driving a car formerly owned by real Chadians, so in a way I just considered myself an intermediary between them and Percy.

I returned to my room, showered at a shared bathroom down the hall, and left the hostel. I was warming up my car in the back when Edgar, the guy who checked me in, asked me if I'd done my chore. I didn't know what he was talking about, and he explained that every hostel guest has to do a chore the next morning.

"Would you like to sweep the breezeway, wipe down the breakfast tables, or strip the beds?"

"I wouldn't *like* to do any of them," I said. "I'd *like* to get on the road and get as far away from this stink pit as possible."

"If you don't do a chore, I'll have to put your name in the computer and you won't be able to stay at another youth hostel," Edgar threatened softly.

At first I thought, *Great, I hated it anyway*, but then I quickly realized I had a long way to go and there was no sense in burning my bridges in Beantown. So I caved to Edgar's demands, picked up a broom, and brushed off the breezeway.

I drove north up Interstate 95, which crosses into New Hampshire for twenty miles or so and gives you just enough time, to say, "Hey, I'm in New Hampshire"—but you better say it fast. Along the way I noticed the diplomatic Hyundai's brake warning light was on. I pulled over into the parking lot of a state-run liquor store, called "Live Free or Die Liquor." I put up the hood and, not being mechanically inclined in the least, began looking for one of the parts in the engine to stand up, wave a little red flag, and tell me where the problem was. Once the car's hood was up, though, it didn't take long for liquor-store shoppers to come by with a diagnosis for the car. A stocky man chewing on a cigar and who looked like he had just come from the racetrack noticed that the brake fluid was out.

"Here's the problem," he said with a heavy New England accent. "Your caw's brake fluid is leaking."

"What should I do?" I asked.

"There's an *Otto Pawts* shop down the road. Hop in and I'll give you a ride."

I opened the passenger's side door as the man picked up the assorted papers and junk that filled the seat and set them on the floorboard.

"Go ahead and put your feet on that shit," he instructed.

The man started his car and together we drove off. "Chaw-lee Paw-ka," he said, sticking his large hand out. "So where you headed?"

"Up to Maine," I stated.

"Oh yeah, what *pawt*?"

"I don't know. I'll probably just cross the border, take care of business, and get out."

"What business?"

"I'm sprinkling my dad's ashes in every state."

"What?!"

"See this urn? My dad's ashes are in here. He wanted his ashes sprinkled in every state."

"You're shittin' me."

"No, that's the truth."

"Come on. Is this a fraternity prank or something?"

"Nope."

"*Candid Camera*?"

"No, it's the truth. I'm spreading my dad's ashes around the country."

"Well, I'll kiss your ass! This has got to be the strangest thing I've ever heard of," Charlie said.

After a moment of contemplative silence Charlie asked me if I'd sprinkled the ashes in New Hampshire yet.

"Not yet. I'm trying to find a quality location. At first I was just dumping them anywhere, but now I want to try to find a special place if I can."

Charlie insisted that he knew a great place and offered to drive me there. I agreed when it looked like I didn't have much choice anyway. Charlie drove down a small country road through green, rolling farm hills surrounded by forest.

"My buddy has a great lake on his *prop-aw-ty* that would be a perfect place to sprinkle the ashes. I've sprinkled in the lake myself on occasion," he said with a nudge to my ribcage.

Just then a crop duster flew overhead, spraying the car with fluid.

"That no-good *bastawrd*," Charlie laughed. "That shit's going to peel my paint."

"Do you know him?" I asked.

"Yeah, that's my buddy whose farm we're going to."

"Cool," I said. "Do you think he'd take me up in the plane to drop the ashes?"

"Probably, but let me tell you, he's a crazy son of a bitch. I won't fly with him anymore."

"Why not?"

"Well, a couple years ago another *fawmaw* hired him to dust his fields and he asked me to ride along with him. We get about halfway done with the job and he *stawts* showin' off. He's doin' barrel rolls and loop d' loops and he clips a wing on the *fawmaw's* silo and the plane crashes into a field of soy beans. I was all messed up—cuts, bruises, broken *collawbone*—and that son of a bitch walked away without a scratch. You know what, he even had the balls to ask that *fawmaw* for payment for the part of the field that got sprayed."

"So you haven't flown with him since?"

"Nope. He claims he's mellowed, but you know, once bitten, twice shy."

We turned off the country road to the man's farm and pulled up to the farmhouse.

"Grab that hose over there. We've got to spray this shit off before it dries."

The plane landed and taxied up between the big, red barn and the farmhouse. The pilot climbed out and, laughing, walked over to where we were washing the car.

"That was a direct hit," the man exclaimed.

Charlie introduced me to Wes, the farmer/pilot. He was a middle-aged man with a thick, dark handlebar mustache and a tattoo of an eagle on his shoulder that read "Eagles Fly, Turkeys Walk." Charlie gave Wes the *Reader's Digest* version of my trip and my idea to drop the ashes from the plane.

"Sure, I'll take you up," Wes said cheerfully. "You gonna go too?"

"Hell, no," Charlie said. "I'm stayin' here on the ground."

"Well, kid, let me grab a drink and I'll take you up."

He reached for the flask in the pocket of his overalls and quickly tilted it up for a swig. "Let's fly, boy."

I poured a spoonful of ashes in my left hand and then crawled into the front seat of the open air bi-winged crop duster. Wes climbed into the driver's seat in the back and started the engine. We taxied down the dirt runway past Wes's John Deere tractor and his garden vegetables. Within a few minutes, we were airborne.

After a few minutes, I was able to stop being scared and actually enjoy the flight. I looked down over the farms, woods, roads, and small towns below. I thought about the sudden change of events. A half hour ago I was staring at a broken-down car in front of a state-run liquor store, and now I was flying with a pilot who looked like one of the Village People.

I was enjoying the ride so much that Wes had to remind me to drop the ashes. I extended my left arm out of the plane and fought to hold it there as the wind rushed against my arm. I opened my palm. A very small bit of the ashes blew away, but most of them stayed in the center of my clammy palm, having formed a quarter-sized lump of gray paste. Using my right index finger, I scraped the ash paste out of my palm and the clump fell to earth. Not exactly the picture perfect way I envisioned the ashes being released, but the end results were the same. I was one state closer to fulfilling the promise.

Charlie drove me to the auto parts store to get the brake fluid, then back to the state liquor store. He showed me where to pour the brake fluid and said, "Keep that stuff handy and check it every day or so."

He wished me well on my trip and even gave me his business card. "Keep this in case you get yourself in a shit mess."

He waved as I drove away, heading for the Maine state line. I drove to the shoreline at Kittery Point, parked my car, and walked down to the rocky shore carrying the urn. I stumbled and skinned my knee on one of the rocks and nearly spilled the urn's entire contents. Just that fast, the whole trip could have been over. I managed to keep the urn upright, but the lid fell off and was lost to the sea. With blood streaming down my leg into my white sock, I continued toward the waterline where I took the spoon and sprinkled the ashes into the water.

I walked back to the small seaside resort town. I decided to splurge and have lobster for dinner. I couldn't really afford it, but I justified it with an "Oh well, I'll scrimp somewhere else on the trip—when in Rome" thought. I went into a restaurant and sat down with the open urn on the table. I ordered lobster and the waitress sent me out of the restaurant to select my dinner. Outside was a large but shallow water tank with a few dozen lobsters in it. Hanging around the tank were the executioners: four teenage boys with bad skin and backwards baseball caps just waiting for tourists to select a lobster so they could toss it in boiling water. I pointed at a medium-sized lobster that was missing one of its antenna. One of the boys reached into the tank, grabbed the lobster, weighed it, and gave me a plastic number marker to identify my lobster.

"Did we get a call from the governor?" yelled the guy holding my lobster.

"Nope," shouted several of the other workers in unison, and then the lobster was thrown into a large vat of boiling water. The lobster's screams sounded like air being released from a punctured tire, but they grew more faint as I turned and walked back into the restaurant.

Shortly thereafter the waitress returned to my table with a bright-red lobster, a small wooden mallet, and a nutcracker. She tied a lobster bib snugly around my neck and said, "Let me know if you need anything."

I began pounding on the exoskeleton with repeated blows from the mallet. I followed that with a few squeezes with the nutcracker, which helped to expose some of the cotton-white flesh. I again smacked the lobster, but now I had the added enthusiasm of knowing that the goal was within sight. I slammed the mallet down across its back and hit a pocket of trapped water, and water shot out a side crack and splattered onto the cheek and glasses of the lady sitting at the table next to me. I offered her my napkin and apologized profusely. She was nice about it, but her crotchety old husband with a shiny chin from all the melted butter running down his face made a big deal out of it. The restaurant's manager ended up apologizing and giving them a complimentary meal for my overzealous crustacean attack. Once I heard that, I purposely leaned into the line of fire, hoping to be splattered when any neighboring table started the cracking process.

When things settled down I noticed a long green vein running down the back of the lobster tail. When the waitress walked by I asked, "What's the deal with this green stuff?"

"It's a delicacy," she said.

"Really?"

"Well," the waitress said quietly, "they make us say that. Between you and me, it's really lobster poop."

"Thanks for the warning." I scraped the digestive track off the meaty flesh before continuing to eat. At the end of the meal I asked the waitress for plastic wrap and a rubber band. She brought out some aluminum foil, which I placed over the urn and held down with the rubber band.

I asked the waitress if she knew of a cheap place to spend the night. She told me about some little beach bungalow that the owner rents out for real cheap but usually only by the week. I decided it was worth a try, so I followed her directions and found it. The old man gave me the once-over and wasn't very keen to the idea of just a one-night stay. "I'm going to have to clean the room and wash the sheets. It ain't worth it to me for just one night."

"What about if I wash the sheets and clean the room before I leave?" I asked.

"You'll still pay full price?" he asked. I agreed and paid him the nightly fee of eighteen dollars. The room smelled like Grandma's house, none of the furniture matched, and the nineteen-inch black-and-white television received only channel seven, and that was only when the rabbit ear antennas were forming a 180° angle. The shower walls had several flourishing bacterial colonies, and let's just say the toilet had not been "Sanitized for Your Protection." The room was a hole, but even with all that, it still beat sleeping curled up in the fetal position in the Hyundai Hotel.

The next morning I got up, washed and dried the sheets, and remade the bed. The room looked better than when I had checked in, but the old man still grumbled about my only staying one night. I drove through Kennebunkport, the summer home of former President Bush. I strolled down a business strip with a view of the ocean crashing against the rocky coastline. In front of one of the shops, a cute teenage girl was handing out free samples of the saltwater taffy they were selling inside the store. I took one and put it in my pocket for later.

I drove back across the Maine border, west to Manchester, New Hampshire, and then northwest on Interstate 89 toward Vermont. I hadn't eaten in several hours and there weren't many options in the middle of New England's farmland, but my hunger helped me recall the saltwater taffy. After being nestled in my pocket all afternoon, it was now in that indistinguishable, gooey, middle-ground condition between a solid and a liquid. I popped it in my mouth and started chewing. I was enjoying the free, tasty treat when all of a sudden, off came the crown on my back left molar. I spit the tangled taffy and crown mess into my hand and looked for somewhere to stop. Twenty miles later near New London, New Hampshire, I saw a road sign for an English pub called (I kid you not) the Crown & Goblet. I went to the restroom to try to separate the crown from the taffy and was soon joined by a jolly ol' bloke who used the pub's one urinal right next to me and splattered his piss on my leg. I grabbed a paper towel to dry my leg. "Sorry chap, I guess my aim's a bit off today," he said. "Just one of those day," I shied as I continued my taffy pull.

To compare the odor emanating from the inside of the crown to the stench of a decaying corpse would be an insult to decomposing bodies everywhere. I washed the crown in the sink and attempted to put it back over the weird-looking, yellow, ground-down stump my molar had become. People came in to use the restroom and there I stood in front of the mirror with my mouth wide open and my fingers down my throat, trying to reattach the crown. I would place the crown on the tooth, then give it a quarter turn if it wouldn't go over the tooth. It was like putting together a puzzle blindfolded. After ten minutes of adjustments, I got the crown back on, though it just sat on top of the tooth and I could easily jiggle it around with my tongue. I bought a steak and kidney pie to go, said "cheerio" to no one in particular, and left the Crown & Taffy as I was now calling it. I ate in the car, being careful to chew only on the right side of my mouth. About an hour later, I still felt the crown wasn't on properly. I wasn't able to bite all the way down. So back into my mouth my fingers went for an adjustment.

I pulled the crown off. When I did, the slickness of my saliva caused the crown to shoot out of my fingers' grip and land somewhere in the car. I pulled over at the first exit, which was smack dab in the middle of Vermont's cow country. There were green fields and fences as far as I could see. I began searching for the small white porcelain poser tooth. I looked in every nook and cranny in the car. I looked inside my backpack, the creases of the seats, under the seats, and in my pockets. If there was one redeeming thought, it was that I knew the crown had to be somewhere in the car because I'd had the windows closed. I searched that car from top to bottom like a drug agent at a border checkpoint. Twenty minutes after the search began, I found the crown nestled into the hard plastic inner workings of the seat belt. I washed the crown off with the melted ice in the cooler and put it back in my mouth.

It was nearing midnight when I pulled into a rest stop on the outskirts on Lebanon, New Hampshire. I decided to try to sleep in the car's front seat, using it like an easy chair, so I tilted the seat back and fell asleep to the humming of the neighboring eighteen-wheelers' cooling systems. I woke up around six the next morning, filled my cup with water from the drinking fountain, and brushed my teeth in the car, spitting out the window. I started the car, crossed over the Connecticut River into Vermont, and continued toward Burlington, driving through the Green Mountains. The car chugged along up the slow grade, being passed by nearly every car on the road, including the eighteen-wheel transport trucks whose drivers flashed their lights at me to get over to the road's shoulder.

With an I-think-I-can attitude, my four-cylinder Hyundai eventually reached the pinnacle of the mountain. Trucks pulled into the slow lane and the air was filled with the smell of burning brakes. Other, more adventurous motorists sped down the twisting mountain road, passing cars like they were on a race track. Occasionally I pumped on the brakes as I worked my way down the hill. Then, without explanation, the car's brakes completely gave out. The diplomatic Hyundai began to pick up speed and I continued to pump the brakes to no avail. The twists and turns of the road were approaching faster and faster, and the tires screeched as the car sped around each turn. Keeping my eyes on the road, I reached down and felt for the lever of the emergency brake, but instead pulled the knob for opening the car's hood. The hood sprang up and I had to crouch down in the driver's seat to watch the road through the small crack between the car's body and its hood. Adrenaline filled my body. My heart palpitated and sweat beads formed on my forehead. I continued speeding down the hill, now taking each turn at fifty to sixty miles per hour. I noticed a sign that read "Runaway Truck Pullout 3/4 mile." I knew it was my only chance and prepared for the pullout. I was swerving from the inside lane to the outside lane to avoid rear-ending other cars. Around the sharp turn I spotted the turnout; unfortunately, several eighteen-wheelers were following each other one-by-one down the mountain in the far right lane. They were so close together I didn't think I'd be able to squeeze between them. I began honking the car horn and flashing my headlights to attract the truckers' attention. I noticed another sign announcing that the pullout was in one-eighth of a mile. I drove out toward the far outside lane and then stepped on the gas: I shot through the small hole of daylight between two trucks like an all-pro running back. A cloud of dust kicked up as my car traveled off the road and into the sand and gravel of the pullout. The car rolled two hundred feet up the embankment before it came to a stop.

Exhausted from the experience, I threw my arms up over the top of the steering wheel and leaned forward, resting my head on the center of the steering wheel, which honked the horn one last time.

"Thank you, God," I sighed as I got out of the car to look around. The car's tires were halfway buried in the thick sand and gravel. I decided that this was a perfect place to drop some of Dad's ashes. I sprinkled a spoonful of the ashes in the sand and then walked back to the highway to get some help. I hiked back up the hill to a nearby call box.

Half an hour later a tow truck showed up and towed the car to a garage. After a brief consultation, Rocky, the Asian mechanic, determined the car needed new front and back brakes and a new brake fluid reservoir. He quoted me $280, repeating several times, "*Berry* cheap. *Berry* cheap. Good price I do for you."

"Could I help you? Maybe hand you the parts or something and then maybe you could knock a little off the price?" I asked.

"You help, I charge you $350," Rocky shot back sharply in his thick accent.

"Well, I don't have that much on me," I said.

"You no have money, you get car out my shop," Rocky stated louder.

"Maybe I should get a second opinion."

"Rocky give you best price in town. *Berry* cheap. Good price. You go get money, Rocky fix you car."

I walked down the street to a shopping center and pulled $300 out of the ATM. I ate lunch at Wendy's, where I updated my journal for an hour. I walked back to Rocky's garage to see how the car was coming along. When I returned, the Hyundai was six feet up in the air on the hydraulic lift. An older white man chewing on a Swisher Sweets cigar told me it was still going to be a couple hours. I sat in the waiting room perusing some of Rocky's outdated and dog-eared magazines. After I had spent an hour catching up on recent history, Rocky entered the waiting room and said the car was finished. I counted out $280 in twenties and Rocky handed me the keys.

"*Sank* you. *Sank* you *berry* much."

"No, *sank* you," I said.

I drove the car out of the shop and Rocky pulled down the garage's metal door behind me. This delay had put me a day back on my schedule and a week behind on my budget.

I had planned to take a trip into Canada to visit my cousin Russ, who was living in Montreal while attending a trade school to learn how to make stained-glass windows. Russ was my favorite cousin, mainly because we were very close in age and he could make me laugh until

I cried by burping the theme songs of television shows. Though I was disappointed I would miss hearing any new songs he had added to his repertoire due to my recent money-and-time setbacks, I had to change my plans, and instead headed west into upstate New York.

I drove eight hours, then stopped for gas just outside of Schenectady, New York. My late-night dinner consisted of beef jerky, fried pork rinds, and a large Gatorade, which I ate in the car. I was still chewing on the right side of my mouth as I drove southwest into Pennsylvania.

I drove another few hours through a wooded area, noticing various road signs warning about the wildlife in the area. My head had begun to bob from exhaustion and I had been looking for a rest stop to spend the night. I was learning the hard way that there aren't many rest stops on the road less traveled. I made a deal with myself that if I didn't find a rest stop within half an hour, I would pull over and sleep on the side of the road. It was very dark on the two-lane highway. The only light was from the occasional vehicle coming toward me. Its lights would shine in my eyes, especially if the other driver wasn't courteous enough to flip off the high beams. On a straightaway, a tractor truck was headed toward me; although the driver did turn off his high beam headlights, the regular headlights shone right into my eyes, temporarily blinding me. Just then an enormous elk attempted to cross the highway and my car plowed into it.

The impact was like crashing into a wall. The Hyundai's front end folded like a timid gambler with a pair of twos. I was wearing my seat belt, but the impact caused my head to lunge forward, and I chipped my front teeth on the steering wheel. I sat in the crushed car a bit dazed, but basically unhurt. The car had been knocked into a ditch by the impact, and the mangled car's engine smoked slightly and leaked its vital fluids out onto the dirt below. The elk got up and hobbled off into the woods. The sound of its cries grew faint as it disappeared into the dark of the night. It was nearly twenty minutes before another car passed and almost an hour before someone stopped to help. By then dawn was breaking.

A farmer driving a large John Deere spotted me and called 911 on his cellular phone. An ambulance came and took me to the hospital for observation. When the admitting attendants realized I had neither medical insurance nor money and didn't appear to be suffering from anything except looking like a first grader who'd fallen off the monkey bars, they decided to observe me from the emergency room waiting area. I was released after eight hours of talking to other patients whose injuries weren't serious enough to be seen immediately. I held remnants of the chips from my two front teeth in my hand. They looked very much like two spearmint Tic-Tac breath mints. Of course, my loose crown had stayed perfectly on the molar throughout the whole ordeal. I spoke with the local police by phone; they told me my car had been towed to the only gas station and repair garage in town.

After being released around three o'clock in the afternoon, I took a bus to the service station to get a look at my car, worrying the entire time whether Dad's urn would still be in there. I got dropped off in front of the service station, which looked more like a junkyard, and walked toward the mangled Hyundai. "Totaled" was scribbled across the windshield in bright-yellow grease pencil. I went into the office of the gas station and rang the bell on the counter. I heard a voice say, "Yeah, hold your horses. I'm in the can." I looked around at the cluttered shop, which offered an eclectic mix of business cards taped to the wall, the famous Farrah Fawcett swimsuit poster, and a bumper sticker stating "It used to be wine, women, and song. Now it's beer, the old lady, and TV." A man came out from the back, wiping his hands with a blue paper towel. He was wearing a greasy blue-collared shirt with a white oval patch stating "Herb" over the pocket.

"Yeah, can I help you?"

"That's my red Hyundai out there."

"Oh, you're the fella that tried to drive through the deer this morning?"

"Yeah, I guess that would be me," I said, forcing a smile. "But I think it was a moose."

"It couldn't have been a moose," he said. "You'd be crushed flatter than a pancake if it had been a moose. It was probably a deer or a bobcat."

"It sure looked like a moose to me," I said.

"Well, we made you up a repair estimate, but I doubt you'll want to see it."

"Fifteen hundred dollars?" I said with amazement. "The whole car isn't even worth that."

"That thing has shit its dyin' turd," Herb said. "There is some salvage value, though. I can give you two hundred dollars for it minus the towing and storage charge."

"How much was the towing?"

"One hundred and twenty-five."

"You're charging me $125 to tow a $200 car?"

"We had to pull it out of the ditch. That's extra. Tell you what," the man said, thinking and readjusting his cap, "I'll give you an even hundred dollars for the car. I probably shouldn't go that high, but hell, I was young once myself. Just consider it a gift from my generation to yours."

"Well, on behalf of my generation I gladly accept the extra $25. Oh boy, what should I buy first?" I asked with sarcasm in my voice.

"Look here, smart-ass, no one is twisting your arm. You can take it or leave it. It sure doesn't make a rat's ass to me whether I get a totaled Hyundai or not. This deal isn't going to make or break me, but I think you should look at our parking rates while you're making up your mind."

He pointed to a sign on the wall that read "Car Parking for Unreasonable Owners $25 a Day."

"Sold," I said.

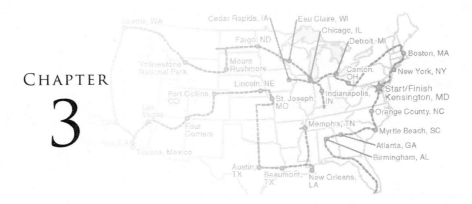

# CHAPTER

# 3

THIS WAS MY FIRST TRUE low point of the trip. Tired, hungry, and holding chips from my two front teeth in the palm of my hand, I seriously contemplated using the salvage money to buy a bus ticket home. I had a cup of vending-machine coffee and thought about the old, chipped coffee cup with which Dad drank his morning coffee. It had a saying printed on the side: "If it's going to be, it's up to me." The memory brought a smile to my weary face, and when it came time to make a decision, I decided to press on with my pilgrimage.

I bought a bus ticket to Detroit where my brother Mark was in a medical-residency program. Stress from the recent events had taken a toll on my complexion. I arrived in Steel City for a two-hour layover with a bright-red zit in the center of my forehead, which made me look like a worshipping Hindu. Without knowing anything about Pittsburgh, except that it's home to the Steelers, I decided to take a look at Three Rivers Stadium. I walked down Liberty Avenue toward Point State Park where the Monongahela and the Allegheny form the Ohio River, and thought this would be a great dropping point for Dad's ashes. I carried Dad's urn down to the waterline by an impressive fountain shooting forty feet into the air, and sprinkled some ashes into the water.

I returned to the station and caught the bus for Detroit. Within an hour after leaving downtown Pittsburgh we had crossed the state line into West Virginia.

West Virginia's shape has a striking resemblance to those "we're number one" over-sized foam-rubber hands that only the most rabid football fans possess. A short ribbon of Interstate 70 passes through the state at the knuckle area of the index finger for about fifteen miles before it crosses the Ohio River into the Buckeye State. I would have to be quick with my West Virginia drop.

The bus was climate-controlled, so all the passenger windows stayed in the locked position. I knocked on the bus's bathroom door, thinking that there'd be an operational window in there. A lady's voice answered, "Be out in a jiff." I don't know how long a jiff is, but I was hoping that it wouldn't be more than the five minutes we had left on our brief visit to the Mountain State. After standing there a few moments, I noticed a road sign stating "Wheeling, Next Four Exits," and I knew from studying the atlas that after Wheeling was Ohio.

"Ma'am?" I said, pleading to the bathroom door. "Are you just about done?"

"Just about."

"Cause I'm in a real big hurry."

"Just another jiff," she said with some struggle to her voice.

"Ma'am, I can't afford any more jiffs; we're just about out of West Virginia."

I looked toward the front of the bus and saw a large iron suspension bridge in the foreground. I figured it was the bridge that spanned the Ohio River. If we crossed that bridge without an ash drop it meant a return trip to West Virginia.

"Ma'am, please!" I said with desperation in my voice. She opened the door and I rushed in. There was a small window with obscured glass next to the toilet. The window was locked with just a one-inch opening at the top. As the bus neared the entrance to the bridge, I reached into the urn with three fingers and grabbed a small clump of ash and thrust it out the window with all the zeal my fingers could muster. The gust of wind produced by the speeding bus sent the ashes back toward West Virginia and I added another state to the completed list.

The bus driver soon traded Interstate 70 for Interstate 77. We headed north through eastern Ohio, stopping at a roadside buffeteria on the outskirts of Canton for a thirty-minute dinner break. A buffeteria, as far as I can tell, is simply a cafeteria that lets diners push their plastic trays along brass rails instead of stainless steel rails. The added touch of elegance allows buffeterias to charge an extra quarter per item.

I pushed my tray along the impressive and recently polished brass rails, and picked out a few items from the greasy and lumpy selections. The cashier sat at the end of the line totaling the bill on an archaic manual cash register.

"That'll be three-oh-three," said, the cashier girl with her hair pulled back by a teal-colored polyester scarf. I handed her three one dollar bills then searched through my pockets for some change.

"Marva?" I asked, pointing to her name tag. "That's a name you don't hear every day. Is it Greek?"

"It's short for Marvelous," she said with an aw-shucks awkwardness. "'Cept all my friends call me Marva Larva."

"Well, that's a catchy nickname," I said. I didn't have any change, but I noticed a small Styrofoam coffee cup next to the cash register that had a few pennies in it. I started to remove three cents.

"What the hell are you doing?" Marva exclaimed.

"Just taking a couple pennies from your 'Take a penny, Leave a penny' cup."

"That's my tip jar," she stated with a how-dare-you tone in her voice.

"Oh, sorry," I said, pulling out another dollar to settle my bill. She gave me ninety-seven cents change and I put two pennies in her tip jar, which really seemed to brighten her spirits.

"Thank you, have a nice meal, and a great trip."

Most of the tables were full, so I asked if I could sit at the table with a small placard stating "Driver's Table."

"Sure, sit down," said my bus driver through a mouthful of salad. After a few bites, a jury of my tastebuds concluded beyond a reasonable doubt that the food was just awful. I pushed my plate away and snacked on the free crackers.

"I was wondering," I asked the driver, "Could I use my ticket to catch tomorrow night's bus to Detroit instead?" I slid my ticket across the table toward him.

"Yeah, your ticket is good for a week. You can get back on the bus tonight, tomorrow, whenever," he said with a mouthful of food. He shoveled in another spoonful of mashed potatoes and gravy and then out of nowhere added, "Have you ever considered the lucrative opportunity of multilevel mass marketing?"

"Uh, I'm still in college."

"That's the best thing about this system! You can do it part-time or full-time; it's so flexible it can fit in with anybody's lifestyle."

"I'm really not much of a salesman," I said, trying to work my way out of the situation.

"You don't have to be; these products practically sell themselves." He reached for his briefcase to show me the newest Amway catalog.

"Thanks anyway," I said as I grabbed my things, exited the buffeteria, and walked across the street into the lobby of the Xavier Motel.

I hadn't slept in a bed or taken a shower in three days and was so tired that, believe it or not, price was not a concern. A young Middle Eastern–looking teenage girl came to the counter. She spoke with a British accent. I filled out the guest register card, paid $25 cash for a single room, and was given the keys to room number five.

The room was stale smelling and decorated in an "Early American Garage Sale" style, but I couldn't have been happier. You never appreciate how great a shower feels until you go a few days without one. The next morning, I awoke well rested with a face and pillow drenched in slobber. The Xavier Motel offered its guests free coffee in the lobby, which I drank while browsing at postcards in the spinning postcard rack. The postcards were mostly busts of Football Hall of Fame inductees. I bought postcards of Johnny Unitas, Art Donovan, and Y. A. Tittle and dropped a note to friends back home.

I wrote a card to Charlie in New Hampshire saying, "No sign of a shit mess yet, but you'll be the first to know."

"Isn't the Hall of Fame around here?" I asked the counter man who was working on a crossword puzzle.

"Yes, it's for American football. We've got discount coupons," he said, offering me a half-priced voucher. With eight hours to kill until I needed to reboard the bus, I decided to visit the holy grail of the gridiron. I asked the motel manager if he had a storage area where I could keep my things for a few hours.

"Oh yes, my friend," the manager said with a slight falsetto to his voice. "It's no problem. Your things may stay there as long as you like." I placed my things on the floor of the closet behind the front counter, but brought Dad's urn with me for safekeeping. I arrived on the grounds of the Football Hall of Fame around noon to find two boys dreaming of glory as they threw a Nerf football back and forth. I spent the next few hours browsing the exhibitions, the busts of the inductees, and various items of memorabilia, including the half shoe that Tom Dempsey wore on his stubbed kicking foot, and Billy Johnson's famous pair of white shoes.

I was strolling down a corridor toward the museum's gift shop when I was stopped by two security guards of differing proportions. The tall and skinny security guard calmly asked me if I would follow them to their office.

"Why?" I asked.

"We'd prefer to speak with you in private, sir," whispered the stout security guard.

"Okay," I said with a shrug of my shoulders.

I walked with them down a few flights of stairs until we came to the security office in the basement. I sat in a chair in front of a desk. The skinny security officer sat behind the desk and the portly officer sat on the corner of the desk and started clipping his fingernails.

"Where'd you get your trophy?" Skinny asked.

"It's not a trophy, it's my dad's urn."

"Urn, huh?" Portly said under his breath.

"Well, we had an alarm go off in the storage room where we keep the trophies that aren't on public display. Ten minutes later we see you walking the halls with this silver cup."

"It's my dad's urn. Look, his ashes are inside."

"Ashes, huh?"

"Well, sir," Skinny said. "Your so-called urn looks just like our 1934 championship trophy to me, but we'll see whether your story checks out. If you'll just sit tight while we view the surveillance tape, we'll get to the bottom of this whole mess."

The time in the office passed very slowly with nothing to do except dodge flying nail clippings as Portly continued to trim his fingernails. Forty-five minutes later, Skinny reappeared.

"After further review," Skinny stated like a referee. "The video tape didn't show any break-in."

"No break-in?" Portly responded. "Was the '34 trophy there?"

"Yeah, they couldn't find anything missing. It must have just been a short in the wiring."

"So can I go now?"

"You're free to go. Sorry for the inconvenience, sir."

I'd had enough of the Hall of Fame and their security force that didn't know a championship trophy from an urn, so I left the museum and casually strolled back toward the buffeteria. I noticed some guys playing basketball in a park, and with three hours yet to kill before the Detroit bus would arrive, I walked over to see if I could get in the game. I played a three-on-three half-court game with the shirtless guys who, I found out later, were coworkers at a nearby machine shop. I set Dad's urn on the grass near the corner of the court. We played for about ten minutes before a player on my team named Big Mike took a twenty-foot jump shot from the opposite corner. The ball hit off of the far side of the rim and took a big bounce toward the corner where the urn sat. Two players grabbed for the rebound, tipping the ball out of bounds. The ball bounced twice in a beeline for the unprotected urn.

"Oh no," I screamed. I could tell that the next bounce was going to knock the urn over, but there was nothing I could do but watch. The urn spilled a pile of ashes onto the grass, and I ran over to save as much as possible.

"What is that, an ashtray?" one of the players asked.

"It's my dad's ashes! Can you give me a hand? I need something to scoop them back into the urn," I said, while covering the pile with both of my hands to shield it from the occasional breeze. One player took a credit card out of his wallet, bent down, and began scooping the ashes up with the credit card and placing them carefully back in the urn.

"It's funny how times change," the man said. "Fifteen years ago, I would have been leaning over a pile of blow with a razor blade, and now here I am cleaning up some dead guy's ashes with a credit card."

I had now sprinkled more ashes than I wanted to in the Buckeye State, but we were able to get most of the ashes back into the urn. I then moved the urn behind the pole that held up the basketball hoop on the next court over and we resumed our game. After an hour, and with dusk settling in, I decided I'd better get back to the motel and pick up my stuff and then wait for the bus to arrive at the buffeteria.

I bought a Pepsi and sat down at a table to wait for the Detroit bus. As I watched the other buses arrive, and the restaurant would fill to near capacity and the noise level would soar, and then in flash the passengers would reboard and leave for destinations unkown, and I'd again be sitting in a nearly empty restaurant. This happened three times before my bus arrived. I showed my ticket and was allowed to reboard. The bus was nearly full, so I looked for an available seat in the rear. Next to the onboard restroom was an elderly woman wearing pink plastic curlers in her hair. Her reading glasses hung down nearly to the tip of her nose, and around her neck was a blow-up neck support that resembled a miniature life preserver. She was shuffling cards on the fold-down tray in front of her.

"Excuse me, is this seat taken?"

"Next victim," the lady said, picking up some of her things off the seat.

I sat down and exchanged pleasantries with the woman, and then pulled out my notebook and began adding up my available funds for the trip. The lady shuffled her cards and kept asking me to play. Eventually I gave in and agreed to play.

"What game did you have in mind?" I asked.

"How about Gin at a penny a point?"

"Okay."

She shuffled and dealt the cards.

"How 'bout some jerky bits?" she asked, handing me a plastic sandwich bag filled with jerky.

"Boy, you've really got this traveling thing down to a science: neck rest, pillows, and snacks."

"Well, I should after three years of traveling back and forth once a week."

"You take the bus every week?"

"Yeah, but I'm going to have to find some other way, with the strike."

"What strike?"

"The bus drivers might be going on strike at midnight; that's why the bus is so full tonight."

"Why are they striking?"

"The usual things: money, fringe benefits, Gin!" she said, laying her cards on the tray table.

"Damn," I said. I added up the cards in my hand. "Twenty-six."

"Did you count that jack?"

She kept score on the back of a gold-colored Social Security envelope.

"So why do you go back and forth once a week?" I asked.

"I live in Canton and work at a tropical-fish supply shop in Toledo."

"Couldn't you find a job where you live?"

"I suppose I could, but I really like the people I work for, and they say when they retire they'll sell me the business."

"Aren't you getting close to retirement age yourself?"

"Heck no, I love to work. It keeps me young. You want some more jerky?"

I reached into the bag and popped a few pieces of the dried meat into my mouth.

The bus pulled into the station in Toledo at 11:00. I paid her the two dollars and thirty-two cents that I owed her from the card games. She collected all her things and left the bus. The driver announced that the bus would be leaving in fifteen minutes, so I got off to use the restroom and buy some coffee from a vending machine. When I got back on the bus, a man was sitting in my seat. He wore a beat-up tweed blazer with the felt elbow patches barely attached and drooping like wilted flower petals.

"Uh, sir," I said politely. "I was sitting there."

"Oh, sorry, son," the man said, "but I've got to sit here. I've got the runs somethin' fierce and I need to be close to the ter-let."

Upon hearing that news, I was only too happy to give up my seat and sit elsewhere.

I grabbed my things and walked back up to the front of the bus and sat in the seat across from the driver. The bus pulled out for Detroit a little late. Once we were back on the Interstate, I asked the driver about the strike.

After glancing down at his watch he said, "We go on strike in twenty-two minutes unless I hear different."

"Can we get to Detroit in twenty-two minutes?"

"We'll see."

I leaned back in my chair to rest. I heard the "beep beep" of my digital watch's alarm that signified the arrival of a new hour; soon thereafter, the driver received a call on his CB radio.

"Greyhound 147," the dispatcher said.

"147, go ahead."

"No settlement, 147. I need you to pull into the nearest station. What's your 10-20?"

"I'm twenty-five miles outside of Detroit. I just passed Monroe."

After a brief pause, the dispatcher said "147, we want you to return to Monroe. We've got buses backed up at Detroit Main with nowhere to park. "

"Copy that," the driver said. He pulled off at the first off-ramp for the return trip to Monroe, Michigan. "Sorry folks, but we're on strike. We're stopping at the bus station in Monroe until further notice."

There was a collective groan from the passengers.

When we pulled into the station just after midnight, the driver told all the passengers they would have to get off the bus. Many passengers tried to finagle their way into staying on the bus to sleep, but he said that policy dictated that the bus be empty.

A few lucky passengers had friends or relatives close enough to come and get them. The rest of us hung around the chaotic bus depot waiting for any news. Hours passed without any updates. People were sleeping on chairs and benches, and then as space filled up, the floor.

The population of the bus station looked like a carnival sideshow. It was people-watching at its finest—an eclectic mix of nomads in suspenders, vagrants bumming smokes, derelicts with muttonchops, and parolees telling jokes. Across from me sat a sad-looking young mother. I tried not to stare as she flopped her milk-swollen breast out of her blouse to feed her unruly toddler who seemed too old to still be nursing. Our eyes briefly met, so I quickly looked away. As I watched a black man, wearing a navy-blue suit with no shirt walk by, my eyes again met those of the breast-feeding mother. I again looked away, but not before she hollered at me, "It's the most natural thing in the world!" I got up and found another seat out of gawking range.

After numerous middle-of-the-night phone calls to my brother went unanswered, I crawled under a row of permanent plastic chairs and, using my duffel bag as a pillow, slept. Early the next morning, the station's cleaning woman began vacuuming and either not seeing me sleeping there, or just annoyed at all the deadbeats using the station as a motel, jabbed me in the ribcage with her vacuum.

"Ouch!" I screamed.

The women muttered something back in Spanish and continued vacuuming the carpet. I crawled out from underneath the chairs and, still half asleep, staggered to the restroom to splash some water on my face and hair. An old man shuffling his feet behind a four-legged metal walker entered the restroom to check the change-return slot on the condom dispenser. He found nothing and shuffled back out without saying a word.

I walked back into the station's waiting area and examined the Michigan state map mounted with four thumb tacks on a bulletin board.

A "You Are Here" sticker pointed to Monroe, and someone else had written in permanent black marker "Wish I Weren't."

I walked across the street to a diner and sat at the counter next to a man holding the Life section of *USA Today*. He had the biggest pair of hands I'd ever seen. I set Dad's urn by the napkins and salt and pepper.

The waitress came over, handed me a one-page laminated menu, and looked curiously at the urn.

"You a bowler?" she asked.

"No," I answered, looking at the menu. She began pouring me a cup of coffee. When the cup was full she looked at me and said, "You did want coffee, didn't you?" I nodded and asked if they had any specials.

"Honey, everything we make is special."

"Well, what do you like?" I asked.

"I like the chili, cheese, and onion omelet."

The man behind the newspaper, without setting the paper down, said, "The omelet of death."

"You be quiet, Phil," the waitress retorted. The man folded down the top half of the newspaper and said, "Go ahead kid, it's your colon."

I ordered the two-egg special. The waitress turned around and, although the fry cook was two feet away and she could have easily handed the order slip to him, backed up about four feet and screamed out the order loud enough that everyone in the restaurant could hear.

Phil resumed reading, and I sipped my coffee and sneaked peeks at Phil's newspaper, which he was holding up near my face. The restaurant was loud with the sound of local diners chatting over their breakfasts. The restaurant smelled of bacon, maple syrup, and just a hint of Aqua Velva.

I tried calling my brother again, but he still wasn't answering. When I returned to my seat, my meal was waiting for me.

"Hey, this is supposed to be a bottomless cup," Phil blurted out, "and I've been staring at the bottom for the last five minutes."

"Phil, isn't it time you get out to your job?" the waitress asked.

"What do you do?" I asked.

"Well, I used to be in long-haul trucking, but my wife got my rig in the divorce settlement, so I guess right now I'm a government employee, if you know what I mean. In fact, I gotta get up to Detroit today to talk to my employer about my last check."

"Hey, I know I just met you, but do you think I could grab a ride with you to Detroit?"

"Tell you what, you pick up my breakfast and you got yourself a ride."

I thought that sticking me with the cost of his breakfast was a little cheap, but I didn't have a lot of options, so I agreed and soon we were headed for Detroit. Phil dropped me off at St. Abernathy's Hospital, where my brother Mark was a doctor in a one-year residency program. After sprinkling some of Dad's ashes in the hospital's rose garden, I went into the lobby to page him. Five minutes later, my brother, dressed in aqua-colored hospital scrubs, walked into the lobby. He look tired and disheveled like he'd been working for twenty-six hours straight, which he had.

"What happened to you?" Mark asked, pointing toward my missing teeth.

"I could ask the same of you," I answered.

"I've been working twenty-six hours straight."

"I've been crashing into deer and sleeping in bus depots."

"I gotta hear about this," he said. "Listen, I'll be off in two hours. Just wait for me here."

I sat around the waiting room reading magazines and thinking that there's a lot of "hurry up and wait" involved in traveling. After I spent two hours perusing U.S. News & World Report with waning interest, my brother showed up with a hearty, "We're outta here." We walked over to the residence hall where he stayed. Since I was a guest, I had to sign in and show my driver's license. There was a big sign on the wall stating "No guests after 10:00." We walked up to the third floor to the room that he shared with a resident dentist from Pakistan named Jamar Babbar. The room contained two twin beds, a dresser, and one window, which had been left open all day to air out the room, which smelled of curry and dirty socks. The trash can overflowed with to-go food containers, and piles of dirty clothes covered the floor.

After talking for an hour, we both pushed more clothes onto the floor and slept until nearly midnight, then went out to a sports bar-and-grill for a late dinner. When we returned to the residency house at two AM, the security guard wouldn't let me back in. We told the man I had been there earlier in the day visiting a relative. We even tried to offer him money, but he stood his ground and refused. We both walked back outside and brainstormed. We considered sneaking me in the backdoor, but Mark remembered that an alarm sounds when that door is opened after hours. It was either sleep in my brother's car or try to get pulled into the room by a rope up the outside of the building. My brother had had success with this during his undergraduate years sneaking into a sorority house, so we decided to try it.

My brother went up to his room and woke his roommate. Together they tied two sheets to each other and threw the line out the window. I tied it around my waist and they pulled me up into the room, seemingly undetected.

"If there's a will, there's a way," my brother said when they had successfully pulled me into the room.

Five minutes later, there was a knock on the door from the night watchman who had watched our entire break-in on a security camera. He escorted me out of the building. My brother threw his car keys out the window and I spent the night in his mid-80s model, maroon, soft-top Chrysler LeBaron. The seat only reclined a few inches and, as I had no blanket and it was an unseasonably cool night, I woke up shivering every forty-five minutes. My only relief came from the car's heater, so when I couldn't take the cold any longer, I'd start the car's engine to run the heater until I thawed out. Then I'd go back to sleep until the cold or a blaring car alarm woke me again. It was the worst sleeping night in my life, and I longed for the comfort of the previous night's bus station. At six AM, visitors were allowed back into the resident's hall. I went to my brother's room and slept like a baby for six hours in a beanbag chair. Mark was at work when I awoke, but Jamar was there watching cartoons on a small black-and-white television.

"How did you chip your teeth?"

"Oh, I got into a little crash and hit my mouth on the steering wheel."

"May I see?"

I opened my mouth; he examined me as if he were a horse breeder. I reached for my crown in the pocket of my pants to show him my other dental needs.

"It's not bad," he said. "I've seen much worse. One of the students or residents could do it for you."

"Well, I don't have any dental insurance. Or any money," I added.

"Come on down to the clinic and maybe they'll work something out."

It was nearly one o'clock when I met Mark for breakfast in the cafeteria. Over the daily special plate of franks and beans, I sheepishly asked him for a loan.

"I'm $40,000 in debt from medical school," he said. "I can't afford to finance your vacation."

"This isn't a vacation. I'm fulfilling Dad's dying wish."

"He didn't even know what he was saying. He thought he was FDR for Christ's sake!" He went on to tell me what a stupid idea the whole trip was. The only encouraging thing he had to say was that he could probably do some trading with Jamar for the cost of my dental work, and he knew of a free ride to Iowa.

"I've got a patient named Stacey Fusenlogin who just had a baby. Once she's discharged, she's driving to Iowa to meet up with her husband. I told her about you and she said she'd love to have someone help with the driving."

After a series of setbacks, things were again starting to go my way. My teeth would soon be back in working order, and if Stacey's episiotomy stayed free of infection, the road again would be mine.

CHAPTER

4

THREE DAYS LATER, I set out with the Fusenlogin family for a straight-shot, twenty-hour drive across America's midway. Their forest-green minivan was loaded down with all their worldly belongings, including a four-year-old boy named Trevor, a two-year-old girl named Amanda, and the new baby, Seth.

"Remind me in my next life not to have a baby during baseball season," Stacey told me. Her husband was a minor-league pitching coach for the Cedar Rapids Kernels. She slammed the van's sliding door closed and got in the front seat. I backed the car up and almost made it to the end of the driveway before the first fight broke out between the two older kids.

Stacey popped a Disney sing-along cassette tape into the stereo, hoping music would soothe sibling tensions. Interstate 94 took us across the green fields of the Wolverine State. We passed by Battle Creek, the breakfast-cereal capital of America, and took a rest stop in Kalamazoo. I had been to Kalamazoo once before to visit my dad's sister, Aunt Bernice. She wasn't able to have any kids of her own because she had an "incompetent cervix"; even as a little kid, I thought that was a terrible name for a medical condition. I halfway expected other relatives to have lazy-liver disease, a good-for-nothing kidney, or a ne'er-do-well spleen. Her inability to have children caused her to spoil us rotten when we visited, which naturally made her our favorite relative. She used a three-wheel electric cart for getting around town. On a good day, fully charged and going downhill with the wind at her back, the cart, which she called "Miss Lillian," could reach a top speed of twenty miles an hour. Aunt Bernice would use the cart for running errands around town, but, most important, she would let us drive it when we came to visit. As preteen kids, my brother and I would cruise the neighborhood trying to impress the local girls with our "wheels." I'm sure some of those girls still laugh at those geeky Maryland guys trying to act so cool in their aunt's electric cart.

Aunt Bernice died two years ago and her funeral was on the day I was scheduled to take the SAT, so I couldn't attend her funeral. She died a tragically comical death by choking on a cherry tomato during a performance of *Oklahoma!* at a dinner theater. She apparently waved her arms and slapped her back, trying to dislodge the tomato, but no one took notice. Everybody thought she was just really enjoying "The Farmer and the Cowman" song-and-dance number. If I'd been traveling alone, I would have stopped to visit her grave, but I couldn't justify it in this situation.

We pulled into a rest stop and parked next to a navy blue four-door sedan with fenders rusty from years of traversing Michigan's salty winter roads and a license-plate holder that stated "My other car is a Zamboni." Stacey and I played with the kids at the rest stop. We tricked them into burning up as much energy as possible with wagers, such as "I'll bet you can't do twenty-five jumping jacks in a minute" or "Run and touch that pole and I'll time you, then you can do it again to try and beat your first time." We got back in the van and drove off for northern Indiana, only to discover that all that running around had resulted in one of the kids stepping in some fresh dog poop and tracking it all over the carpet of the minivan. We rolled down all the windows and tried to deal with the smell until Stacey pulled off at a Sinclair gas station. She ordered the kids to take off their shoes and then wiped the shoes down with moist towelettes. She threw away the tainted towelettes in the dumpster behind the gas station and told the kids to put on their mukluks.

"Do you think they have a Prozac shake in there?" she asked, gesturing toward the station's convenience store. I smiled as she gasped for a final breath of fresh air before cleaning the soiled carpet. She splashed some cleaning solution on the stains, creating an ammonia/dog-poop kennel smell.

Stacey gave me ten dollars and sent me inside the store to get drinks for everybody. After making my selections, I got in line at the checkout counter behind a guy with enough dirt under his fingernails to plant corn. He was buying a bag of chips, a pack of nonfiltered Camel cigarettes, and one sixteen-ounce Budweiser. His black leather wallet was connected to his sagging Levi's with a shiny chain that nearly hung to the floor. He pulled a twenty-dollar bill from his wallet and handed it to the checker saying, "Put the change on the Powerball, would ya?" The checker tapped a few buttons on the lottery machine and handed him a ticket and a few coins in change. While watching this scene play out in front of me, I couldn't help but hear Dad comment, "Not a lick of sense. That guy'll be shovelin' shit against the tide the rest of his life."

I returned to the parched peripatetic pip-squeaks in the minivan. Stacey decided she wanted to drive, so we switched places and got back on the road. Soon thereafter, the little girl fell asleep chewing on the foot of her naked Barbie. With two sleeping siblings, Trevor no longer had to share the attention, and he talked my ear off. He started by letting me know my place: "My dad could beat you up."

"You think so, huh?"

"You're a wimp."

Stacey asked me to take the Barbie out of Amanda's mouth. I grabbed the naked doll. Looking at it, Trevor said, "They call privates 'privates' because they're private."

Interstate 94 took us through Gary, Indiana, a city of urban decay with a peppy show tune named after it. We picked up Interstate 80 heading west toward Des Moines. Stacey told the kids we'd left Indiana and were now in Illinois, and soon we'd be in Iowa.

"Mommy, why did they put all the "I" states together?" Trevor asked.

We'd been in Indiana such a short time, just over an hour, that I forgot to sprinkle any of Dad's ashes. I immediately dropped some ashes out the window to make sure the same thing didn't happen in Illinois.

By the time we arrived in Iowa, the land of corn and caucuses, I was fed up with family life. The incessant crying and fighting and screams of "Mom!" so annoyed me that after twenty consecutive hours on the road, I began contemplating a vasectomy.

"I'll drop you off anywhere you want," Stacey said.

"I'll just walk from wherever you're going."

"Well, we're going to stop by the stadium first to see their dad. Hey," Stacey said with surprise in her voice, "would you like to see tonight's game? I could have my husband leave a ticket for you at the box office."

"Sure," I answered, not being one to turn down a free ticket, even to watch a team named the Kernels. We said our good-byes and Trevor stuck his tongue out at me. The game didn't start until seven o'clock, so I killed time by walking around the neighborhood. It was late Friday afternoon and residents were either starting to mow their lawns, mowing their lawns, or resting on the porch after having recently mowed their lawns. Besides that observation, I thought Cedar Rapids looked nice. I didn't see any cedars or rapids, but maybe they kept those on the other side of town.

The stadium gates opened at six o'clock and I was one of the first fans inside to watch the teams take batting practice. The grandstands were covered by a corrugated tin roof supported by large steel beams. The beams had been painted so many times over the years that the different layers were noticeable from several feet away. The air was filled with a comingling of aromas: hot dogs roasting, stale beer, cigarette smoke, popcorn popping, freshly mowed grass, and cotton candy, with just a hint of cow manure from the distant stockyards.

"The Star-Spangled Banner" was performed at home plate by a teenage girl wearing a navy blue corduroy Future Farmers of America jacket and flanked by her award-winning hog on a leash. The beer vendors stood at attention, or used the opportunity to wipe the sweat from their foreheads on what had turned out to be a muggy night in Iowa.

The ceremonial first pitch was tossed out by a ninety-five-year-old man, who the public-address announcer introduced as "The Kernel's favorite season-ticket holder, Henry 'Lefty' Reynolds." Over the loudspeaker, the stadium's announcer shouted, "Play ball!" and the Cedar Rapids Kernels ran out onto the field to the delight of the crowd and their mascot, a six-foot-tall corn-on-the-cob.

The game remained a scoreless tie after the first four innings, so to create some excitement for the spectators, several fans were invited onto the field between the fourth and fifth innings to participate in a game. They had to lean over, place their head on the butt end of a baseball bat, spin around ten times, and then attempt to run to first base. The crowd howled with laughter as the fans fell down from dizziness as they attempted to reach first base and claim the prize of dinner-for-two at Chico's Crab Shack.

During the between-inning entertainment, community volunteers were walking up and down the aisles selling fifty-fifty raffle tickets. The proceeds, they said, would go half to the raffle winner and half to a local bodybuilder going to New Orleans later in the summer to compete in the Mr. America competition. A home run by the Kernel's third baseman had the fans dipping into their wallets to reward him for his two-run blast to left center by "passing the hat for the home run."

Later in the game, the public-address announcer said, "Folks, we're taking up a special collection to help a young man in attendance tonight, who is traveling around the country fulfilling his late father's wish of having his ashes sprinkled in all forty-eight contiguous states. During the seventh-inning stretch, we'll bring him down on the field to receive our donation. Thank you."

"Oh, no," I said to myself. "Stacey, it had to be Stacey."

I wanted to disappear into the Iowa night, but an approaching middle-aged usher with a salt-and-pepper flat-top haircut was already waving for me to follow him. We walked down a long hallway under the stadium and ended up in the Kernel's clubhouse. There, several representatives of the team introduced themselves to me.

"Did you bring your dad's ashes with you to the game?" one of the media relations guys asked.

"Yeah," I said with curiosity in my voice.

"Would you be willing to spread some on the field?"

"Sure," I said. "I haven't dropped and ashes in Iowa yet."

After the third out of the inning, they walked me through the clubhouse to the dugout and onto the field. I was announced and received a nice response from the crowd. "Roastbeef Hume, we at the Cedar Rapids Kernels respect and admire your dedication to your father and would like to present you with the donation that we've collected tonight:

$263." The man handed me a Kernel's baseball hat filled with mainly one-dollar bills. I shook hands with the team president, and then he handed the microphone to me.

"Um," I muttered, hoping something of substance would come out of my mouth. The Kernel mascot put his cornstalk arm around my shoulder for support, and I uttered a few nervous words. I gave the microphone back to the man, reached into the urn, and sprinkled some of the ashes onto the field. I waved to the crowd, then walked back through the dugout. One of the players yelled, "Hey, man, can I have a dip of your dad?" and spat tobacco juice against the dugout steps. Several other players laughed. I just walked into the clubhouse.

I returned to my seat in the stands. Some of the people sitting around me acknowledged my return with handshakes, high five's, and gifts of free hotdogs and beer. A more cynical fan sitting behind me muttered under his breath just loud enough for me to hear, "Great scam. Empty your ashtray on the field and walk away with two hundred bucks."

A group of four little kids came up to me with their programs and asked me for my autograph. This was my first such request since the great Chad debacle with Percy's cast in Boston. "Stay in school. Your friend, Roastbeef" I wrote on each of their programs. A reporter from *The Cedar Rapids Gazette* asked me a few questions about my trip.

"I love your story. I think that's so special what you're doing for your dad," a lady two seats down from me said. She introduced me to some of the others in her group of about twenty people. They worked together at a local dog-food plant. The woman introduced me to the man sitting next to her. Lonnie was a soft-spoken giant of a man with a bushy goatee that had just a hint of gray peeking through on each side of his chin. He had crow's feet around his eyes and generally appeared more weathered than his forty years. My hand nearly disappeared in the grasp of his enormous paw when we shook hands, though he squeezed my hand very daintily.

"I like what you're doin' kid. It's real sweet, touching, you know."

"Thanks," I said.

"I never knew my ol' man. He split on us. My mom did too, if you can believe that."

"That's too bad," I said, with an empathetic series of nods.

"Yeah, but at least I got to grow up on a farm with my uncle."

"Oh, that's good. Do you still live on a farm?"

"Nope. My first wife didn't want to live on a farm, so, fool that I am, I sold it and moved to the city. If I had a lick of sense I would have divorced her right then."

"You like farming, huh?" I asked.

"Yeah, I do. I really do. There's just something rewarding about growing things from the ground up."

"What do you do now?"

"I work quality control at the plant. It's shit work, but it pays the bills."

"Do you think you'll ever get back into farming?"

"I don't know. It's a pretty tough nut to crack, 'specially when you're out tryin' to get back in."

Lonnie asked me whether after the game I'd like to join them for a drink at the Stadium Lounge, a small bar just across the street from the right-field fence. He barely got the question out before a pinch hitter named Mickey McLaughlin hit a two-out solo home run and the Kernels beat the Clinton LumberKings 3-2. At the gates on the way out, volunteers were collecting money to give to the game-winning hero. Cedar Rapids had been good to me, so I passed on a Susan B. Anthony dollar coin that someone had donated to me and walked with Lonnie to the post game watering hole.

The Stadium Lounge was so close to the stadium that its distance from home plate was painted on the front of the building: 443 feet. The storefront sported dents and scuff marks where past home-run balls had rolled or bounced up against it. Being a Friday night, the bar was crowded. There were two open stools at the bar, so Lonnie and I sat there and ordered a beer. I noticed, and found it odd, that entire families were in the bar. Kids were playing video games while their parents smoked and tossed back a few.

The man on the other side of me was a dignified-looking gentleman in his mid-sixties wearing a tweed blazer, he looked like a college professor. The man spoke eloquently and seemed to be well known and liked by the other bar patrons. He sat on the barstool drinking a beer and apparently found it easier or more comfortable to drink without his false teeth, which rested on a cocktail napkin next to his bottle of Old Style. Soon a young woman in her early twenties came up to the man and gave him a hug. He asked her, "Have you met Roastbeef yet?"

"Hi, I'm Angie, Arnie's honey," she said with a slight lisp in her speech. "Come dance with me, Arnie."

The old man raised his eyebrows at Lonnie and me, but got off his seat and headed toward the dance floor. Arnie rocked his shoulders back and forth and clapped to the beat of "My Generation," while Angie danced around him spinning, kicking her leg in the air, and occasionally dropping to the floor in the splits with screams of "woo!"

I called the bartender over and ordered another beer. Lonnie told the bartender to put it on his tab.

"So where are you staying while you're in town?"

"I haven't figured that out yet," I said.

"Well, it ain't much, but you're welcome to stay at my place tonight if you want," Lonnie said.

"Oh, that's okay. I don't want to put you out."

"No, no trouble at all. I've got a pull-out sofa in the living room."

"If you're sure it's no trouble."

"No trouble at all."

We stayed at the bar until last call at a quarter 'til two, then walked to Lonnie's house, four blocks away. Each street had a streetlight on each corner, but Lonnie's house was near the middle of the block and the only light came from the full moon overhead.

"Here it is," he said, as he went to the mailbox near the street and picked up his mail. "Home, sweet home."

We walked up the cracked and uneven concrete walkway to the front door. He unlocked the three locks on the front door.

"Why do you have so many locks?" I asked.

"Oh, my roommate is a big security freak."

Lonnie turned on the entryway light and began locking the three door locks behind him. He turned on the overhead light in the living room and said, "It's not much, but it's home until I can get a place for myself."

The living room looked very well lived-in. The walls were bare except for two black glow-in-the-dark posters. One had a large marijuana leaf with a slogan at the bottom reading "Don't criticize it, legalize it." The other poster was Led Zeppelin's album cover for "The Song Remains the Same."

"The couch pulls out," Lonnie said. "I'll get you a blanket and a pillow."

He returned shortly with a Mexican-style woven blanket and a pillow with a faded *Alf* pillowcase. I thanked Lonnie for his generosity, and with a "No sweat," Lonnie disappeared to his room.

I quickly fell asleep and slept very deeply until I was awoken just before dawn by a huge thud on the front door. This happened two more times before the door flew violently open, followed by loud footsteps and hollers of "Police!" Before I could even rub the sleep from my eyes, I was looking straight into flashlights and guns pointed at my face. "Get on the ground," an officer screamed at me.

"Okay, don't shoot," I repeated several times as I crawled off the sofa bed and onto the floor. I laid on the floor with one of the officer's knees jammed into my upper back. I could hear the other policemen yelling down the hallway. After a moment an officer shouted, "All secure," and at that point they handcuffed me and sat me up on the sofa bed. Two officers brought Lonnie, who was completely naked except for the handcuffs, into the living room. They sat him down on the pull-out sofa bed next to me.

"Lonnie, what is this?" I asked.

"Shut up," a policeman replied sharply.

From down the hall we could hear the police talking and moving objects out of the way. After a few moments, a voice from down the hall yelled, "Score! The basement is full of it. There must be two hundred plants down here."

Lonnie looked at me and said, "Sorry. I had no idea we'd get raided or I never would have invited you over."

The police went through the pockets of my pants and found the rolled up wad of more than two hundred dollars.

"I suppose this is your allowance?" an officer asked sarcastically as he placed the cash in a clear plastic bag labeled "Evidence."

"Hey, what are you doing? That's my money. I can explain it."

"It was yours, but we've got some strict drug-forfeiture laws, my friend, and we gladly accept your contribution to our worthwhile cause of getting slime like you off the streets." Another officer noticed the urn by my clothes and opened it, finding the powdery ashes.

"Oh, what have we got here?" the officer sneered. "You fellas not in enough trouble already?"

He gingerly stuck his pinkie finger into the urn and dabbed it into the ashes, and then touched the tip of his pointy, pink tongue to his powdery finger. He ran his tongue back and forth across his front teeth and gums.

"I can't place it," he said. So several of the other officers did the same thing.

"It's too bland to be crack, but too sweet to be smack," one officer said in a confused tone of voice, unaware he had made a clever little rhyme.

"It's not coke," another said.

"Well, it sure ain't crank!" said a young officer confidently.

"It's my dad's ashes," I stated matter-of-factly.

All the officers started spitting and washing their mouths out with water.

"We'll book it and let the crime lab tell us what it is," said the officer in charge. The officers then pulled Lonnie and me up by the handcuffs and walked us out of the house to two waiting cars. I sat quietly in the backseat on the ride to the county jail. I contemplated the recent decisions I'd made that had put me in this mess.

If I'd only said no when Lonnie invited me to stay at his house. If I hadn't gone to the bar. If I hadn't gone to the baseball game. If I hadn't taken the ride with the Fusenlogins. *Answer no to any of those things and I'd be a free man right now*, I thought.

The silence of the ride was broken when the officer driving the car turned around and looked at me and said, "How do you sleep at night knowing that shit you grow is polluting young kids?"

"I didn't gr—" I started to explain when I was interrupted.

"Tell it to the judge, you stupid bastard," the officer yelled back in a hostile tone.

The car pulled into the county jail's driveway and we waited as a large-screened electrically operated parking-lot fence topped with razor wire closed behind us. The officer opened the door and pulled on the sleeve of my shirt to get me out of the car. He yanked me up too soon, purposely bumping my head on the inside roof of the car.

The first rays of sunlight were breaking through as I was led into the jail's booking area. We walked down a long white corridor lined on both sides of the walls with framed eight-by-ten photos of the county's past sheriffs.

"Well, he's all yours," said the arresting officer. "The other basement farmer will be along any minute."

I was put in a holding cell with a group of drunks, vagrants, and petty thieves. After two hours, we were all lined up, ordered to strip for "delousing and shower," and told to place our clothes in a large blue-mesh satchel. After the shower, we were given a tuberculosis screening X-ray and issued bright orange, oversized, county-jail jumpsuits that made us look like we were going parachuting. One by one we had our mug shots and fingerprints taken. After my turn in front of the camera, I was put back in the cell and left for another six hours. I had an overwhelming feeling of boredom. Minutes passed like hours. I realized how truly bored I was when I noticed an inmate mopping the floor and envied him—at least he had something to do.

The Linn County Jail had a constant and overwhelming stench of body odor and bleach. As I sat on the floor with my back against the wall and my knees pulled against my chest, I wondered if I'd ever get used to the pungent and irritating smell. I placed my folded arms across my knees and laid my head on my arm to sleep. As I was just starting to doze off, another prisoner with a job I envied rolled a bi-level stainless steel cart by the cell, yelling, "Breakfast!" He passed out brown-paper lunch sacks, each containing a peanut butter and jelly sandwich, a bag of generic-style cheese doodles, and a carton of milk.

The next day, I saw Lonnie for the first time since we had been incarcerated when we were loaded on a prisoner bus and driven to the courthouse.

This was not the way I had planned to see Cedar Rapids. We were hand-cuffed by one wrist to another inmate. My bracelet brother was a black guy with cornrows who called himself Ice. Inside the courthouse build-ing we were put in holding cells. Ice kept complaining to the other black inmates about being handcuffed to me.

*Like you're my first choice, Ice*, I thought, but for my own safety never uttered.

I saw Lonnie again in the afternoon at a bail hearing. We were several seats away from each other in a caged-in section inside a courtroom. I tried to get his attention, but the bailiff barked at me, "Shut your stupid ass up."

The nameplate on the judge's bench read "Judge Maureen Ferber." When the judge walked in from her chambers and took the bench, I could hear the grumbling of some of the prisoners who'd had dealings with her before.

"Oh no, we got Judge Furburger again," said one disappointed inmate.

"Damn, I always get Furburger. I hate that stupid hole," said another prisoner.

I thought that she looked nice, like one of my friend's moms. She seemed to me to be the kind of lady who believed that "boys will be boys" and punished bad choices with yard work. I was counting on her maternal spirit and middle-America good sense, hoping she would take one look at me and state for the record, "This clean-cut young man could never do such a thing. Release him from custody immediately."

Instead, Judge Ferber, without hardly looking up from her paperwork, set my bail at ten thousand dollars, and I started grumbling to myself about what a hard-ass Judge Furburger was.

I was returned by bus to the county jail, where my prisoner status was changing from temporary guest to resident. I was told I was being trans-ferred to the general population, which required a cavity search before entry. Doctor Plastic Gloves told me to drop my jumpsuit and lean over the examination table. With those few words as foreplay and a finger saturated in lubricating jelly, he gave me the once-over with the enthu-siasm of a pirate searching for buried treasure. When he discovered I didn't have a kilo of cocaine in my colon, he gave me a tissue and told me I could put my clothes back on. He disposed of his gloves and began putting new ones on for the next examination. This experience would stay with me the rest of my life, but for him I was just another notch on his stethoscope.

I went to the next station, where my wardrobe was changed from the temporary-status orange to general-population red. I was escorted to a cell with six other inmates, neither Ice nor Lonnie making the cut. On the way, we passed a guard sitting in a watch station reading a newspaper. I thought I spotted a picture of me, the Kernels' owner, and the corn-cob mascot from last night's game.

"Wait," I said. "Can I see that paper for a second?"

"Oh, we got a reader in our presence," said a guard sarcastically.

"There's a picture of me in that paper. That'll prove I'm not a marijuana farmer." The guard glanced briefly at the picture, looked at me, then turned the page. Later in the day, a guard came to the cell and told me I had a visitor. I was led down to the visitor's room where a nicely dressed young Hispanic woman sat waiting. She introduced herself to me as Stella, my court-appointed lawyer.

"Finally, I can tell my story. I didn't do anything," I insisted. "I was just spending the night at this guy's house, and next thing I know I'm in jail. My picture's in today's paper; that'll prove everything. You can call the Kernels, you can call—"

"Wait," Stella said, interrupting me. "We'll get to all of that in time. First I want to find out about you."

She folded back a piece of paper on her yellow legal pad and pulled a pen from her purse and said, "Okay now, I have your name. What is your address?"

"1501 Johnston Knoll, Kensington, Maryland."

"Maryland? Oh, boy, you're a long way from home."

"Yeah, I'm supposed to be on vacation," I said, looking around disgustedly at my surroundings.

"So what is your favorite number?" she asked.

"What?!" I asked, astounded by her question.

"What is your favorite number?"

"What difference does it make? Can't you see I'm in jail? Just get a copy of today's paper and get me outta here."

"All right, I will," she said calmly, "but I need to know your favorite number to present the best defense for you."

After a long and awkward pause, I scratched my head and said, "Uh, five, I guess."

"I had you pegged for a five." she said smiling. "Favorite color?"

"Stella, come on, this is ridiculous!"

"That's where you're wrong. There is a distant correlation in criminology between colors and numbers and convictions and acquittals."

I sighed deeply and said, "Uh, green, I guess."

"Oh, good," she said happily. "Green is a good acquittal color. I haven't lost a green case yet."

Thinking for a moment while placing the ball-point pen back over her ear, she said, "I lost an aqua, but that one is on appeal."

I was then able to tell her my whole story without being interrupted with any further new age–style defense questions.

"This is simple," she said. "I'll speak with the D.A. about getting the charges dropped. If they understand you were just passing through Cedar Rapids, then you're free and easy, down the road. If they don't let you off, we'll have to get Lonnie to sign an affidavit saying you had nothing to do with the pot and get Mrs. Fusenlogin to testify that you drove with her from Detroit. You tell your story, and we'll show the judge the newspaper article. The planets will align for us."

"How long will all this take?"

"Could take a week, could take a month," she said. "Can you afford to raise bail?"

"Ten thousand dollars?!" I said with amazement. "No."

"Do you have any friends or family who might be able to raise the money?"

"No," I said dejectedly. "Wait, Charlie said he'd help me if I got in a shit mess."

"Who's Charlie?"

"He's a guy I met earlier in my trip, but I can't ask him for that kind of money."

"I'll see what I can do. I'll be back tomorrow."

"Thanks for your help," I said as she got up and walked away.

Stella was able to get Lonnie's affidavit saying I didn't know anything about the marijuana in the basement. But Stacey had split her episiotomy stitches open and was hospitalized and unable to give her testimony. I told my whole story, starting with Dad's delusional FDR rants and then highlights from the trip, and I finished with the story of me bent over the examination table. Judge Ferber ordered me released. My money was returned, but Dad's ashes were held as evidence in Lonnie's trial and put through a series of toxicology tests.

Although free, I couldn't continue on the trip without Dad's ashes. I had seen more than enough of Cedar Rapids, so I decided to wait out the trial, which they figured wouldn't start for another month, elsewhere. I thought perhaps there would be more short-term opportunities for me on the big shoulders of Chicago, so using the one-way bus ticket I was given upon my release, I headed for the Windy City.

# CHAPTER
# 5

IT WAS A HOT, HUMID Memorial Day weekend when my bus pulled into the bus station at Clark and Randolph in downtown Chicago. The heat was so oppressive I figured the only relief would be at the water, so I headed for the lakefront. I soon found myself on Michigan Avenue in front of The Art Institute. On the steps next to one of the well-hung lion statues sat a middle-aged, long-haired, hippie-looking guy who appeared to have been loitering around Chicago since the riots of '68. He played an acoustic guitar and repeatedly sang, "Don't shoot the animals, the animals are our friends. Don't eat 'em, Don't shoot 'em, Don't wear 'em, the animals are our friends."

I strolled north on Michigan Avenue across a bridge that spanned the Chicago River, and I continued walking the length of the Magnificent Mile. I found a copy of the *Chicago Sun-Times* resting on top of a trash can as I approached Oak Street Beach. I sat on the sand and read the classified section, looking for lodging or job opportunities. I circled the probables with a pen borrowed from the obese woman in a flower-print muumuu who sat on a blanket nearby. I had difficulty concentrating on the ads due to her incessant high-pitched screams, "Stop throwing sand at each other!"

A Puerto Rican man strolled the beach carrying a large ice chest filled with soda. In broken English he chanted over and over, "Cokes, Pepsi, Mountain Dew, Fanta Orange," then he raised his voice, squealing, "and Yoo-hoo!" I bought a soda and asked the man about his business, as I considered becoming a soda entrepreneur myself. The man repeated a few times, "Me no speaka English," but I had the feeling he just didn't want any competition.

After completing the job search, I found a pay phone and began calling some of the leads. The only place still hiring was a gimmicky two-in-one-type business nearby that fixed cameras and sold hot dogs. The ad stated the business was being "wildly welcomed by hungry Chicagoans with broken cameras."

The manager offered me a job over the phone if I had an address and could work that night. The first thing I needed to do was get an address, so I looked up cheap motels in the yellow pages. I phoned the Cicero Sandman Motel and asked the receptionist if they rented rooms by the week.

"Honey, we rent 'em by the month, week, day, or hour."

I ended up renting a room for a weekly rate of $125 at the Midway Motor Lodge, an upscale flophouse on the northwest side of town near the JFK Expressway; it had a red neon sign stating "Transients Welcome." It seemed like the perfect place for a plotting assassin to call home. At least it was an address; first problem solved.

The hot dog/camera shop was near the intersection of Clark and Division and had a line that stretched halfway down the block. I entered the store and introduced myself to the manager who, upon making my acquaintance, said, "No time for small talk now." He tossed me a paper hat and apron and pointed toward the back of the shop.

"Get back there and start filling those used film canisters with condiments for the to-go orders."

I walked to the back of the shop past the camera supplies and stacks of film to the grill where a crew of five were working at a slave's pace preparing hot dogs next to a photo-developing machine. The whole thing seemed surreal. How does somebody one day decide to open a hot dog–and–camera shop? And why that combination? Why not a dog grooming/sushi bar? Maybe it was just the novelty factor, but the place was doing great business.

"Finally, some help," an exhausted old man said while taking a moment to wipe the sweat from his brow.

"The manager told me to fill the condiments," I said.

"Forget that for a minute; I need some help with this Nikon," said an older man with a green visor and glasses with a tiny magnifying glass attached to them. "The shutter is jammed and the guy needs it back by five! By the way, the name's Ingmar," he said, extending his hand toward me. "What do you know about cameras?"

"Well, frankly," I confessed, "I think I might be more help with the hot dogs."

Ingmar blurted out what sounded like Scandinavian profanity as he turned to work on the camera. The manager busted through the swinging doors and saw me talking to Ingmar.

"This isn't the social hour. Let's go! I got the DePaul photo club out there and they want twenty-six dogs with the works!"

I had a new job and a renewed feeling of excitement. I tried to work as much as possible, volunteering anytime there was extra work. This got me in good with Dino Salvatore, the shop's owner. He was a tall man with deep-set dark eyes who suffered from a case of premature baldness. He was a no-nonsense, business-is-business, bottom-line sort of boss who got flustered and couldn't remember the name of anything when things got busy. Everything in the shop was a "thing-a-ma-bopper" or a "doohickey." He called the employees "what's her face" or "fuzzy britches."

One morning about two weeks after I started work, Dino called a mandatory morning employee meeting. We were fed donuts and coffee in trade for listening to Dino's short-, middle-, and long-term business plans. He said he was opening another business in Indianapolis and needed four or five of us to go down there to help set up the business and train the new staff. He offered the volunteers an extra dollar an hour and payment for our lodgings. When he asked for volunteers, mine was the only hand that went up. Everybody else had other commitments or excuses. Dino offered two dollars an hour more, then three. Finally Jerry, this quiet guy who was always just in the background, volunteered to go.

We left the Land of Lincoln headed for the Land of Quayle on a Saturday, just the three of us in Dino's Chevy Blazer. It was my second time through Gary, Indiana, and the industrial smokestacks/metal-and-concrete skyline was still as impressive as my first time through in the Fusenlogin's dog-poop minivan.

We drove south on Interstate 65 through the flat, green heart of middle America toward the metropolis of Indianapolis. We stopped at a Bob Evans Restaurant in a town called Fickle. When our well-endowed waitress brought over the menus, Dino quickly opened his up and said, "Well, I see that melons are in season." Jerry and I both hid behind our menus in embarrassment. I tried to be extra nice to her the rest of the time, hoping that she'd only spit on his meal and not on all of ours. Dino paid the check and left her an eighty-seven-cent tip, so Jerry and I each added a dollar to it.

We arrived in Indianapolis in the early afternoon and Dino drove us downtown around the roundabout Soldiers' and Sailors' Monument in the middle of Meridian Street. He pulled up in front of a store with white-painted windows that obstructed the work that was taking place inside.

"There it is," Dino said proudly. "The next gold mine. There's nothing like this down here. It's all tuna salad on white bread. We're gonna clean up."

A long white canvas banner with red block letters announced "Coming Soon: Dino's Chimichangas."

He parked the car down the block and gave us a walking tour of the area, finishing with a tour of the shop. Sheets of drywall and debris littered the place but Dino assured us we'd be selling chimichangas within a week, and in the meantime we'd be searching for employees, training the ones who had already been hired, and marketing the new shop.

He took us to a small motor lodge on the south side of downtown near the former train station that had been converted into a shopping mall. We pulled into the parking lot of the Hoosier House with its bright green sign that read "Vacancy." Dino got two rooms: a single for himself and a double I had to share with Jerry. Dino told us we were on our own and to meet at the car the next morning at seven. We unpacked, which took all of five minutes. The room was silent as we both wondered, "Well, what do we do now?"

"You wanna go get a beer?" I asked, hoping this would loosen up my roommate.

He shrugged his shoulders and said, "Yeah, sure, why not?"

We went into a pub on Meridian Street and split a pitcher of Budweiser. They had a weekend happy hour that featured free chicken wings, so I challenged Jerry to a chicken-wing eating contest—loser buys the beer. He shrugged, "Yeah, sure, why not." We each got a plate of ten wings and began. We both finished the plate of wings and got ten more. I maxed out at twenty-three wings and Jerry finished at over thirty. When I complimented him on his achievement, he said, "I wasn't even hungry. If I was hungry I could have eaten fifty of those things."

At about two o'clock that morning, I rushed from my bed to the bathroom to vomit. Sweat dripped from my face and tears fell from my watering eyes as my body convulsed. I sat on the floor with my head in the toilet. Following my lead, Jerry rushed into the bathroom with his hand covering his mouth and threw up in the sink. We both looked at each other and said simultaneously, "The chicken."

Jerry's chunky chicken vomit stopped up the sink, and the smell was so bad we called the front desk to see if the maintenance man could come snake the drain.

The night clerk said, "He won't be in until noon, but I have an auger you can use if you want." I had no idea what an auger was, but I knew I couldn't smell a sink full of Jerry's vomit all night, so I went to the front desk to get it.

"Do you know how to use one of these?" the night clerk asked. I said I didn't so he gave me a demonstration. I took it back to the room and gave the same demonstration to Jerry. He forced the snake down the sink as far as he could and spun it around and eventually fought through the vomit clog. We went back to sleep and at 7:05 were awakened by loud knocks on our door. When we didn't answer, Dino started yelling through the door, calling us "drunk deadbeats" and screaming, "We're here to work!"

Dino wouldn't hear any of our excuses and sat there on the foot of my bed until we got up and got dressed. We went to the shop to clean up all the debris before the painters got there. The white chalk dust left on the floor from the drywall work was being kicked up into the air as we cleaned. It seemed to find a home around our mouths and noses to the point where we looked like we'd been to a Studio 54 coke party during the height of disco.

We spent the rest of the day putting mailing labels on postcards that Dino was mailing to everybody in Indianapolis to announce his new business. He showed us the sandwich board and the Styrofoam chimichanga suit we were going to be wearing, as well as the mountainous stack of flyers to be passed out.

We worked long, hard hours with never so much as a thank you from Dino. "Your paycheck is your thank you," he used to tell us. One Saturday he let us borrow his car to drive out and see the Indianapolis 500 racetrack. The immense metal stadium stands could be seen from blocks away as we drove down 16th Street. We bought tickets and got in the last tour of the day. They drove us around the two-and-a-half-mile oval track in a gray bus that could have doubled for an inmate transfer bus. The bus driver stopped at the finish line in front of a strip of red clay bricks—hence the name "The Brickyard." The driver wouldn't let us off the bus but stopped so we could lean out the windows to take pictures. I was suddenly struck with an idea for Dad's Indiana drop, but it would take some preparation, starting with getting Dad's ashes back.

Monday morning I placed a call to Stella's office to get an update on Lonnie's trial. We spent the rest of the week playing phone tag, but when I did talk to her she told me Lonnie had plea-bargained the case and received a nine-month sentence at an honor farm. I smiled at the irony of Lonnie, the farm boy who unwillingly left the farm for the city, now returning to the farm, albeit an honor farm.

"The evidence," Stella said, referring to my dad's remains, "was released by the court and can be picked up. You need to do it right away, though. They'll only hold personal property for thirty days."

"What happens if I don't pick the urn up in time?" I asked.

"The Sheriff's Department has a property auction."

"Oh, no!" I imagined a frenzied auction scene with my dad's remains going to the highest bidder. "How much longer do I have?"

"The urn was released on the sixteenth, so it looks like you have about eleven more days."

"Well, as my attorney, couldn't you pick it up and send it to me?"

Stella didn't really want to, but she finally agreed to claim "the evidence" and FedEx it to me. The package arrived five days later with Dad's urn and ashes safely tucked inside and blanketed in layers of bubble wrap. After five weeks of separation, I had Dad back in my possession, and the trip to fulfill the promise could continue, starting with a drop in Indiana.

The next day at Dino's I mixed a spoonful of Dad's ashes with a few ounces of white paint inside a plastic sandwich bag. I found a small paintbrush and sealed off the top of the bag around the handle of the paintbrush with a rubber band. I bought a disposable camera and returned to the racetrack and joined a bus tour. When the bus driver stopped for us to take pictures at the finish line, I leaned out the window and dropped my camera on the racetrack. I frantically raced up to the front of the bus and pleaded with the bus driver to let me off to retrieve my camera.

"I'm not supposed to let anyone on the track," he said in a dopey way.

"Come on, please," I begged.

"Well, hold on. I'll go get it for you."

"No, I have to get it. It's a very sensitive camera and if you happen to touch the wrong button you could expose the film."

"Well, make it quick," he said, pulling on the manual lever to open the bus door.

I walked behind the bus, pulled the saturated paintbrush out of the plastic bag, and added a thin strip of Dad to the finish line. I quickly put the brush back inside the bag, shoved it in my pocket, grabbed my camera, and returned to the bus.

"I got it," I told the bus driver, with a big smile on my face.

"That's the camera that's so sensitive?"

"Yeah, that's it. Thanks for letting me get it." He just shook his head and closed the bus door. I returned to my seat feeling giddy with pride. "That performance was worthy of induction into the Ash Dropper's Hall of Fame," I told myself.

A few days later I was standing on the corner of 15th and Meridian, wearing a heavy wooden sandwich board. Dressed in the chimichanga suit and passing out flyers, I thought, *What has my life become?* I'd been in Indianapolis for nearly three weeks working from morning to night and waiting for events to unfold in Cedar Rapids, but now I had Dad's ashes back. What was I doing still making chimichangas, marketing chimichangas, selling chimichangas, and cleaning up after people who had just eaten chimichangas?

The business was up and running, so I told Dino I'd be quitting.

"You can't quit. We just started this thing. I need you to stick around at least for a month until I've got a fully trained, dependable crew."

"Sorry," I said, "Friday's my last day."

"You're just gonna let the team down, huh? Quit at halftime of the big game?"

I just shrugged my shoulders.

"I thought you were a team player."

"I *was* a team player," I said, mocking his words. "I came down here to Indianapolis. I worked nights and weekends. I did every job you told me to."

"I, I, I," Dino said slowly, shaking his head. "There is no 'I' in team, my friend."

"Whatever, Dino, but I'm still quitting on Friday."

"No, you're not, you're outta here right now! I'm not gonna have your piss-poor attitude poisoning the rest of the crew."

"Fine," I said. "Give me my check and I'm out of here."

Dino's face turned red, a surly look came over his face, and in a rushed and fluttered voice he screamed, "You'll get your last thing-a-ma-bobber on Friday when all the other fuzzy britches get paid!"

I took off the sandwich board and dropped it on the tile floor, which made a crash. I got my belongings from Hoosier House and decided to take a short trip until Friday. I rented a dented, purple Duster from Ugly Duckling Rent-A-Car and drove down to Louisville, Kentucky.

I found a motel in Jeffersonville, Indiana, just across the Ohio River from Louisville. I had stayed in some pretty bad motels, but this one had to be the worst. The drapes were held together with several strips of duct tape, and water and drain pipes ran from the floor to the ceiling, fully exposed, in the middle of the room. It was the kind of motel that drug addicts and prostitutes checked into under aliases, not to hide from the police, but to avoid ridicule from their peers.

A bridge spanning the Ohio River connected Jeffersonville to Louisville, and after I got settled into my nineteen-dollar-a-night squalor, I walked across it to explore Louisville. I stopped for a drink at a few seedy bars in the downtown area. At one place called The Alibi, I played a game of table shuffleboard against a hunched-over barfly named Claire. The hump of her osteoporosis-affected spine stood up higher than her head, but despite her condition, she was able to beat me twenty-one to six, so I bought her a beer. I walked back to the bridge, stopping in the middle to pee into the Ohio some fifty feet below.

The next day I drove around Louisville to check out the sights. My first stop was to see the twin spires of Churchill Downs—the most hallowed ground of the Sport of Kings. I took a tour of the grounds with a hodgepodge of tourists. One teenage kid in my group had a T-shirt that read "My Nana and Papa cruised through the Panama Canal and all I got was this crummy T-shirt." I had to agree with him it was a crummy T-shirt. No self-respecting teenage boy would be caught dead in a Nana and Papa T-shirt. This kid was either retarded, being punished, or had lost every other shirt he owned in a fire.

Naomi, our tour guide, showed us the area where they bury the heart and hoofs of some of the greatest racing horses. The rest of the body is apparently sent to the dog-food processing plant where the also-rans meet their fate. Dog food is the great horse equalizer.

Our next stop was at the grandstands, where I walked up to the rail and sprinkled a spoonful of ashes onto the sacred mile-and-a-quarter track. A small gust of swirling wind whipped the dirt and ashes around toward the infield grass.

Listed on the traveler's guide pamphlet of things to see in Louisville was the Colonel Sanders Museum. This small, one-room museum displays the Colonel's knickknacks and tells the story of the guy with a snow-white goatee and eleven herbs and spices. The museum was within the corporate offices of KFC, and I was intently watching a video of the Colonel being interviewed. When I turned around, a full-sized replica of the Colonel was there, which startled me. I left the museum inspired by what I had seen and bought some KFC for lunch. The Colonel was buried in a cemetery nearby, so I thought, why not have lunch with the Colonel? What could be a finer tribute? Why bring flowers when you can bring a two-piece extra-crunchy meal with side dishes and a buttery fresh-baked biscuit? A small monument stood over the Colonel's grave with a small bust of his likeness. I expected the epitaph on his gravestone to read something like, "He had a finger lickin' good life," but all it read was "Harland Sanders 1890–1980."

The only other thing I wanted to see in Louisville was the factory where Louisville Slugger baseball bats were made. The traveler's guide said that some years ago the factory had moved to Indiana. *When did this happen?* I thought. All those years in Little League I thought I was striking out with a Louisville Slugger, but actually I was striking out with a Southern Indiana Slugger.

I spent another night in Jeffersonville, except I decided to save the nineteen dollars and sleep in the back seat of the Duster. I parked for the night at the Down by the Lazy River Trailer Park in a space marked Guest that backed up to the ten-foot-tall flood walls. Kids had cut out the bottom of an orange plastic milk crate, nailed it to a telephone pole, and were using it for a basketball hoop. I watched them play as I sat on the hood of the car and updated my journal.

I returned to Indianapolis on Friday. My check was waiting for me but Dino was nowhere around, which I was happy about. The bad part was that he used to always cash the checks for Jeff and me; now I had to go to one of those check-cashing places that take a percentage of the check as a service charge.

I had been in touch with a Driveaway car-transport service in Chicago, in hopes of obtaining a vehicle with which to continue the trip. After a two-month hiatus, I was excited about the possibility of again heading west. First, I had to get back up to Chicago. I took a Greyhound bus to Chicago and then a Chicago city bus to the car-transport business. The bus was crowded and the only available seat was next to a homeless-looking man wearing a dingy "Lose weight now, Ask me how" T-shirt. The man had his stringy, shoulder-length grey hair pulled back into a ponytail and a sour smell encompassed him. He passed his travel time by picking wax from the inside of his ear with a pair of flat tweezers and wiping his golden findings on his sock.

The Driveaway business office was on Wabash Street underneath the elevated tracks. I walked in the door and noticed two young men with backpacks standing in front of a man's desk. I waited at the front of the office until the two backpackers left.

"Hi, I called about the car you have going to Santa Barbara," I said.

"Sorry, it's gone. Those guys just got it," the man said.

"Oh, great," I said dejectedly. "Well, have you got any others?"

The man opened a manila folder and thumbed through the papers inside. After a few moments he said, "We've got a motor home going to New Orleans, or a Cadillac going to Ogden, Utah."

The thought of a big motor home rambling down the highway to the Big Easy intrigued me, but the practical side of my brain thought better of it. Although not an economical car, the Cadillac would be more fuel efficient than a motor home, and it was headed in the general direction I needed to go.

"I'll take the Cadillac."

The man handed me a stack of papers to fill out and asked to see my driver's license. After signing some papers and receiving instructions, I was given directions to the house where I was to pick up the car.

"You've got five days to get it there," the man said.

As I approached the pick-up point, I saw a pink convertible Cadillac with a "Me & Mary Kay" bumper sticker parked in the driveway. I parked the Duster, and after I rang the doorbell, a lady wearing a pink babushka, housecoat, and slippers answered the door. She looked like a human cotton candy. Her name was Harriet Conrad and she was very protective of her car, which she referred to as "the Pink Lady." She explained it had been given to her for her outstanding success in cosmetic sales by Mary Kay herself.

In an effort to establish some rapport, I asked why she needed the car taken to Utah, but little did I know I was opening the floodgates to a wasted afternoon. She rambled, almost without breathing, for an hour, as I stood staring at her with glazed eyes. I never found out the reason she needed her car transported, but I wasn't about to add a follow-up question. She didn't need any prompting anyway. She segued right into a painfully long spiel of praise for her merchandise.

"Why, Mary Kay is a premier line of cosmetics and personal-care items. Just take a look at this catalog," the woman said, handing me a slick-looking glossy-paged magazine. "Tell you what, I've got catalogs and supplies in the trunk; anything you sell on the way to Utah I'll split with you fifty-fifty."

"Uh, okay" I said. I would have said anything to get out of there. Imagining myself as one of those department-store perfume-spraying assaulters was a small price to pay for the freedom of the open road. So I backed the Pink Lady out of the Conrad driveway as the newest foot soldier in the Mary Kay cosmetics army.

"No smoking in the Pink Lady," she hollered at me.

I got on a small two-lane highway that eventually led to Interstate 94 and was on my way northwest toward Wisconsin. As I ventured out into the more rural areas, the Chicago radio stations grew more and more faint or static-ridden. Soon I found myself listening to crop reports because they were the only stations coming through clearly and I figured knowing the current price of corn and soybeans couldn't hurt anyone.

After six hours, I stopped in Eau Claire, Wisconsin, for gas. As I drove through the small downtown, I noticed a large, yellow banner hung over Main Street announcing this year's Polka Festival, which was being held now. I drove over to the nearby fairground, where I found thousands of cars in the dirt parking lot. Many polka lovers had yet to go into the festival and were having tailgate parties, which were the most elaborate and well-planned tailgate parties I'd ever seen. Some of the revelers had towed rotisserie barbecues the size of trailers to the parking lot. They had set up folding picnic tables and chairs and had already tapped their kegs of beer.

I wandered around the parking lot hoping someone would invite me to join their barbecue. I pretended I was asking for directions and would slip in something like, "Can you tell me that again? I'm all alone and I'm so hungry I'm not thinking clearly." As bold and obvious as I was, no one picked up on my pathetic attempts to obtain a free meal, or they just wanted to keep their bratwurst for themselves.

I headed into a wooded area next to the parking lot to sprinkle some of Dad's ashes, only to find I wasn't the only one sprinkling. I headed away from two guys at the urinal tree and made Dad's Wisconsin ash drop far back in the woods, where I was relatively confident excreters wouldn't venture. I put the urn back in the Pink Lady and entered the Polka Festival.

It cost twelve dollars to get in, which I contemplated spending until the ticket seller said, "It comes with a souvenir beer mug and three beer tickets." I paid and entered a banquet room with a large wooden dance floor. The band played a loud polka and the mobile elderly ruled the dance floor. I tore off one of my drink tickets and had a bock beer, made at the on-site microbrewery. They had long tables set up stretching from one side of the room to the other. I sat down near an old man dressed in lederhosen and a Bavarian-style hat with a mustache-duster sticking out of the back. He was cooling off by sitting in front of a fan he had rigged up to run on a motorcycle battery. He was so proud of it that when I asked him about his invention, he talked for twenty minutes straight. I thought if I showed interest and sat right next to him he'd at least offer me some cool air, but he turned out to be an air-conditioning grinch. I'd try to lean in toward the oscillating fan, but invariably it would turn back toward him just as a hint of a breeze blew my way. So I sat listening to his story, sweating in the heat of a Wisconsin summer.

The man's name was Mickey Dennis. He was a retiree in his late seventies who had never married, and he came down to the Polka Festival every night to dance. He lived across the state in Appleton but spent his retirement traveling around in his motor home attending polka festivals, Octoberfests, and dances. "If they're playing a polka in the Midwest, I know about it."

"I dance at least four nights a week," he told me. His regular schedule was to get into the town where they were holding the festival, find a place to park or camp, ride his bike for six to ten miles, rub down his legs with rubbing alcohol, take a nap, and then polka 'til the band went home.

I was impressed, and offered to buy him a beer. "Nah, I drink iced tea when I'm dancin'," he said. "Here, you can have my drink tickets, too." He told me the festival used to be free, but there were so many old people coming in and not buying anything that they went to the admission with free-drink-coupons plan. "Most of these old-timers pay the money and never even have a beer. The tickets just go to waste."

When he told me that, my entrepreneurial juices began flowing. *Whenever those young partiers out in the parking lot come in*, I thought, *most are going to imbibe more than the three beers included on their admission ticket. They'll have to buy more tickets for three dollars each. If I get these unused tickets and sell them for two dollars each . . . chi-ching!*

There were two old ladies nearby, so I asked if they had any leftover drink tickets. They each gave me one. I walked around the room and addressed anyone I suspected of being a teetotaler. I received a few "buy your own beer" comments, but more often than not the old-timers freely handed over the tickets. Within twenty minutes, I had over fifty free-drink tickets in my pocket. All I had to do now was listen to polka and watch the bar for people paying for beers.

Whenever I saw people pay for a beer, I went over and asked them if they'd like to buy discounted beer tickets. I wish I'd had a million of those tickets because selling discounted beer tickets at a polka festival is as easy as, well, selling discounted beer tickets at a polka festival.

Soon I had dollar bills bulging out of my shorts, dangling off me like I was a bachelor-party stripper. I had an overwhelming sense of happiness and pride in my effort. The festival closed at midnight. I walked back to the Pink Lady and counted the money in the front seat: eighty-eight dollars, mostly in ones. I put some of the money in my wallet but stashed most of the bulky stack in the Pink Lady's glove compartment for safekeeping.

After an evening of excessive bratwurst and beer consumption, I was in no condition to drive, so I crawled into the backseat and went to sleep for about an hour and a half, when I was awakened by a loud knock on the windshield.

"Let's go, Mary Kay. You can't sleep here," said a parking lot attendant in a bright orange vest.

Dazed, I looked around and noticed all the other cars were gone.

"We've got to lock the gates before we can leave," the man said.

I crawled back into the front seat, yawned, rolled down the driver's side window, turned on the radio, and drove off into the night. I stopped at the first rest stop I could find, which was near the Wisconsin-Minnesota border. I crawled back into the backseat again and tried to go to sleep. Just as I was nodding off, a van drove up and parked right next to my car. I heard the driver open his door and say "Keep revvin' the engine or it'll die. I just got to take a quick leak." For the next three minutes, someone in the car would mash down on the gas peddle and rev the engine every ten seconds.

*This is ridiculous*, I thought, as I looked at my watch. It was 2:30 AM. The driver came back and peeled out toward the interstate, and I tried again to fall asleep. The only sounds were crickets, the low humming of a tractor-trailer's cooling system, and the occasional car noise from the freeway.

I awoke the next morning at about eight o'clock mildly hungover, my body suffering from drought-like conditions to the point that the inside of my mouth and throat were chapping. I took my toothbrush, towel, and hairbrush to clean up in the rest stop's bathroom. There was a drinking fountain on the way and I stopped to drink for so long that a kid waiting behind me said, "Save some for the fish."

Inside the restroom, another traveler was washing his hair in one of the two sinks. The man was bent over the sink hitting the soap dispenser with the open palm of his left hand while holding down the water tap with his right. I wet my hands and ran them through my increasingly greasy hair. I cupped my hands and splashed water on my face, then began to brush my teeth.

"What ya haulin?" the man washing his hair asked me.

"Uh, nothing," I said tentatively. "I'm just passing through in a car."

"Oh," he said. "You clean up like a trucker. You know you can get a shower at a truck stop for just a couple bucks."

"Then why aren't you?" I shot back at him.

"Don't have time on this run," he said. "I gotta be in Seattle in twenty-six hours."

"Is that possible?" I asked.

"Well, we're sure as hell gonna find out."

I finished up and dried my face off with a piece of the most abrasive paper towel ever made.

"Keep on truckin," I said with my thumb up in the air as I pushed the bathroom door open. The man kept his head down in the sink but waved with his right hand. He was in the rinse cycle and nothing was going to distract him.

In the lobby area of the rest stop, an elderly husband and wife team were offering free coffee to weary travelers. They were doing this as a community service and also to get donations for their service club. I got a cup and put a quarter in their coffee can, sprinkled some of Dad's ashes on the rest stop's grassy picnic area, and got back on the road.

Next stop was Minneapolis. I pulled into the campus of the University of Minnesota, my dad's alma mater. Even before my dad had contracted Alzheimer's, he had told me he wanted to be cremated and sprinkled on the running track where he had some of his fondest memories. I wandered around the campus and eventually found the running track, which had been replaced by a spongy all-weather turf. I walked away with the urn under my arm to locate a better spot. As I walked through the middle of the quad area, I decided this grassy tree-lined area would be a nice spot, so I took the rubber band and aluminum foil off the urn and sprinkled two spoonfuls of ashes onto the lawn.

I drove away over a bridge that span the Mississippi River and stopped at a small sandwich shop in downtown Minneapolis. The shop was filled with business people in dark blue suits. I sat at the counter and ordered the specialty of the house, the Hubert H. Humphrey Hoagie.

Back in the car, I looked at the map and decided to head for Fargo, North Dakota. By the end of the five-hour drive, my sun-beaten left arm, which I'd hung out the window for most of the trip, was the color of red-clay brick and the back of my sweat-saturated T-shirt stuck to my body like cellophane wrap.

The most notable Fargo listing in the travel guide was the Celebrity Walk of Fame, which sounded like an interesting drop point for some of Dad's ashes. I arrived in Fargo just before sundown as the day's warmth was giving way to an evening chill. I've never felt such a quick and steady drop of temperature. Suddenly, the sweat dripping off my back was crystallizing into icicles.

I drove through the town and began noticing small metal signs posted on street lamps directing the way to the Walk of Fame. I parked down the block and walked over, carrying the urn. I noted some of the celebrities who had been honored: Bob Costas, Dr. Ruth Westheimer, and Charley Pride. Not quite the biggest names in show business, but it can't be very easy booking celebrities in the land of frozen sweat; you've got to take who you can get. I half-heartedly sprinkled some of Dad's ashes across the handprints and footprints of the mildly famous, carried the urn back to the car, and drove off.

Tired from the day's drive, I decided to spend the night in Fargo. I checked out prices at a few hotels downtown. The cost seemed a bit out of line, so I parked the Pink Lady on a quiet residential street a few blocks from downtown. Although a pink Cadillac doesn't exactly blend in, it certainly stood out in this working-class Fargo neighborhood. I figured it would be safe enough to sleep there, although street signs showed it was a snow-removal day and the weather wasn't getting any warmer.

I cleaned up with melted water from the ice chest, changed shirts, and had dinner at Rose's Bar and Grill. I sat at the bar in front of a television showing a cheerleading competition. The bartender waddled over toward me with the most severe limp I'd ever seen and set a cocktail napkin down in front of me. "What'll it be?"

I decided to give my liver the night off and sheepishly ordered a Sprite and the daily special, Salisbury steak. When Gimpy brought my drink, I asked if Rose was working tonight. "Nah, Rose died. We just ain't changed the sign yet is all."

"Tony, can you turn this goddamn pep rally bullshit off?" asked an older man in a disgusted tone. The bartender channel surfed through sitcom reruns, news broadcasts, and eventually settled on a Twins baseball game.

Later in the evening, just as I was getting ready to leave, a man loud and excited thundered into the bar, flinging Marlboro Red packs to friends across the room from a carton he carried like a football.

"It's a boy!" he shouted. "It's a boy! Can you believe it?!"

The bar patrons erupted with joy. They all circled around him with congratulatory pats on the back. "Seven pounds, eight ounces, with balls red as fire and a pecker as big as his ol' man's," the new father said with an ear-to-ear grin.

"I knew if you stuck to it long enough you'd get a boy," the old guy who hated cheerleading said. Gimpy offered a free drink to the house to celebrate, so I decided to double-cross my liver and have a free beer. After lots of celebrating and toasts, the new dad was drunk. He was pawing at the bottom of his pack of cigarettes only to find he was out.

"Damn," the man slurred. "I'm all out of smokes."

"Here you go, you can have my pack," I said.

"Darn nice of you, kid. Let me buy you a drink."

"Oh, you don't have to."

"I know I don't have to, goddamn it," he barked. "I'm a navy man and we always repay a good deed. What are you drinking?"

"Old Style."

"Tony, get this kid a shot of somethin' and an Old Style."

The bartender came over. "What do you want?"

"Uh, tequila, I guess."

"Tequila?" the new dad sneered. "What are you, some kind of goddamn Mexican? This is America. We drink whiskey around here."

"Okay, uh, whiskey then."

"What kind? J.D., Jim Beam, Wild Turkey, Yukon Jack."

"Yukon Jack," I said tentatively.

"Good call, my friend. Yukon Jack, now that's a real drink. An American drink. Tony, put that Mexican piss water back on the shelf and get this American man a shot of Yukon Jack. And give me a double while you're at it."

"Haven't you had enough?"

"Hey, I'm drinking for two now, goddamn it."

The bartender waddled off and brought back the drinks. The man lifted his shot glass and said, "To our wives and lovers. May they never meet."

"And to your son," I added.

"Yeah, I had a baby boy," he happily slurred, his eyelids barely halfway open.

We clicked our glasses together and drank the shot. My face felt like it was on fire as I gasped for air.

"Smooth," the man said.

I took several swallows of beer and wiped my eyes, which had begun to tear up.

"What's the matter with you?" the man asked. "When I was your age, I could drink a whole bottle of that shit and outfight or out fuck anyone."

"I'm just not much of a hard drinker," I said. Then trying to change the subject, I added, "Have you decided on a name yet?"

"After seven girls, we haven't even considered a boy's name."

"You have seven girls?"

"Yep. We've got every damn Barbie ever made."

"Well then, why don't you name the kid Ken."

"Nah, Ken is a pretty-boy faggot's name. I want my kid to have a man's name."

"What about Jack?" I said, looking at the empty shot glass. "That's a good name."

"Jack," he said, thinking it over. "I like that. That's a rugged name. Jack."

"Yeah, like Jack London or Jackie Robinson, even Yukon Jack," I said. "What's your last name?"

"Offerman."

"Offerman? Jack Offerman?" I said out loud. "You can't do that to the kid. The school bullies will have a field day with a name like that. You might as well name the kid Master Bates!"

# CHAPTER

# 6

I AWOKE IN THE BACKSEAT of the Pink Lady just after six the next morning. Again suffering from an acute case of cottonmouth, I drank some of the multipurpose melted ice water from the ice chest, crawled into the front seat, and started the car. I rolled down the driver's side window to feel the cool, crisp, early morning air. The streets of downtown Fargo were nearly empty. I pulled into a Sinclair gas station to fill up before I got back on the interstate. While pumping the gas, I noticed an elderly woman dressed in her "Sunday Best" complete with a powder-blue hat with a small, fake yellow bird perched on top. She was muttering to herself and carrying a gas can in one hand and her black leather Bible in the other. She went into the gas station's convenience store, paid for one dollar's worth of gas, and came out to pump next to me.

"May I fill that up for you?" I asked.

She handed me the gas can and said "My car ran out of gas and I'm already late for church."

"Don't worry about it," I said, "Whenever I go to church it seems like I'm always late. I just sneak into one of the back pews and sit down real fast."

"You don't understand, son. I'm the organist. If I'm not there playing 'Bringing in the Sheaves' by seven o'clock, they'll know."

"Do you want a ride to your car?"

"Oh, that would be nice," she said.

We got in the Pink Lady and drove about a quarter mile down the street.

"Are you a Mary Kay girl?" the lady asked.

"Well, kind of," I admitted sheepishly.

"Oh, I just love Mary Kay. The makeup, the body lotion and powder, the perfume. I have on some of her antiperspirant right now," the woman said, raising her left arm and fanning at her underarm with her right hand so I could catch a whiff. I appeased her with a reluctant lean toward her.

"Oh, yeah, nice," I said with a forced smile.

"There it is, that tan Oldsmobile over there," she said, pointing at her car. We put a gallon of gas into her car. I sold her some undereye firming creme for three dollars and threw in an age-defying moisturizer for free. Then with a wave and a "God bless you," she was gone.

I took Interstate 94 heading west across North Dakota. The scenery was beautiful, if you are particularly fond of wide-open prairies. Mile after mile and hour after hour, nothing but wide-open hay fields. The monotony of the drive was briefly broken when the interstate was closed for road repair. Westbound traffic was redirected onto a single eastbound lane for about four miles so road crews could lean against massive road-paving equipment and smoke cigarettes.

The Missouri River ran along the west side of the capital city of Bismarck. When we studied state capitals in elementary school, for some reason I could never remember this one, so I drove through ol' whatchacallit without even glancing at the capitol's dome.

I gained an hour as I crossed the imaginary line dividing the country between Central and Mountain Time. I reset my watch while driving the Pink Lady with my left knee firmly pressed against the steering wheel. In my head I could hear Mr. Munson, my high-strung high-school driver's education teacher, screaming at me to keep both hands on the wheel, "Driving is a privilege, not a right, people!"

I stopped for some gas at a Rip Griffin Travel Center in Dickinson. This is the kind of place where travelers can buy every product and service ever known to man. If you want to buy a Conway Twitty CD, Chicken in a Biskit crackers, naked-lady mudflaps, a bronze fourteen-inch figurine of John Wayne, butterscotch Life Savers, a radar detector, pitted or non-pitted olives, a key chain that reads "Beauty is in the eye of the beer holder," a replacement bulb for a Volkswagen dome light, a sixty-four-pack of crayons, and then take a shower and have your tires rotated, you've come to the right place.

There was a buffet restaurant inside the travel center that catered to the trucker crowd. The restaurant was equipped with phones on the tables to assist the truckers with phoning their contacts. I took a seat at the counter and ordered the all-you-can-eat breakfast buffet. A pot-bellied black man with a bushy white beard sat on the stool next to me and used the phone. I couldn't help but eavesdrop on his conversation since he was talking loudly and the stools were positioned so close together that Siamese twins would be comfortable.

"Produce outta Philly?! There ain't no money in that. You gotta be gettin' me somethin' headed south. I ain't been home to *Nath* Carolina in weeks and the ol' lady be gettin' pissed."

The waitress left my bill on the counter. Under the total she had written "Thank you, Tracy" and drawn a picture of a smiley-faced cartoon character with its tongue protruding from one side of its mouth. I left the counter feeling bloated and lethargic, so I browsed around the travel center until I felt better. In the rear of the building by the showers and laundromat was a large room filled with sofas called the Trucker's Lounge. A couple dozen truck drivers in various stages of alertness were watching *Caddyshack* on a big-screen television. I stopped to watch from the hallway even though a husband-and-wife trucking team encouraged me to "go on in and have a seat. They won't bite."

I was instantly intrigued by the laugh of one man near the television. He had a long-lasting, hearty belly laugh followed by a loud gasp for air at the end that sounded exactly like Dad's laugh. I became anxious waiting for something in the movie to tickle his funny bone so I could hear him laugh again. Every time he laughed, I had this strange feeling of simultaneous joy and sorrow. I took a seat on the couch behind the man and closed my eyes and tried to imagine I was home watching television with Dad. I never said a word to the man or even looked him in the face, but for a tear-filled half hour in a travel center in North Dakota, I had my dad back.

It was early afternoon when I crossed into Big Sky country. There was a rural-route school bus in front of me and several kids on the bus took turns flipping me off out of the back window until the bus exited the interstate. I tried to get a picture of their unique "Welcome to Montana" gesture by holding my camera out of the window, but when I had the photos developed I ended up with a blurry picture of the Pink Lady's side mirror.

I didn't see another vehicle for at least a half hour. Driving alone in eastern Montana is like serving time in solitary confinement. There's no one to talk to, nothing to look at, and nothing coming in on the radio. I started to get excited about any small thing that proved humans had been there. "Todd '71 Rules!" was spray painted on a cement pillar of an overpass. I thought, "I wonder how Todd's doing? I wonder if he still thinks '71 rules? I wonder if he still goes out spray painting?" But then I was out of Todd-related material and I had to just stare at the long ribbon of highway that lay in front of me.

I passed a slow-moving Volkswagen Beetle with enough dirt on it to plant grass and a license-plate holder that read "My other car's a Rolls-Royce." I was so happy to see another human being that I smiled and waved at the driver. He momentarily looked at me and then quickly turned his eyes back to the road.

Another half hour passed and the only sign of life was a roadside memorial where I assumed one or more lives had been lost. There, forlorn in the Montana wilderness, stood a two-foot-tall, homemade, white cross with a few weather-beaten stuffed animals affixed to it. That was the last sign of life I saw until I came across a man lying on the soft shoulder of the highway with a motorcycle lying over him. He was frantically waving both of his arms back and forth in the air.

I pulled over to the side of the road and backed up about one hundred yards to where the man was lying with his legs pinned under his motorcycle. I put the car in park, flung the door open, and ran back to the man. He was a rough-looking biker, dressed in all black leather, with a thick, furry black beard, and a teardrop tattoo near the corner of his left eye.

"Thank you," he said. "Thank you so much for stopping. I've been trapped under my bike for a half an hour and you're the first car to stop."

"What do you want me to do?" I asked.

"If you'll just lift up the front with the handlebars, I'll push on the back and pull my leg out."

"One, two, three!" we counted in unison and then lifted with every bit of strength we could muster.

The man was able to pull one leg out. We tried again, this time with me lifting the back of the bike, and we were able to free the other leg. The man sat on the road rubbing both legs and stretching them out.

"Can you stand up?" I asked.

"Yeah, I think so," he said, wincing with pain.

I leaned down, and the man put his arm around my shoulder and I hoisted him up. Once on his feet, he took a few steps in each direction then stuck out his hand and said, "The name's Mad Dog." He wore a black leather jacket with several patches sewn on to it, riding gloves, Levi's covered by leather chaps, and scuffed black boots.

While we were talking, Mad Dog started his bike and revved the engine a few times. A man dressed just like him must have taken the revving as a signal. I saw a flash of long hair and leather sprint out from the irrigation ditch, jump in the Pink Lady, and leave me chasing a cloud of dust and car exhaust. Mad Dog quickly followed the car and yelled at me as he passed, "Thanks for the Caddie, mother fucker!"

I stood there on the side of the road and watched as the Pink Lady faded off into the Big Sky distance. I was twenty miles from even the smallest of towns; with no other options, I was forced to start walking. Occasionally I would see a car approaching and stick out my thumb, but no one stopped. The enormous gusts of wind created by semis as they passed me at eighty miles an hour almost knocked me over.

After walking for a few hours, the sun began to set and I was getting scared that I might be out in the vast wilderness all night. My mind started playing games with me. I was thinking about how months from now, when the road crews come through, one of the crew members will notice bits of clothing and bone fragments in some old animal droppings and wonder, "Who was this guy? What was he doing out here without a car?"

The lights of a small roadside town up ahead began to come on. *I'm saved*, I thought, as I began to jog. The oasis was much farther off than it appeared. It took me nearly an hour to jog to the little town that consisted of a cafe on one side of the street and a gas station on the other.

I walked up to the gas station. A sign on the door stated "At the cafe, be right back." I walked over to the cafe; a sign there read "At the gas station, be right back." I peered through the cafe's glass door, but I didn't see anyone inside. I looked for a telephone but didn't see one. I knocked loudly on the cafe door. After a while, a man came to the door, pulling his suspenders up over his shoulders, and unlocked it.

"Sorry to keep you waiting," the man said. "I didn't hear you knockin'. I swear I'm gettin' as deaf as a post."

"You got a phone?" I asked.

"Over there in the corner next to the john," the man said, pointing toward the back of the restaurant.

I hurried in to use the phone. The man shouted, "The soup of the day is navy bean," while I dialed.

I dialed nine-one-one and reported that the Pink Lady had been stolen. The operator told me to stay at the diner; a sheriff would be out to take a report.

"Can I see a menu?" I asked. I ordered a sandwich and bowl of soup, and I was finished and on my third cup of coffee by the time the sheriff arrived.

"Are you the guy that got his car stolen?" the policeman asked me, the only customer in the restaurant. I looked around and nodded yes.

"Well, when you called it in, we radioed ahead, so it'll only be a matter of time until we find it. We don't get a lotta pink Cadillacs up this way," the officer said.

"What's a kid like you doing driving a pink Cadillac for anyway?" the officer asked, then ordered a piece of pecan pie and a cup of coffee.

"It's a long story," I said.

"Well who's stoppin' you from tellin' it?"

"Well, basically I'm driving around the country sprinkling my dad's ashes in every state. It was his last wish. I don't really care about the car, but Dad's ashes are still in it."

"I admire that," said the cook. "God knows my kids wouldn't even come to my funeral let alone haul my dead ass around the country."

The conversation then turned to a debate over burial or cremation, which lasted until a woman's voice came through on the officer's hand radio. She reported that a stripped pink Cadillac had been found in Glendive.

"Where's Glendive?" I asked excitedly.

"Just up the road, maybe thirty-five or forty minutes from here," the officer said, still writing down the details in a small notebook.

"Can you take me there?" I asked.

"Of course. You're gonna have to identify it."

We got onto the interstate and headed west. About twenty minutes into the trip, a car sped by doing at least a hundred miles an hour. The officer said, "Sorry kid, but duty calls."

The officer turned on the car's lights and siren and we set off chasing the law-breaking vehicle. It took a few miles for us to catch up to the car and pull it over. It was a cherry-red Corvette with Idaho plates. I watched from the squad car as the driver was arrested. The officer walked the offender back to the squad car and had him share the backseat with me.

"We got company," the officer said. "Speed Racer here can just come along for the ride."

Twenty minutes later, the officer pulled into a poorly lit industrial park in what appeared to be the bad part of town, unless, of course, the whole town of Glendive was a dump. He drove back through the rows of graffitied buildings to the back corner where abandoned couches and tires littered the area. Two Glendive police cars were parked in front of a pathetic pink carcass. The Pink Lady had been raped of every part not welded to her frame.

"You see that, Speedy?" the officer said. "This is what we do to the cars of out-of-state law breakers."

We walked over to the stripped car to examine it, but Speed Racer remained in the backseat of the squad car curiously looking on. I examined the car for any of my personal belongings but found none. The bikers had taken everything: the glove-compartment beer money, my clothes, my journal, the ice chest—even the Mary Kay catalogs were gone. Dad's urn had been taken, and his ashes dumped on the floorboard of the front passenger's side. I tried to scoop up as much of the ashes as I could and then brushed out the remaining particles onto the ground. This would have to suffice as Dad's Montana drop.

I brushed the ashes into the center of the Pink Lady's pink rubber floor mat, which looked like finely stretched bubble gum. After collecting as much as much of the ashes as I could, I folded the four corners of the mat together to create a makeshift carrying case and walked back to the car. The officer gave me a small, white plastic trash bag to put the ashes in.

Another police car pulled up and an officer photographed the Pink Lady while another dusted her for fingerprints. The Glendive officers asked me questions about the theft. The officer who had given me a ride wished me well and took Speed Racer to face his day in court. I was given a ride to the Glendive police station to file a report and to make all the necessary phone calls. I dreaded having to call the car-transportation service and tell them that the car they had entrusted me with was now nothing more than scrap metal.

Sergio, the on-duty sergeant, allowed me to use the police department's courtesy phone to make the dreaded call. I was pleasantly surprised when Ashley, the young-sounding Driveaway representative, was very empathetic to my situation. Her gum popped and crackled as she spoke to me, saying things like "no way" and "what a bummer," as I explained the demise of the Pink Lady. She told me it was "no biggie" then requested the police report number and some other contact information and wished me a "nice day." I thought for sure I was going to be yelled at and was so relieved at the outcome.

I thanked Sergio as he handed me my copy of the police report, and I walked out of the police station. I had no idea what my next move was, so I started walking toward Interstate 94 about a mile away. I noticed a Sinclair gas station and convenience store and I walked toward it. On the back of my copy of the police report I wrote "Will Work for a Ride," and I sat on a curb in front of the store's entrance to wait. A middle-aged man driving an old pick-up truck with a battered-looking camper pulled up next to me after pumping his gas.

"Where ya headed?" the man asked.

"I don't care," I said.

"I'm headed for South Dakota and could sure use a hand unloadin' my truck."

"Great," I said, grabbing for the door handle.

"The name's Fred Filmore," he said, extending his hand. I introduced myself and off we went back into North Dakota to catch Highway 85 south.

"So what do you have in there?" I said, gesturing behind him.

"Souvenirs, collectibles, knickknacks—you know, your basic useless crap, but the tourists eat it up."

"What do you do?"

"I run a souvenir shop just around the corner from Mount Rushmore."

"Cool," I said. "I've never seen Mount Rushmore."

"Well, you will today."

Fred had driven all the way from Regina, Saskatchewan, to buy his souvenirs. This was a trip he made about four times a year to save on shipping costs.

"It's a nice drive this time of year," he said. "But I've been caught in some bad storms where the snow was asshole high to a tall Indian."

"Can't you get this stuff made in America?" I asked.

He chuckled disgustedly under his breath, "They don't make anything in America anymore. This country is goin' to hell in a handbasket."

Four hours after I'd met Fred we were pulling into a small town with two blocks of shops. Fred pointed to his as we drove by. "That's mine, right there." The building looked like a log cabin that had a miniature version of Mount Rushmore on the roof. "See that sculpture on top? I made it myself from papier-mâché," Fred said proudly.

I complimented his art even though it barely resembled the presidents. Washington looked like a woman and Roosevelt's glasses were much too large for his face, causing him to look like a 1970s-era Elton John.

"It really helps bring in the customers," stated Fred.

He pulled his truck around the back of the store and parked it. Together we started carrying box after box into the shop's back storage area. When we finished unloading, Fred thanked me for the help.

"You wouldn't have any other work around here, would you?" I asked.

"Sure, I've always got work. All this stuff needs to be priced and put on the shelves; I could at least give you a couple days of work."

"That would be great," I said.

"Okay then, open all these boxes and let's see what we've gotten ourselves into."

Inside the boxes was every kind of Mount Rushmore souvenir imaginable. Salt-and-pepper shakers, shirts, buttons, bumper stickers, posters, postcards, plates, games, and mobiles, all depicting Mount Rushmore. In the store's front window was a display of presidential shot glasses stacked in a pyramid, a sign in front of the display said "Drink with Your Founding Fathers!"

We worked for two more hours, until eight o'clock, when Fred closed the shop and invited me to dinner at his house, just outside of town.

When we walked in the door, Fred's wife, Eunice, a masculine-looking woman who I figured was probably the model for George Washington in the papier-mâché sculpture, looked me over and said, "Did you bring home another stray?"

"This is Roastbeef," he said, introducing me to his family.

"Oh, Roastbeef, ooh la la," said Eunice sarcastically. "I hope you're not lookin' for some fancy roastbeef meal cause tonight's spaghetti night."

"That sounds great, I love spaghetti."

Fred's wholesome-looking, all-American family resembled a Norman Rockwell painting until Fred's twelve-year-old son turned around from watching television to get a look at me. He was a strawberry-blond, freckled-faced kid who had a port-wine birthmark the size of an apple on his forehead. It started at his hairline and continued to his eyebrows, then trailed off on the side of his face just below his eye. I tried not to stare, but I couldn't get over how much the shape of the birthmark resembled the continent of South America.

The birthmark didn't seem to bother the boy, who was very outgoing and personable. His family had nicknamed him Port, which didn't seem to bother him in the least.

Besides Port, Fred had an eight-year-old precocious daughter named Faye and twin five-year-olds. Fred's eighty-five-year-old mother, Hazel, also lived with them.

"Is dinner ready?" Fred asked.

"Just waiting for you, as always," Eunice said, straining the noodles into a colander in the sink.

We sat at a large picnic table in the center of a very spacious kitchen. Resting at the center of the table was a one-gallon plastic container with a green-and-red label that read "Real Tomato Ketchup." Eunice poured the ketchup over the noodles, added salt and pepper, and mixed the contents with two wooden spoons.

"Voila!" she said, looking at me. "Just like the Eye-talians."

"Who wants to say the blessing?" Fred asked. Both the twins raised their hands, then a fight broke out over who had said it the previous night.

"Ah, for Christ's sake, would you just say the prayer?" Hazel said with disgust for the situation. Fred responded with a quick blessing that included a special thanks for me joining them.

Hazel seemed younger than her years, but she was just as cantankerous as she could be. She wore dark black eyeliner, which, being the end of the day, had cracked, flaked, and smeared all over her upper cheek to the point that she looked like she should have been playing center field at Yankee Stadium on a sun-drenched afternoon.

Everyone else in the family drank milk or water, but Hazel had a bottle of Miller beer. Her reddish-orange lipstick was smeared all over the mouth of the clear glass bottle. "Do you drink beer?" she asked me.

"Sure," I said.

"Port, get Potroast here a Miller."

I took a bite of the spaghetti and was pleasantly surprised by the taste. "Wow, this is really good. I never thought ketchup could make such a good spaghetti sauce."

"Oh, yeah," said Fred. "This is the best ketchup ever. It's restaurant quality."

"Yeah, we really go through it," Eunice added. "We put it on just about everything. Monday night it's our taco sauce, Tuesday night it's spaghetti sauce, Wednesday it's on burgers, you name it."

"I could eat this much ketchup," said one of the twins with his arms open wide.

Besides their slightly overzealous affinity for ketchup, the family was pretty normal. They listened as I told them about some of the adventures I had had over the past few months. Faye got a bit mixed up when she thought that the Pink Lady was a real woman. It took most of the dessert for me to get her straightened out.

After dinner, Fred and Eunice got the kids bathed and in bed while I sat out on the screened-in back porch with Hazel.

"They make me come out here to smoke," she said, scanning the area like a little kid about to swipe some candy. When she was sure nobody was watching she clipped the filter off her cigarette with a pair of sewing scissors. "They also make me smoke these goddamn filtered cigarettes, but this'll be our little secret, eh, Potroast?"

"Your secret's safe with me," I said.

"Do you smoke?" she asked.

"No, not really. Maybe an occasional cigar, but that's about it."

"Yeah, my second husband smoked cigars. White Owl Tiparillos," Hazel said very matter-of-factly. "He'd smoke 'em all the way down to the plastic tip."

"What happened to him?"

"Smoked himself into an early grave," she said as she lit her filterless cigarette.

"When was that?"

"I don't know. I've buried so many of 'em, I've forgotten all the dates."

"How many times have you been married?"

"Five times."

"Five times?!"

"Yep, five times. I always made 'em marry me," she said. After a long pull on her cigarette she continued, "I wasn't about to just shack up and give 'em the milk for free. No, sir, you gotta buy this cow."

"You think you'll get married again?"

"No, siree, been down that road enough times. Anyways, the men that are interested are deadbeats. They want me to support them. I ain't supportin' no man. Oh, did you hear that?" Hazel asked hurriedly.

"Hear what?"

"We just got a big one," she said pointing to an electric bug-zapper light outside the screened porch. Hazel quickly snuffed out her cigarette with the sole of her house slipper when she heard Fred, Eunice, and Port coming out to the porch after putting the younger kids to bed. Port took his T-shirt off and sat on the floor with his back at his mother's feet. While the family conversed, Eunice picked blackheads out of Port's back and shoulders, wiping the harvest onto her apron.

"Well, we better call it a night. We've got a big day tomorrow. The park service is expecting a record crowd for Labor Day," Fred said. He gave me a blanket and pillow and told me I could sleep on the sofa in the living room.

"Oh, no," Hazel interrupted. "We can't have our guest sleeping on the davenport. He can sleep in my bed."

"And where are you going to sleep?" Fred asked.

"In my bed," Hazel said with a smirk.

"I'll be fine here on the davenport," I said with a smile.

The next day, and for the next two weeks, I worked at the souvenir shop. I never knew selling souvenirs could be such exhausting work. From sunup to sundown I was unpacking boxes, pricing items, stocking shelves, ringing up sales, and helping tourists find just the right souvenir to remember their Mount Rushmore vacation.

Because I only owned the clothes on my back since the theft of the Pink Lady, Fred gave me a full collection of clearance Mount Rushmore merchandise including, I kid you not, "My Foster Parents went to Mount Rushmore and all I got was this stupid T-shirt."

My favorite assignment was strolling around the parking lot of the Mount Rushmore viewing area dressed as Uncle Sam. I wore the traditional Uncle Sam costume, including the red, white, and blue top hat with the phrase "Uncle Fred Wants You to Get the Best Souvenirs" printed on the front. I also wore a large wooden placard strapped across my shoulders and handed out small maps and handbills describing Fred's wares, services, and location. My chimichanga days proved to be valuable training for this job. As much as I liked the Uncle Fred assignment, as it was known, I had to give up doing it because the glue they used to apply the fake white goatee irritated my skin to the point that my chin looked liked raw meat. I wore a large gauze bandage over my chin for several days and Hazel resumed her role as Uncle Fred.

Fred had recently installed a photo booth displaying a painted wooden picture of Mount Rushmore with the faces cut out. Tourists could put their heads in through the cut-outs and have their pictures taken with their faces on Mount Rushmore. The photo booth was very popular despite its exaggerated price tag of $9.95 for an instamatic color snapshot.

By now I had established a very good rapport with Fred's family. I knew their set dinner menu by heart and had eaten more ketchup in the past two weeks than I had in the previous two years. Things had become very comfortable between all of us. Hazel had for the most part stopped hitting on me, except for the occasionally friendly pat on the tush. Fred was a great boss, completely different from Dino back in Indianapolis. Eunice, suffering from pre-menopausal hot flashes, didn't seem embarrassed in the least to shed her blouse and cook or perform other chores around the house in just her bra.

It was a difficult decision to tell them I was going, but my first duty was to complete Dad's wish and that could not be done staying in South Dakota. If I didn't get moving before the first snow, I'd be stuck there for the winter—and if I had to spend the winter somewhere, South Dakota wouldn't be my first choice. Over dinner one night, I broke the news that at the end of the week I would be leaving.

I hadn't yet sprinkled any of Dad's ashes in the state of South Dakota and was planning on doing it on my last day at the base of Mount Rushmore. When Port heard of my plan he immediately chimed in with a "bor-ring!"

"I've got a better idea," he said. "I know a good trail, up the back side of Mount Rushmore. I go up there with my friends sometimes and shoot eggs at the tourists below with wrist rockets. You should see them run for their tour buses."

"How do we get up there?" I asked.

"There's only one fence to climb. It says 'No Trespassing,' but no one's ever bothered us. Then you just hike up the hill for about an hour and this trail dumps you off right next to George Washington's sideburn.

You could sprinkle your dad's ashes off the top of the mountain. It'll be like dandruff."

The plan was set. We decided to leave early Sunday morning before anyone in the house had gotten up. I placed two spoonfuls of Dad's ashes into a plastic sandwich bag, zipped the bag up and stuck it in my front pocket, and off we went.

The sun was just breaking the horizon when we arrived at the fence. It was a four-foot barbed-wire fence with red-and-white painted metal signs affixed to each of the wooden posts spread out ten feet apart. The signs stated "No Trespassing" and "Violators will be prosecuted to the full extent of the law."

"Oh, don't let that worry you," Port said. "They just put those up to scare off people." We walked along the fence for a few hundred feet until we found a slight crevice under the fence where a mountain spring had eroded the ground enough so that we could slide under the fence. We took turns holding up the bottom strand of barbed wire while the other slid underneath it and onto the forbidden side.

"See, I told you it was easy," Port said with confidence. "Come on." As we walked up the hill, there was a slightly noticeable path cut through the grass, but it was obviously not the most traveled road.

"There wasn't even a fence up until just a few years ago," Port explained. "That's when a Girl Scout troop hiked up here for a picnic and some Brownie girl was trying to show off and fell. Luckily for her, she landed on Lincoln's cheek and was able to hold onto his birthmark until the rangers came."

By the time we neared the top, the sun was beating down on our backs and we were sweating. The shade of the trees was a cool relief. As we came out of the small clump of woods, we saw nothing but rock in front of us.

"We just climb over that way," Port said, pointing to the right. "And voila, George Washington's temple." We climbed over and up and then stood up to see the valley below us. The Black Hills looked beautiful from the crown of Washington's head.

"If you go over by Jefferson's ear and look back this way, you can see my dad's shop." Together we hiked over to Jefferson's ear and Port

pointed out Fred's souvenir shop. I noticed that vandals with spray paint
had been to this spot. Jefferson's inner ear had been painted yellow, and
in black spray paint they had written "Get Tommy a Q-Tip!" As much
as I dislike graffiti and vandalism, I couldn't help but laugh. We walked
over to Roosevelt to get a closer look and then on to Lincoln. There on
the top of Lincoln's head I opened the plastic baggy and let the ashes
scatter in the breeze. The ashes swirled around like a miniature cyclone
and slowly dissipated as they blew toward the head of Washington.

"Cool," Port said.

"Yeah, I'm glad you told me about coming up here."

Just then a loud horn was blown, followed by an amplified voice saying, "Suicide is not the answer. Things are never as bad as they seem.
Come down and find Jesus." We looked around, then looked at each
other. We saw a man in a navy blue suit climbing up the rocks toward us.
He wore a black fedora hat and carried a Bible in one hand and a bullhorn in the other. "You're young, you've got a long life ahead of you,"
he said, now starting to sound out of breath. "Jesus turns lives around,"
he said, panting. He then stopped and sat on a rock, and took off his hat
and wiped the sweat from his brow with the left sleeve of his jacket. We
hurried down the rocks toward him.

"Are you okay?" I asked him.

"God is good!" he yelled through his bullhorn, now only a few feet
away.

"Are you okay?" Port asked.

"Hey, who's savin' who here?" the man snapped back sharply.

"I don't know," Port stated.

"Aren't you guys trying to kill yourselves?"

"No, are you?" I said.

"No, I saw you coming up here and I thought you were going to jump
off."

"Oh, no," I said.

"My name is Reverend Roy Regan and I conduct a sunrise service up
here on the first Sunday of each month."

"I don't see any other people," Port said.

"I preach to the universe. The earth is my church, the trees are pews,
and the animals are my congregation."

"An all-squirrel choir," I said under my breath to Port. "Do the squirrels drop a couple of nuts in your offering plate?" I asked aloud.

"Son, I don't believe it's proper to make jokes at the expense of the man who just saved your life."

"You're right, I'm sorry, pastor," Port said, acting remorseful.

"It's reverend, not pastor."

"What's the difference?"

"Reverend sounds better. Reverend Roy Regan, it has those three R's. 'Pastor Roy Regan' screws up the flow."

We walked back down the hill with the reverend, thanked him for saving our lives, and walked home. The reverend invited us to come worship on the mountain anytime.

The day before I planned to leave, I was working in the shop and it was very busy. A tour bus had stopped, and the tour group had fifteen minutes to make their souvenir purchases. The store was nearly filled to capacity. Through all the customer questions and chaos I spotted a couple of preteen boys grabbing things and putting them in their pants pockets, then looking around to make sure no one was watching them. I screamed across the store, "Hey, put that back!"

The two boys ran out of the shop and down the street. I took off after them in my best cops-and-robbers style.

"Stop them!" I yelled out to anyone on the sidewalk ahead, but the window-shopping tourists only clutched their packages and cleared a path for the thieves. At the end of the second block from the shop, the boys split up. I followed the smaller of the two. He was clutching a handful of Mount Rushmore plastic rulers in one hand and running as fast as he could. I was catching up to him, and when I got close enough, I leapt on his back, tackling him from behind. As we hit the ground, several of the plastic rulers fractured into jagged pieces. One of them, with a point as sharp as a knife, penetrated my chest between my eighth and nine rib and punctured a lung, though I didn't know it at that point. In fact, it hardly hurt at all. I'd had paper cuts and charley horses that had hurt more than this, but when I looked and saw a sharp plastic stick halfway impaled into my flesh, I knew it was probably pretty serious. Being the good Samaritan that he was, the young thief got up and ran away.

Port, following behind me, had seen the accident and quickly called the paramedics. I was rushed to the hospital in Deadwood for an operation. The doctors were able to reinflate my lung and stop the internal bleeding. After a five-day stay in the hospital, I was released.

I spent another two weeks convalescing on homemade tomato soup at Fred's house until the doctor gave me the okay to travel. As I improved, I tried to help with chores, but the family wouldn't allow me to lift a finger. Hazel caught Port and me taking down the window screens and putting up the storm windows, and when she hollered at me to get back in bed, there wasn't even a hint of sexual innuendo.

As a going-away gift, the family had restored their old moped into working order, placed a big red bow on it, and set it on the front porch for me to find as I walked out the door. After lots of hugs and promises to keep in touch, I peddled down the driveway and started the engine with a twist of the handgrip. The family waved until I was out of sight, speeding along at a breakneck speed of twenty-two miles per hour.

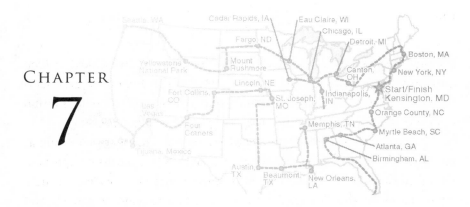

# CHAPTER
# 7

IT TOOK ME THREE AND A HALF HOURS to reach the Wyoming state line, which was only about sixty miles away. I didn't have a pair of gloves, and without them my fingers had become numb. I would take turns holding the handlebars with one hand while trying to warm the other by blowing into it or sticking it underneath my sweatshirt.

I saw a roadside bar near Beulah, Wyoming, with dozens of motorcycles parked in front of it. Now feeling a certain kinship with the easy riders, I parked my moped next to an impressive collection of Harley Davidsons and went into the clapboard shack. It took a few minutes for my eyes to adjust to the darkness of the bar, but once they did, I could see thousands of one dollar bills pinned, glued, stapled, nailed, and taped to every inch of wall and ceiling space. Some of the bills had been written on with clever statements such as, "Doreen & Frank Forever" and "Mike '89." Most of the dollar bills were discolored after years of being saturated with cigarette smoke. I made my way over to the bar and found an empty stool. I asked Donna, the wig-wearing barmaid, if they served food.

"It's all right there in front of you," she said, while lightly scratching her hickey-ridden neck. My eyes were drawn to the faded black tattoo over her right breast that read "I Love Dick."

I scanned the selection of food items that sat on the back counter behind the bar: potato chips, Slim Jims, and a jar of hot-n-spicy pickled eggs.

"I guess I'll have one of each, and a beer."

Donna tossed the Slim Jim and potato chips to me and placed the pickled egg on a cocktail napkin saying, "Don't let that sucker roll away.

These are slippery li'l devils, and if that one hits the floor, you don't get another."

There were a dozen or so biker guys playing pool and hanging out. Two of the men were participating in a pain-tolerance contest. One man suffered from male-pattern baldness and pulled the few sad strands of hair that held steadfast to his scalp into a stubby and pathetic-looking ponytail. The other man was stocky with a thick, furry black beard. The contest was for them to each hold their hands about three inches over the flame of a small globe candle. The first one to pull his hand away from the slowly scorching flame had to buy the other a drink. I watched the competition and was soon treated to the grotesque smell of burned flesh. These two masochists were able to hold the palm of their hands over the flame for about a minute before a champion was crowned.

"Fuck!" Balding-Ponytail screamed, as he hurriedly pulled his hand away from the fire and shook it like he was doing the hokey-pokey. He spit a large dangling glob of saliva into his burned hand to cool the now medium-rare palm.

"I own you, bitch!" Beard Man shouted. "I can't be stopped!"

"Double or nothing on the back of the hand?" Balding-Ponytail asked.

"It's your hand and your money," Beard Man stated matter-of-fact before they simultaneously placed their turned-over hands back above the flame. Seconds after the sequel commenced I noticed little puffs of singed hair smoke rising from both of their hands, and grimaces came to both of their faces. They were unable to sustain the pain as long as in the first contest and started to coerce the other into quitting.

"Come on, man, your hand's melting; pull away," said Beard Man.

"No," Balding-Ponytail said with struggle in his voice. "I could go all night this way."

"You know you wanna quit, man. Just quit."

"You quit."

"You wanna quit together?" Beard Man suggested.

"No, you quit."

"Come on, we'll both pull out on three, okay?"

"Okay. On three."

"One, two," Beard Man counted slowly and then shouted, "three!" Neither man pulled his hand away from the flame.

"You lyin' whore," Balding-Ponytail exclaimed. "I knew I couldn't trust you."

"Okay, it's a draw. Say it's a draw. I said it's a draw. Just say it's a draw and it's over."

"It's a draw," Balding-Ponytail said. They both pulled their hands away from the flame.

"Still undefeated," Beard Man stated proudly. "And you still owe me a drink from the first ass-kicking I gave you."

The bald man ordered two draft beers from Donna and placed one in front of the bearded man.

"Thanks for the cocktail, Mother Fucker," he said with a tone of arrogance.

I was taken aback. It sounded just like what the car-jacking biker had said to me when he drove off in the Pink Lady. I looked closely at the man, wondering if he could be the same guy who stole the car. I listened and continued to discreetly watch him. When I was convinced that this was in fact the car thief, I called the police. I met the officer down the street at a thrift shop and explained the situation. The policeman went into the bar to investigate and returned to the thrift shop where I had since purchased a pair of red, white, and blue ski gloves with the Lake Placid 1980 Olympic symbol on the back. The officer assured me he wasn't the robber.

"They're a motor cycle club of dentist bikers from Nova Scotia; they're clean as a hound's tooth," the officer said.

"Dentists?!" I said with amazement. "Those guys who were cussing like sailors and burning holes in their hands were dentists?"

"Yep. Showed me their Canadian Dental Association cards and business cards. Real nice guys. Hell, one of 'em even gave me a couple new toothbrushes for my kids." I guess the officer didn't want to be outdone by the generosity of the dentist bikers because he reached into his motorcycle's side locker and gave me a reflective "McGruff the Crime Dog" decal sticker as a parting gift.

I rode the moped on the shoulder of the interstate across northern Wyoming and spent the night in a town called Gillette. No razors or shaving cream, just a small downtown area and a seventeen-dollar-a-night motel. On the next day's ride, I got pulled over by a state trooper who told me it was illegal to drive the moped on the interstate. The officer let me off with a warning and gave me a state map to help me plot my way out of Wyoming.

The small country roads I was forced onto were less dangerous and more scenic than Highway 190, but at this pace I'd be finishing the trip with coarse gray hairs growing out of my old-man ears.

Two days of ten hours of riding got me to the east entrance of Yellowstone National Park. Once inside, I joined hordes of other gawking tourists at the world famous hole in the ground known as Old Faithful. A park ranger named Mitch stood guard near the landmark, awaiting the next blow. He was a little pip-squeak of a guy who wore braces with a thin, metal headgear strip around the front of his face, which made him look like an NFL kicker. He was certainly no overwhelming figure but his authoritative presence caused me to rethink my idea of sprinkling some of Dad's ashes down the Old Faithful hole.

"I didn't come this far to just litter Dad's ashes on the ground, like a tourist discarding an empty bag of potato chips," I told myself. So I devised a plan to distract Mitch long enough for me to hop over the rail that encircled Old Faithful and sprinkle Dad's ashes before the next eruption. I thought a bear scare would do the trick but wondered whether it's moral to scream *bear* in a crowded national park.

Instead, I told Mitch that a kid was carving his name in a tree. Mitch, a tree hugger, looked at me with fixed eyes and coldly asked, "Where is he?" as if he had a score to settle. I pointed toward the edge of the woods and Mitch raced over, leaving his Old Faithful post long enough for me to sprinkle some ashes down the hole. When Mitch came back he asked me for a description of "the tree-tagger."

"Uh," I said, stalling, and then I described a tree-carving suspect using visions of Dennis the Menace as my template. Mitch passed along the information via walkie-talkie to the other rangers.

The Old Faithful eruption went off like clockwork, and Dad had been successfully sprinkled in another state. As I returned to my moped, I saw a group of rangers talking to a blond-haired kid in a red-and-white striped T-shirt. I eavesdropped on their conversation and discovered that, to my dismay, they were accusing this kid of being my imaginary tree-tagger.

I couldn't let this kid be my fall guy, so I approached the rangers with the truth. After a brief scolding and warning about never doing this again, they let us go. I exited the national park on the west side and rode north on Highway 191 toward Bozeman, Montana. I was in good standing with the Montana state police, so I tried to ride on the interstate shoulder. I made it through Butte and Missoula before my next encounter with the law. The Montana officer gave me the same spiel I'd heard in Wyoming almost verbatim. He, too, let me off with a warning, but no map. I only had about 100 miles to go to reach the Idaho state line, so I decided to risk it and stay on the interstate. I only got about ten miles before I was spotted by the same officer, and he pulled over and gave me a thirty-five dollar ticket.

"And if I catch ya out here again, I'll impound your little scooter," he warned me. I figured that I'd pressed my luck enough so I stopped for dinner at a family restaurant called the Big Sky Cafe. I sat at a booth next to an overwhelmed mother of three small children. The kids pounded on the table with their silverware, and when the mom focused her attention on cutting one of the kid's meat, another used the opportunity to pick some chewed gum from underneath the table and start chewing it.

"No! No!" the mother hollered. "That's poo-poo gum. If you want some gum, I'll buy you some gum. Don't eat that."

After a cold but beautiful two-day ride out of Montana and into Idaho, I sprinkled Dad's ashes in Coeur d'Alene, which I believe is French for, "Damn, it's cold up here." That night I stayed at tthe Lucky Inn Motel in Opportunity, Washington. It all sounded so positive and inspirational I expected Tony Robbins to be the desk clerk.

I acquired a Washington state map the next morning at a gas station and set out for Seattle on a rural two-lane highway with tree farms on both sides of the road. There were acres of saplings next to acres of mature trees followed by a stump-ridden field, its harvest now on sale at a Home Depot near you. The highway meandered in every direction all the way to Seattle, taking me nearly a week to cross the state. Most of the money I'd saved from working at Fred's had been spent on damp and musty motels. I longed for the inexpensive and surprisingly comfortable backseat of the Pink Lady.

At the end of a particularly cold and gray day's ride, I stopped for the night in Govan, Washington. The motel in Govan was appropriately named the Govan Motel and used letters and numbers interchangeably on their marquee board. Hey, who needs to buy more E's when a backwards 3 works just as well?

For nineteen dollars I purchased the one-day exclusive rights to use Room 6. I pulled the moped into a parking space next to a Winnebago sporting a red silhouette sticker of a square-dancing couple in the back window. My new neighbors were sitting in folding chairs in front of Room 5. They were a middle-age couple huddled over a hibachi barbecue. I smiled at them as I unlocked the door and said, "Smells great, what time do we eat?"

They smiled back and said, "We'll letcha know," which ninety-nine times out of a hundred means, "Leave us alone."

I took a hot shower to wash away the chill of the road and was toweling off when there was a knock on the door. I looked through the peep hole and saw my barbecuing neighbor standing there.

"Yeah?" I said through a closed door.

"What do you want on your burger?" asked the man, who looked surprisingly like Don Ho without a lei.

"Oh, you shouldn't have," I said.

"Too late now. They're almost done. What do you want on it?"

"Hold on. I'll be right out." I quickly browsed through my bag to find the cleanest of my dirty clothes and went out to meet the neighbors.

"So, did we talk you into a burger?" the man asked.

"Sounds great, if you have enough."

"Oh, sure, plenty." He introduced himself and his wife as Rod and Winnie Kapitolo and the lazy bassett hound resting on a blanket at their feet as Mai Tai. They were a retired couple from Hawaii traveling around the states in a motor home, and they couldn't wait to tell me stories about where they'd been and who they'd met. "We've met the nicest people," Winnie said with just a hint of a Japanese accent.

"Salt of the earth," Rod added. "You care for a glass of wine?"

He poured me some wine in a small clear plastic cup from a five-liter box of Franzia Mountain Chablis. I swished the wine around the glass and then smelled it.

"Oh, nice bouquet," I said, as if I was some kind of a wine connoisseur.

Rod didn't pick up on my sarcasm. "Oh, yes, they really put out a nice box of wine."

We ate hamburgers, Fritos corn chips, and macaroni salad, and drank from the box of wine. I listened while they talked and argued points of minutiae for three hours straight. I was reminded of the old saying, "There's no such thing as a free lunch"; the price of this one was listening to the endless insipid travel tales of Rod and Winnie. *No wonder Mai Tai looks so exhausted*, I thought to myself. Around ten o'clock my politeness wore off and I said good night.

"Well, let us get your address so we can send you a Christmas card," Winnie asked. I scribbled Port's name and address on the paper and wrote, "Keep in touch," at the bottom. I went into my room and I heard Winnie tell Rod, "What a nice young man."

"Salt of the earth," Rod added.

I slipped out of Govan without another Winnie and Rod encounter and headed for the Cascade mountain range. I worried about how the moped would handle the elevation and the cold, but both turned out to be nonissues.

Two days later, the moped and I successfully rode into downtown Seattle. There were signs pointing to a place called Pioneer Square, so I followed them. I stopped in for a "warm-me-up" coffee at the Caffeine Junkie coffeehouse, which seemed to be run by new age crystal creeps, near Pioneer Square. I walked into the shop and was instantly greeted by the smell of incense, roasting coffee beans, and cigarette smoke. One of the shop's walls was painted with a colorful mural of faceless, floating body forms suspended around a bright yellow star. There was a small group of coffee drinkers milling around, reading newspapers, and playing checkers. A community bulletin board near the front door was cluttered with flyers for items for sale, roommates wanted, and upcoming shows for such local bands as Guava Girl & The Stoic Balding Brothers, The Ass Dents, Shrinking Spleens, and The Pan Scrapings.

I took a seat at the counter next to a man dressed completely in black and hunched over a notebook. He sported a small hoop through the side of his nose, and a cigarette dangled precariously from his mouth. I ordered a coffee from the counterman, who had a silver stud pierced between his lower lip and chin, and suddenly I felt like that one family on everybody's block that doesn't decorate their house with Christmas lights. I asked Silver Stud to pass the cream from in front of Hoop Nose.

"Oh, don't worry about him, he's just depressed because his muse has cancer," Silver Stud said matter-of-factly.

"Hepatitis!" Hoop Nose hollered. "Why must you always misdiagnose the condition of my muse?"

I picked up my coffee and found a table near the window. Someone had scratched into the formica tabletop the words, "What the world needs now is a good plague." I drank my coffee and updated my new journal, which was now several days behind. I ordered another coffee and noticed that the poet at the counter with the sick muse had been given some divine inspiration because he scribbled frantically in his notebook for a half hour without looking up. Then, with desperation in his voice he suddenly shouted out to the room, "What rhymes with *gonorrhea*?"

Trying to assist in the creative process, Silver Stud suggested, "Sopapilla?"

"Nah, too ethnic."

I went into the restroom to wash my face before I left to tour the Space Needle. I rode over to the World's Fair complex, where Seattle keeps its most famous landmark, and parked my moped at a bike rack. I walked through the area where the World's Fair had once been. It now resembled a carnival with kiddie rides and carnival-style games. I stopped briefly to listen to a busker who was playing a small toy piano and singing "Climb Every Mountain" incredibly off key.

I walked over to the Space Needle's ticket office when I could no longer take any more of the man's singing. The price to go up in the Space Needle was five dollars, but a family of five or more had a flat rate of fifteen. In an effort to defray my cost, I waited in the lobby until I saw a family of four arrive and then approached them with my money-saving idea.

"Excuse me," I said to the man. "If you buy my ticket and we go in as a family, you'll save five dollars."

The first few families I approached thought I was pulling some sort of streetwise scam and refused my offer. I was in no hurry to go up. I had more time than money, so I patiently waited for the next family.

After waiting another half hour in the lobby, a portly man walked in holding the hand of his daughter, while his wife attempted to control their spastic toddler son on a harness and leash. I approached the man with my offer and when the man didn't immediately refuse the offer, I continued.

"It'll work. Families of five or more are just fifteen dollars. I save five and you save five," I said. "It's a win-win situation," I added to close the deal.

The man looked confused, then pointed to a picture of the Space Needle in a glossy pamphlet he was holding and in an inquisitive voice he uttered, "Space Needle?"

"Yes," I said smiling. "Do you speak English?"

"Space Needle."

"Come with me," I said, beckoning toward me like a traffic cop, hoping the family would follow me to the ticket counter. When we got to the counter the lady behind the glass asked, "How many?"

"There are five of us in my family," I proudly stated.

"You don't look very much alike," she said.

"You know, a lot of people say that, but I think I'm a dead ringer. Look, I've got my father's, uh, ears!"

"Okay, that'll be fifteen dollars."

I turned to the man and slowly and clearly enunciated, "Fifteen dollars." The man looked at me with a frozen expression as if he were an unprepared student being called on by the teacher.

I then held my right hand up toward the man's face and rubbed my thumb across the other four fingers of my hand, hoping that the man would know my sign language for money. I opened and closed my hand three times, extending all my fingers in hopes the man would figure out I was counting to fifteen, but instead he just mimicked the gesture.

"You and your dad sure don't communicate very well," the woman said.

"Yeah, I know, that's what our counselor tells us," I responded, admitting defeat. I paid the five dollars and went through the turnstiles.

The elevator ride took one minute to climb fifteen-hundred feet to the Space Needle's observation deck. The family stopped at the snack stand near the elevator, and I walked outside to the south-facing guardrail to look at downtown Seattle. The view was beautiful. The combination of nature and man-made structures was impressive. *This is the place*, I thought to myself. I reached into the coffee can, grabbed the Mount Rushmore souvenir teaspoon and scooped up some ashes. I carefully pulled the spoon out of the makeshift urn, protecting it from the wind by cupping my other hand over it. Just then the family walked up to me with the little girl holding a cotton candy fluffed up to twice the size of her own head. The man smiled and again performed my fifteen-dollar hand signal, which I think he thought was some sort of American greeting. He pulled his camera out of its case and handed it to me. I turned to take the man's camera just as a gust of wind grabbed the ashes and blew them back toward the Space Needle, with most of the ashes sticking to the billowy sides of the little girl's cotton candy.

I was then left with one of the great moral questions of life: When your father's ashes blow into the cotton candy of a little girl who doesn't speak English, do you try to tell her what happened?

I briefly thought about this dilemma while posing the family for the picture, and I decided that ignorance is bliss. After I took their picture, we exchanged fifteen-dollar hand signals and went our separate ways. I walked around to the west side of the Space Needle, which faced Mount Rainier, and again let some of Dad's ashes fly. This time the drop was successful and the ashes drifted out and down toward the ground. I questioned whether I had done the right thing or not, but justified it by thinking, *I ate a lot of weird stuff as a kid. Cremated human ashes can't be that bad for you, can they?*

I returned to ground level only to wonder what I should do next. I was nearly out of money, and I told myself it's just as easy to be poor in a warm climate as it is in a cold and damp climate, so I turned the moped south on the shoulder of Interstate 5 toward sunny California. I reached Tacoma two-and-a-half hours after leaving Seattle and continued south into logging country. The moped got a flat tire and, without any equipment to fix it, I started pushing it along the highway's shoulder to the first exit, which in these parts are few and far between. Step after step and mile after mile, I pushed the moped along the roadside shoulder littered with gravel and cigarette butts, which, I believe, is the name of Ben & Jerry's worst-selling ice-cream flavor.

The World's Strongest Man Endurance Event that I felt I was now competing in was getting even more strenuous on the mountain inclines. Too tired to push any farther, I stopped for a break near a makeshift roadside memorial. A two-foot-tall white wooden cross stood in front of a pine tree that had had a clump the size of a volleyball taken out of its side. A tattered red ribbon that hung on the cross stated, "In Loving Memory of Li'l Joker." There were dried bouquets of flowers lying near the cross, and weather-beaten cards and letters were nailed to the tree. I read some of Li'l Joker's mail, figuring Li'l Joker wouldn't mind. Family and friends of Li'l Joker had poured their hearts out in those letters, telling stories of family parties and trips, what he meant to them, and how much they would miss him. After reading the letters, my struggle of pushing the moped didn't seem so tough.

I continued on the moped marathon for two more miles without spotting an exit but with a renewed appreciation for just being alive. I spotted a road sign in the distance that I hoped would announce a freeway exit with services, but which instead read, "This stretch of highway is kept clean by the Wong Driving School," whose motto was "Learn to drive the Wong Way."

After pushing the moped another mile, an older-model gray Chevy pickup passed me, then pulled over to the side of the road and started backing up. The truck looked like a crumpled ball of aluminum foil due to the multiple dents all over it. I walked up to the passenger window.

"You need some help?" the driver asked. He was a middle-aged man with brown, stringy, shoulder-length hair and a red bandanna tied around his forehead, resembling a "Born in the USA"-era Springsteen.

"My bike broke down. Do you know how far it is to the next town?" I asked.

"A good eight or ten miles," the man said. "I'll give you and your bike a ride if you want."

"That'd be great," I said.

"One, two, three," we both counted and then lifted the moped into the bed of the truck. The moped was much lighter than I'd expected and it nearly flew out of our arms as we lifted with all our might. One of the moped's pedals struck the driver just under his right cheekbone, opening a small cut.

"Damn it," he yelled, clutching his cheek. He grimaced in pain and let loose with a string of expletives.

"Sorry," I said and reiterated countless times before the driver reassured me it wasn't my fault.

"You don't have to give me a ride if you don't want to," I said.

"We've already got that bike in there, I might as well give you a ride," he said, tying the tailgate closed with blue climber's rope. We both got into the cab of the truck. "The name's Al," he said, extending his hand while simulating chewing in an attempt to regain some feeling in his cheek. "Al Baumgardner."

Al started the truck, pushed a Frank Sinatra eight-track tape in his stereo, and off we drove.

"So, how's your cheek feeling?" I asked.

"Oh, it's okay, don't worry about it. So, what's the matter with your bike?"

"Flat tire."

"They'll fix you up; they've got a twenty-four-hour truck stop with everything."

"Are you pretty familiar with this area?"

"Sure. I've lived most of my life in the Northwest."

"Where are you heading now?"

"Medford, Oregon. I got a job down there in the morning."

"You're gonna be drivin' all night?"

"Most of it. I figure I'll be there by about 4:00. That gives me a couple hours to stretch out once I get there. I don't have to be on the site until 6:00."

"What do you do?"

"Ah, a little bit of everything. I'm a handyman type. Down there, though, we're building a shopping center."

"Do you work for a company?"

"This time, yes, but most of the time, I find my own work. What do you do?"

"I'm traveling around the country sprinkling my dad's ashes. It was kind of like, you know, his last wish."

"You've been traveling the country on that?!"

"Well, not the whole country, just since Mount Rushmore."

"Wow, that's a far-out story. Traveling the country on a moped. Now that's one for the boys on the site tomorrow."

"Gas, Food, Lodging, two miles," a sign stated. "Is this the place?" I asked.

"Yep," Al said, and then again paused. "You know, I was just thinking, since you're not going anywhere in particular, you're more than welcome to ride along with me to Medford."

"Are you sure you wouldn't mind?"

"Oh, hell no, you'd be doing me a favor, helping keep me awake."

"Great!" I said. "Thanks a lot."

"Hey, no sweat off my balls. Grab a drink or a sandwich; they're in that cooler behind my seat."

I lifted the lid off the cooler and saw about fifty ham-and-cheese sand-wiches on white bread, individually wrapped in cellophane. I grabbed one for each of us. It was starting to get dark now as we neared the Oregon state line. As we drove through the city of Portland, Al turned the radio dial from station to station, eventually stopping on an oldies station where the disc jockey used the term "one-hit wonder." Al turned down the music and very seriously asked me, "Would you rather be a 'has been' or a 'never was'?"

I thought about it for a moment. "I guess I'd rather be a 'has been' because at least at one time I would have done something."

"I used to think that way too, but the older I get, the more I think it's better to be a 'never was' because you don't know what you're missing."

"What do you mean?"

"Well, if you do something great, you briefly reap the rewards: fame, fortune, power, whatever. But it's fleeting. It's gone before you know it and then you spend the rest of your life trying to recapture that brief moment of glory. Personally, I think ignorance is bliss. I mean right now there are natives on South Pacific islands who've never heard of a Nobel Prize or a Super Bowl and would probably use an Oscar to open a coco-nut. They're happy just fishin' with a spear and bangin' their old lady in a bamboo hut."

"Wow, I've never really thought about it that way," I said, laughing under my breath. "But what if you did something great and then were able to stay at that level for your lifetime."

"Impossible," Al stated. "All things have cycles. There are peaks and valleys to everything. The only thing constant in life is change."

"Well, maybe another peak will come."

"Yes, but sometimes the peaks are molehills and the valleys are Grand Canyons."

"Yeah, I guess so," I said. "I guess I'll worry about it once I do some-thing worth noting."

It was nearing midnight and the highway that cut through the wilder-ness was dark and had very few other travelers. I sensed Al was grow-ing weary and offered to drive and let him sleep for awhile. With a long yawn and a shake of the head, Al agreed. He pulled over and we exchanged places. We buckled up and I drove off into the Oregon night. Al was asleep before we entered the Eugene city limits. He began to snore and occasionally speak some incomprehensible gibberish. I slowly began to feel myself getting tired. I rolled down the window just a crack to get some fresh air in the car, but Al's teeth began to chatter and without a blanket, he hugged himself for warmth. I rolled up the window and turned on the radio.

The highway's white lane line began to seem endless and appeared foggy to my tired eyes. I felt my head nod a few times. I slapped myself in the face and continued to drive. I nodded off again and was awakened by the feeling of the truck leaving the paved road and venturing onto the gravel on the side of the road. Instantly alert, I pulled the steering wheel to the left and was able to get back on the road with just a slight fishtailing of the back of the truck, but my moped was thrown from the truck's bed. We pulled over and put it back inside, but although neither of us said anything, I think we both knew the moped hadn't survived the fall. I started apologizing to Al again, but all he said was, "I think I'll drive."

"Well, that was a deja vu experience," Al stated calmly.

"What do you mean?"

"I rolled this truck once, that's how it got all dented up. I fell asleep at the wheel and rolled it about five times."

"When was this?"

"A couple years ago. It thrashed the body and broke the windows, but it didn't hurt the engine. Still runs like the day I got her."

"How about you?"

"Fine. Cuts and bruises, nothing major."

"You're lucky."

"Yeah, I am. In the police report they said they found my ham-and-cheese sandwiches scattered hundreds of yards in every direction."

We talked the rest of the night just to help each other stay awake. I told Al how expensive the last couple of weeks had been from staying in motels every night.

"You don't have to tell me," he said emphatically. "I spend my life in motels. The key is you gotta make 'em work for you."

"What do you mean?" I asked.

"If you pay thirty bucks for a room, you gotta get your money's worth. Lots of times I'll roll into a town early in the morning, just after daybreak, and check-in. Then I have thirty or so hours before check-out the next day. That morning I'll sleep until noon, and then that night I get another night's sleep. Boom. Fifteen bucks each."

"What if they won't let you check-in that early?"

"A lot of 'em won't but plenty will, usually the mom-and-pop-type operations, and if they won't, well screw 'em, there will be other motels in town."

The sun was still a few hours from showing its face when we arrived in the greater Medford area. The streets were empty. Al drove me by the construction site, which seemed to be a giant fenced-in mud hole. There were dozens of Hispanic men loitering next to the fence's gate.

"What are they doing?" I asked.

"Those are the day laborers."

"What do they do?"

"Whatever the foreman tells them to. Some days he'll hire twenty, some days none. It just matters how much grunt work there is that day."

"Do they get paid at the end of each day?"

"Yeah."

"Do you think I could get a day's work there?"

"You don't want to do that. It's hard work. It's all digging, lifting, mixing, and carrying, and they only get five or six bucks an hour."

I eventually talked Al into putting in a good word for me with the fore-man. Al had worked with the foreman before and said the foreman didn't like hiring white day laborers because he thought they were all booze-heads or drug addicts. The foreman arrived at five-thirty and hired ten of the men standing around the gate and me, thanks to whatever Al had told him. All of us day laborers were given an orange hard hat with stenciled black letters across the front that screamed "DAY LABOR."

For the first four hours, I had the job of loading the freestanding cement mixer. My job description was as follows: split a ninety-pound bag of cement mix down the middle with a box cutter, pick the bag up and empty the contents into the mixer, repeat several hundred times until my arms became as limp as noodles. During our morning break, I sprinkled a dash of Dad into the cement mixer. I was happy knowing he would be part of the foundation, because in life that's what he was to so many people.

I was so exhausted that during lunch I fell asleep in the bed of Al's truck while he dined on his premade ham-and-cheese sandwiches. In the afternoon, I think the foreman could see I was wiped out, and he gave me the easier job of building cement forms. I carried lumber to the mason workers and drove stakes into the ground with a sledgehammer.

This seemed like a pencil-pushin' job after lifting ninety-pound bags all morning. At three o'clock the foreman called the day laborers to his office/trailer to give each of us forty-eight dollars cash.

"Will we be seeing you tomorrow?" the foreman asked me, with a smirk on his face.

"I don't think so," I said and walked out to Al's truck. Al was removing his tool belt as I approached, looking like a beaten horse.

"I told you it was hard work," he said with a grin. "So what are you gonna do now?"

"Sleep for a week."

"Sleep?! It's cocktail time."

"My arms are so tired I don't think I could even lift a glass."

"We'll get you a straw—now hop in."

Al joined the motorcade of work trucks to a nearby watering hole called Sam's Palace. They had schooners of Old Milwaukee beer on draft for sixty cents. I felt like such a big spender ordering a schooner, paying with a one-dollar bill, and telling the bartender to keep the change. Al sat at the bar and talked to his coworkers. None of my coworkers showed up, which was fine since I hadn't said a word to them all day due to the fact that my Spanish was limited to *taco, tortilla, Cinco de Mayo,* and *Julio Iglesias.*

After a couple of beers and a scan of the jukebox, I decided to go lie down in the back of Al's truck. I quickly fell asleep and was awakened sometime later by Al and five other guys throwing buckets of water on me and laughing uncontrollably.

"We're just messin' with ya," said one of the culprits, as he playfully rubbed my saturated head.

"Come on, let's get some dinner. I'm buyin'," said Al.

We drove off to a twenty-four-hour mini mart, where he purchased a packet of Farmer John hot dogs and a twelve-pack of Coors Light. He stopped at a motel near the job site and went in to talk to the desk clerk.

"Here's the deal," Al said. "A single is twenty-eight dollars, a double is forty-two dollars. If you want to pay the difference you could get your own bed, or you can sleep on the floor for free."

"The floor is fine with me."

"You cheap bastard," Al chuckled with a big smile on his face.

Once inside the room, Al started preparing dinner. He placed a clean five-gallon joint-compound bucket under the bathtub faucet and turned on the hot water. He opened the packet of hot dogs and dropped them into the bucket and let the hot water run.

"You don't need a hot plate or an oven, all you need is running hot water to cook," Al told me. "In fifteen minutes you'll have a boiled hot dog just as good as Wienerschnitzel." He carried plates and utensils in a plastic shopping bag. In the glove compartment of his truck, he had an enormous variety of condiment packets he'd collected from fast-food restaurants. When the hot dogs were piping hot, we ate them hunched over the dresser while watching a rerun of Hogan's Heroes on the television. While applying some Taco Bell mild sauce to his hot dog, Al said, "Did you know that somebody killed Hogan? Strangled him, I think."

"Really?" I said matter-of-factly, while mixing an Arby's horseradish sauce with a Wendy's ketchup.

"So what do you think of the dogs?" Al asked, fishing for a compliment.

"Good. Real good."

"You can cook so much in the bathtub. I should write a cookbook for the motel traveler."

"Yeah, bathtub cookin', that'd sell a million copies," I said.

"You wouldn't believe how much stuff you can cook with a bucket and hot running water. Poached eggs, spaghetti noodles, cup of soup, instant coffee, and those are just the staples. If I really thought about it, I'll bet you I could make a gourmet meal in that bathroom."

I just nodded and said, "Did they ever catch Hogan's killer?"

"I don't think so."

"I'll betcha it was Schultz."

"Yeah. Nazi bastard."

CHAPTER

8

AL LEFT FOR THE SITE at a quarter to six the next morning. On his way out, he accidentally stepped on my hand with his steel-toe work boots, which is a great way to start any day. He wished me luck and I sleepily thanked him for everything.

It was Christmas Eve morning and the thought of being alone for Christmas depressed me. The only person I knew on the West Coast besides Al was Uncle Spud, who lived in San Luis Obispo, California. He wasn't actually an uncle, but a close family friend and former army buddy of Dad's.

I called Uncle Spud from the bus station to see what he was doing for Christmas. "Just roasting my chestnuts by an open fire," he said. He knew what I was doing and extended an invitation for me to come stay for the holidays. I didn't need to be asked twice. I bought a bus ticket along with the rest of the masses trying to get somewhere for the holidays, and within a couple of hours we had crossed the state line into California. The Land of Milk and Honey was gray and drizzly, nothing like what I envisioned California to be. I imagined it sparkling with sunshine, palm trees lining the roads, and long-haired surfers in red-and-white striped shirts chatting with nubile blond movie stars. Instead, we were driving through dull little mountain towns with names such as Yreka, which I think is the Indian word for "Oops, I forgot to wear deodorant today."

Our first stop was in Redding and our second was in Sacramento, where I had to change to the coastal bus that traveled on Highway 101. On our way to San Francisco we passed a small town called Vacaville, where the chief industry is a state prison. A sign on the freeway read "State Prison next right. Do not pick up hitchhikers." Come on, just one, pleeeease!

We stopped for half an hour at the downtown terminal in San Francisco. I took a quick stroll around Market Street, hoping to find an elderly beatnik still snapping his fingers to poetry or some burned-out flower children smoking banana peels and protesting something, but all I saw were business people in overcoats scurrying about in the freezing cold wind.

The bus stopped once more in San Jose, then arrived in San Luis Obispo at ten o'clock. Uncle Spud met me at the South Street Greyhound station and wasted no time in asking me to "pull his finger." We walked back to his house, which was only a few blocks away. I hadn't seen Uncle Spud in eight years, but besides being heavier and grayer, he didn't seem any different, still a free spirit. Despite now being in his early seventies, he was vibrant and seemed as energetic as he had been in the stories Dad used to tell about him.

Uncle Spud was a short and stocky man with a pocked face from a bad bout of teenage acne. He signed up with the Army in 1944, the day he turned eighteen and was legally able to do so. He met Dad in the service. Fighting side-by-side, they created a soldier's bond that was closer than brothers.

Uncle Spud received his colorful nickname when one day, near the end of the war, he was ordered to secure a Berlin apartment building to make sure there weren't any booby traps, bombs, or snipers lying in wait. He and my dad were inside the building executing their orders, just about to give the "all clear," when a Nazi woman sprang out of the pantry in her apartment and stabbed Uncle Spud in his lower back with a potato peeler. The potato peeler barely penetrated his flesh, but the wound was considered an injury from hand-to-hand enemy combat, so he was awarded the Purple Heart. One of the guys in his unit called it "the million-dollar tater wound" and gave him the nickname of Spud.

Despite the passage of time since the war, the guys from the unit remained very close. As they started to die off one by one, the others would meet at the funerals to show their respect for their fallen brother. Basically it was a time to get together and get drunk and raise hell and act like the kids they never got to be. When Dad died, six of the guys who lived up and down the East Coast met in Baltimore and went to an

Orioles game. They got so drunk at the game that afterwards they were down at the restaurants on the bay, urinating for distance off a dock into the water and singing "Boogie Woogie Bugle Boy" at the top of their lungs. They were arrested on charges of being drunk and disorderly, but after a night in jail, no charges were ever filed.

Uncle Spud wasn't able to make it out for the festivities due to the travel distance and his job at Cal Poly University chairing the agricultural department. He had written several textbooks that were used at agriculture schools all over the country and had made a good living doing so. He would joke, "I could retire right now just on the royalties of *Growing Legumes in an Arid Climate.*"

He never married and lived alone about a mile from campus in a remodeled Victorian-style house with a large wooden front porch. He was something of an institution in town. People called him Professor Spud whether they had gone to the university or not. People would stop him on the street and ask to see his war wound. He'd always stop, no matter where he was or what he was doing, and lift up the back of his shirt to expose the tiny scar on his lower back just above his buttock, then invariably he'd loudly pass gas and say, "Watch out, bombing raid."

He wore short pants and sandals year round, adding socks and a sweater if the weather warranted extra protection. He carried his keys on a plastic pink shower-curtain ring latched around the belt loop of his shorts. The keys clanged back and forth, and each step he took could be heard a block away. He carried a large collection of keys to his house, cars, school office, and farm equipment, and the weight of the keys would eventually wear out the belt loop on his shorts. When a loop would break, he would carry the ring on one of the remaining belt loops until all of them had given way, and then he would donate the shorts to the local thrift store and buy a new pair. Though he never left his name on the donated clothes, the local charities always knew when they were getting a donation from Spud.

His style of dress was so notorious around town that a local bar advertised a Professor Spud look-alike contest, and nearly two dozen people showed up. The winner had concocted a way to have a potato peeler sticking out of his lower back and had a sign around his neck that read, "Watch out, bombing raid." Professor Spud agreed to judge the contest once the bar's owner offered him complimentary scotch-and-waters all night long.

I remember one visit when I was about ten. Uncle Spud laughed with Dad and insisted that when I turned fifteen, I was going to come spend the summer with him so that he could take me down to the border city of Tijuana, Mexico, to get me my first "piece of tail." They laughed so hard they cried. I can still remember them wiping the tears from their cheeks as they tried to regain their composure. I reminded Uncle Spud of this story, which still had the same effect on him. "Ol' Peggy Lynn," he said, wiping his eyes. "I really miss that no-good son of a bitch." He was silent for a minute, then boldly said, "What's all this blubberin' shit?! I got a promise to keep. I've got to get you a piece of tail in Tijuana."

"Oh, that's okay," I said. "That was just talk, and it was a long time ago."

"Nonsense, I told your ol' man that I was going to get his boy laid and goddamn it, that's just what I'm going to do."

"That's okay, Uncle Spud. Dad's gone and I don't really want—"

"How old are you?" Uncle Spud interrupted.

"Twenty-one."

"Good God, I'm six years overdue. Your ol' man died wondering why his son wasn't getting his promised pussy."

"He had no memory at the end."

"Hey, you're keeping your promise to him, the least thing I could do is keep mine. So we agree, Tijuana tomorrow. We'll consider it a Christmas gift," he said, extending his hand, which I reluctantly shook.

"All right then, let's go get us some dinner and by dusk tomorrow, I'll have you knee-deep in Mexican muff."

After breakfast we were walking on Higuera Street. Uncle Spud stopped in front of a small walkway no more than six feet wide between two buildings.

"This is Gum Alley," he stated proudly, opening both arms. I looked around, and on both sides of the buildings chewed blobs of bubblegum had been stuck from the ground to the top of the building, some twelve feet high. There were tens of thousands of pieces of chewed gum in various colors stuck to the walls.

"This is the place," I said. "I'll sprinkle some of my dad's ashes here."

"Wait," Uncle Spud said. "You can't just sprinkle him here. We've got to make a bubblegum monument to your dad. Come on."

We walked around the block to a drugstore, grabbed a handful of Bazooka Joe gum, and hightailed it back to Gum Alley. We each chewed several pieces, one by one, until they were all pliable. Once we had about a dozen chewed rubbery pieces piled in a mound on one of the Bazooka comic strips, we formed the gum into an arrow, sprinkled some ashes into the middle, and folded the gum over. I then climbed up Uncle Spud's back and stood on his shoulders to put the arrow pointing toward Heaven as high as I could reach. Once I affixed the gum to the side of the red brick wall with all the force I could muster and posed for a photo from a passing tourist, Uncle Spud set me down. We shook hands and complimented each other on a job well done.

"Are you okay?" I asked.

"Yeah, fine," Uncle Spud said confidently after taking a deep breath.

"Your face is really red."

"I'm fine," he said, with a hint of hostility in his voice. "Just a little tired. Give me a second to catch my breath, would ya?"

The next morning we left San Luis Obispo in Uncle Spud's orange Chevy van with a bumper sticker that read "Gas, Cash, or Ass, nobody rides for free." I started to climb in the passenger's seat, but Uncle Spud quickly put a stop to that.

"What are you doing?"

"Getting in the car."

"No, no, you're driving."

"I'm driving?" I said, with surprise in my voice.

"For Christ's sake, I'm seventy-three years old. I'm three times as old as you and you expect me to chauffeur you all the way to Mexico? I gotta save my strength for later, when it counts."

Oak trees dotted the light brown rolling hills on both sides of the freeway as we worked our way south. Well-placed billboards scattered intermittently along Highway 101 counted down the mileage to a restaurant called Andersen's Split Pea Soup in Buellton. Though I appreciated them letting me know I was making progress toward their fine restaurant, when its exit arrived we chose not to take advantage (mainly due to the fact that we both hate split pea soup).

We passed through Santa Barbara, Ventura, and a place called Oxnard, presumably named after the testicles of a beast of burden. In Hollywood we bid adieu to Highway 101 and "re-upped" with Interstate 5. From the interchange we could see the skyline of downtown Los Angeles, then thirty minutes later the exit sign for Disneyland. I was nervous about what awaited me in Mexico, so I suggested we stop at all the aforementioned places.

"If you don't get down there early," he insisted, "you end up with all the scabies-ridden leftovers."

Seven hours almost to the minute after we left San Luis Obispo, we were waved across the international border by an unconcerned guard, continually motioning for the steady stream of cars to pass through into Mexico without as much as a question from him. We followed the signs to downtown Tijuana. Peddlers filled the streets, selling woven items, ceramic statues, and candy. As we strolled down Revolution Street, barkers stood at the entrance to their shops, trying to draw tourists into their establishments.

"Amigos, cold beer, naked senoritas," said a seedy-looking man wearing a white tank-top with red letters reading "Tijuana Sex Patrol." We paused briefly in front of the topless bar, so the man continued with his sales pitch. "Cheap cerveza. Friendly ladies."

"You want to try it?" Uncle Spud asked.

"Maybe there's a better one down the block," I said, stalling.

As we strolled down the street, each of the bar's barkers continued with their short, choppy, Spanglish catchphrases, "No cover, grande boobies."

When we got to the end of the block, there stood the oldest-looking donkey wearing a woven palm-frond sombrero with cutouts on each side of the hat so his ears could stick through. The donkey wore a wooden nameplate around its neck identifying him as "Oscar" and stood in front of a scenery-drop of a beach setting with the name Tijuana, B.C., Mexico at the top of the painted canvas. By the donkey stood a man with an archaic-looking camera around his neck. He repeatedly hollered out, "Have your souvenir photo taken with the world-famous Oscar the donkey."

"You think if I went to India, they'd know that donkey?" Uncle Spud said jokingly.

"Probably. He is world famous. I don't think that guy would lie."

We both laughed.

"Boy, Tijuana sure looks different since the last time I was here," Uncle Spud admitted, then turned to the photographer. "Hey, there, Ansel Adams. Where can we find some real fun around here?"

"Real fun?" the man said in a broken mix of Spanish and English. "Real fun *es un photo con*." He increased the volume of his voice to play to a group of passing Asian tourists. "Oscar, the world-famous donkey."

I then said to the photographer, "If that donkey was really world famous, wouldn't those Asian people already know about him?"

"*Oscar es muy popular en el mundo*, the world," the photographer said.

"So, for example, what are some of the countries currently experiencing 'Oscar-mania'?'"

The photographer angrily snapped back, "*Quieres photo o no*?!"

"No, we don't," Uncle Spud interjected. "We're looking for some real fun, you know, a little female company."

The photographer threw open his right arm in a sweeping motion across his body. In a frustrated tone he said, "Any of these bars have women."

"Yeah, I know, but we're looking for a place where only the locals go."

"Yeah, we got a place like that, and I could take you there."

"Great," said Uncle Spud.

"But you pay for me, too."

Reluctantly, Uncle Spud agreed.

"And you have picture taken with"—he increased his volume again—"Oscar, the world-famous donkey!"

Uncle Spud and I each put on a sombrero and stood next to Oscar. The photographer positioned us and then loudly counted to three in Spanish, "*Uno, dos, tres.*"

We both said, "*Queso,*" and when both of our mouths formed the "O" sound, he took the picture, making us both look like fish. The photographer then hailed a cab. He sat in the front seat next to the driver and we got in the back. The photographer began speaking to the driver in Spanish. The driver pulled out and I looked back through the rear window at a forlorn world-famous, sombrero-wearing donkey standing all alone on a street corner. The driver drove only a couple of blocks, then pulled over to the side of the road.

"He said he won't go into that part of town unless you pay for him, too," the photographer explained.

"Goddamn, doesn't anybody screw their wife any more?" Uncle Spud barked. He then reluctantly agreed. After ten minutes of driving through twisting and turning streets littered with potholes, the driver pulled up and parked on the sidewalk in front of a small store.

We walked into the storefront, where a man sat behind a row of glass showcases displaying piñatas. The photographer, who was named Ernesto, spoke to the man in Spanish, then told Uncle Spud, "Give him eighty dollars."

"Eighty dollars?" Uncle Spud questioned. "What for?"

"Cover charge, twenty dollars each," Ernesto said.

"For twenty dollars they better have a frickin' buffet in there."

Uncle Spuds pulled off four twenty-dollar bills from the roll of money he kept clipped in the front pocket of his shorts. The man then led us to the back of the shop where music with a loud bass played in a dark room. A disco ball overhead occasionally sprayed flecks of light around the room as it spun.

"Two for the show?" asked the maitre d' as we entered the back room.

"Three to get ready," Uncle Spud said.

"And four to go," I added with a smile.

The man looked at us with his expressionless face.

"There's four of us," Uncle Spud said, sensing the man was not in the mood for weak American humor.

The maitre d' grabbed four plastic-coated menus from a large stack and walked us down front to an over-stuffed couch next to the stage, where a naked dancing girl was hanging upside down by her toned and muscular legs from a brass pole that stretched from the floor to the ceiling. The man handed us each a menu, then snapped his fingers toward the naked cocktail waitress, who brought over four bottles of Corona beer with a lime wedge floating inside each bottle. She also set down four shot glasses and an unopened bottle of Jose Cuervo tequila.

I was the first to open the menu and see pictures of two dozen women in sexually explicit photos. Below each picture was their name, measurements, and a price list for various activities. The turnover for the girls at the establishment must have been pretty high, because on several of the photos new faces had been pasted over the original face, but the picture of the original body remained.

Ernesto broke the seal on the tequila bottle and poured a shot for everyone, then raised his glass. He thought about a toast for a moment and then said, "To United States President Abraham Lincoln." We raised our eyebrows at Ernesto's unique choice for a toast but hoisted our glasses and together said, "to Abe," and then downed the shot in a swift motion.

Uncle Spud poured four more shots and toasted to Pancho Villa. The scene continued for the next hour with each of us making at least two toasts to the heroes of the other's country. The bottle was nearly empty, so I poured half shots for everyone, spilling some of the tequila on the table. I raised my glass and in a slightly slurred speech toasted "Here's to Juan Valdez, the best damn coffee grower in the world."

"He's Colombian!" Ernesto protested.

"Well, whatever, he sure grows some damn good coffee," I sloppily retorted.

The maitre d' approached us saying, "Your women are ready now."

We all started to get up, staggering just a bit. The maitre d' ordered a boy of perhaps ten or eleven to show us to the women. A sense of nervous tension grew inside me as I knew that the time had arrived. My heart began to beat faster and my palms turned moist. I took a deep breath and followed the boy upstairs. There was a long corridor with doors on each side with numbers and a woman's name on each door. In Spanish the boy told Ernesto and the taxi driver, "*Ocho y diez*" and pointed toward the end of the corridor. He paused to study the piece of paper the maitre d' had given him, then said, "You're in three and you're in four."

Uncle Spud opened the door that had a number three above a small plastic stick-on sign with a picture of a teddy bear that said "Rosa's Room." I was sent directly across from Rosa's to room 4 with no name on the door.

"This is Margarita's room," the boy told me. "She hasn't got her name on the door yet." I took a deep breath, ran my fingers through my hair, and knocked on the door.

"You don't need to knock, just go in," the boy said.

I walked in and stood near the door. There before me, sitting up naked in bed, was an overweight woman in her late forties or early fifties, holding her rosary beads.

"*Buenas tardes,*" she said with a big smile, rolling over to the side of the bed to place her rosary beads around a pair of white porcelain praying hands on the nighstand.

"*Hola,*" I said, my voice cracking between syllables. I cleared my throat and tried it again with a deeper, more confident tone. "I mean, *hola.*"

"Oh, you speak Spanish very well," she said.

"*Gracias,* but I don't think my high-school Spanish teacher who flunked me two semesters would agree with you."

"Oh, you're funny," she said with a big smile. "I like funny men, they make me laugh."

"You know, you don't look much like your photo on the menu."

"I'm new here. In fact, this is my first time."

"Your first time?" I said, my voice raising in astonishment.

"Well, my first time getting paid for it," she explained. "Oh, no, my first time was nearly thirty years ago. I've got nine kids."

"Do they know you're doing this?"

"Yes, we've all had to do extra things since my husband passed on."

That was the final straw; there was no way I could continue with what we had come to do. "You know, ma'am, nothing against you, but I can't do this," I said.

"Oh, it's okay," she said, "you're just shy. My husband was shy at first, too. I've got a way to help you get over it." She reached into the top drawer of the nightstand and pulled out a deck of playing cards.

"Strip poker will help get you in the mood," she stated proudly.

"It seems to me you've already lost," I said, gesturing at her bare breasts.

"I'll put on some clothes, then we'll play." She put her clothes back on, and we both sat on the bed with our legs crossed as she dealt the cards.

"Five-card draw, no junk," the woman said as she began dealing the cards. We played for fifteen minutes. I enjoyed a string of good luck, losing only both shoes and one sock, while Margarita sat naked again.

"You know, this just really isn't going to work, but I really appreciate your efforts at getting me in the mood."

"No, you can't go," she commanded. "I don't get paid if we don't do it."

"I'll tell them we did it; you'll get paid," I insisted.

"No, that's no good. We have to make it more believable. They're right outside that door."

"I have an idea," I said. I stood up on the bed and started bouncing on it. The wooden legs of the bed bounced off the floor and returned repeatedly with a loud crash. Margarita and I held hands for balance as we jumped up and down on the bed, all the while with big smiles on our faces.

"*Si, si, si, oh mi Dio, si!*" Margarita screamed out, and we both laughed.

When I left the room I hugged Margarita good-bye and said loudly so the words would carry down the hallway, "Thanks for the great sex, Margarita. That sex was the best sex I've ever had."

Again we laughed and hugged. Then I walked away from the room down the hallway.

"Be careful getting back to your car," Margarita advised in a motherly kind of way. "And put on your jacket, it'll be cold outside."

I walked down the stairs and returned to the showroom, where another naked dancer was hanging upside down on the stage's brass pole. *Must be a standard move*, I thought to myself. I sat in a booth to wait for Uncle Spud to finish. A few minutes passed, then a woman came running down the stairs screaming, "*La Diabla! La Diabla! Yo soy la Diabla!*" and continually crossing herself.

Every head in the place turned, including that of the upside-down naked woman on the pole. I didn't understand what she had said, but I could tell from her reaction that she hadn't just won the Mexican lottery. The woman ran to the maitre d' to explain what had happened. The maitre d' shook his head as he listened, then wiped the sweat from his forehead back across his wet black hair. He found the young kid who had taken us upstairs and slapped him across the face with violent force. The boy sat on the floor, huddled against a wall like a wounded animal as the maitre d' continued to yell at him in Spanish. I asked Ernesto to translate for me.

"'I told you not to put the old man with Rosa,'" he translated. "'She's too much for any man, especially an old man. Now she's not going to be able to work for a month. She thinks she's the devil. And who do you think has to get rid of the body? Dumping bodies in Tijuana isn't as easy as it used to be.'"

The maitre d' walked up the stairs, still apparently a bit confused about what had happened. The door to room number three was open; I followed him through it to find Uncle Spud lying on his stomach on the bed, totally naked with his war scar prominently on display. I stood there stunned.

"What happened?" I asked Rosa. She answered in Spanish and the young boy translated for me.

"Rosa said they were doing the hoochie-coochie—," he stopped to check on the translation again with Rosa, then continued, "yeah, hoochie-coochie, and your friend grabbed his chest and his eyes rolled back in his head."

Then, with a very matter-of-fact tone to his voice, the maitre d' turned to me and said, "What are you going to do with the body?"

"Huh?" I said, shocked by the question.

"I gotta get this guy's dead ass out of that bed and get a paying customer into it."

"Well, what do you usually do?" I said with flustered confusion.

"Take it down past Ensenada and bury it in the mountains."

"No, I can't do that. I can't just leave him there."

"Well," said the maitre d', "the other option would be to cremate the body, and then you could take the ashes with you. A customer of mine owns a kiln where they make souvenirs. He could cremate your friend there."

"A kiln?"

He put his arm on my shoulder, "It's a huge kiln. It works great, and since you're a friend of mine, I bet he'd do it for a couple hundred bucks."

"What if I put the body in the trunk of the car and drive it back across the border?"

"You could do that. Frankly, I don't care what you do with it just as long as you get it out of this bed in the next three minutes, but I have to tell you my friend, taking a dead body across the border is a bad idea. If they catch you, they'll put you under the jail."

I bit down on the inside part of my lower lip as I contemplated my next move. Rosa continued sobbing and incessantly repeating, "*La Diabla, Yo soy la Diabla.*"

"Come on, kid, I got a room full of horny hombres with freshly cashed paychecks sitting down there; what's it going to be?"

I was getting fairly used to carrying human ashes around the country, so I decided to have Uncle Spud's body cremated. I took Uncle Spud's wallet and key ring. I gave the boy Uncle Spud's clothes to be discarded. Uncle Spud's naked body wrapped in dark-brown piñata paper resembled a large Tootsie Roll. It was carried out the back door to the dirt alley and an awaiting van. I rode alone in the back of the van.

Drunk, tired, depressed, and confused, I sat on the bump of a wheel well, overwhelmed with numbness. I looked down at Uncle Spud's lifeless body stretched out before me and began sobbing uncontrollably.

The ride across town took nearly an hour due to the poor conditions of the cobblestone and dirt roads. I looked at our picture with Oscar from just a few hours ago and just couldn't believe that Uncle Spud was dead. The driver pulled up to the plant. I looked out of the small, oval, tinted window on the side of the van to read a sign saying, "*Ceramicas de Cisco.*" The driver stopped at the chain-link fence to open the locked gate. A mean-looking rottweiler barked endlessly at the van as we drove up to the back loading area.

"So, Rosa killed another one, huh?" the man said to all of us. They lifted Uncle Spud's body from the van's floor to a rickety gurney. As they pushed it toward a ramp to wheel it into the building, the unstable gurney hit a hole in the dirt driveway and crashed down on its side. Uncle Spud's body rolled off into the dirt. The brown tissue paper encasing his body ripped, and Uncle Spud laid on the ground like a smashed piñata waiting to be attacked by party-going children seeking a sweet treat. Taking this as a cue, the rottweiler attacked the body, biting and tearing at Uncle Spud's feet.

"Hey!" I shouted. "Call him off, call him off!"

"Princess, no!" the man shouted. "*Mal pero*, *mal*, Princess!"

But the dog continued. The driver kicked the dog in the ribs with the pointed toe of his snake-skin cowboy boots. The dog let out a yelp and ran back toward the front gate with one of Uncle Spud's toes dangling out of its mouth.

"*Lo senito*," the man said very casually.

"So, how long will the, uh, procedure take?" I blurted out.

"*Mañana.*"

"Tomorrow?! What do you mean tomorrow?"

"*Es un kiln, no es un crematorium*," he said. "*Kiln es* little hot, *crematorium es muy caliente, mucho* hot."

"It takes twenty-four hours?"

"*Mas o motos*," he said with a shrug of his shoulders, then added, "*dinero por favor.*"

"Two hundred dollars, right?"

"*Tres ciento*," he said.

I repeated the price to myself several times until I figured out he was asking for three hundred dollars.

"Three hundred dollars?!" I exclaimed. "They told me you'd do it for two hundred."

"No, no, tres ciento," he said, slowly shaking his head.

I looked through my wallet and Uncle Spud's money clip. "Two hundred and eighty dollars, that's all I have. No mas dinero," I stated while turning my pockets inside out.

"No, no, mas dinero en el zapatos," he repeated several times while pointing at my shoes. I eventually took off my shoes and socks to prove I had no secret stash, and he reluctantly agreed to the price.

I waited in their waiting room all day long. I passed the time looking through books about ceramics and Spanish newspapers. Day turned to night, and I tried to stay awake, but I kept nodding off. The next morning I awoke on their sofa, which smelled like oily tortilla chips, when the man set a plastic container holding Uncle Spud's ashes on the coffee table. He handed me a colorful breaded Mexican pastry that was dry and bland and tasted like four, but it was still a welcome treat after going without dinner the night before.

"Quieres en ceramic statue?" he asked, pointing to the ashes and then to a ceramic donkey on display in the lobby. "Es more easy go over border."

The man showed me a laminated sales catalog that had ceramic statues of everything from Jesus on the cross to Porky Pig. I decided on making Uncle Spud's ashes into a surfing monkey statue because I felt it captured his laid-back California attitude.

I watched the women pour the ashes into a small mixing vat, then into a iron mold, and then into the kiln. An hour or so went by before the Uncle Spud surfing monkey statue was finished. The man agreed to drive me back to Tijuana. As we drove, I noticed the surfing monkey was actually a savings bank. There was a small coin slot at the back of his head and a larger capped hole at the bottom of the surfboard to remove the money. I pulled off the black rubber cap and, holding the statue upside down and covering the coin-slot with my thumb, started filling the bank with Dad's ashes. The van ride wasn't as bumpy as the previous ride, but the constant stops and starts of the downtown Tijuana traffic made the job difficult. I was able to get most of the ashes in with just a few slight spills onto the van's floor.

The driver pulled over to the side of the road about a half a mile from the international border and pointed out the way to get there. I decided to leave Uncle Spud's van behind, figuring it might be too risky to try and sell it or drive a car registered in someone else's name across the border. I walked past stand after stand of vendors hawking just about any conceivable kind of souvenir.

"You want a friend for your surfing monkey?" one man said. "You should never surf alone."

My stomach felt nervous as I entered the checkpoint building. The "Midnight Express" theme song played in my head and my heart began to pound faster. There were two dozen tourists in a single-file line in front of me. One by one, they would approach the counter and talk to the border guard. The man in front of me was wearing an over-sized sombrero and carrying three woven blankets in his hand. The border guard asked him a series of questions and apparently wasn't satisfied with the answers, so he sent the man into an enclosed glass office with writing on the door that read "Secondary check."

"Next," the border guard said. I approached the counter. "Citizenship?"

"United States."

"Reason for being in Mexico?"

"Uh, vacation."

"How long were you in Mexico?"

"One day."

"Are you bringing anything back with you?"

"Just this souvenir piggy bank."

The guard waved his hand for me to pass through. I walked a few feet further and stepped over a red line painted on the floor. I was back in the United States. I felt like dropping to my knees to kiss the ground, knowing there would be no Mexican prison in my immediate future.

CHAPTER
9

WITH THE LAST DOLLAR I had hidden in my wallet's photo gallery, I rode the street trolley from the border town of San Ysidro to downtown San Diego.

"Downtown San Diego Train Station, connections to all trolley lines and Amtrak," a voice on the intercom stated as the trolley began to slow to a stop."

I crossed the tracks heading for the terminal building and sat down on the front steps to contemplate my next move. It was the last day of the year, I was tired, flat broke, hungry, carrying the worldly remains of two people, and perplexed as to what to do next. As I sat there below the mission-style bell tower, an Amtrak train arrived. I watched with curiosity as an eclectic array of passengers disembarked the train. Many struggled with their bulky carry-ons as they cautiously stepped down off of the train. My entrepreneurial spirit was instantly awakened and I went over to offer my baggage-carrying services. After two rejections, I was hired by a middle-aged woman in a carmine-colored business suit to carry her expensive-looking luggage from the train to the nearby taxi stand. After I placed her bag safely in the trunk of the waiting taxi she handed me a one-dollar bill.

"Thank you," I said enthusiastically, and then hurried back to the train to offer my porter services to others. By the time I got back, most of the passengers had dispersed or rented pushcarts from a nearby machine for seventy-five cents.

*Damn carts, taking all my business*, I thought to myself until I saw a kid return a cart to the row of pushcarts for a twenty-five-cent deposit return. I scouted around the terminal and its surroundings for stray carts. Within half an hour of being in San Diego, I had increased my net worth to $3.75. I took my earnings to a nearby convenience store and bought a premade ham sandwich encased in a plastic container, barbecue chips, and a Coke, and returned to the station to await the next train. I was just about finished with my meal when another train pulled into the station. I offered my baggage-carrying services and had three takers for a grand total of five dollars. I then returned about a dozen pushcarts for an additional three dollars and had a nice little cottage industry going.

Unfortunately, my business was quickly yanked out from under me by an Amtrak official who informed me that Amtrak's liability insurance didn't allow non-Amtrak workers to help passengers with their luggage.

"Consider this your warning," the man said. "If I see you doing it again, I'm calling the cops."

I was disappointed in losing half my revenue source, but I still had the cart-return gig. I returned carts the rest of the day, usually making somewhere between one to four dollars each time a train came through. The last train arrived at 11:05 PM and I finished the day with $29.25. I figured a few more days of this and I'd have enough money to restart the trip in an easterly direction.

I decided to sleep on the depot's wooden benches with newspapers as blankets, like a quintessential cartoon hobo. I had just started tucking myself into a cozy corner of the San Diego Union Station when a security guard came through the terminal and tapped me on the shoes with his nightstick.

"Can't sleep here, Bub."

"Where can I sleep, Bub?"

"There's a YMCA down Broadway."

"How far is that?"

"Four or five blocks."

I gathered my things and began searching out the YMCA building. A young man with horned-rim glasses wearing a brown and yellow '70s-era Padres cap sat behind the counter. After a brief discussion via the intercom, he buzzed me through the door into the well-lit lobby. I asked for the cheapest room they had, which was a bed in a shared dormitory-style room for $18. I hadn't had a full night's sleep since I was at Uncle

Spud's house, which seemed like a week ago, so I gladly handed over the cash, mostly in quarters.

"You break your piggy bank for this?" he asked, with a smirk on his face.

I continued counting out the quarters, forming them into one-dollar stacks on the counter.

I filled out the guest registry card and was handed a key to room 215. At first I was pleasantly surprised to find no one else in the room, but soon a deep sense of melancholy overtook me. I felt so lonely. I'd been alone 90 percent of the last nine months, but had never felt lonely. For some reason, it hit me that night. Maybe it was Uncle Spud's death, a lack of sleep, and being in an unfamiliar city on New Year's Eve in a dorm room that smelled of Ajax, but I felt like I had to get out and be around people. I strolled the empty streets of downtown San Diego. Anybody who was going out was already where they intended to be. It was ten minutes to midnight and I walked briskly, hoping to find somewhere, something, or somebody to at least wish a happy New Year to.

On the corner of Ninth and Broadway, I spotted the red-and-green neon sign of a little bar called the China Doll tightly wedged in between two discount furniture stores. The sound of an extremely poor rendition of "Harper Valley PTA" flowed out of the bar's wide-open front door. I walked inside to find a crowd of late-middle-aged people tooting horns, spinning noisemakers, and wearing paper party hats, anticipating the coming of another year.

"Here's Chuck with the last song of the year," the karaoke emcee announced.

Chuck, a Mexican man with a salt-and-pepper Poncho Villa mustache and a tattered blue-mesh baseball cap with yellow letters that asked the profound question of the 1980s—"Where's the Beef?"—approached the small stage in the corner.

"You gonna do your standard?" the karaoke emcee asked.

"Yeah," Chuck hollered into the microphone, causing a piercing ring. "Habby New Year, everybody," he slurred slowly.

The emcee cued up the music for the Rolling Stones' classic "Satisfaction." Chuck made the song his own by replacing the word "I" with the name "Chuck." Then every time he sang, "Chuck can't get no satisfaction," Chuck thrust his hips forward in a provocative way.

I ordered a beer and was given a green, pilgrim-style paper hat with "Happy New Year" written on the front in gold glitter. I glanced up at the clock to check the time. Every number on the clock face was a five, and it said "Cocktail Time 5:00."

"Help yourself to the buffet, if there's anything left," the bartender said.

I walked to the back of the bar to find dozens of homemade dishes on a long folding table. An older woman eating a drumstick told me that anybody who brought a dish of food had gotten free drinks until 9:00.

"I brought the fried clams," she stated proudly, "but those were gone hours ago."

"Ten, nine, eight, seven, six, five, four, three, two, one, Happy New Year!" the revelers in the bar hollered in unison. The old lady hugged me awkwardly, and as we unclenched she accidentally rubbed her half-eaten drumstick against the back of my neck.

"You sing?" she asked.

"Not very well."

"Oh, come on and do a duet with me. My regular partner has a snootful, and I haven't sung all night."

"What duet would we sing?" I asked.

"'Reunited,'" she said. "I always sing 'Reunited.'"

"I think this is going to take a little liquid encouragement," I said in jest.

"Oh, absolutely," she said with enthusiasm. "Get whatever you want and tell 'em to put it on Big Helen's tab."

Her nickname struck me as a bit peculiar because she was a woman of very modest size.

"You're Big Helen?" I asked. "Why do they call you Big Helen?"

"There's another Helen that hangs around here, too, so they call us Big Helen and Little Helen."

"Is Little Helen here tonight?"

"Yeah, she's around here somewhere, but she's tough to spot in a crowd. I'll look for her while you chase us down a couple drinks."

"What do you drink?" I asked.

"Greyhounds," she answered, as if I was the stupidest man on earth. "Everybody knows Big Helen drinks Greyhounds."

I ordered our drinks and headed back to the buffet table where Big Helen was lighting a new Steno flame to keep a tray of chicken enchiladas warm.

"So did you spot Little Helen yet?" I asked with a smirk on my face.

"Not yet. Well, Happy New Year, Sailor," she said as we clanged our drinks together in a toast.

"I'm not a sailor," I said.

"Oh, I just call all the men 'Sailor,' and all the ladies 'Toots.' It's simpler that way."

"Big Helen," the karaoke emcee announced, "you're next."

"Showtime, Sailor," she said, grabbing my arm and leading me toward the stage. I chugged down my beer on the way there. I couldn't believe I was nervous about singing in a bar full of middle-aged drunks, but I was.

"Give it up for Big Helen and—" the karaoke emcee said, pausing to stick the microphone in my face.

"Ah, Sailor," I answered.

The introduction music started, and as the lyrics were highlighted in pink for the Peaches part and blue for the Herb part, we belted out our tune.

"There's one perfect fit, and, sugar, this one is it. We both are so excited 'cause we're Reunited, hey, hey . . . "

During the instrumental bridge in the middle of the song, Big Helen whispered in my ear, "There's Little Helen coming out of the restroom." I lost my place in the song as I stared at the smallest woman I'd ever seen walk across the floor and be lifted up onto a barstool by another patron. I finished the song with my petite partner, knowing, and agreeing with the nicknames given to the Helens.

At closing time Big Helen, in a motherly style I hadn't seen all night, insisted I take some food with me for my trip.

"It's just gonna go to waste if you don't take it."

She dumped about half a dozen pieces of fried chicken into a brown paper bag and handed it to me.

"That'll make a nice lunch for you tomorrow."

I thanked her for the beers she had bought me, and headed back to the YMCA. I was buzzed through the front door by the late-night counterman who was watching a small black-and-white television.

"What room you in?" he asked, looking over the counter.

"215," I said as I walked by.

He noticed my bag with multiple grease stains on it and said authoritatively, "Can't keep food in the rooms."

"It's just some chicken," I said. "I'm not eating it here, just keepin' it 'til tomorrow."

"Food attracts bugs and mice. Can't do it."

I turned and walked back outside and sat on the stoop where I ate two wings even though I wasn't hungry. Suddenly inspiration hit. I loaded up my party hat with the four remaining pieces of chicken and put the hat back on my head. I threw the bag away and slowly walked back into the lobby, trying to keep my head and neck as straight as possible. I strolled by the counterman carefully balancing my poultry contraband.

"Goodnight," I said.

"Thank you for your compliance, sir." the counterman answered. "This place works because we all work together."

"It sure does," I agreed. "Well, Happy New Year."

"Same to you, sir. Goodnight."

I awoke the next morning at 11:00 upset with myself that I had missed the arrival of all the New Year's Day morning trains. I checked out and walked back to the train station eating my soggy fried chicken along the way. There was some commotion on the station's front steps, but the 11:35 train was just arriving and duty called. I was able to corral eight pushcarts. As I was returning them and collecting my money, a Hispanic man approached me. His hair was slicked straight back and a spider web tattoo covered three-quarters of his face.

"You've either got balls the size of grapefruits or you're just plain stupid," he said in a cold, slow monotone.

"What?" I asked with amazement.

"The cart return is mine, *muchacho*."

"I've been returning them since yesterday."

"I know, my boy told me. He said some gringo chased him off."

"I didn't chase anybody off. I've just been returning carts, that's all."

"I didn't come to argue," he said, as he pulled up the sleeve of his plaid flannel shirt exposing a switchblade knife affixed to his forearm with a white sweatband. "You don't want to take a paying job away from a little kid, do you?"

"Uh, no, no, I don't," I said. "How 'bout I finish returning these and I'll be on my way."

"That was half right."

I just nodded and walked away, abandoning six pushcarts within inches of the deposit return. I walked dejectedly like a beaten dog over to the station's front steps, where a man was talking through a bullhorn to a small crowd of people.

"We will complete our journey and insist that elected officials do something to further our cause," he told the crowd with his distorted, static-ridden voice.

There was a smattering of applause from people standing behind the man. A ten-foot-long vinyl sign with Old English lettering that read "ABBA, American Bicyclists for Better Air" hung above him.

"We will leave here today and crisscross the country for two months. We'll arrive in Washington, D.C. with numbers behind our message."

"Woo hoo," one of the sign holders yelled, followed by the chant of "ABBA, ABBA."

"Brothers, brothers," the man with the bullhorn said, trying to quiet his supporters.

A man in a blue pin-striped business suit shouted out, "Hey, ABBA, do 'Dancing Queen!'"

"Friends, we are a small group of idealistic bikers, but if you feel the way we do and want to take a stand with us, we have extra bikes waiting for you to join us right now. You needn't worry about food or shelter. We've taken care of everything. Join us and help us help the world breathe safer, cleaner air."

With little money, my business opportunities gone, and a death threat as my motivating factors, I decided to join the group. I walked down the stairs to a van and introduced myself to the bullhorn man.

"So you want to join our group, brother?"

"Yes, I do. I love clean air."

"Good, good, I'm glad to hear we are of like minds. That's good enough for us. Welcome aboard, brother."

He pulled an aluminum bike out of the van and said, "Here's your bike. State-of-the-art aluminum frame, strong and light. Oh, by the way, what's your name?"

"Uh, Fernando," I said with a smirk on my face.

"Well, welcome to ABBA, Fernando."

All the riders got onto their bikes and huddled together for a brief moment, then the leader announced, "Next stop, Washington, D.C.!" Then they pulled out and headed through the downtown area led by a motorcycle police escort. The group rode about two blocks before the leader ordered everyone to stop.

"Hold on, my tire's flat," he insisted, but everyone rode by him including me, already pulling up the rear. The van stopped to help change the tire and within a few minutes, the leader had passed me and was back among the pack.

The plan for the day had us heading east on streets that ran parallel with Interstate 8, then north along Interstate 15 to Riverside, approximately one-hundred miles away. The van that followed us serviced the bikers' needs for food, drink, and repairs, and picked up the bikers who couldn't continue.

With Surfing Monkey safely stowed away in my backpack, I rode thirty miles along the freeway to Escondido, where I saw the support van pick up two of the bikers. Their bikes were loaded onto the trailer and the bikers got into the heated van to eat oranges and play cards.

My back ached and I had friction burns on my inner thighs from the bike's seat. *What the hell am I doing riding when I could be in the van?* I thought. I pulled over at the next underpass and waited for the van to pick me up. It pulled up a few minutes later with a couple more riders inside. The driver rolled down the passenger-side window and a gust of warm air blew into my cold and exhausted face. "What do you need?" asked Wayne, the support van driver.

"I think I'd better call it a day."

"Are you injured?"

"No, just tired."

Wayne laughed and told the other passengers, "He's tired." They all continued to laugh as I rolled my bike into the trailer and got into the van. The van continued heading north toward the day's final destination. The other bikers and I ate all the orange wedges and drank most of the bottled water.

Wayne set up a drink stop for the bikers about ten miles ahead of the pack and was very angry at us for eating the orange wedges.

"I've got my eye on the three of you," he warned.

All Wayne could do was quickly cut the few remaining oranges into wedges before the pack arrived. With only a handful of oranges, he had to cut them into slivers to try and make them stretch so every biker could have at least one. The other incapacitated bikers and I asked him to leave the engine running so the heater would perform at full capacity. We sat in the van and continued our card game.

By the time the van pulled into the Wagon Wheel Motel just after dusk, I'd collected eight dollars in poker winnings. Wayne got out and took care of the arrangements. He passed out room keys to the guys in the van, then waited for the bikers to pull in. Those of us riding in the van got our own rooms, while the last bikers to straggle in were forced to share a room. An inequitable flaw in the system, but I wasn't going to be the one to complain about it. By the time the last biker arrived at the motel, I had already taken a shower, watched some TV, and was ready for dinner.

There was a family-style restaurant next door and each biker could order whatever he wanted; ABBA was footing the bill with the donations it had received.

During dinner, the leader tapped his knife against his water glass to call everyone to attention.

"Well, we've made it to our first stop. Tomorrow we've got a long uphill climb over the Cajon Pass. Then a seventy-five-mile ride to Barstow, where we will be welcomed by the mayor and the Barstow High School band. We should have some news coverage there, so it's bound to be a big day. You'll be given a wake-up call at five o'clock, followed by breakfast right here between five thirty and six, and then we're on the road by six fifteen. All right, everybody, it was a good ride today; let's get a good night's sleep and have a good ride tomorrow."

The next morning, the wake-up call came at five o'clock. I answered the phone, then immediately rolled over and went back to sleep. At six o'clock a loud, hurried knock came to the door. When the stubborn knocker refused to stop, I got out of bed and dragged myself to the door.

"It's six thirty, everyone is gone but you. I'm starting to think you're not ABBA material, Fernando," the group's leader declared.

"Just give me a second," I said. I closed the door and hurriedly splashed some water on my face, dressed, grabbed my bike and backpack, and put it in the van with the leader. The plan was for the van to drive us to catch up to the pack, which was nearing the base of the mountain pass.

Wayne sped past the pack and drove ahead two miles to let me and the leader off to set up the first refreshment stop. The leader immediately got on his bike and rode off while I stayed there waiting for the pack. All the bikers in the pack stopped for water and orange wedges, then continued on their climb up the mountain.

While Wayne was concentrating on handing out the supplies, I put my bike back in the trailer and hid behind the van's backseat. The next refreshment stop was at the top of the pass. There, among the commotion of dehydrated bikers, I reappeared huffing and puffing from my imaginary ride up the hill and joined in on the orange-wedge feeding frenzy. I felt a little guilty for my lackluster effort, so I got on my bike and rode downhill for eight miles, the cool wind blowing on my happy face.

The late morning sun was beginning to warm the desert and I was already feeling like I'd had my fill of biking for the day. Near Victorville, I pulled up to one of the bikers who was out of water and waiting for the van to pick him up. I gave him one of the bottles I was carrying and decided to stay with the man until the van arrived.

"What's wrong?" Wayne asked as he pulled up to us.

"He's dehydrated," I explained. "I gave him some water, but I think we better ride in the van for a while."

"Why do you need to ride in the van? You tired again?"

"No, uh, I pulled a groin," I said, having learned it was easier to get in the van with an injury than with an "I'm tired."

Wayne just shook his head and opened the van's sliding door. The dehydrated biker and I climbed into the back of the van and began eating and drinking.

"Don't you have anything else but water, granola, and oranges?" I asked.

"You shouldn't eat anything heavy while you're riding, you'll cramp up."

"Well, were not riding anymore today," said the other biker.

"Yeah," I added, "let's stop for a burger."

"No. I am not stopping for food," Wayne said emphatically. "That's not what this van is for."

"Come on, Wayne, you've got the money. No one will know," I said.

"And there's an In-N-Out Burger at the next turnoff," the biker said excitedly.

"I am not stopping for burgers!"

"Come on, we'll use the drive-through, and we'll be back on the road in a second."

"No!"

We then started chanting, "In-N-Out! In-N-Out! In-N-Out!"

"Oh, for Christ's sake, okay, we'll stop," Wayne said, slowing down for the turn off the freeway.

He pulled into the drive-through and ordered our food. The drive-through was very narrow, and the trailer carrying the bikes went up on the curb and ran over a small flower bed of pansies before coming down with a thud onto the pavement. We ate our hamburgers while Wayne tried to make up the time he had lost. He was driving about eighty when he got pulled over and cited for excessive speed. Wayne was fuming mad at us. His precious schedule was put even farther behind when he had to stop a half dozen more times to pick up other weary bicycle riders who had decided to call it a day. We all agreed the view of the barren California desert, spotted with yucca, cactus, and sagebrush, is so much nicer when you're inside a support van traveling at a high rate of speed.

By the time we pulled into Barstow, the van was full of bikers and three others rode in the bike trailer. Wayne pulled the van up to the steps of City Hall where the leader and three other bikers stood with the mayor, attempting to explain why most of the bikers on the cross-country bike trip were being driven in a van. The leader was furious but tried to mask his feelings during the presentation. The media event turned out to be one cub reporter from the *Barstow Bee* and a field trip of third graders.

After the twenty-minute reception, where the leader was presented with a key to the city of Barstow, we road two miles to our motel on the north side of town. Several pizzas were delivered to the leader's room and we all ate there while watching a rerun of *Gilligan's Island*.

It was time for the leader's daily "State of the Ride" address and although he didn't name names, it was clear to everyone he was blaming me for several of the problems the group had endured. The next morning I woke up to a phone call, but instead of the 5:00 AM wake-up call, it was the front desk informing me that check out was in ten minutes. I looked at my watch to see that it was 10:50. I looked out the motel room window and saw no sign of the ABBA van or any of the bikers. I called the front desk to ask whether ABBA had left.

"Who's ABBA?" the desk clerk asked.

"The bikers, the group of bicyclists, have they left yet?"

"Oh, yeah, hours ago."

I quickly got my things together and set out for the road. I knew from the previous day's ride there was no way I was going to catch up with the group, especially since they had a five-hour head start, so I stood near the freeway's eastbound entrance with a sign I had written on the back of one of last night's pizza boxes that read "VEGAS."

I stood there for a few hours. Occasionally someone would slow down and have a closer look at me. One lady even offered me a ride to Whiskey Pete's, a casino just past the state line, but she was scared that my bike would scratch the paint of her car. When I refused to leave the bike behind, she wished me good luck, rolled up the window, and sped off.

Before the trip, I had always thought of the desert as scorching hot. As another hour went by sitting out there exposed to the bone-numbing wind, I couldn't remember a time I had felt colder.

*I should have left this stupid bike and taken that ride to the state line,* I thought. At least I'd be sitting in a heated casino instead of freezing out here in the middle of nowhere.

A tan-colored Toyota truck with Arkansas plates pulled up alongside me. Inside the cab was a young couple who couldn't have been any older than me.

"Vegas?" the driver said.

"Yeah, Vegas," I answered, trying not to seem too excited at my first opportunity in hours.

"Hop in."

I lifted the bike into the truck bed, set my backpack in the corner, and hopped in. "Okay," I hollered, and the truck took off, leaving a cloud of dust where I'd spent most of the day sitting.

The driver turned and opened the small, sliding back window and yelled to me, "Why ya goin' to Vegas?"

"I'm meeting up with some friends there," I screamed back, trying to compensate for the loud flapping sound of the wind as we shot through the desert at eighty miles an hour.

"I'm Quincy, and this here's Kitty," he said, pointing to the young woman sitting in the bucket seat next to him. Her neck was checkered with reddish-purple hickeys the size of walnuts.

"Hi, I'm Roastbeef."

"Well, kick back. We'll be in Las Vegas in a couple hours."

I laid low in the bed of the truck to stay out of the wind chill as much as possible. We passed Baker, California, and its eighty-foot-tall thermometer which read forty-four degrees at dusk. Twenty minutes later, I heard Quincy yell, "Shit!" I realized we were slowing down as he started to pull the truck over to the side of the road.

Quincy got out of the truck cursing at life. He had sandy-blond hair cut in a flat-top style and was wearing a blue-and-white sailor suit. Kitty was a pie-faced redhead wearing a white frilly wedding gown and just about ready to pop with motherhood. They both spoke with a Southern drawl.

"What's wrong?" I asked.

"I reckon I ran out of gas," Quincy said dejectedly.

"I've been tellin' him to get that gas gauge fixed for months," Kitty added.

"Tell you what, I saw a call box only a mile or so back. I'll ride my bike back there and call for some help."

"That would be great, we'd sure appreciate it. See honey, I knew pickin' this guy up was an all right thing to do."

I got on my bike and rode back to the call box. I picked up the phone and plugged my other ear to try to drown out the sound of the cars as they sped by. The operator said that running out of gas was given the lowest priority of all traffic-related occurrences and it could be two hours or more before someone came by with a can of replacement gas.

"Two hours! Ah, forget it. I'll go back to Baker and get my own gas."

The lights of Baker were visible perhaps five miles down the flat barren road that cut through the night. I set off riding as fast as my legs could peddle. It took me just over half an hour to get to the first gas station on the highway. I explained to the man behind the counter that I'd run out of gas.

"All right then, we'll get you fixed up. You gotta gas can?"

"No."

"Well, then, you got two options. I've got one you can borrow, but there's a ten dollar deposit, or you can buy one here. They're just five dollars, but with any purchase of five dollars or more you get a snow globe of our world-famous thermometer." He took one in his hand and turned it over to allow all the small, white particles to go to the top of the clear plastic case before turning it again to watch them sink past the miniature replica of the thermometer back to the bottom. "Ain't that somethin'?" he added.

"Yeah, it is, but I'm a little low on cash. In fact, I only brought a couple of dollars for the gas. I didn't even think about the gas can."

The man thought for a moment then said, "If ya want to, you can go out in the back to the trash bin and find some pop bottles in the dumpster, and you can put your two dollars worth of gas in them."

I dug through the top layer of garbage: cigarette butts, candy and potato-chip wrappings, soda cups, napkins, and crumpled-up day-old newspaper. I found three two-liter plastic bottles and gave the man his two dollars. The man said, "I know I'm not supposed to, but here you go," and handed me one of the promotional items.

My two-dollar purchase filled up two and a half of the plastic bottles. I placed two of them in my backpack next to Surfing Monkey and cradled the third on my forearm as if I were a running back in the open field. I hadn't realized it on the way to Baker, but there had been a slight downhill grade. Riding back to Quincy and Kitty, it took me over an hour to climb the slight incline carrying the extra weight.

"I thought you'd ditched us, boy," Quincy said upon my arrival back at the truck.

I went on to tell the whole story as Quincy unscrewed the cap and and emptied the gasoline-filled Mountain Dew bottle into the tank, and flung it into the dirt and sagebrush.

"I reckon we got enough gas to get us to the state line."

"No," said Kitty. "You fill this truck up. I'm not running out of gas again on my wedding day."

"Oh, you guys are getting married? Congratulations."

I lifted my bike back into the truck's bed and started to climb in myself when Kitty said, "Why don't you get up here in the cab with us. It's freezing out there."

"Are you sure we can all fit?"

"Sure, sure, no problem. We ride like this all the time back home." Kitty sat in the middle with her legs around the truck's stick shift. She pulled her white dress up to her crotch so Quincy could get the car in gear. He drove across the freeway into the dirt, rocks, and tumbleweed of the median and then pulled out on the southbound highway back to

Baker for a fill up. We arrived in Baker five minutes later. Quincy filled the tank with gas.

"Damn, the gas is expensive out here," Quincy stated before getting back into the truck. "I hope I still have enough for the preacher."

"Where are you getting married?"

"In Vegas, duh!" Kitty said.

"I know, I know, but do you already have a church or what?"

"Q's been out here before. He says there's all kinds of churches that'll marry ya, no questions asked."

"That's right, a buddy of mine in the service got married out here and he said if you got the money they'll marry you, no problem. I hear they'll even marry queers out here if they got the money. It sure ain't like the Church of Christ back home, no sir."

Quincy checked his wristwatch. "Nine thirty-five," he said. "We're really going to have to hurry this thing up. I got to be back in lineup by zero six hundred."

"Well, if you hadn't run out of gas," Kitty said in an accusatory tone.

"Well, if you didn't have to stop every frickin' twenty minutes to pee or eat or barf."

"Well, if you'd worn a damn condom."

"Well, if you weren't such a Fertile Myrtle."

There was an awkward silence for several minutes. We were heading down a long straight stretch of highway. Miles off in the distance were the multicolored twinkling lights of the state-line casinos.

"Well, there's the state line," I said, trying to play peacemaker. "It won't be long now until your at the altar."

We neared the state-line turnoff and Kitty timidly asked, "Q, can we stop? I really gotta pee bad."

He just sighed and exited the highway. We parked next to a large Winnebago with Texas plates and a license-plate holder that read "We're spending our kids' inheritance." Kitty ran into the casino holding her pregnant stomach as she hurried to the ladies' room.

Quincy and I sat down at a blackjack table. Quincy laid down a twenty and was betting five dollars a hand and playing two hands simultaneously. He was holding his own with the dealer who wore a red-and-white checkered shirt and a name tag that read "Howdy Partner, My Name is." Attached to the name tag was a cheap-looking red strip from a label maker that read "Jeff from Guam."

After Quincy had won a few hands in a row and was starting to build an impressive pile of five-dollar chips, I felt the bite of the gambling bug and dug down into my shoe and pulled out a folded, moist, ten-dollar bill and placed it on the table.

"Cashing ten dollars," Jeff announced to no one in particular. He dragged the ten-dollar bill across the blackjack table with the wooden poker he used to push it into the cash drop. He gave me a stack of ten one-dollar chips. I laid one chip in the circle, and sat back confidently on the stool.

"Minimum bet is two dollars," Jeff said in a monotone without making any eye contact. I increased my bet with another chip. Jeff dealt the cards and I grabbed them with my right hand and sheltered them with my left so no one could see my hand.

"Please only hold the cards with one hand," Jeff said.

A waitress came by our table chanting her mantra, "Cocktails, cocktails." We both ordered a beer and continued playing blackjack. I bet two dollars each hand and lost five in a row. I sat there watching Quincy continue on his lucky streak, waiting for the cocktail waitress to return with my complementary ten-dollar beer.

"If you're not playing anymore, you need to make way for someone else," Jeff told me.

"Jeff, were you this bitter in Guam?" I asked.

"I'm just doing my job, sir."

"It seems to me you could do it a little nicer. You've been on me the whole time."

"We have rules all the players must follow."

"Come on, let's go," Quincy said, starting to collect his chips.

"No, I'm waiting for the ten-dollar beer I ordered," I said.

"That's fine, but you'll have to give up your seat."

"Jeff, if everyone on Guam is as big of an ass as you are, I understand why your crappy little island never became a state."

"We don't care if we're a state or not."

"Yes, you do. You know you want to be a state," I taunted him as if I were a second grader.

The cocktail waitress arrived with the beers. Quincy cashed in his chips, coming out thirty-five dollars ahead. We jumped in the truck and headed out for Vegas. There was a nervous energy in the car the closer that we got to Sin City. Quincy pulled off the freeway at Tropicana Boulevard and cruised north up the Strip past all the flashy, bright, glittering houses of legal theft. Ten-story-tall marquees screamed about Wayne Newton this and Prime Rib dinner that. The city was a spectacle, and we were enthralled with the sights and the hordes of people on the sidewalks. Quincy pointed out the different points of interest while he drove.

Just north of the strip on the way toward the downtown area was a small group of wedding chapels side by side. Each of the sad-looking little chapels had a signboard or glittery marquee to entice those lovebirds who were still sitting on the fence.

"Michael Jordan and Joan Collins were married here," one of the chapel's signs proudly stated.

"I didn't know Michael Jordan was married to Joan Collins," Kitty said.

Another chapel called Lee's Discount Marriage Service was housed simply in a mini-mall store wedged between a doughnut shop and a liquor store. "Tyin' the knot shouldn't cost you a lot" was painted on the window, and a red neon light below it incessantly flashed "Come Get Hitched!"

"Do any of these look okay to you, honey?" Quincy asked, without a reply from Kitty. We passed another chapel with a marquee signboard rolled out on wheels to the edge of the street. It read in large, black, block letters, "We've Married Two Popes," then in smaller letters at the bottom, "Sally and Bob Pope, June 18, 1988."

"It's going to have to be one of those, honey, we've about come to the end."

"What about that one?" she said, pointing to a white building with Roman columns in front. "That looks like a good one."

The sign on the building read, "Celebrity Ceremonies. Let Legal Legend Look-alikes Bind Your Love." We pulled into the driveway just before midnight, went into the building, and waited in the lobby for assistance. The lobby looked like a doctor's waiting room with couches, coffee tables, and magazines, but in each of the four corners they had mannequins dressed like famous celebrities: Laurel and Hardy, Marilyn Monroe, Cher, and Mae West.

From behind a red velvet curtain came an old man who supposedly was a W. C. Fields look-alike, but his large, fake rubber nose kept slipping off as he tried to talk.

"So are you the happy couple?" he said, looking at me and Kitty.

"No, they're the happy couple," I said, giving them a slight nudge toward the counter.

"Very well," the man said. "Are you both of legal age?"

"Yes," they said simultaneously.

"Do you both come here freely without mental reservations?"

"The sign out front said 'Come on in.' I didn't think we needed reservations," Quincy said.

"No, no, I mean do you both want to get married."

Again they agreed.

"Well then, have you decided on a celebrity look-alike to conduct the service?"

"No," Kitty said.

"Well, then, what you need to do there, little lady, is take a look through our portfolio of the celebrity look-alikes. I will tell you, though, that our Lucille Ball, Mr. T., and President Reagan are all unavailable tonight. Oh, and Mother Teresa fell and broke her hip, so she's out too, but I think we have everybody else. Go ahead and have a look-through. I'll set up the chapel."

They flipped through the book of pictures. Each celebrity look-alike had a close-up and full-body picture and the price to conduct the service. The book started with the most expensive, Elvis, and worked its way down.

"Look at their Marilyn Monroe," I said. "She looks more like Ethel Mertz."

"$250 for Jesus Christ!" Quincy said.

"How about Robert Blake? You watch those reruns of *Baretta*," Kitty suggested.

"Ah, but look," Quincy said, pointing to the book, "it's twenty-five dollars extra for the cockatoo."

They looked through the whole book, going back and forth with different suggestions.

"I don't really care which one we get, Kit, I just don't want to spend very much money unless we really like the celebrity. I mean, I'm happy with Shecky Greene or Nipsey Russell; they're only twenty dollars."

"I don't even know who they are. If we're going to get married by a celebrity, I'd like to at least know the celebrity."

"How about Boy George?" Quincy said, with a sigh of desperation in his voice. "He's only thirty-five dollars, and you like that chameleon song he does."

"Okay," Kitty agreed.

"Boy George it is," I said, and rang the bell for the man to return. The man had washed the W. C. Fields makeup off his face and had a towel over his head when he came out.

"Did you decide on a celebrity?"

Putting his arm around Kitty, Quincy proudly stated with his chest sticking out, "Boy George, please."

"Ah, Junior McCalister," the man said. "Good choice, I'll give him a call. In the meantime, you can start filling out the paperwork."

I excused myself to go buy a bottle of champagne, a bag of rice, and a disposable camera with the few dollars I had left. The liquor store didn't carry just plain white rice so I bought two boxes of chicken-flavored Rice-a-Roni.

When I returned, Kitty and Quincy were each in their own dressing rooms waiting for Boy George to arrive. I knocked on the door with a small, brown engraved plaque that read "Bride."

"Come in."

"Hey, how's everything going? Do you need anything?"

"Oh, I'm glad you came by. I wanted to ask you if you'd walk me down the aisle."

"Sure," I said.

"You're the best hitchhiker we've ever picked up," she said, giving me a hug.

"Thanks. Well, I better go check on Quincy."

I walked into the groom's room without knocking to find Quincy pacing the floor. He said, "Is Boy George here yet?"

"No, not yet."

"I'm so damn nervous. I didn't think I would be, but I am."

"Well, I bought this for after the ceremony, but if you want to pop it now, go ahead."

We opened the bottle of André Brut champagne and took turns drinking it straight from the bottle, finishing each drink with a robust burp. The old man knocked on both doors and said loudly from the other side, "Junior, I mean, Boy George is here."

"Thanks a lot for hanging out with me," Quincy said.

"What are you talking about? This is one of the highlights of my trip."

Quincy walked into the empty chapel and the old man told him where to stand. Kitty took my arm and I led her back into the lobby. We waited at the entrance to the chapel.

The old man started the music "Here Comes the Bride" on his tape player. The aisle was only ten-to-fifteen-feet long and the chapel had only six pews, three on each side. We walked down the aisle and the three of us stood before the altar. The old man changed tapes quickly and started playing "Karma Chameleon," and down the aisle dancing and twirling around in a circle, his multicolored hair swinging around from side to side, was the conductor of the ceremony, a dead ringer for Boy George.

He spoke softly with a slight British accent. He read the marriage passage from the Bible and then asked, "Who gives this woman to this man?"

There was a pause, then I gestured with a slight wave of my left hand, "Ah, that would be me, I guess."

I placed her hand on Quincy's arm and took a seat in the front row and began taking pictures with the disposal camera. Boy George read from three-by-five index cards, asking each of them if they took each other for better and worse.

"You may kiss the bride," he said, then pointed to the old man, who started the tape player again to "Karma Chameleon." Boy George danced back down the aisle in a red, gold, and green whirlwind into the lobby.

"You've got five minutes if you'd like to get some pictures," the old man told them, then yelled out to the lobby, "Junior, get back in here."

I took pictures of the couple with the minister standing in the middle with his arms around both of them. A pregnant bride, a groom in a sailor suit, and a Boy George impersonator/minister; it was all I could do to snap the picture without laughing out loud.

The old man handed them a bulging manila envelope and said, "Here you go. A little something to get your life together started, with our best wishes for a long happy life."

I waited out in the lobby where I mixed some of Dad's ashes into the box of Rice-a-Roni and saved the flavor packet for some soup down the road. When they came through the Old West saloon-style swinging doors of the chapel into the lobby, I started tossing the rice on them. They laughed and tried to shield themselves from the falling grain and human ashes.

"Hold it! Stop! Hold it!" the old man screamed. "Stop throwing that goddamn rice!" I stopped and looked at the man timidly like a toddler who had spilled his milk. "Do you know how hard it is to get rice out of shag carpet? Go throw that shit out in the parking lot."

It was nearly midnight, just six hours until Quincy had to be back in San Diego or he'd be considered AWOL.

"Do you guys want to do something before you have to head back?"

"Yeah," Kitty said quickly.

"So what's in the envelope?" I asked.

They opened it to find it was stuffed with every kind of Las Vegas promotion, come-on, and coupon imaginable. They sifted through the stack.

"Free shrimp cocktail for the bride and groom," Quincy read.

"Let's go get one," Kitty said, rubbing her mound-like stomach. We all got in the truck and drove into the old downtown area of Las Vegas along Fremont Street. The Golden Gate Casino offering the free shrimp cocktails was on the corner. We stood in line at the buffet-style restaurant in the back of the casino and ate their free shrimp cocktails to the incessant ringing and rattling of the slot machines.

We decided to visit the other casinos and cash in on whatever their wedding packet entitled them to. They got their picture taken in front of $1,000,000 at the Golden Horseshoe Casino, a free roll of nickels at another, and their names in the headlines of a promotional newspaper. The headline read, "Quincy and Kitty Strike It Rich in Las Vegas."

CHAPTER

# 10

I STOOD NEXT TO MY ALUMINUM BIKE in the casino's parking lot, waving as Quincy and Kitty drove out of sight. Other than the roll of nickels Quincy had insisted I take, I was again completely broke. It was almost two o'clock in the morning, nearing the wee, small hours when the average tourist surrenders the night to the compulsive gamblers and blacked-out drunks.

While riding around aimlessly, I noticed a flashing yellow-and-black pawnshop sign near the freeway. I rode my bike over to the pawnshop. I walked into the shop to the sound of ringing bells clanging against the glass door. The barrel-chested shopkeeper stood behind thick, bullet-proof Plexiglas and asked me over the microphone, "Whatcha got?"

"Well, I really hate to part with it, but I've got this lightweight racing bike. It's almost brand-new."

"Are you one of them goddamn clean-air people on your aluminum bikes?"

"Ah, well, in a way . . . " I said, my voice trailing off at the end.

"They rode through here today, blockin' traffic, and causing an uproar."

"They were here today?"

"Yeah, all hot and bothered about clean air."

"You wouldn't happen to know where they're staying, would you?"

"Hell no, how would I know where they are staying?"

"Would you be interested in this bike?"

"You think I'm stupid? What would I want with an aluminum bike? You'd probably get more for it at the recycling center."

I rode around through all the parking lots of the hotels and motels in the downtown area looking for the ABBA van. After two hours of unsuccessful searching, I was too exhausted to search anymore.

I hopped the wrought-iron fence that surrounded the swimming pool at a small, gimmicky independent motel called "Motel Six-the-Hard-Way." A list of pool rules hung on the lifeguard stand: No jumping or diving, no horseplay, no glass bottles, no pets.

*Why not save us all the reading and just get a sign saying "No fun in or around this pool"?* I thought.

I quietly lifted the top reclining lounge chair off of a stack of about six others, pulled it inside the pool attendant's bamboo hut, and, with my backpack for a pillow, folded my arms and went to sleep.

I slept for a few hours until the mullet-haired, morning cabana boy arrived on the pool deck carrying two freshly laundered bundle of towels and tossed them into the hut, hitting me on the chest. With a groan of surprise, I was instantly wide awake. The cabana boy walked into the hut to explore.

"Dude, you scared the crap out of me."

"Oh, sorry," I said.

"No problem, bro. It's cool. I've crashed here myself when the ol' lady is givin' me a hard time."

"Yeah, it's not bad," I confessed. "I've definitely stayed in worse places than this."

"Oh, hell yeah. This hut's the kind, Dude."

"It sure is the kind," I agreed. "Well, thanks for being cool about this."

"No sweat, bro. We all gotta watch out for each other, huh?"

"That's right," I said, collecting my backpack and exiting the hut.

"Maybe someday you'll save my life or somethin'," he said with a smirk.

"Maybe, you never know."

"Hey, but if I need CPR, get some chick to do it," he said, chuckling.

"You got it; no CPR from me," I said.

"You take 'er easy, bro," he said, as I walked off the pool deck to retrieve my bike from behind the hibiscus bush where I had hid it for the night.

I hopped on my bike and rode back down Las Vegas Boulevard toward the Strip. I stopped at the donut shop near the discount chapel and spent half of my nickel roll on a caked doughnut and small coffee. I browsed through the morning newspaper some early bird had already read and discarded. I scanned the classifieds for any kind of opportunity that would help my dire situation.

There was an ad for the Waste Not/Want Not Recycling Center. "Just two blocks from McCarran Airport," it read. "Top prices paid for all recyclables." I ripped the ad out of the newspaper and asked the Vietnamese doughnut maker, who was wearing a maroon Pizza Hut cap, for directions. He had sugar granules stuck to his eyebrows, a thick accent, and a poor sense of direction, so I thanked him for his help and decided to find the recycling center on my own.

I figured I had a 25 percent chance of going the right way, so I gambled on south and continued riding down toward the Strip. I stopped for a while in front of Caesar's Palace and asked passersby if they'd like to buy a bike. The only offer I had was from a teenager with spiked hair and a "Rage Against the Machine" T-shirt who offered me two one-dollar chips from the Slots-O-Fun Casino. After nearly an hour of old men in Bermuda shorts saying things like, "Did those one-armed bandits take all your money?" I decided the bike was headed for the scrap heap. It took me about an hour to find the recycling center, but my gamble had paid off.

The recycling center looked like the morning after a really good party, with loose cans and bottles scattered everywhere. I approached a man sitting in a trailer with a window cut out of the side and metal security bars covering the opening.

"I want to sell my bike. It's aluminum."

"Aluminum is ninety-five cents a pound," the man said, "but you'll have to take the seat, tires, pedals, hand grips, and reflectors off. They ain't worth nothin'."

"What'll you give me for it the way it is?"

"You think this is a bike shop? I don't want no bike."

"Okay," I said. "Do you have some tools I could use to take the other stuff off?"

"You think this is a tool library?" he said, before turning toward his desk to pound the keys on an adding machine. I tried to reason with him, but he abruptly cut me off. "Don't want no bikes, ain't got no tools!"

I turned and left the scrap yard, temporarily defeated. I rode around the area looking for a mechanic's shop where I could borrow a wrench and a screwdriver. I pulled into a quick-service oil-change shop called Friendly Dan's. I stood in the small lobby that had a few vending machines and an old-style nickel slot machine. While waiting for someone to acknowledge my presence, I dropped a nickel into the machine, pulled the handle, and nothing happened. When the man, who was not Friendly Dan, came in from the service area, I said, "That machine ate my nickel and nothing happened."

"That machine is just for show, it's an antique from the original Flamingo."

"Well, I want my nickel back."

We argued back and forth a few times, then the man reached into his pocket, grabbed his change, and held it in his open hand before him. He didn't have a nickel, so he picked out a dime and put it in my hand. "There you go, you just doubled your money. Now you can leave Vegas a winner." At that point I didn't have the nerve to ask to borrow the man's tools, so I got back on my bike and rode off.

Behind the shop was the start of a bread-and-butter, Joe Six-Pack, working-class housing tract. I rode through the streets and eventually came across a man working on his car in the driveway. I asked the man if I could borrow his tools. The man agreed, but he insisted I use them there. I promised I'd bring them back, but he started in with some hard luck story about people ripping off his tools before. I worked alongside him in his driveway, loosening the nuts on the wheels and seat so they were just hand-tight, and I took the reflector and grips off with the screwdriver. I thanked the man and carefully rode off on the loose, wobbly bike. I was able to arrive back at the recycling center in one piece. I unscrewed the bike with my hands to the satisfaction of the man in the trailer, who paid me just over eleven dollars for the aluminum bike frame. I carried the other parts with me and tried to sell them on a busy street corner. After an hour standing in the burning sun with a sign that read "Bike parts for sale," I gave up and tossed them in the trash bin behind an AM/PM mini-market.

Now on foot, I walked over to a supermarket to buy something to eat. I bought a sourdough roll from the bakery section and asked the lady behind the counter for a cup of hot water. The hot water was free, but she charged me twenty-five cents for the cup.

"That's the way we keep inventory," she told me.

I paid for the roll and cup of water, added the chicken flavoring from the Rice-a Roni packet and had my meal near the front of the store, leaning against a row of shopping carts.

There were several free publications on a rack by the automatic sliding doors, so I grabbed a few to browse through while I was eating. I opened the papers and spread them across the top of a few shopping carts.

In *The Rebel Yell*, the UNLV student newspaper, there was an advertisement for a ride-share going to Seattle. Although not the direction I wanted to go, it gave me hope there were rides going other ways. My college had had a ride board in the student center; maybe there would be one at UNLV.

I was excited about the chance to get moving again. I asked a box boy for directions to the campus and, with the sourdough roll in one hand and my cup of soup in the other, set out for the nearby campus. I found the student center and located the ride board. There were several offers heading to all parts of the United States. I took down many of the phone numbers and used the rest of my nickels calling them from a pay phone.

Many of the rides had already been filled or were still weeks away. One woman refused me a ride because of my sex, and a man refused me because I didn't have enough money to contribute. I called a woman who was going to a small town in northeast Arizona called Teec Nos Pos. It certainly wasn't my dream ride, but she was leaving in the morning and would let me ride along for ten dollars. We agreed to meet in front of the campus at six the next morning.

I had about fifteen hours to kill before then, so I went to the campus library and updated my journal, did some reading, and slept in a small reading cubical with my head on the desk until the library closed at eleven.

I had to save the ten dollars for the ride, so I had no money for food. I walked back to the Strip just to kill some time. It was now after midnight and my stomach was growling with hunger pains. It seemed to moan its displeasure even louder as I walked past the casinos with their bountiful midnight-buffet marquees. I decided to go in and see if I could somehow get some food. I surveyed an all-you-can-eat midnight buffet and thought, *If I could just get by the lady at the front counter, I'd be in.*

I walked to several other casino buffets to see if any of them were less secure, but I found them all impenetrable. I sensed an opportunity at the Frontier Casino when I noticed that the buffet's dining room was surrounded by a five-foot-tall planter box filled with leafy green artificial plants. I devised a plan and put it into action by flipping my backpack over the dining room's planter. The backpack landed next to an unoccupied table. I waited a few minutes and then rushed up to a painted-on-eyebrow lady holding the crushed velvet entrance rope. I explained that I had left my backpack in the dining room.

"Oh, by all means," she said, as she allowed me to pass through the gates of gluttony. I picked up the backpack and went and hid out in the bathroom for a half an hour. Though hunger is a great motivator on its own, I had to give myself a pep talk to work up the courage.

"It's now or never," I told myself, "You can either have some balls and eat prime rib, or you can walk out of here scared and hungry. No guts, no glory."

I took a few deep breaths, walked back out to the dining room, set my backpack down on a table, and quickly walked over to the salad bar area. I browsed at the selections while looking around the room for a reaction from anyone who might have spotted me.

After a few minutes standing there, occasionally moving to the side to allow other customers access to the salad bar, I began to feel comfortable that I had penetrated the food fortress. Just then a busboy approached me and my heart began to race.

"Do chew nee da plate?" he asked in a thick Mexican accent.

"Yes, that would be great, thank you." I took the plate and walked over to the steam table and piled on fried chicken, beef ribs, mashed potatoes, and gravy. I sat down at a table for two in the corner by the planter. There was a two-dollar tip left there by the last occupants of the table, and since I'd already stolen dinner, I continued my crime spree by pocketing it. I ate as fast as I could and was nearly done with the first plate when the waitress walked up. My heart again raced. Could she have spotted me stealing her tip?

"Slow down, this is an all-you-can-eat ," she said with a chuckle. She was a sweet-looking woman of forty with big, full, pink cheeks. She smiled from ear-to-ear, not the least bit embarrassed about her chipped front tooth. "So what can I get you to drink?"

"Oh, nothin', I'm fine," I said with my mouth still full of food.

"Well, I'll bring you water just in case."

"Okay, thanks," I mumbled between chews.

"I'll need your ticket."

"Oh, uh," I said, stalling for something to say. "You know what, it was on my tray and it, uh, it uh, blew into the meatballs, and there was sauce all over it so I, I, ur, just threw it away."

"Oh, okay," she said. "That happens sometimes." She smiled and walked away. I figured she knew I hadn't paid for the food, but would she rat me out to security? I watched her every move as she strolled around the dining room doing her job, but I never saw her tell anyone. Later, she brought me a glass of water and winked at me.

*What a nice lady*, I thought. *I can't believe I stole her tip*. I put the two dollars back on the table and slid them under the salt-and-pepper shakers. I went up to the carving station and had a slice of thick, juicy prime rib with a glob of horseradish on it. I went back again and again for more food, gorging myself to the point of being uncomfortable. I put an apple, orange, and dinner roll in my pocket for later.

"Thank you," the waitress said with a friendly wave from across the room. That did it. I was already feeling bad about stiffing her and that "thank you" only made the guilt multiply. I felt "lower than whale shit," as my dad used to say, so I walked back to the table, opened my wallet, and laid out a one-dollar bill on the table. I knew doing so would drop my net worth below the critical ten-dollar mark, but I was riddled with guilt from the whole experience.

I now had nine dollars and fifty cents and about five hours before my ride arrived to beg, borrow, find, steal, earn, or win fifty cents. I strolled the Strip checking pay phones and newspaper racks for forgotten change. I spotted a bank of pay phones in front of the Imperial

Palace and stuck my index finger inside each phone's coin return receptacle, only to saturate my finger in a disgusting mystery liquid hidden behind the last of the silver-plated, swinging coin-return doors.

After an unsuccessful half an hour of this, I decided to go against the good sense that God gave me and bet fifty cents on one spin of the roulette wheel. I walked up to a roulette table and took my place between the perfumed-soaked blue-haired ladies on a turnaround bus tour and the tattooed, drunk idiots blowing their paychecks. I put two quarters on the solid black strip, then picked them up when the dealer told me the minimum bet was two dollars. The dealer pushed the ball out between his thumb and index finger and sent it racing around the roulette wheel. The ball landed on black.

*If I'd only had the guts to bet two dollars*, I thought. I stood and watched for several minutes as the ball continued to fall in one black trough after another. I reached into my wallet and placed two dollars on the solid black strip.

"Money plays!" the dealer shouted out to no one in particular. He spun the ball around the roulette bowl and waved his arm over the field of numbers saying, "No more bets." The ball hopped and jumped, landing in the green double zero. He shouted out, "Double zero!" to the displeasure of everyone at our table. He placed the clear pyramid-shaped marker on the number and wiped all the losing bets, including my two dollars, back toward him. Seeking to reclaim my lost money, I took casino oxygen and doubled my bet to four dollars.

"Red's overdue," I mumbled repeatedly, trying to convince myself as I placed my money on the table's solid-red marker. "Red's due. It's got to be red this time."

The next roll of the ball rejected my theory; it landed on number seven black. My financial empire had crumbled to three dollars and fifty cents.

*Well, three-fifty's not going to do me any good, might as well risk it*, I thought. I cashed it in for seven fifty-cent chips that I scattered on numbers five, six, ten, twenty-three, twenty-five, thirty-one, and thirty-six. I crossed my fingers and repeated in my head, "*please, please, please, please, please . . .*" as the ball spun around.

"Twenty-one!" the dealer shouted as he slid the marker across the table. My head fell into my hands with disappointment. Not because I had lost, but because the ball had landed on my dad's birthday. The whole reason I was even in Las Vegas was because of Dad and I hadn't even bet on his birthday! I felt so stupid. I had placed bets on my birthday, friends' birthdays, even Michael Jordan's uniform number, but the omission of Dad's birthday was a frustrating oversight that cost me the equivalent of the ride fare and a morning breakfast.

I stood there for a brief moment until the dealer told me to make room if I wasn't going to place a bet. I had no money, what was I going to play with?

I walked out of the casino suffering from a recurring bout of abject poverty, and stood forlorn on the sidewalk, considering my next move. I meandered my way up to the corner of Tropicana and Las Vegas Boulevard and waited for the light to turn green to cross.

"Hey, man, check it out," yelled a man handing out handbills. I took one and read it over while waiting for the light to change. When I crossed the street, another man was passing out the same handbill for a strip club but on different-colored paper.

"Check it out," the other man said, and I took one of his handbills, too.

"Hey, I need a job. Are they looking for anyone else to pass out these flyers?" I asked.

"Yeah," he said eagerly. "Just take this handbill to Big Steve and tell him you want to work. But make sure you give him my handbill and tell him Fast Ronny sent you, cause I get a kickback for bringin' in new blood."

The club was just a few blocks east of the Strip. A red neon sign flashed "Live Nudes" and "Nude Nudes," which I thought was an interesting advertisement instead of all those other strip clubs that offered "dead nudes" or "clothed nudes."

It was certainly no time to be picky, so I walked up to the front door where two thick-necked thugs wearing black tuxedos with red bow ties guarded the door. I asked them if I could speak with Big Steve.

"What for?" said one of the goons.

"I want a job. Fast Ronny told me to come over here and talk to Big Steve."

"Okay, what's your name?"

"Uh, Broke Roastbeef," I said, trying to fit in. A few moments passed until the door swung open and a guy too big to be a midget but too small to be considered a normal-sized man came out wearing a blue suit with a red-and-yellow paisley ascot. "I'm Big Steve," he said with a squeak to his voice.

"Oh," I said, trying not to seem too surprised by his size. "I was wondering about a job passing out flyers."

"They're not flyers, they're handbills. There's a big difference, and if you wanna make it in this game, Jack, you'll learn this PDQ"

"Okay."

"Well, first, let me tell you we work on commission. For every guy who brings your handbill in here you get three bucks. If you pass out one and it gets in here, you get paid. If you pass out a thousand handbills and none of them make it in here, you're S.O.L., my friend. You want the job?"

"Yeah, but can I get paid by five o'clock in the morning? I'm leaving Vegas at six o'clock."

"You bring some business in and I'll settle up with ya."

Big Steve grabbed a handful of handbills printed on lime-green paper.

"Okay, the green ones that come back tonight are yours. A word to the wise, kid. If you see someone else passing out the handbills, pick a new corner. A lot of those guys are very territorial and for Christ's sake, I don't need another employee stabbing."

I took the handbills and walked back out to the Strip. I walked north out of the range of the other hand-billers and ended up on the sidewalk in front of Bally's just after two in the morning. Holding the stack in my left hand, I grabbed one handbill with my right and held it out in the path of the late night gamblers strolling by. I said nothing and no one took one of the handbills.

"Free handbills, take one," I said, as the next group passed by. They at least looked at me but didn't take one. Then I remembered how the other guys down the strip were doing it.

"Check it out," I said in my best New York City accent. I became more and more assertive, stepping in front of people and nearly shoving the handbills into people's hands. After twenty minutes of this, the sidewalk was littered with the handbills that people had briefly taken possession of before they dropped them and continued on.

"Check it out," I said to an elderly man.

He replied in a distinct Irish brogue, "What's a nice young lad like yourself doing passing out this kind of rubbish?"

"I'm just trying to get ten dollars together so I can get outta town," I told him. His wife and her friend followed a few steps behind, chatting with such thick accents that it was hard to believe they were speaking English. The old man showed his wife the handbill and said, "This young lad needs ten dollars to get out of this cesspool of sin."

"If I be givin' you the ten dollars lad, will you be throwin' those bloody pamphlets in the litter box?" she asked. I nodded my head and she opened up her purse and handed me a ten-dollar bill.

"Do you believe in Jesus?" she asked before releasing the bill from her hand.

"Yeah," I said, putting the ten dollars in my wallet and looking around for a trash can to throw the handbills away.

"You can't say you believe in Jesus, and then not be livin' a Christian life. You're draggin' down the name of Jesus with this smut. One day, dear lad, Judgment Day will come and you'll be standing in front of St. Peter sayin' 'I shoulda, woulda, coulda,' and it'll be too late."

"Yes ma'am," I said, nodding my head. I figured she was entitled to ten dollars worth of hell-fire-and-brimstone rants.

"Don't be playin' fast and loose with Jesus," she ordered in a scolding tone, waving her wrinkled bony finger just inches from my face.

I thanked her for the money and began my walk back toward the UNLV campus. I arrived at the campus an hour later and spent the remaining hours sitting on the steps of the administration building waiting for my ride to show up. I was exhausted and would occasionally nod off.

At five minutes to six, a woman drove up in a small, red Toyota Celica with an Indian dream catcher hanging from the rearview mirror. The backseat was filled with clothes and boxes to the point where it was impossible to see out of the back window. She introduced herself as Charlene Gargle, which sounded like a lie to me. I was tempted to respond, "Yeah? Well, I'm Ted Mouthwash. How ya doin'?"

She shook my hand firmly and I complimented her on the bent-fork bracelet she wore on her right wrist. "That's cool," I said. "I wish women would wear more silverware jewelry."

"Oh, thanks," she said. "Made it myself. Well, hop in."

She took an isolated four-lane highway to Kingman, Arizona, where we got on Interstate 40 headed east. The woman talked incessantly about herself and what was waiting for her in her hometown of Teec Nos Pos. I would try to be polite and listen to her stories or at least at random intervals say things like, "yeah," "wow," "really, how 'bout that" and "are you serious?" I tilted my head back to the headrest and closed my eyes.

"Hey, man, wake up," Charlene said. "This isn't a sleeping car. I brought you along to keep me company."

"Oh, sorry," I said, sitting up and shaking my head around, then slapping myself in the face a few times. "I didn't sleep at all last night."

"Gambling?"

I was too tired to go into the whole story so I just said, "Uh huh."

"I don't gamble," she said. "I work too hard for my money to just give it away to the casinos."

"What do you do?"

"I'm an assistant softball coach for the Rebs."

She was a large, stocky woman with short, highlighted hair. She had dense, blond peach fuzz growing on her cheeks and scattered dark, coarse hair growing on her upper lip and chin. I listened politely to her stories and when she was all talked out she said, "Would you like to listen to a book on tape?"

"Sure," I said, thinking *anything to shut her up for a while.* "What do you have?"

"I only listen to romance novels," she said, popping the cassette into the car stereo. The book was *Passionate Partners* and was written by some author with a flowery pen name. I paid some attention at first to the story of Cheryl and Tony but as the book continued and the love scenes between the two business partners were developing, it became evident that Tony was actually Toni. We were listening to a lesbian romance novel.

We passed through Seligman, Ash Fork, and the snowy mountain town of Flagstaff. Thirty minutes later we drove through Winslow, Arizona, and, contrary to the Eagles song, I didn't see anybody standing on any corners or, for that matter, any girls in flatbed Fords, but I'm sure if we would have gotten off the interstate and actually explored the sleepy little desert town we probably would have found both.

"Well, I take this small highway north now," Charlene explained as she pulled off of the interstate just before the Petrified Forest at the interchange of Highway 191. "You're welcome to come along, but I'll tell you, Teec Nos Pos is way out in the sticks."

I looked around and saw nothing here except a roadside Indian souvenir shop. "Sure, I'll ride along with you. But could we stop here for a second, I need to use the restroom."

"Good idea," she said. "I'm due for a squirt."

She pulled the car up to a wooden building with several multicolored giant Teepees on the roof and hand-painted signs affixed to the sides of the walls: sand painting, moccasins, Indian jewelry, ice cream. It reminded me of Uncle Fred's souvenir shop back at Mount Rushmore.

"Ugh!" A large white man with a half-smoked cigar in his mouth said. "Welcome to Indian City."

"Have you got a restroom?" I asked.

"Restrooms are for customers only."

"We'll buy something when we come out."

"Sure, that's what they all say, then they stink up my restroom and drive off to Flagstaff. If you want to use the restroom, you buy something."

"Well, how much is this belt?" Charlene asked.

"Six-fifty," said the shopkeeper.

Charlene looked at it closely while I began fidgeting to ease the pressure on my full bladder. "Six dollars and fifty cents?" she asked. "But it says it's made in the Philippines."

"So what, it's a nice belt."

"But you call this place Indian City, and you're a white guy selling Filipino belts."

"Correction!" he said with a sharp, firm voice. "I'm one sixty-fourth native American."

"Well, that doesn't change the fact that this belt was manufactured in the Philippines."

"You think they don't have Indians in the Philippines? I know several Filipino Indians."

It looked like this conversation was going to last a while, so I went out behind the shop to relieve myself in the tumbleweeds. When we returned to the car, Charlene said, "It's about a two-hour drive from here. Do you want to hear another book?"

"Oh, no," I wailed. "Not more Cheryl and Toni."

"Don't you like romance novels, or are you just some kind of homophobe?"

"Me? No, romance novels, lesbians, it's all good."

"You might like this one, *Closeted Coworkers*," she said, shuffling through her collection of books on tape. "This one is a lot like my own situation. It's so real to life, it's like the author knows me."

"What do you mean?"

"Well, my family doesn't know. I've come out to everyone except them."

"Do you think they have any idea?"

"No, they're always asking me about the men I'm dating."

"What do you tell them?"

"I make up dates with make-believe men. You know, karaoke with John the CPA or a movie with Bill the lawyer. Then the next time I talk to them, I say that things didn't work out. John was a bore or Bill was a deadbeat. They think I'm just too picky."

"Do you have a lady friend," I said, struggling for the correct term.

"Yeah, I've got a partner," she said with a husky chuckle.

"Have you come up with a story for this time?"

"No, not yet," she said, then startled by inspiration, shouted out, "How 'bout you be my boyfriend for the weekend?"

"Uh, I don't know."

"Come on. You can stay at the house, free food, free party. It'll be easy. Besides, what else are you going to do in Teec Nos Pos?"

"Well, I don't know. I mean we barely even know each other. How could we pull it off for a whole weekend?"

"We've got two hours. Let's create a relationship."

# CHAPTER
# 11

WE ARRIVED IN TEEC NOS POS, ARIZONA, in the early afternoon with the details of our relationship fresh in our minds. We drove through a two-block downtown business area of mostly vacated storefronts with boarded-up windows and then into a small neighborhood of weather-beaten adobe haciendas.

Charlene's parents' house had a white rock-garden front yard with just a few colorful garden gnomes for accent. Charlene parked behind an old camper shell that was resting on cinder blocks. It had a faded and peeling Good Sam sticker on the back window. Her parents had seen the car pull into the driveway and came out to meet us. Her mother hugged Charlene as her father stood there, holding a small fluffy Pomeranian dog that yapped continually. The man looked at me and said stoically, "You want a dog?"

I grinned. Charlene hugged her standoffish father and said, "Hi, Chopper," to the dog while scratching him behind his ears. "Mom and Dad, this is Roastbeef. Roastbeef, this is my mom and dad, Dick and Eliza Gargle."

"Roastbeef?!" the man shouted. "What the hell kinda name is Roast-beef?" I just smiled politely and thought that a guy named Gargle shouldn't be making fun of other people's names.

"Ohhhh," Eliza whispered to Charlene. "Is this the young man you've been telling us about?"

"Kinda young for you, isn't he?" Dick queried.

"Oh, Daddy," Charlene whined while taking my hand in hers. "You're a couple of years older than mom."

"That's right. That's the way it's supposed to be. The man is supposed to be older than the woman, even says so in the Bible. Thy woman is subservient to thy man."

"Don't start, Dad," Charlene pleaded.

"All's I'm sayin' is God set up the right way of doin' things and the wrong way of doin' things, but fools like you think you know better than God."

"That's a bunch of crap," Charlene stated. "God doesn't care who's older in a relationship."

"Oh, get a load of this girl? Not at my house five minutes and she's cussin' like a sailor and spittin' on the Lord's word."

"As long as they're both happy," said Eliza, trying to smooth things over.

"Well, you and your young fella aren't sleepin' together in my house," Dick said, shaking his finger at Charlene. "Junior here can sleep out in the trailer."

Charlene and Eliza walked into the house and Dick unlocked the camper's padlock and let me in.

"Well, it ain't the Holiday Inn, but the price is right," he said to me as I stepped into the humid camper. It was just like walking into a sauna, except I didn't have to make small talk with a fat, sweaty guy wearing nothing but a towel.

"Don't worry, Eliza will fix this up for you real nice."

After I got settled into the trailer, I decided to take a walk into downtown Teec Nos Pos. There was nothing in town of particular interest to me, but at least browsing around got me away from the uncomfortable family conflict at Casa de Gargle.

The plywood that covered many of the storefronts was stenciled with black block letters stating "Post No Bills." The bill posters paid no attention and posted freely. The small cafe had a sign in the window stating "Closed for one week for roach spraying."

About the only store in town that was open was the Better New & Used Thrift Store. I browsed through old Barry Manilow record albums, crutches, pup tents, bowling shoes, fondue pots, paperback books, and a ceramic coffee cup stating "I owe, I owe, so off to work I go."

"Can I help you find anything?" the lady behind the counter asked.

"No, I'm just looking around."

"Are you coming or going to Four Corners?" she asked.

"Uh, neither," I said. "I'm here staying with the Gargles. Do you know them?"

"Sure. Known 'em for years. You must be their daughter's boyfriend."

"Uh, yeah, that's me, the boyfriend. I'm the boyfriend," I said with an unconvincing stammer.

"It's funny, I would of thought she was as queer as a three-dollar bill. I guess that shows ya that you can't judge a book by the cover."

That night in the Gargle's kitchen nook we all dined on Stroganoff-flavored Hamburger Helper and canned peaches. When Charlene innocently asked her mother to pass the salt, the father/daughter conflict reappeared.

"That stuff'll give ya high blood pressure," Dick blurted out.

"I like high blood pressure," Charlene answered.

"You got sucha mouth. You think people like that wisenheimer mouth of yours?"

"I don't care if they like it or not," she answered, salting her food.

"Good God, will ya look at how much salt she uses?! Look at that, mother, we've got a salt addict for a daughter. Maybe we should put up a salt lick in her bedroom."

"Who wants some peaches?" Eliza asked, coming to the rescue. The rest of the meal was eaten in silence until Dick finished, stated that he'd have his Ding Dong in the living room, and adjourned to his Lazy Boy.

The next day a crush of Gargles converged upon the sleepy desert town to celebrate their common DNA strands. I spent all afternoon swishing around the backyard, mingling with several different generations of Gargles. When I was introduced as Charlene's boyfriend, most of them told me something similar to what the thrift store shopkeeper had said. The reunion was fairly uneventful for me. I listened to a lot of old stories about people I didn't know. I did find out that the family's real name was Gorgonzola, as in the pungent Italian cheese. The name had been changed at Ellis Island to help them acclimate into turn-of-the-century American society.

Lunch was served potluck style with hordes of casseroles, the likes I hadn't seen since Dad's death. In the late afternoon, two of Charlene's uncles, who smelled like they had bathed in bong water, got into a quarrel about who was going to get the last of the extra-extra-large "Gargle Family Reunion" T-shirts. They started wrestling and pulling hair and calling each other "son-of-a-bitch" and eventually rammed into the side of the aboveground pool, spilling the green, pond-like water across the yard.

When it was time to take the group photo, I offered to take the picture, but they insisted I be in the photo next to Charlene. I stood there and smiled, knowing that one day when the closet door swung open and the Gargles discovered they had a gay daughter, out would come the scissors and my face would end up on the editing-room floor.

I slept in the camper one last night and had chorizo and eggs for breakfast with the Gargles the next morning. I left Charlene there to explain to her parents the reason for our breakup and caught a ride to Four Corners with a Gargle cousin who was heading home to Durango, Colorado.

It was a dry and gusty day, but occasionally there were other cars forging their way through the desert for their passengers to experience the thrill of standing in four states simultaneously. Charlene's cousin had seen the Four Corners monument so many times that he didn't even glance over toward it as he let me out. The actual sight was a disappointment. I walked up to the monument, which was a large circle on the ground made of a red polished stone. Within the stone were inset brass state line markers that intersected in the center of the circle at a baseball-sized brass plaque that marked the exact spot. One by one, tourists got down on all fours and had their pictures taken. I stood by at the outer edge on the Land of Enchantment side of the circle, waiting for my turn. A family with six kids showed up and started contorting their bodies every which way over the state lines while their fanny-pack-wearing father snapped photos with an Instamatic camera. The fun was short-lived, and soon the kids were loaded back in the van and away they went. I was temporarily left there alone, so I took Surfing Monkey out of my backpack and sprinkled some of Dad's ashes through the coin drop at the back of the monkey's skull. I made sure to pour the ashes right at the intersecting mark. Just as I completed the four-state sprinkle,

I heard a van racing toward the parking lot at what must have been nearly fifty miles an hour. The driver suddenly slammed on the brakes in the dirt parking lot, causing a huge dust cloud to engulf the whole van and make it temporarily invisible. The doors of the van all opened, and ten college-aged guys wearing Greek-lettered T-shirts came sprinting toward me, yelling and screaming at the top of their lungs. I got out of the circle on the Utah side and watched as a stocky fraternity brother slid on his belly across the marker while his brothers chanted, "Otto, Otto, Otto!" He had skinned up his chin on the dive but got up to wipe the blood on his shirt and receive high fives from his admiring brothers. I noticed that Otto had a charcoal-colored stain on his white T-shirt.

"Excuse me," I said to Otto, "but you just slid across the ashes I sprinkled there."

"So what."

"Well, those are my father's ashes, and I'm sprinkling them in every state."

The fraternity boys burst out laughing.

"Otto's got a dead guy's ashes on his shirt," one of the fraternity boys said once the laughter started dying down. Otto took the shirt off to shake it out.

"Don't just shake it all toward Colorado," I said hurriedly. "Give it a shake in each direction."

The laughter grew again as Otto obliged and took a quarter turn toward a different state after each shake.

The fraternity boys were heading back to Colorado State University after a national-chapter convention in Los Angeles.

I asked them for a ride and away we went. The fraternity members had animal nicknames, such as Gopher, Goat, and Weasel. The designated driver was known as W. P., and as the trip progressed, I came to find that W. P. stood for Whale Puke. He drove the fifteen-passenger rental van, and it was fairly evident the fraternity members wouldn't be getting their security deposit on the van returned. They planned on arriving in Fort Collins, Colorado, by early Monday morning, which gave them nineteen hours to get there. The fraternity boys had two ice chests full of beer and full twelve-packs under the seats waiting for their turn in the cooler.

They were already drunk and incessantly offered me beers and ordered me to catch up. I was thirsty from the heat and dust of the desert so the first beer went down very fast.

"Damn, this boy drinks like a brother," one of the fraternity members said. It was either Toad or Squirrel; I can't remember.

"Do it again, I was pissin' and missed it," said another member. He had just added a few ounces to the five-gallon Sparkletts water jug that was serving as their onboard restroom.

Someone threw another beer to me and I again drank it down, but slower than the first.

"Ah," said a dissatisfied fraternity member. "He doesn't drink like a brother, he drinks like a G.D.I. pussy."

Then they all began chanting, "G.D.I., G.D.I., G.D.I.," which I found out later stood for God Damn Independent, someone who's not in a fraternity. I drank yet another beer just to shut up their endless chanting.

The desert scenery was changing to a mountain setting as we drove the Rocky Mountain highway toward Denver. The van began to become more quiet as the fraternity guys started feeling the effects of one thousand miles, three days, and constant partying. One never-say-die brother named the Rat tried to rally the troops.

"Let's play 'Stump the Oaf.'"

The Oaf was a large boy-man who sat in the back of the van, taking up the entire backseat, which was made for three. I learned later the Oaf was actually in another fraternity and had been forced to go "inactive" for some reason that was unclear to everybody. The Oaf claimed he knew every song of the rock-and-roll era. The brothers would challenge him on his claim and hence the game "Stump the Oaf" was born.

"I've got one," Weasel said and started singing a song. He sang two lines and then stopped and said, "Name it." The Oaf thought about it for a couple seconds then answered correctly.

"Damn," said Weasel, "he's unstumpable."

"I was born in the wagon of a travelin' show," W. P. sang out from the driver's seat.

"You insult me," the Oaf said. "Gypsys, Tramps and Thieves."

This went on for over a half an hour without a successful stumping. Just as the van was approaching the road sign announcing the continental divide, I challenged the Oaf with a song. When the Oaf answered correctly again, I asked, "How do you know all these songs?"

"We didn't have a TV set in my house growing up, so it was either play my parents' record collection or read a book. So I played every album in the house a dozen times until I got a portable TV for my twelfth birthday."

The five-gallon piss bottle was filled to the top, so W. P. pulled over to empty it along the side of the road. The bottle emptied, making a loud "clug clug" sound as its contents seeped into the dirt and snow patches alongside the road.

It was the middle of the night, and the road was straight and empty except for the occasional big rig that W. P. would pass. He had the cruise control set on eighty, and as everyone else slept, he wore his Walkman headset with the music so loud the sound spilled out from the headphones and was slightly audible several rows back. We pulled into the driveway of a fraternity house just before eight o'clock in the morning. A few of the more ambitious brothers grabbed their books and headed off toward campus for their classes. Everyone else headed for their bed.

So much had happened in one day. It was hard to believe that twenty-four hours before I had been in Teec Nos Pos, Arizona, eating chorizo and eggs.

The fraternity house was actually two four-plex apartment buildings facing each other, with a common area courtyard between them. All the apartments were two bedrooms, and each bedroom housed two fraternity brothers. Their yearly "International Night" party was coming up the next weekend, and although it was just Monday morning, preparations were already being made. They told me I could sleep on the couch, but with so many brothers going in and out and building things for the party, sleep was nearly impossible. When I finally was able to doze off, some guy walked by, and kicked the bottom of the couch, and asked, "Who are you?"

In a dazed state I told him, "Roastbeef. I came in the van with the frat guys."

"Frat guys?!" the guy hollered. "This is a fraternity. Do you call your country a cunt?"

"Uh, no, not often."

"Well, this ain't no motel."

"Oh, it ain't?"

He ordered me off the property. I was so tired I decided to walk over to the campus and sleep in the library for a few hours. On the way I ran into one of the fraternity brothers from the road trip. He asked me where I was going and when I told him he said, "Oh, don't listen to that little prick. He was a legacy, we had to take him. You can't leave yet, International Night is this weekend. It's a real scene. You can crash in my room."

We walked back to the fraternity house, and I slept for four hours on the floor in his sleeping bag with a bunch of clothes shoved into a pillow case as a pillow.

International Night was the talk of the fraternity. Every room was responsible for representing a different country. It was not just a party but a competition among all the brothers, with each room wanting to out-do the other with decorations and that country's traditional music, food, and liquor.

Without any other plans and not being one to turn down a party, I decided to stay for the week. Most of the guys were very welcoming, and I worked on the party effort to help compensate for my free lodging. I bounced from job to job, building a miniature Eiffel Tower in one room in the morning, then painting the Great Wall of China in another room in the afternoon. The guys in the Russian room sent me on a borscht-buying mission, and let me tell you, buying borscht in Fort Collins is no picnic.

Sometimes we'd work through the night and sleep when we could, but there wasn't much sleep the whole week. Aside from setting up for the party, the most exciting thing that happened during my week as a make-believe frat boy was being invited to do an interview on the college's cable television station. A couple of the brothers were Radio-

Television-Film majors and worked at the on-campus station that, although it offered only four hours of programming each week, seemed very desperate for material to fill the time. I was interviewed on a talk show called "The Doug & Greg Show," except neither Doug nor Greg were there, because, I was told, they were "cramming for midterms." Inside the studio were a lot of granola guys with beards and ponchos who looked like they should be following the Grateful Dead around the country.

"I'm Cathy," said a girl in a navy-blue business suit as she started to pin her microphone to the lapel of her blazer. "I'll be interviewing you today." I looked at her, a bit taken aback, finding it hard to believe she was the first-choice replacement for Doug and Greg, because she definitely had a face better suited for radio.

For the first few minutes of the interview, we talked about meeting up with the fraternity brothers at Four Corners and their housing me during my Fort Collins stay, but it soon started to become evident that she was an aspiring Barbara Walters type. Through her questioning I could see she was hell-bent on bringing out a lot of emotion in the interview. When I realized she wanted the interview to culminate with me crying about my deceased father, the lying began.

"You must have loved your father very much," she said in a slow, comforting, Bill Clinton I-feel-your-pain kind of tone.

"Ah, he was okay. When he wasn't drinking, he didn't hit us too hard."

She let that answer go and asked me about my promise to Dad.

"Actually, Cathy, I don't even know the man whose ashes are inside this surfing monkey. His family gave me a thousand bucks to dispose of the ashes and I'm gonna do it." Then I sprinkled some ashes into her hair on live television. She called me every dirty word in the book until the director was able to run a poorly made commercial showing the volleyball team's upcoming schedule.

Cathy yelled at the laughing granola crew, telling them to shut up, then stormed out of the studio.

"That's the best television we've ever done here," a crew member told me. "Comedy, action, drama, that was good stuff."

"Maybe those ashes you sprinkled on her will help to kill the bug up Cathy's ass," said another.

They gave me a videotape of my television debut. I returned to the frat house to show them the tape, since the station's signal was only strong enough to spread around the campus and a few surrounding blocks of Fort Collins. My interview was seen by a local citizen, who called me at the frat house with an interesting proposition.

"I want you to take my wife's ashes to Graceland," said the middle-aged man on the other end of the phone. He called himself Vince Vanderboom but told me I could call him "Double V."

"I'm really not in the human-ash disposal business, this is more like a promise I made to my dad."

"I know," he said. "I saw your interview. That's what gave me the Elvis idea for my wife's ashes. She was the biggest gal-darn Elvis fan you ever did see."

"I don't know if I'm going to Memphis. I just kind of take this trip as it comes."

"Well, you think about it, but believe you me, I'll grease your kitty, my friend. How does a thousand dollars sound?" asked Double V with a cockiness about him.

"Why don't you just do it yourself?"

"I got another year of house arrest 'fore I can stretch my wings again," he said, confessing this was his fourth drunk-driving conviction. "The first two they got me dead to rights, cause I was drivin' when I couldn't find my ass with both hands, but I swear the last two were nothin'. Maybe a wet reckless at worst."

I told him I'd think about it and get back to him.

"Sure, sure, no hurry. She's been sitting on my mantel since eighty-seven, she ain't goin' nowheres."

The frat guys told me I was a fool if I didn't take him up on his offer, so the next day I went over to meet Double V in person and we agreed that he'd give me $250 up front, $250 when I got to Memphis, and the $500 balance when I sent him back photos of me sprinkling his wife's ashes on the grave of Elvis. Double V gave me five fifty-dollar bills he had hidden in his house slipper. When he took the money out, I got a good look at the ankle brace that monitored his whereabouts.

"Well, here you go," he said, handing me a silver-plated urn. "Aw shit, I forgot to kiss her good-bye. She used to put my balls in a blender if I didn't kiss her good-bye." He kissed the urn and handed it back to me. "I'll look forward to seeing those pictures," he said as we shook hands at the front door of his house/jail cell.

I generously, or foolishly, donated $100 to the frat brothers for their international party and padded my wallet with the other $150. On Friday night, the night before the party, the fraternity members had a big meeting to vote for who was going to be named the King of the World. It was the King's job to visit every country and then objectively select a winner. The meeting went on several hours, so I took the time to catch up on some much needed sleep. I was awakened by a bowl of ice cold water being thrown on me and was informed that the brothers had broken with tradition and named me, an outsider, to be the King of the World. I was shocked, not so much by the honor they'd bestowed on me, but from the freezing cold water that had taken my breath away.

"This is going to be the best one yet, King," one of the fraternity members said to me, and from then on they always referred to me as King.

On Saturday, people began arriving in the early afternoon. There were former fraternity members, chapter members, and sorority girls from other schools who had come from as far as Florida, Texas, and Arizona for the party.

I was handed a makeshift trophy of an old world globe nailed to a four-by-four board to give to the winner.

Party guests were given cards—called passports—and were supposed to get stamps in each country visited. I was led around the party by Greenbean, whose job for the night was to make sure I visited every country.

At first I was kept in their garage, which they had converted into a dance club with the help of one reflective disco ball in the center of the room that one of the members had recently stolen from a dance club in town. Tradition had it that four members carried the King around the courtyard a few times while the men bowed and the women curtsied as I passed. They then carried me up the stairs to visit my first country, Japan.

Four girls dressed in brightly colored kimonos met me at the door and welcomed me to Japan. A red-haired girl with green eyes seemed to speak in slow motion with her heavy Texas drawl when she asked, *"How j'all* get to be the King?" while handing me some hot sake in a small cup barely larger than a thimble.

"I don't know, really, they just threw some water on me and told me 'you're the King.'" I took a drink of the sake; it was terrible. It tasted like warm rubbing alcohol, but it was booze and it was free, so I drank it and then quickly washed it down with a swallow of beer.

"My name's Roastbeef, by the way," I said. I liked being around fraternity guys because they all had nicknames, too, so my name seemed like the norm.

"My name's Heiii-deee Bri-iiiight."

"Heidi Bright? Say it again."

She repeated her name and I fell in love right there. It's always the smallest little things that attract me to girls and with her it was those green eyes and the way it took her a half hour to say her name.

She and the other girls in the kimonos were from the University of Nebraska and had driven all the way to Fort Collins for the party because one of the girls was dating the chapter president.

"Have you been to the South Africa room yet?" she asked.

"I, I, I, I, ain't gonna play Sun City," I answered.

She didn't get it, but her green eyes sparkled with stupidity, and I was smitten.

"I'll see you in a little while," I told her as I was led away from Japan toward the French room upstairs. The odor coming from the room was the first signal that I was entering France. The stench seeped out of the room and down the hallway. Upon entering I saw they were cooking broccoli on a hot plate and had dirty socks and workout clothes hanging on a wash line with three fans behind them to spread the disgusting smells. They had spray-painted "WE SURRENDER" in large, red block letters on the white bedroom wall. Two swarthy fraternity members were dressed up as cancan girls, and when I came in, they handed me a glass of French wine and said in an attempt at a French accent, "Welcome, Monsieur, to the Moulin Rouge." Then they put their arms around each other's shoulders, exposing their huge patches of dark underarm hair and their lumpy fake breasts, and started doing leg kicks.

They offered me a tray of what they called escargot, but what truly looked like Omaha garden snails. I'm pretty sure I saw one move. I had to give France a good score on originality but also for having the most disgusting display.

The night continued. Every twenty minutes I was escorted to another room to experience the flavors of that country. I kept asking to go to Japan so I could talk to Heidi some more, but the countries had drawn numbers for the order of the King's visit, and Japan was second to last.

I hopped countries and continents like a jet-setting playboy: fish, chips, and ale in England; a real, live sacred cow in India; tequila, nachos, and contaminated water in Mexico.

As it neared midnight, we arrived in Japan to continue my gluttonous task. I was already full way past a comfortable level, and my slurred words were revealing the effect from imbibing boozes around the world. When I walked into the room, I noticed Heidi was asleep on the bed.

"What happened to Heidi?"

"We were all shootin' sake and she just barfed all over her kimono and passed out on the bed," one of her friends said.

"Hey, that's my bed," said a frat guy dressed up like a sumo wrestler. He had his hair pulled back into a ponytail and was wearing a large bladder-control adult diaper.

"Hey, nice diaper," I said.

"Man, these are great. I haven't used the can all night. With these things on there's no down time." Then for no apparent reason he screamed out, "Party!" and chugged from a bottle of sake.

The sake still tasted like warm rubbing alcohol, which was a good gauge for me because if I could still taste its nastiness, I hadn't lost all my senses.

The final room of the evening was the same room I had been staying in for the week, revamped into Greece. We had feta cheese, tomatoes in olive oil, pita bread, ouzo, and retsina. The floor was scattered with broken plates that the brothers had bought from every thrift store, flea market, and garage sale between Denver and Fort Collins. When the floor got so full you couldn't see the carpet anymore, one of the brothers raked the larger pieces out of the way and into the closet. The Greek music played, and everyone in the room danced around in a large circle, going forward then reversing position haphazardly. At the end of the song more plates were broken and shots of ouzo were downed.

When the last plate was broken, the crowd started looking around the room for other things to break. Before I could stop him, I saw a frat guy raise Surfing Monkey over his head.

"No!" I screamed from across the room, but I was too late. Surfing Monkey broke into hundreds of pieces and a cloud of Dad's ashes covered the smashed plates, carpet, and shoe tops of the revelers. I got down on my hands and knees and started sorting through the chunks of broken pieces, separating them into piles of broken plates, Surfing Monkey/ Uncle Spud, and Dad's ashes. Greenbean emptied the contents out of a coffee cup that he kept his change in and handed it to me. I dusted the ashes from each plate fragment into the cup.

"Everybody with dusty shoes stand still," I ordered.

"Why are you doing that? It was only a crummy monkey statue," Ramrod said.

"It was filled with his dad's ashes."

One by one, I swept the shoe ashes into the coffee cup, then continued trying to save as much as I could from the plates and carpet. Some of the other guys picked up all the Uncle Spud pieces and put them in a shoebox. When I'd picked up as much of the ashes as I thought I possibly could, nearly three-quarters of a coffee cup full, I dumped the ashes into a plastic shopping bag, placed it in the shoebox, and resumed my King duties.

They ordered me to go out to the courtyard to announce the winner. Despite the crushing blow to the worldly remains of Uncle Spud and the loss of much of Dad's ashes to the shag carpet, I presented the pathetic attempt at a trophy to the Greek room. There were cheers and boos, and I heard somebody heckle me with a "you suck," but at least my King duties were over. Or so I thought.

There were mattresses spread out and stacked two or three high in the middle of the complex, and I was informed, it was the King's final duty to jump from the second-floor balcony down to the mattresses, which was approximately a ten-foot jump.

They started chanting, "King, King, King," so I reluctantly obliged. I landed feet first on the mattress and then tried to ease the impact by rolling onto my side the way a skydiver lands, but I still hit hard enough to re-sprain my ankle on the landing. I was slow to get off of the mattresses until I looked up and saw the Oaf preparing for his jump, after which I quickly scampered off to safety. I think they would have jumped for most of the night if the campus police hadn't shown up around two o'clock demanding silence and ordering everyone inside. They all seemed to know the routine. "Quarters in the kitchen!" someone shouted.

"Playin' King?" Greenbean asked, as he threw his arm around me and put me in a headlock.

"No, I've had enough."

"Pull up your skirt and have a beer," he said while he walked me through the apartment, still in a headlock, and sat me down at the table.

"The King gets the first shot."

"I'm not the King anymore," I stated. "I'm back to G.D.I. serf status."

They slid the quarter across the table and I closed one eye due to blurry double vision, then aimed for the cup. I bounced the quarter off the brown Formica table top; it flipped over and over in the air, hit the rim of the cup, and fell in.

"Greenbean," I said proudly. He took the cup, halfway filled with beer, gulped it down in a quick fluid motion, and caught the quarter between his front teeth. I shot again and missed, and another brother took his turn. We played until we ran out of beer around four o'clock, although the details from the final few hours are sketchy in my head.

I do remember waking up around eight o'clock still very drunk with some asshole walking in and out of the apartments playing "Charge!" on his trumpet. During my drunken sleep, the fraternity brothers had stacked piles of trash all over my body. I awoke covered in beer cans, plastic cups, and paper plates, with the letters G.D.I. scribbled across my face in lipstick. Like a defenseless freeway overpass, I'd been tagged during the cover of night.

I tried to roll over and go back to sleep in the trash pile that was my bed, but the crinkling of the trash and the wetness from the spilled beer cans made it all seem hopeless.

I got up and took a long, hot shower. The lipstick markings didn't want to come off my face. I scrubbed my face with soap. Occasionally I peeked my head out of the shower to look in the mirror for an update, and then tried again. Each scrub slightly diminished the bright red lipstick on my pale, white, hungover face. Eventually I settled for just looking like I had a minor G.D.I. sunburn and felt comfortable enough with my appearance to get out of the shower.

I dressed and gathered my belongings and poked my head inside the Japanese room to see if Heidi Bright was still there, but she was gone. All that remained was an orange vomit stain on the pillow where she had laid her head. A few fraternity brothers were up nursing their morning-after beers and watching the European Curling Championships on ESPN. I thanked them for their hospitality and on the way out took one last shot at stumping the Oaf.

"I love, I love, I love, my Calendar Girl . . . each and every day of the year."

"Neil Sedaka," he quickly responded.

*Damn, he's good*, I thought as I walked out of the fraternity complex.

The bus station was about a one-mile walk from campus, and it felt great being outside in the cold Colorado morning air. It was Sunday morning, and except for the occasional car on the way to or from church, the streets of downtown Fort Collins were nearly empty. While walking, I was passed by a red convertible BMW with the top down. Inside was Heidi Bright and the other sorority girls from the University of Nebraska, who were on their way back to school.

"Hey, it's the King," yelled Carolyn, the girl in the front passenger seat, pointing at me as they passed. I waved and they pulled over. I ran up to their car.

"Where ya headed, King?" Donna, the driver, asked. I told her I was going to the bus station.

"Well, you're welcome to ride along with us if want to," Donna offered.

Only a fool would turn down a free ride with three beautiful sorority girls, so I hopped in the backseat next to Heidi and off we went toward Lincoln. All the girls had their hair pulled back into ponytails, slid through the snap-together opening of their adjustable baseball caps.

The girls were suffering the effects of too much International Night, and Heidi looked pale enough to drop off at the morgue. Within a few minutes I could tell that the party girls were going to be no fun at all. They didn't even want to carry on a conversation.

They slept, looked through magazines, and listened to the radio. I had big plans of telling my friends back home about being picked up by three sorority girls in a convertible. It sounds like a great set up for the *Hustler* mailbag, but these girls were duds. Major embellishments would be needed to make anything out of this story.

Our first stop was at a Blimpie's Burger in a little town just after crossing the state line into Nebraska. The stop was fairly unremarkable except for evidence of a small graffiti battle on the wall of a bathroom stall. Someone had scratched into the paint, "Jesus is Lord." A respondent answered below it in red ink, "I don't shit in your church, don't preach in my shit house."

When I returned to the car, I told the girls about my discovery, but they didn't seem to find it too amusing. I sprinkled a spoonful of Dad's ashes under a tree on a median strip of nature within the asphalt confines of the parking lot.

The weather that had been unseasonably clear and warm for Nebraska in early February was turning colder and cloudy, so I helped Donna put up the convertible top. We ate our greasy burgers and french fries and drove east on Interstate 80 through southern Nebraska. The National Weather Service constantly interrupted the music programming with reports of severe thunderstorms and tornado warnings in the area. *The Wizard of Oz* came to mind, and I envisioned cows and tractors flying through the air. The girls were just annoyed by the interruptions, especially when they "like, really liked" the song. Thankfully, the storms stayed well to the north of us as we sped across the plain.

The girls in front were chatting about friends with benefits and some guy named Brandon, and Heidi was reading a book titled *What Color Is Your Parachute?* I decided that for now, my time could best be used sleeping, so I wiggled around in the backseat trying to get comfortable, but I found a hard object sticking in my back. It was an empty wine cooler bottle that had been halfway pushed down the seat. I pulled it out and set it on the floorboard.

"Don't lay it there," Carolyn said.

"What do you want me to do with it?"

"Get rid of it. If we get pulled over with a wine cooler, we're busted."

When I didn't do anything about it, she reached back, grabbed it, and flung it out of the car window onto the patchy snow of the road's shoulder. Apparently some upstanding-citizen crime fighter saw her throw the bottle and notified the police, because we didn't get ten miles before we were pulled over by a pair of Nebraska's finest.

"What the hell is he pulling me over for?" Donna asked in a very hostile tone, sounding more like a sailor than a sorority sister. "I wasn't speeding. I did nothing wrong."

The policeman approached the car and was very nice and polite until Donna went off with the same rant. We all tried to cool her down, but she was a firecracker with a lit fuse and all we could do was sit back and wait for the explosion.

"I demand that you let us go immediately. You have no right pulling me over. I was doing nothing wrong. This is harassment," she continued while the officer attempted to interrupt her with a series of "ma'ams."

"Ma'am, we stopped you because we got reports of littering on the highway."

"We didn't throw any bottles out of the car," she answered.

"I didn't say it was a bottle."

"Well, I didn't throw it. It was him," she said pointing at me. They all turned on me in an instant, saying that I had thrown the bottle. The officer asked for all of our driver's licenses and walked back to his squad car to check us for any outstanding warrants.

While we sat in the car waiting for him to return, Donna asked, "How could you be a donor? I could never do that." She had noticed the organ donor card I had attached to the back of my driver's license.

"What's the big deal, you're dead anyway," I barked back hostilely.

"It's creepy," said Carolyn.

"I know," Heidi added.

"I don't want my exceptionally cute hazel eyes ripped out of my head and given to some grumpy ol' blind man. Ick!" Donna declared.

The officer walked back to our car and handed the girls their licenses back, then started writing me a $250 ticket. Since I was from out of state, the officer told us we'd have to follow him to the station to pay the fine. I was so furious at being double-crossed by the backstabbing sorority sisters I wanted to smack each one of them upside the head. Instead I sat there with my arms folded, my blood boiling.

"I can't believe you did that to me," I said with disgust.

"Don't worry, we'll pay the fine," Donna reassured me. "I just can't have it on my record, I've already got two wet recklesses."

We pulled off the interstate, crossed the South Platte River, and followed the officer to the police station in Hershey, Nebraska. The girls, true to their word, ponied up the money but came up a bit short.

"Do y'all take American Express?" Donna asked the officer, who nodded without saying a word. "Oh good, Daddy'll write it off as a business expense," she said smugly.

Shortly thereafter we were back on the interstate, with only Donna's credit card the worse for the experience. The days were getting longer with the arrival of spring, and we drove in the dark for only the last few hours of the trip. By then all the girls had enough energy to gossip about their sorority sisters. After listening to them talk for the better part of an hour, I felt like I was listening to a soap opera. By the time we hit the Lincoln city limits, I felt as though I had a pretty good understanding of the pecking order within their sorority. Occasionally I would interrupt when they started speaking in sorority tongue.

"She's cute and ni-i-ice, but she's got a QR, y'all."

"What's QR?" I asked.

"Questionable reputation," Donna answered matter-of-factly while pulling into a parking space behind the sorority house that read "Reserved for Kimmy's Big Sister."

"Well, thanks for the ride . . . and for framing me," I said with a smile.

"Our pleasure," Donna said while taking off her baseball cap, shaking her head and running her fingers through her hair in an attempt to give it some body.

"Where are you staying tonight?" Heidi asked.

"I don't know. Are there any really cheap places around here?"

"Well, we can't put you up here, our house mother's a major bitch," Carolyn stated.

"What about the toolshed in the back?" Heidi suggested.

"What's he going to sleep on?" asked Donna.

"We'll put our futon out there," said Heidi.

The girls agreed on the idea, and of course I was up for any kind of arrangement that didn't require me to open my wallet. They went into the house and told me to stay in the backyard. They opened the window of their second floor room and shoved their futon mattress out of the window. It landed with a loud thud in the flower bed below, wiping out a colorful collection of impatiens, pansies, snapdragons, and begonias, as well as crushing a Malibu light. The thud of the thick mattress hitting the ground started a few neighborhood dogs barking. I dragged the futon mattress into the toolshed, maneuvering some of the tools around to make more room. I laid the mattress out flat and tried to make myself comfortable with the pillow and blanket the girls had thrown to me. As I lay there staring at the corrugated metal roof of the toolshed, I thought about what a difference a day makes. Yesterday I was "King of the World," and today I was going to sleep to the smell of gasoline and grass clippings.

The next morning I was awakened at seven o'clock when the gardener opened the door of the toolshed. He was startled at seeing me sleeping inside the shed and began screaming at the top of his lungs, "Intruder alert! Intruder alert!"

In an instant I went from a sound sleep to a state of panic as adrenaline shot through my veins. I came out of the toolshed with my hands up in the air, trying to calm him down. All I could think to say was, "I'm in the sorority!"

He continued screaming, "Intruder alert," pulled a pair of garden shears from his leather tool belt, and lunged at me, stabbing me right on the point of my hip bone. It hurt like crazy but didn't bleed a drop. I took off running around the backyard, holding my hip and hobbling along due to my sprained ankle while repeating, "I'm in the sorority, they know me."

He followed close behind waving his clippers in the air screaming, "Intruder alert!" By now all the girls in the house had been woken up by the commotion and were watching the chase from their windows.

"Carl, we know him," the girls shouted. He looked at them as he slowed the chase to a walk but still kept pursuing me. Carl, I found out at this point, was a few letter tiles short of a Scrabble game. The girls came down into the backyard and Carl apologized and allowed me back into the toolshed to get my backpack. Together we shook the dirt and grass off of the futon mattress and carried it back into the house. The house mother stood on the front porch in her bathrobe with her arms crossed in front of her sagging chest, looking like she had just eaten a shit sandwich.

I thanked the girls and got on my way. I started walking down the street toward the campus when I heard a distant, "Wait!" Heidi ran down the sidewalk in her robe and baby-blue furry bedroom slippers to give me a piece of paper.

"This is my brother's address," she said, slightly out of breath. "He's a bit of an oddball, but I betcha he'll put ya up if you're goin' through Atlanta and need a place to stay."

I tucked the piece of paper into the front pocket of my Levi's and stood there for an awkward moment wondering whether I should kiss her, hug her, shake her hand, or just thank her and walk away. To this day I wonder what would have happened if I had laid a big kiss on her. Would she have kissed me back? Would she have slapped my face? Would she have turned her head when she smelled my morning breath?

What-ifs can drive you crazy. I learned an important lesson that morning: losing, rejection—even humiliation—is easier to live with than what-ifs.

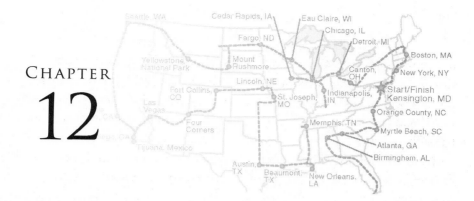

CHAPTER

12

I WALKED THROUGH THE CORNHUSKER campus and stopped on a grassy quad area to plot my next move. I needed to head south and then east to pick up states still on my "need 'em" list. My "got 'em" list now totaled thirty-four states, and I decided I could easily add two more by visiting both Kansas City, Missouri, and Kansas City, Kansas, which settlers courteously placed side by side.

I'd had good luck picking up rides, so I set out for the interstate to see if my luck would continue. It was late in the morning when I stopped in for a quick lunch at a McDonald's.

Inside the restaurant's vestibule hung a picture of a dozen smiling McDonald's employees of every race, sex, and age, with a slogan that read "Now Hiring Friendly People." I bought my lunch and sat in the plastic dining room decorated with an "eat up and get out" attitude about it. I read a complimentary issue of the local *Thrifty Nickel*, a free advertisement paper that is basically a garage sale without all the driving around. One ad in particular piqued my interest: "Vanity mirror, pick, and shovel—twenty dollars." That seemed like a bargain to me. I'd think the vanity mirror and pick alone would be worth twenty dollars, but a shovel, too?

I was about halfway finished with my meal when a family sat down at the table across from me, joined hands, and gave thanks for their tray full of Big Macs. I thought it was touching, real down-home Americana but also a little bit strange. At my house we used to pray before important dinners—Christmas, Easter, Mother's and Father's Day—but never once at a fast-food restaurant; it just never crossed our minds to do so. The whole situation intrigued me and I began wondering what their prayer must have sounded like.

"Dear Lord, bless these Value Meals to our bodies, and help Junior be worthy of his Happy Meal toy. Amen." Who knows, maybe they were just praying that one of the friendly McDonald's people hadn't spit on their burgers.

I stopped at a gas station near the Main Street exit to Interstate 80 and asked customers for a ride. Eventually a nicely dressed man in a double-breasted blue pin-striped suit agreed to let me ride along in his tan Oldsmobile Cutlass. He took his leather briefcase out of the front seat so I could sit down.

"Looks like we're gonna be gettin' some rain here soon," he said looking up toward the clouds. "Yep, not a good day to be out hitch-hikin'."

The hint of cologne I smelled while talking to him outside became overpowering inside the car with the windows rolled up. It was like being held captive at a department store perfume counter. I attempted to roll down the window to get some fresh air, but he quickly took control of the master button on the driver's side saying, "You want some air? I'll put the air on. Just don't be monkeyin' around with the car's buttons."

I introduced myself and held out my hand. Reluctantly he shook my hand and muttered a name that sounded something like "Roy Guttum," though I couldn't be sure. There was a long break in the conversation and the silence made me nervous.

"So, what do you do?" I asked.

He looked over at me with a cold stoic stare. "You're a nosy little son-of-a-bitch." He then turned his head back to watch the road and muttered to himself, "Not in my car five minutes and already tryin' to pick my brain."

"Sorry," I said, trying to ease the tension. "I was just trying to make small talk to pass the time."

"You wanna know about passing time? I'll tell you about passing time. I passed eight-and-a-half years at Leavenworth. Now that's pass-ing time, my friend," he said. He reached across me, opened the glove compartment, found a box of mint-flavored toothpicks, popped one in his mouth, and tossed one toward me that fell into my lap.

"You in the service?" he asked.

"No."

"You know anyone who went to Vietnam?"

"Not really. This one guy who was a friend of the family went, but I was just a baby then, so I don't really remember him, and unfortunately he didn't make it back."

He shook his head and was silent for a minute. In a low voice, speaking slowly, he said, "Well, let me tell you about it. Someone who did make it back. You know what I miss? The violence. The power and the violence."

My stomach sank to my knees and I thought about how many times my mother told me never to take a ride with strangers.

"You got a gun?" he asked.

I shook my head no, and he reached around his lower back and held his hand under his jacket. "Do you have a gun?" he again asked.

"No," I said in a pleading tone. Roy pulled his hand out from behind his jacket with his thumb and index finger pointing like a child using his hand for a gun. He pointed his finger at my head and made a firing sound with his mouth. I forced out a fake laugh, trying to hide the fact that only seconds earlier I thought I was going to end up as a blurb in the newspaper that read, "An unknown decomposing body found in a shallow grave."

He picked up his sunglasses from the dashboard and put them on. "You think I look different?"

I decided to choose my words very carefully so as not to upset him in any way until I could get out of the car. I smiled and said, "You look like a movie star."

"Guess who gave me these sunglasses. Guess!" he demanded.

"I have no idea."

"Of course, you don't," he snapped back quickly with a hint of sarcasm in his voice.

After a dramatic pause he proudly stated, "Bobby DeNiro."

"Really?"

"You callin' me a liar'?"

"No. I just said really, like I'd really like to hear more about the story."

"Why should I waste my breath, you wouldn't believe it anyway."

"Yeah, I will. Robert DeNiro gave you those glasses."

"His friends call him Bobby."

"So Bobby DeNiro gave you those glasses," I said, again trying to prompt him into his story.

"Are you his friend?"

"Me? No, I've never met him."

"Then don't call him Bobby, asshole."

"Sorry," I again apologized, hoping it would help keep me alive. I noticed a road sign that said "Nebraska City, 10 miles." "Well, Nebraska City's coming up. I'll just get off at any exit that's convenient for you"

"Oh, you don't want to get off in Nebraska City. I was in the county lockup here and this is no place for a little chickenshit like you. You'll be better off in Mizzura, which is where I'm headed."

He was no longer just a weirdo, he was now holding me captive. I was scared and mad at myself for taking the ride. We crossed over a bridge into Iowa and took Interstate 29 south toward Missouri. When we arrived at the Missouri state line there was a visitor's center at the first exit.

"Could we stop at the visitor's center?" I asked.

"Oh, all they got there is stale coffee and old pamphlets. I can tell you everything you want to know about Mizzura."

He proceeded to ramble on with Missouri trivia for half an hour. Outside St. Joseph, the freeway narrowed to one lane in each direction. A work crew in bright orange vests stood around waving a "Slow" traffic sign but not really doing much work. We slowed to about ten miles an hour and I took this as my chance to get out.

Roy's right hand was resting on the center console between our two seats. I took the mint toothpick out of my mouth, and holding the end that was saturated with my saliva in my hand, I jammed the still firm and sharp end down into the back of his hand with all the force I could muster.

"Jesus!" Roy screamed. The toothpick broke in half with the sharp end barely sticking in his hand like an acupuncture needle. The toothpick impaling was enough of a distraction to make Roy lose the mechanical master door controls, and I quickly unlocked my door, opened it, grabbed my bag, and rolled out onto the highway, skinning my right arm and forehead into a raw hamburger consistency. I never thought ten miles an hour was a very fast speed until I rolled to a stop and lay in the dirt and gravel on the side of the road, dazed from my quick farewell to Roy.

I was helped to my feet by several members of the road crew. They took me to the foreman's office, which was actually a plywood trailer shack behind a portable cement guard wall. His office was filled with blueprints and posters of professional wrestlers and the Budweiser girls. They continually asked me how I was, and what had happened. As I told the story, they uttered things like, "Jiminy Christmas," "Heavens to Betsy," and "What in tarnations is this world comin' to?" A guy named Pete washed out my wounds with hydrogen peroxide and gave me a ride into St. Joseph. I wasn't hurt bad enough to go to a hospital, but I wasn't well enough to go sightseeing at the Pony Express Museum, so I got a room at a motel to convalesce.

I was starting to look, and feel, like I'd been to war. My arm and head were bandaged up, my hip was bruised to an eggplant hue, and I limped like a spaghetti western sidekick. After two days of eating delivered pizza, taking naps, and watching television talk shows, I was feeling strong enough to at least cook my own dinner. I walked a couple of blocks to a Kroger supermarket to buy some Cup-a-Soup and hot dogs for a Bathtub Buffet a la Al.

In front of me in the checkout line was a frail older man with a tracheostomy hole in his throat and clear plastic tubing under his nose connected to a small, green tank of oxygen on a hand dolly. He was buying two TV dinners, five Baby Ruth candy bars, and a quart bottle of Budweiser. His medical alert bracelet continually slid down over his wrist, attempting an escape over his emaciated hand, as he signed a check for his purchase. The cashier called him by name and let him slide on the cash-only policy in this line. He struggled to carry his shopping bag and push the oxygen-tank dolly. I finished my purchase and caught up with him just before he reached the automatic door's sensor pads.

"Can I give you a hand with that?"

"That would be great," the old man said. "I've about run outta hands."

But instead of handing me the grocery bag, he placed the dolly's handle in my hand to push. We walked through the parking lot, passing the cluster of cars near the front of the market. He never acknowledged which car was his, so I asked, "Where ya parked?"

"Oh, I don't drive, had to give it up. Damn cataracts," he said. "But I just live down here a few blocks."

"Oh, okay," I said, realizing I had gotten myself into more than I bargained for. I continued pushing his oxygen tank down the sidewalk, making sure to keep it near his body so there was enough slack in the air tube. During a brief stretch of silence as we walked, I chuckled to myself as I imagined myself of running ahead with the oxygen and watching this old man try to keep up with his lifesaving oxygen tank and then playing tug-of-war with the tube, until with a firm last heave-ho, I pulled the tube right out of his nostrils. Of course, I would never do that, but the thought brought a smile to my face, especially since he was walking me all over St. Joseph.

"Are we getting closer now?" I asked after a few more blocks of walking.

"You betcha," he said. "Just a few more blocks." He rubbed his shoulder and added, "Hey, kid, would you mind switchin' with me? These goddamn frozen dinners are about to pull my arm out of its socket."

After we walked a little bit farther, he stopped to sit on a short brick wall around someone's rose garden. "I always stop here," he said. "It's the halfway point."

"Halfway?" I said. "I thought you said it was only a couple more blocks."

"It is," he said as he unscrewed the cap to his Budweiser and took a big swallow. "My house is just two blocks up and one block over at 2613 Evergreen. What do you think I am, senile or somethin'?"

"No, I just thought I was helping you to your car and now you've got me walking all over town."

"You wanna sip? You're old enough, aren't ya?"

"Yeah, I'm twenty-one."

"Good. I don't wanna be contributing to the delinquency of no minors," he said. "Oh, by the way, my name's Wally."

"I'm Jimmy," I said, not feeling like going into the whole nickname story.

"Junior?"

"No, Jimmy."

"Oh, Jimmy. That's good. I thought you said Junior. Nobody should ever be made a junior of somebody else. I ain't never met a Junior yet that wasn't screwed up in one way or another."

We arrived at Wally's white-washed, wood-framed, shotgun-style house that was set back further from the street than the other houses on the block. After my dealings with Psycho Roy, I felt apprehensive about going inside. I looked over at this frail man and figured if he tried anything weird, I could easily take out his air supply.

I helped him into his house, which had a yellow-brown look to the carpet and drapes and everything else from his years of smoking. He had many little knickknacks around the room, most notably a dried-out lump of cat poop resting on top of the television. He asked me to stay and have dinner with him. I thanked him, but declined.

"Oh, come on, I'll let you have the choice: chicken or Salisbury steak," he said, holding out the two different TV dinners he had purchased.

"I don't wanna eat your food."

"I don't hardly get hungry anymore. I just eat to eat. I like breakfast, but besides that I just eat to eat."

"Well, if you really don't mind sharing."

"No, it'll be nice to have some company. You know, I don't know a soul anymore. Not a soul. I used to go into town and I knew everybody."

"I guess that's what you get for living so long," I said.

"Yeah, I'm fortunate. I know that."

"How old are you, if you don't mind me asking?"

"Don't mind at all. I'm seventy-five years old."

"That's amazing."

"You know what's amazing," he said. "I'm seventy-five years old and I can still fit into my army uniform."

"Wow," I said, nodding my head.

"You know why that's so amazing?"

"No, why?"

"'Cause I was in the navy," he said, bursting out with laughter.

We ate our TV dinners on TV trays in front of the TV. "I never miss that *Wheel of Fortune*," he told me. "I guess those puzzles every time. Usually before those numbskull contestants do."

When I didn't answer or compliment his puzzle-solving skills, he said, "So which salt mine do you work in?"

"Huh?"

"Ya gotta job?"

"No, I'm just passing through on a trip."

"Oh, where ya going from here?"

"I was trying to get to Kansas City, but my last ride sort of dumped me off here."

"You hitchin'?"

"I was, but I think I've had a change of plans."

"Good. That ain't no way to be travelin' these days with all those loonies out there "

"Tell me about it."

"'Course in my day, things were different. If you were broke down along the highway, the first car along would stop and help you. Nowadays, I'd be afraid to take help from anybody."

"You took help from me."

"You're no serial killer."

"What, you think they wear a 'Hello, I'm a Serial Killer' badge?"

"I'm just saying it's not safe out there anymore. When I used to ride the rails there was a bond between the fellas. Most of 'em would help you out if they had anything worth sharin'. 'Course anybody that was ridin' the trains didn't have a pot to piss in or a window to throw it out of."

"You rode the rails?"

"Sure did. For most of thirty-eight and thirty-nine I rode them big iron horses all over this country. Hell, I was a buddin' ass kid not more than eighteen or nineteen years old. There wasn't no work at home, and I didn't have but two nickels to rub together, so off I went."

"You must have a lot of good stories from your experience."

"I don't know if I'd call 'em good stories. About all I remember from those years was always being cold, hungry, and tired. But I do, in a way, think those were the best years of my life," he said, breaking a Hostess fruit pie and handing me half. "I sometimes long for the rails."

He offered to let me spend the night on a roll-away bed, but I still had a room at the motel so I declined. We agreed to meet the next morning for breakfast, and when I returned he had coffee and fruit pies waiting on the screened porch.

"You know, I've been thinking about the rails since we talked last night," he said in a tone that sounded like I was about to hear a sales pitch. "You know, if you want to ride the rails, I could help you get your feet wet."

I wasn't thrilled with the prospect of illegally boarding trains with a seventy-five-year-old emphysema sufferer with cataracts, but after my last ride, I had sworn off hitchhiking, at least for a while.

The three nights at the motel had exhausted most of the advance I had received from Double V, though I did still have a small amount of "walkin' around" money, as Dad used to call it. So with a backpack containing the worldly remains of three people, some food, and a few meager belongings, I set off on the next leg of the journey with Wally as my tour guide.

The train yard was a short walk from Wally's house, and the prospect of adventure seemed to add a spring to his step. We walked past the depot and found a sizable erosion hole under a portion of the train yard's chain-link fence.

"Bingo!" Wally exclaimed. "Time to dance the fence limbo."

Wally crawled under first. I handed him all our belongings and followed. He took a seat on a pile of railroad ties that were stacked out of the way waiting for their turn at some action. I sprinkled some of Dad's ashes and tossed a piece of Uncle Spud's monkey remains across the train yard, but Mrs. Double V had to wait for Graceland. "Which one do we ride?" I asked.

"Hold on. Let me study the situation for a minute."

He pointed at the different trains while forming a strategy in his head. "It seems to me that this one's going next. You see, it's being loaded on the side track next to the main line. It's also headed west, most likely St. Louie. How's that one sound?"

I shrugged my shoulders and off we went toward a flatbed car. The dolly that held Wally's oxygen tank didn't roll very well across the rocks, so I cradled the tank in one arm like a baby and carried the dolly in the other. A metal ladder hung down a few steps in the front of the car near the hitch. I gave Wally a boost up. He sat on the metal platform and I handed him his oxygen tank, then the dolly.

"Is this enough oxygen for the trip?" I asked as I climbed up the ladder and onto the car.

"Sure," he said confidently. "Once we get movin' at seventy miles an hour, the air will be whippin' down our faces so fast I'll turn this dad-burn thing plumb off."

"We need to find some cover 'til the train gets moving," Wally said. "If an old bull comes along and sees us, he won't think twice about crackin' us upside the head."

We found an empty open-air car with side walls that were about five-feet tall. We sat down inside and waited for the train to pull out. Two hours passed.

Like a little kid on a family vacation, I kept asking Wally, "When's this thing gonna get goin'?"

"You have to be patient," he told me. "If you want to ride a train that leaves when you want to, you need to buy a ticket on Amtrak. Ridin' freight trains is a hurry-up-and-wait kind of life."

Another few hours went by and still no movement. We snacked on hot dogs straight from the plastic package. Then suddenly, the whistle blew and the train lunged forward and slowly pulled out onto the main track.

"We're moving," I said with glee.

The train chugged along for about five hundred yards until it pulled off on another side track and stopped. We looked at each other in disbelief. We had just waited four hours to travel a quarter of a mile.

"The train that was behind us is probably the next one to go," Wally explained. "That's why they moved our train out of the way."

We hopped off and walked back to the area of the yard where we'd sat all day. We walked along the far side of the train and kept as close as we could to its side to try to stay undetected. We walked far enough back to cross under the train and then dashed across the main line to the other train. As we started to crawl beneath the middle of a boxcar, the train started to move. Wally crawled back out with all the speed and agility of a non-emphysema sufferer.

"Damn, that was close," I said.

"Get on this train!" Wally screamed.

The train was slowly getting started, so Wally grabbed the side ladder on a boxcar and stepped up onto the first step. I walked along the train and handed him his oxygen tank. I ran back to where the rest of our stuff still sat. By now the train was moving fast enough that I had to jog to keep up with it. When I got back to Wally he was sitting on the metal mesh platform on the rear of the boxcar with his legs hanging over the edge. The oxygen tank rested on its side next to Wally's leg. I jogged and handed the dolly and my backpack up to him. As he reached to grab it, the tank rolled off the platform, ripping the oxygen tube right out of his nose.

"Grab the tank!" he yelled.

I quickly stopped in my tracks and retreated to pick up the tank. I grabbed it and made a mad dash to get back to the boxcar Wally was on. I was running as fast as I could, but the train continued to increase its speed, and with the extra weight of the tank, I was losing the race. As I became short of breath I could see there was no chance for me to catch up to Wally. I decided I better just get on any car I could. I tried to grab a ladder of another boxcar further back. I couldn't run, grab the ladder, and hold the oxygen all at the same time. The train was now definitely winning the race as car after car passed me. I continued running, but was dropping farther and farther behind. I looked back over my shoulder and saw there were only about a dozen cars left before I would miss the train all together. I noticed one of the approaching cars was an open-air car with side walls just like the one we had spent most of the day waiting in. I didn't know if it was full or empty, but I saw it as my last chance to get me and the tank on board. When the car got alongside of me, I threw the oxygen tank over the side wall with my best shot-put toss. I didn't hear the sound of the metal tank crashing against the metal car so I figured it must have landed on something reasonably soft. Now it was my turn to board. A ladder with two vertical handrails on each side was approaching on a boxcar. My heart was beating like a meth addict on a two-week binge. I grabbed the handrails with both hands and then jumped for the ladder's bottom step. My right foot landed on the step. I pulled myself closer to the ladder and was able to place both of my feet on the bottom step. I climbed up to the platform, lay down as my body recovered from its intense adrenaline overdose, and thought to myself, *How do I get myself into this shit? All I did was offer to help a guy with his groceries.*

When I calmed down a bit, I went looking for Wally's oxygen tank. I climbed a ladder to the top of the boxcar and walked along the top. The open-top gondola was three cars ahead. I was too scared to jump from one boxcar roof to the next boxcar roof, so I climbed down the ladder on the other side of the car and then up the ladder of the next boxcar. I got to the last boxcar before the open-air car, walked to the end of the car and looked down into the open-air car. Inside the car were about fifty live pigs minus one, which had been hit in the head by a flying oxygen tank. I don't know if the pig was dead or just unconscious, but I wasn't about to jump inside the car to find out. I held onto the side of the car and made my way to the next car, then the next, and eventually found Wally. I was frantic the whole time, worried that he couldn't breathe without his oxygen. Instead, I found him sitting on the platform looking as if he didn't have a care in the world, smoking a cigarette through the tracheostomy hole in his throat.

"Wally!" I screamed from the top of a neighboring boxcar. Wally held his cupped hand up to his ear. I waved my arm for him to come with me, but he didn't budge. I went over to him to tell him about the oxygen tank.

"Ya, let them old hogs have the dad-gum thing. I'm breathin' just fine."

The train was headed west, not east as we had hoped, but by the time we realized this we were already traveling fifty miles an hour. Neither one of us was about to disembark at that speed, so we sat back and ate fruit pies that had been in our pockets during the entire train-hopping ordeal and were now smashed into the consistency of pudding. The train traveled all night through the wheat fields of Kansas, which is the geographical middle of America, equidistant from the bright lights of Broadway and the glittery glow of Hollywood. I've never seen, complete black and total darkness until that night in the middle of Kansas.

The first stop turned out to be the next morning at a place called Fort Hays, Kansas. Since I'd traveled all night in the wrong direction I was only too happy to get off.

"I think I'll stay on and see that ol' blue Pacific one last time," Wally said with a sparkle in his eye. I gave him my address and told him to send me a postcard when he got to the ocean.

"Will do," he said. We hugged good-bye and I scampered off toward the small depot. "Take 'er easy," Wally hollered, "and if she's easy, take 'er twice."

I asked the man at the ticket counter how far away the nearest East-bound highway was.

"'Bout two miles," he said. He had a ballpoint pen hanging out of the corner of his mouth and looked just like Andy Capp smoking a cigarette.

I walked the two miles and came up to the on-ramp for the west-bound Interstate 70. I stuck out my thumb at the entrance to the on-ramp and within twenty minutes was sharing the back of a red Ford pick-up truck with three bundles of hay.

There wasn't much to look at driving along Interstate 70 except fallowed wheat fields waiting for summer to produce their "amber waves of grain."

I reached into the shoebox, tossed a chunk of Uncle Spud out toward the fields, and tossed a clump of ashes into the air, ironically making Dad's ash drop in Kansas "dust in the wind."

We slowly pulled up to another old, red Ford truck, which I was beginning to think was government issue in the Midwest. This one, however, distinguished itself from all the others in the area with a black-and-white bumper sticker that read "When In Doubt Whip It Out." As we approached the truck, I could see the driver wore a straw cowboy hat. It looked like he was hauling a small, white TV satellite dish next to him. As we pulled alongside, the dish turned and leaned out the window and barked at me. It was the face of a shaggy brown dog who'd either recently had surgery or was way too into science fiction. The dog repeatedly leaned out of the truck's open passenger window. A gust of wind from traveling sixty-five miles per hour would catch the plastic cone around his neck and violently push his head to the right. He'd go back inside the cab temporarily and then stick his head back out into the wind and have his coned-in head again smacked against the side of the door. I gave them a thumbs-up as I passed, and the "whip it out" farmer tooted his horn and waved.

A small, blue truck with an old tattered camper shell and an Alaska license plate kept us company for the next hundred and fifty miles. We jockeyed back and forth for position in a noncompetitive way without getting more than a hundred yards apart during those two-and-a-half hours. I felt like we were traveling buddies, and I made up a name and lifestyle for the other driver. It's amazing the things you'll do to keep your mind stimulated when riding through seemingly endless wheat fields. I called my new friend Rex. He was leaving his home in Alaska, where he was a salmon fisherman, for bigger game fish down in the Florida Keys.

We pulled off for gas in Junction City, Kansas. I bid farewell to Rex and silently wished him well landing that marlin down in the gulf stream. My driver, who introduced himself as "Sweet Earl," filled up on gas and even bought a jalapeno corn dog for each of us. Hours later we would run into Rex again. He must have stopped somewhere along the way too. Ol' Rex pulled up beside us and smiled and pointed, and I waved back with a smile on my face. It was the strangest feeling of old friendship with this fellow traveler I'd never actually met. I wondered what name and background he'd come up with for me. As night came, Rex's camper shell slowly disappeared from sight and his red taillights grew fainter as the sky grew darker. We crossed the Missouri state line, leaving Kansas City, Kansas, for Kansas City, Missouri. I spotted a sign for a bus depot and asked Sweet Earl if he'd drop me off there. I hadn't eaten anything since the Junction City jalapeno corn dog, but the bus station at least had vending machines. My dinner consisted of a package of peanut butter crackers, a Slim Jim, and a Pepsi. A balanced diet when you're on the road. I wrote in my journal about Wally, Sweet Earl, Rex, and the corn dog while seated among the finest bus station transients the Show Me State had to offer.

With very limited funds, the time had come again for some creative travel arrangements. I was trying to figure out how I was going to buy a ticket when an angel appeared in the form of a drug addict. I was walking around the streets by the bus depot, which is usually the worst part of every town in America, when a middle-aged black man with salt-and-pepper muttonchop sideburns that stretched halfway down his cheek approached me. He had a "can you spare some change" look about him, but he passed by without saying a thing. I continued to walk and he turned around and came back toward me.

"'Scuse me, sir, can I ax you a question?" Without allowing me time to respond, he segued right into, "I was wonderin' if, from one good guy to another, if you'd be willin' to sell me some urine. Providin' that you ain't also on the pipe, my brother."

My forehead wrinkled with confusion. "You wanna buy what?"

"You see here, I need me some clean urine cause I be fixin' to meet up with my P.O., and let's just say that I had a little relapse last night, and my piss'll put me back in the pen, my friend."

"How much do you pay for, ah, urine?" I asked, stammering with awkwardness.

"Well, as they say, everything's negotiable. How much you want?"

"Is this legal? Could I get in trouble for doing this?"

"No. You don't know what it's for, what I'm doin' widit. Besides, ignorance is nine-tenths of da law."

"I don't think so," I said. "Sorry," I added as I took a few steps away from him.

"Look here, my brother," he said, putting his arm over my shoulder. "I'm a good guy. I don't be rapin' or robbin' nobody. I'm basically an upstandin' citizen, you hear what I'm sayin'? I'z jiz like da pipe. What can I say?"

"Well, how do we do it?" I queried.

"We just go back to the bus station's restroom. I got this here sandwich baggy. You piss it full and make yourself twenty."

Acquiescing to his scheme, we walked back to the bus station. The man introduced himself as "Noodles" then added that he was "a credit, not a debit to society."

*Where was this guy last spring when I was flunking out of accounting?* I wondered. Inside the restroom, he handed me a plastic sandwich bag with a ziplock closing mechanism. One side of the bag's closure was yellow, and the other side was green, and when the two were successfully inner-locked they would both appear blue. Noodles explained this to me: "Make sure the bag is blue. I sure as hell don't be wantin' to take no goddamn golden shower."

I went into a stall and closed and locked the door. At first I was successful filling the bag, but as the experience continued and I had extra product and no more buyers, I had to redirect my stream into the toilet while trying not to spill the flimsy and unstable plastic bag. I ended up with urine on my hands, pants, and dripping down the outside of the baggie.

"Noodles, hold the bag, I've got piss all over the place."

"Close the baggy and wash it off. I don't wanna be touchin' that nastiness."

I closed the bag, pulled up my pants as best as I could with just one hand, and came out to the row of sinks to wash my hands and the baggie. I dried the baggie with a coarse, brown paper towel and started to hand it to Noodles. Then I pulled it back toward me. "Maybe I'd better get the money first," I said.

"You still don't trust me," Noodles said with a chuckle. "I be tellin' you every which way 'til Sunday that I'm a good guy, but you still be wantin' to judge a book by the cover."

"You're a good guy. I know that, but I need the money, and urine doesn't grow on trees ya know."

Noodles again chuckled and walked over to a fold-down baby-changing table and pulled out the contents of his front two pockets, placing his possessions onto the plastic table. There were lots of dollar bills crumpled tightly into balls, coins, a plastic cigarette lighter, and the tattered business card of his parole officer with the words "cock sucker" scrawled across it in red pen. He began unfolding the dollar bills and placing them in a stack to be counted. Including his change, he had $20.53. He pleaded with me to let him keep $1.50 for the bus ride home, so my net profit for one bag of drug-free urine came to $19.03.

"You do know that if this piss comes back dirty and I go down, I will track you down, and you'll wish you'd never made my 'quaintance."

"I understand," I said confidently. "But Noodles, what you've got there is practically Mormon piss, well, except for the Pepsi I just had."

Noodles smiled the smile of a free man, took out a half-used roll of masking tape, and taped the bag of urine to his right inner thigh. "Damn," he exclaimed. "You got some warm-ass piss. You sure you ain't runnin' a fever, boy?!"

"No," I said with a slight smile. "Well, nice doin' business with you," I added as I started to walk out of the bathroom.

"Where ya off to in such a big hurry?"

"Well, now that I've got some money, I need to find a bus."

"Where ya headed?"

"South," I said. "I don't really know where."

"Just wanna get the hell outta Dodge, huh?"

"Yeah. How far do you think twenty bucks can get me?"

"I can get you coast to coast for twenty dollars."

"How?"

"Trailways got this companion fare goin'. Buy one, get one free. One of my boys sells tickets. I grease him with a little kickback and he'll pig-gyback ya as a buddy on somebody else's ticket. Ya want me to see what I can do?"

"Sure," I said, encouraged that I would soon be back on the road.

Noodles, with my pee safely secured against his inner thigh, walked over to the Trailways ticket counter to speak with a light-skinned black man with one gold middle tooth. The tooth shined so bright as he talked I thought wise men might show up. Noodles shook the man's hand and walked back toward me with an ear-to-ear grin.

"He can put you on a bus to Texas, but it'll cost you twenty. Ten for him, ten for me." Noodles said. I agreed and together we went back up to the counter to finalize the deal. Noodles's friend had a Trailways logo necktie and a name tag that read "Mr. Randy." His name made me think of a character from Sesame Street: Oscar, Grover, Big Bird, and their new neighbor, Mr. Randy. I didn't care, though. I just hoped that the phrase of the day was "Discounted Bus Fare."

"Yo, Ran-Dee, this is the gentleman I was tellin' you 'bout. Can you hook him up with that bus goin' to Texas?"

Mr. Randy punched the keys on his computer and found me a companion named Herm Tuttle going to Austin, Texas.

"That'll work," I said.

Noodles slid my ten dollars across the counter to Mr. Randy, who handed me a printed ticket that had my name just below that of my new traveling buddy, Herm.

"Don't say shit to your companion," Mr. Randy warned. "If you start flappin' your gums and Hermie don't wanna play ball, it could fuck it up for all of us."

I nodded. "Don't worry."

"Thank you for traveling with Trailways," he said with a big smile that nearly blinded me. Noodles and I walked away together. I thanked him for his help and wished him well on his drug test. He gently patted at his upper thigh and gave me the thumbs-up sign as he walked out of the terminal.

When the boarding call came for our bus, I got in line and looked at the others to see if I could figure out which one was my traveling buddy. With a name like Herm I was looking for a wimpy, balding man in a fraying cardigan sweater, carrying a briefcase and a sack lunch that his eighty-six-year-old mother had packed for him. I didn't see anyone who resembled my sweeping generalization right off, but I had three states and about 700 miles to find Herm.

The bus trip took us south on Highway 71 through towns called Butler, Lamar, and Jasper. All three names sounded to me like characters on the TV show *Fat Albert*. A right turn on Highway 44 had us heading toward Tulsa on the Will Rogers Turnpike. Will Rogers may have "never met a man he didn't like," but I'll bet he didn't ride the bus much. We stopped for a half an hour in Tulsa, where I was approached inside the bus terminal by a tall, skinny black man with a shaved head. He was wearing a Muslim standard-issue dark suit with a bow tie. He asked me if I wanted to buy a copy of a Muslim newspaper called *The Final Call*.

"Uh, no thanks," I said. "I've already got that."

He then said some words to me in Arabic that were probably either, "Okay, thanks," or "You're such a liar," and thinking back on it now, I'd have to bet on the latter.

*Tough gig*, I remember thinking at the time. *This guy's either the best salesman in the Nation of Islam force or he must have insulted Elijah Muhammad's mama to draw the Oklahoma Bible Belt assignment.*

We were still on Highway 44, only now it was called the Turner Turnpike. Years ago, before the interstate highway system took over, this stretch of road had been part of historic Route 66. Our layover in Oklahoma City, or "OKC" as our bus driver called it, was long enough for me to eat two tacos at a nearby fast-food place called Taco John's. John must have had the day off because I was helped by a girl named Trudy, who was stingy with her packets of hot sauce.

On the walk back to the bus terminal, I decided I'd better make my Oklahoma drop while I had the chance. There was a planter filled with beautiful purple and yellow pansies in front of a convalescent home called Senior Sooners. About a half-dozen old people with translucent skin sat hunched over in wheelchairs on the front porch, wrapped in thick blankets. *Thank God Dad didn't have to sit around waiting to die like that*, I thought, as I sprinkled some of his ashes into the flower bed.

I arrived back at the terminal ten minutes early and spent the time updating my journal. A young brown man with a dark-black bowl haircut that made him look like an Incan Moe Howard dropped a key chain and a small printed card on the chair next to me. I read the card as he placed more key chains near other people. "I am deaf. I sell these key chains to support my family. One dollar donation. God Bless You." I looked around and most people didn't even pick up the card to read it. After a moment, Incan Moe made his rounds again, picking up the key chains. When he came by me I felt riddled with guilt for having all five senses and no Stooge similarities, so I gave him a dollar.

OKC to Fort Worth, Texas, must be a popular route; there wasn't an empty seat on our bus. I sat next to a guy who was about eighteen years old and had a pierced tongue. When I introduced myself, he shook his head and said, "Right on," but he never told me his name. We didn't talk much because he was listening to Poison on his portable CD player and constantly picking at an elbow scab all the way to the Texas state line. I just looked out of the window for my last chance to see "the wind come sweepin' down the plain."

I noticed that Oklahomans enjoy touting their accomplishments to passersby. Water towers, grain elevators, and billboards would proudly state things such as, "Hometown of Congressman Jerry Mandering" or "State Wrestling Champs 1989, 1990, 1992." This left me wondering what happened to the 1991 team. Did they lack drive after their back-to-back titles? Couldn't their best wrestler make weight for the championship bout? Did the coach have a drinking problem in ninety-one? These are the thoughts of a weary traveler on a late-night bus.

CHAPTER

# 13

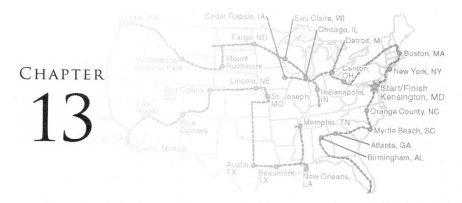

WE PULLED INTO FORT WORTH at midnight. Our next bus would leave at one o'clock for Austin. I decided to stretch my legs by walking around the depot that was neighbored by countless closed businesses and dilapidated buildings. A travel-weary man asked me, "Ya know where I could get a bite to eat 'round here?"

"No, sorry," I said.

The man looked up and down the vacant streets and said, "I'm so dad-gum hungry I could eat the ass end of a skunk."

"Sorry, but I'm not from around here."

"Ah right, well, thank ya very kindly."

"Hey, your name's not Herm is it?" I asked.

"Herm?! What the hell kinda stupid name is that?"

The bus ride from Fort Worth to Austin wasn't as crowded as the previous one, so most of the passengers moved around to get a seat by themselves. The seat next to mine was empty so I stretched out and tried to get some sleep. An older lady across the aisle from me rustled through her purse attempting to locate a much sought-after throat lozenge. She removed its crinkled red cellophane wrapper, neatly folded it into a small square shape, and put it back in her purse to save. It reminded me of Christmas morning when my mother used to make everybody save the wrapping paper. The gift was always secondary to her. The important thing was opening the gift carefully so the wrapping paper could be reused for the next hundred Christmases to come.

The woman actually reminded me a little bit of my mother, if my mother had lived to be an older woman: a wrinkled beauty with a slightly tattered appearance. One of the handles from the sides of her eyeglasses was missing, she had multiple liver spots the size of pennies on the backs of her gaunt hands, and she had saturated herself in perfume that smelled exactly like bathroom deodorizer spray. Again she started rustling through her black canvas open-top travel bag that read "Nana's Doodads." The bag was large enough for a midget and possibly even his friend to stow away in. After a while, the noisy search was over and she pulled out a skinny plastic box the length of a pencil with the initials of each day of the week on the tiny door of each separate compartment.

"Ohhh," I heard her wail. I looked over and she asked me, "What day is today?"

"Today's Wednesday."

"Not today today," she said. "The day we started the trip."

"Where did you get on?"

"Tulsa."

"Well, Tulsa was yesterday, Tuesday."

She looked at her pill box, "Oh, this damn thing." Then under her breath I heard her mumble, "I'll just take the estrogen and sort the whole thing out once I get home."

She put the pill case back into her travel bag without taking any of the pills and found a small, brown prescription bottle. She tried to open the childproof cap, and after watching a few unsuccessful attempts, I offered to help. As I lined up the arrows on the cap with the arrows on the bottle, she said, "These things are old-lady proof. The young kids have no trouble gettin' into 'em."

I noticed on the prescription label that the drugs belonged to Hermione Tuttle. As I handed her back the bottle I couldn't help but chuckle under my breath. I had found my travel partner and she was on estrogen.

The morning sun reflected off the state capitol's pink stone dome in the foreground as our bus pulled into the bus depot in Austin. Soon thereafter, I found myself strolling through the University of Texas campus at seven o'clock as the early birds scurried off to class. In my first semester of college, I took a seven o'clock class and never once made it to class on time. That was my first in a series of "withdrawals" from college courses.

Vendors were setting up their wares in the quad area. I got a free T-shirt for filling out a Discover credit-card application in the name of Al Baumgardner, bathtub chef. I wonder if he qualified?

A man wearing a "Got Beer?" T-shirt underneath an unbuttoned, blue checkered flannel shirt was trying to buy used pairs of Levi 501s.

"How much do you pay for them?" I asked.

"Depends on the condition."

"How much for the ones I have on?" I said, lifting up my shirt and turning around like a runway model.

"I'll give you three bucks for those."

"Three bucks?" I said with surprise in my voice. "How 'bout ten?"

"I can't make any money at ten bucks. I'll give you five."

We haggled back and forth for a while, but I couldn't get him to go higher than five. Eventually I agreed and he held a towel around me so that I could change into a pair of short pants.

"So what do you do with them?" I asked.

"I sell 'em to a company that sells 'em in Japan. They go ape shit for anything American over there," he said while peeling off a five-dollar bill from a wad of money.

On the east side of campus was the LBJ presidential library. I had been to other presidential libraries before and always found them interesting, but I couldn't justify spending the time or the money just to see the cowboy hat LBJ wore when he popped the question to Lady Bird, so I kept walking.

I noticed that Texans seize every opportunity to show their fierce independence, even decorating their sewer caps with the Lone Star symbol. I reached an elevated section of Interstate 35 and walked parallel to the freeway on the street below. I stopped at a diner on Thirty-first Street for some breakfast. A handwritten placard rested against the front window announcing the all-you-can-eat grits for $1.99. All I knew about grits was that on the television show *Alice*, Flo used to tell Mel to kiss hers, but the price was right, so I decided to give them a try. The waitress set the grits down in front of me with a hearty, "Enjoy 'em baby!" I opened up a dozen sugar packets and poured the contents into the grits. I ate the

grits fast, then chased them with a gulp of coffee and ordered another
bowl. I had almost finished the second bowl when I felt my body's gag-
ging mechanism activate, so I called it quits.

"Can I get you anything else?" the waitress asked.

"Well, I could use a ride."

"Can't help ya there," she said. "I'm a bus rider."

"Where ya headed?" asked a middle-aged pot-bellied man sitting next
to me at the counter. Then he spat tobacco juice into his empty coffee
cup.

"East," I answered.

"Oh, yeah? My boy's fixin' to go to Beaumont this afternoon. He'd
be tickled to give you a ride, long as you don't mind riding with a deaf
driver."

"Oh, your son's deaf."

"Yep. He was born that way. But he reads lips real good."

The old man set up the ride for me, and now all I had to do was kill
five hours until he was ready to go. I sat at the counter as long as I could
and read the *Austin American-Statesman* cover to cover. The big local
story was about a family that had put their barbecue inside the house to
keep warm and died of carbon-monoxide poisoning.

The morning waitress crew went home and was replaced by fresh,
midday hash-slingers. The waitresses had time to chat during the lull
between breakfast and lunch. I kept my face nestled into my paper but
didn't read a word for nearly an hour as I eavesdropped on the waitresses' conversation.

"My boy and his wife split again."

"She still doin' him dirty?"

"She's just no good, that one is. Ornery as the dickens."

"Why does he keep takin' her back?"

"Why? 'Cause he's thinkin' with his little head and not his big one."

They talked about everything, jumping subjects faster than I could
keep up. My favorite part of their conversation was when they talked
about out-of-towners coming into the restaurant.

"Once, this family from Canada came in here and they'd never heard
of biscuits and gravy." They all laughed, and then another one tried to
up the ante.

"This guy from Massachusetts thought grits were made out of fish."

Granted this wasn't the Lincoln-Douglas debates, but it did help pass the time until my ride showed up.

At two o'clock on the dot, the man's son pulled into the diner's parking lot. His two-tone El Camino truck had a license plate that stated "Hearing-Impaired Driver" and had a picture of an ear with a circle and a line through it.

"Are you *d'woti dat* wants a *wide*?" he said, speaking pretty clearly for a deaf guy.

"Yes," I said, nodding and trying to enunciate clearly to help him read my lips.

I jumped in the front seat and we shook hands. His name was Greg and I found him to be smart and friendly with a good sense of humor. He drove well above the speed limit and we talked the whole way to Beaumont. It would have been one of the best rides of the trip except I was terrified of crashing the whole time. He would take his eyes off the road for long periods of time to read my lips as I spoke. To protect my own life, as well as others on the road, I tried to keep my responses as short as possible.

He was traveling to Beaumont to meet his friend from Louisiana. Beaumont was the halfway point for both of them and they met there from time to time. We were traveling on Highway 71 through rural Texas where farmers supplemented their incomes with painted barn advertisements: Fisherman's Paradise, freshly stocked, no license, no limit.

Both sides of the highway were decorated with an abundance of colorful wildflowers. Just past the city limits of La Grange, I "messed with Texas" by sprinkling some of Dad's ashes out of the window and tossing a chunk of Uncle Spud into the sea of bluebonnets. We connected to Interstate 10 in Columbus and experienced scattered thunderstorms all the way to Beaumont. Greg exited the freeway and pulled into the dirt-and-gravel parking lot of a country-western dance club called Granny Kitty's. He drove around the backside of the club looking for his friend's car and when he didn't see it he said, "Looks like I beat him here again." He invited me to go in with him, but I declined.

"You only get to see your friend every once in a while, you don't need me here bothering you guys."

He insisted, so we walked up to the entrance.

"Can't letcha in in shorts, sir," said the doorman in a black Stetson cowboy hat.

I told Greg I'd sold my only pair of jeans back in Austin, and after he stopped laughing he said, "No prablum, I've got an extwa pair of Wranglers in my twuck."

They were a couple sizes too small, but as Dad used to say, "Beggars can't be choosers." I stood between the body of the car and the open passenger's door pulling and tugging, struggling to get into the jeans. After a few minutes, Greg asked, "Ya wanna spway your ass with WD-40?"

The jeans were so tight, with all my good parts bulging out noticeably that I looked like a male prostitute character in a *Hee Haw* comedy skit. I followed Greg back up to the entrance, where we were told the cover charge was five dollars for men and two dollars for women.

"That is so unfair," I told Greg. "They are punishing us for having a penis. Where's an attorney when you need one?"

We walked over to one of the six bars located within the cavernous club and found one seat at the bar. I didn't mind standing since I felt like I'd been sitting all day. The cover charge had taken a big chunk of my money, but luckily they had one-dollar Lone Star and Shiner Bock longnecks until eight o'clock.

Greg's friend arrived complaining about "how shitty Texans drive." His name was Charles Thibodeaux and he was a Cajun man from a small town named Breaux Bridge, Louisiana. "It's just a stone's throw from Lafayette," he said. Greg and Charles had grown up together, and despite now living in different states, had maintained a relationship. They talked using a combination of lipreading and sign language. I left them alone and walked around the club, looking at the rodeo memorabilia and the faded and smoke-damaged photos of country singers on the walls. I got another beer and leaned against the railing around the immense dance floor. A sea of cowboy hats and belt buckles two-stepped by me like a parade passing through town. All the women looked beautiful being spun around the dance floor, even the matronly types wearing square-dance dresses. I was fixated on a college-age girl in a red-and-white checkered baby-doll dress with fire-engine red cowboy boots and long, sandy-brown hair. Her knee-high skirt constantly curled and twirled back and forth around her trim, tan legs to the sweet down-home twang of the country music. I stood there envying the bolo tie–wearing redneck that had his hand pressed tightly against the small of her back.

I felt a tap on my shoulder, and when I turned around, a young, portly Native American woman asked me to dance. I remember being told by my father to never turn down a dance from a lady. "Walking across the floor to put yourself on the line deserves a three-minute dance no matter who's doing the asking," he used to say.

Despite wearing the world's tightest-fitting jeans and not knowing the dance, I led her onto the dance floor. In the center of the dance floor, which was the size of a football field, was a sort of free zone for two-step novices. Here, the incompetents were routinely lapped by the good ol' boys and girls. I tried to make small talk with the woman to break the awkward silence between us. She was a student from Regina, Saskatchewan, studying horse husbandry.

"I hear that they make a lot of Mount Rushmore souvenirs up there."

She just shrugged her shoulders. I asked her name and it sounded like she said, "Dah." I asked again, but it still came out sounding like "Dah," so I dropped it. Apparently she didn't care much for my chit-chat, because she dropped her right hand from mine and placed it up on my shoulder near her other hand and we bear-hug danced the rest of the song. It just felt wrong, and I couldn't wait for the song to end. When it did, I thanked her and she just stoically walked away.

The band, Big Bubba Joe & His Black-eyed Peas, plugged in and gave us a few, "Check one, two, check, check, check, one, two." I went to the bar for another beer. Dah, or whatever her name was, just disappeared into the crowd. Greg and Charles were out on the dance floor. The band played a song called "Boot Scootin' Boogie," and Charles signed to Greg to tell him the song and the line dance. Greg followed the other dancers and, without hearing a note, didn't miss a beat. He was a really good dancer. You would have never known he wasn't hearing one note of that song. He stuck his thumbs through the belt loops of his Wranglers as his legs went every which way in unison with the other dancers. I stood by the rail and smiled through the whole song in my admiration for him.

Afterward, I went down on the dance floor to shake his hand and tell him how great I thought he did. Another song started and he convinced me to try. I stood behind him and tried to follow what he was doing. Up and back, side to side, point, clap, turn, up and back. Without question, I was the worst line dancer in the history of country music. I got mixed up and stepped forward when I should have stepped back and stepped on the feet of all the people around me. The favor was returned when a cowboy boot stomped on my foot. I screamed in pain and hopped around on my other foot like I was on a pogo stick; the in-sync country ballet went on, unfazed by my pain. I hobbled off the dance floor toward the restroom where I had to choose between Pointers (Men) or Setters (Women). Luckily, I guessed right.

"Howdy, partner," the restroom attendant said as I opened the door. I was able to say "Hi" brusquely through my pain. I put my foot up in the sink and ran some cold water over it.

"What hap'n to you foot?" he asked me.

"It got stepped on."

"Where boots?"

"I don't have any boots."

"Why?"

"Why what?" I said, frustrated with his questioning.

"Why no boots."

"I just don't."

"But why?"

This went on and on. He just couldn't grasp the concept that somebody might not own a pair of cowboy boots. Fortunately someone else came into the restroom and he went back toward the door to say, "Howdy, partner." I read the small sign someone had obviously helped him write: "This restroom kept clean for tips only. Thank you, Ben."

"Hey, Ben," I said. "Could you get me a bag of ice for my toe?"

"Can't leave. It's my job."

"Ben, you're helping me. I'm a paying customer. This is just doing your job."

"What if other boys come in?"

"I'll take care of them, Ben, just please get me a bag of ice. I think my little toe might be broken."

Ben finally agreed and ran off to the bar to get me a bag of ice. The man in the restroom washed his hands, grabbed a piece of wrapped candy, and set a dollar bill next to Ben's sign. I picked up the dollar to put it in his tip jar and when I did, the door opened.

"Howdy, partner," I said. There in front of me was a security guard for the nightclub who was the size of three men. He had a well-groomed goatee, piercing light blue eyes, and a silver stud earring.

"You stealin' from Ben?!"

"No," I stated. "I'm putting a dollar in, not stealing."

"Where is Ben?"

"He went to get me some ice for my toe."

"So you lured him away so that you could steal a retarded guy's tip money?"

"No, no," I reiterated.

The bouncer then grabbed my arm, twisted me around, and slammed me into the wall. My upper two teeth bit down on my lower lip and cut it wide open. My blood was now splattered and dripping down the white tile wall. While holding me against the wall, he reached into my pockets and took out all my money, which totaled about $4, and put it in Ben's tip jar. He told me to get out of there and threw me out of the restroom back into the bar. I limped over to the bar and grabbed a cock-tail napkin from the waitress station.

"What happened to you?" the bartender asked.

"Oh, one of your security thugs beat me up in the restroom."

The bartender picked up the phone and called someone, and in a few minutes some older white-haired man in a three-piece blue pinstriped suit came up to me and asked me to tell him what had happened. I told him the whole story and he asked me if I could identify the guy. I pointed at the bouncer, who was standing on the corner of the dance floor. The man fired the guy on the spot and two other security guards escorted him out of the club. The older gentleman then asked me to come back to his office. We walked through the kitchen and down a long corridor where old beer kegs lined the walls.

"Sit down," the man said. "You want something to drink?"

"No, but I'll take some ice for my lip."

He called someone and told them to bring some ice and a couple of beers to his office.

"You know, we run a nice place here, but like any other place, sometimes things go wrong. And what that bouncer did to you wasn't right, wasn't right a'tall. We've had trouble with him in the past and I just want to let you know that he's been fahr'd. But here at Granny Kitty's, we take care of our customers, so I wanna know how we can make this unfortunate incident up to you."

"What do you mean?" I asked.

"We don't need the police or no damn lawyer rufflin' our feathers here. We want to make you happy, and we want you to forget all about this unfortunate situation. So why don't you tell me what'll it take to make you happy?"

There was a knock on the door, and in walked a young Mexican man in a long plastic dishwasher's apron carrying a small metal pail filled with four beers and ice. "Well, this is a good start," I said.

The man opened one of his desk drawers and thumbed through a file, eventually pulling out a release-of-liability form with a crisp one-hundred-dollar bill on top of it. "If you'll sign that form saying that we here at Granny Kitty's did nothing wrong, you can put that one-hundred-dollar bill in your pocket."

In all honesty, before he said that, I thought somehow I was in trouble. I never thought they would offer me money, but since they did, I knew enough not to accept their first offer.

"You know, I appreciate your offer, but I really think I'd better talk to my lawyer before signing anything." I felt funny saying that, as if I had an attorney waiting on a retainer.

"Okay, then, you tell me what you want. Maybe we can make a deal."

I told him my situation and we settled on two hundred dollars cash, a hotel room for the night, and an unlimited bar tab for me, Greg, and Charles. We shook hands and I signed the release form. I knew he was getting a good deal, but I'm not the suing kind and I hadn't had two hundred dollars in my pocket since meeting with Double V in Colorado. We spent the rest of the night drinking and dancing and avoiding security guards. I gave Charles the *Reader's Digest* version of the trip, and he offered me a ride to Louisiana in the morning, which I gladly accepted. After their last song, the lead singer encouraged us to "tip our bartenders and waitresses," and then added "drink 'em up cause she's pickin' 'em up. You don't have to go home, but you can't stay here." The house lights were turned on, but before our eyes could acclimate to the light we were already being rounded up by the security force and herded toward the exit. Along the way, one of the matronly women in a square-dance dress patted the backside of my skintight Wranglers and said, "You gotta sweet li'l caboose there, cowboy."

The next morning we were awakened with a knock on the door by an unseen maid shouting, "Housekeeping."

"Yeah?" I screamed out from bed.

"I'll come back," she responded, and then we heard her knock and shout "Housekeeping" on the door across the hall.

We were all slow getting started, motivated only by the smells of coffee and bacon coming from the Waffle House next door. We had breakfast there and ended up sitting at the counter because there was a wait for a booth. There weren't three seats together, so I sat between some guy reading a USA Today and a little old lady who seemed to know many of the workers and engaged them in chitchat to the point where they were neglecting their work.

A sign hanging on the wall above the grill read, "No firearms on the premises," which I thought was a good idea. I had eggs over easy and their specialty, hash browns smattered, smothered, covered. The jukebox blared out a tune called "Waffle House People." You've just got to love a joint that has its own theme song.

"Hey, y'all," the waitress announced in a deep husky voice. "Today's Trevor's birthday." She started singing "Happy Birthday to You," and everybody joined in. Greg and Charles performed the song using sign language, and one of their gestures led to a spilled glass of water on the lap of the guy reading the newspaper. He didn't seem to care about his jeans getting wet, but he threw a big fit about his Life section getting drenched.

We paid our bills, and I wrote down Greg's address on the back of a Waffle House pamphlet that lists all of its locations around the country. We said our good-byes and I was again headed east.

Charles drove a charcoal-gray Monte Carlo that had obviously been well taken care of over the years. It wasn't long until we were crossing the state line into Louisiana and were welcomed to the Pelican State by a large road sign. Charles rattled off one joke after another, most of which featured Budroe and Hebert as the butt of the joke. When we passed Lake Charles, he told me it was the town he was named after. Sometime later in the conversation, when I was staring out the window just half-way listening to his ramblings, I heard him say something about "this wife" and it stuck in my head as sounding so temporary.

"What do you mean 'this wife'? How many wives have you had?"

"Dis wive's, numba tree," he said in his thick Cajun accent.

"Do you think she's the right one?"

"I don't know. I don't believe dat dare is just one right one. I think you could pretty well blindfold yourself and pick one. It don't matter much, they all the same."

We pulled off Interstate 10 just past Lafayette into his hometown community called Breaux Bridge. Charles ran a little bed-and-breakfast place on a bayou. He described the cabins as "slave quarters," but added that "tourists eat up that realism shit." He told me I could stay in one for free if there was one empty by nighttime. Charles had to do some work around the property because he'd been away for two weeks taking classes in an effort to obtain his master electrician's license. I offered to help him, but he told me to have a look around town.

I walked through the old downtown area along the flood-evacuation route shown by an occasional street sign. I stumbled upon the bus station and went in to read the schedule board. They had six buses a day going to New Orleans, and I took out my notebook and wrote down the departure times for later that night and the next day. They had a post-card rack in the station and I bought five for a dollar and stamps from the man behind the counter, who was much more interested in watching the small-screen black-and-white television than selling me stamps. I looked for somewhere to write the cards. I stopped at a middle school and sat on the cold metal bleachers. Two teams of kids in their checkered school uniforms played basketball on the blacktop in front of me. I wrote to the fraternity guys, Al, Port, Greg, and to Double V to let him know I was getting close to Memphis.

I returned to the cabins on the bayou to find Charles sitting on the porch of one of the cabins with his feet resting elevated on the rail.

"Dare you is," Charles said when he saw me approaching. "Why you ain't come here 'fore dis?"

"You said you needed to work."

"Well, all work and no play makes Charles a dull boy. Let's go get some crawfish." We walked about a quarter of a mile down a dirt road that ran parallel to a slow-moving stream. Up ahead was a small shack with a hand-painted red-and-white sign that read "Jean Paul's Crawfish Shack." When we got there, Charles introduced me to Jean Paul as "a good ol' boy," which I'd never been called before—or since, for that matter. We sat on a wooden picnic table in front of the shack. Jean Paul came out with a roll of white butcher paper. He rolled it across the table and tore it at the other end. A moment later, he returned with a huge metal colander filled with boiled crawfish, miniature potatoes, and corn-on-the-cob broken in half.

"Enjoy," he said, pouring the contents out onto the table. "I be right back witda extras."

The top of the table immediately changed from pale white butcher paper to a pile of crimson crustaceans. There seemed to be a million of the tiny lobster-looking things, all no bigger than your thumb.

"You ever had crawfish?" Charles asked me.

"Nope."

"Boy, you in for a real treat today."

Jean Paul returned with a bottle of Tabasco sauce, a plate of lemon wedges, and a pitcher of beer.

"Jean Paul, this boy ain't never had no crawfish."

"Well, let's pop dat cherry," Jean Paul responded. "Well, boy, whatcha do is pull that nasty li'l some-bitch's head off, and then jus shuck dat shell off like you's eatin' peanuts. Give him a shot of dat Tabasco and lemon and you in business."

I watched Charles do the first one, then tried it myself. He finished about five of them before I got the first one in my mouth. The crawfish's juicy flesh exploded with flavor, but it was so small that it was gone before my brain had time to register the flavor sensations.

"Boy, that's a lot of work for not much meat."

"We'll stay 'til you're gooden full. Don't worry, you'll get your fill."

We continued eating the crawfish, throwing the heads and shells into a pan in the center of the table for proper burial at a later time. I got much better at shucking the longer I worked on it, and by the end, Charles was only beating me at a rate of about three-to-one. Charles had an interesting way of buttering his corn-on-the-cob. He'd put a spoonful of butter in his mouth, then eat across a few rows of corn, and then mix the butter and corn together in his mouth. "That way you get the right amount with each bite," he explained.

Without asking us, Jean Paul brought out another colander full of crawfish and spilled them out across the table. I had eaten a few potatoes and corn halves, plus I'd polished off most of the pitcher by myself in an attempt to cool my mouth from the Tabasco fire. Jean Paul brought another pitcher of beer and said, "How you likin' them li'l fellas?" I nodded my approval. "Dats right, they good. Shore is, they good."

We continued eating and Charles told me about the tailgate parties they would have in the fall before the LSU football games. "Kick off is Saturday 'round one, so we get started tailgatin' 'round Thursday. Wednesday for a big game. Yes, sir, we know how to have a good time down on da bayou."

We finished our meal and I reached for my wallet, but Charles, in an authoritative voice and pointing his finger at me said, "You put dat away. Your nasty ol' money's no good down here. You's my guest." I thanked him and shook hands with Jean Paul, and we started heading back toward the cabins. When we got there, we saw a man and woman standing on the porch knocking on the door. They were looking for a room for the night. Charles introduced himself as the owner and then introduced me as "Roastbeef, the bellboy." I had to bite my bottom lip to keep from laughing, which was still very sore and tender from the night before.

"Yes, sir," I said, "at your service."

Charles gave me the key to their room and said, "Take them to Room 5, bellboy." He knew I had no idea where Cabin 5 was, and I guess he just wanted to see how long I'd go along with the farce. I led the people down the path until it came to an end, and I had to turn either right or left. It was a fifty-fifty shot so I turned right. The first cabin I came to was number seven. I walked to the next one hoping the numbers were declining, but it turned out to be number eight. I made an about-face and led them back the other way.

"Sorry, I'm still kind of new here," I told the couple. I opened the door to Cabin 5, handed them the key, and wished them a pleasant stay.

"Oh, son," the man said. "Would you please fetch the two big suitcases from my trunk? Here are the keys."

After getting the suitcases, I walked back toward the cabin while Charles pointed at me and laughed. I put the suitcases down and handed the car keys to the man. He reached into his pocket and handed me a quarter. "Thank you," he said with a big smile. "We'll let you know if we need anything else."

When I told Charles about the man's generous tip, he laughed to the point where he had to wipe the tears away with the sleeve of his shirt. When he regained his composure, he said, "Looks like we ain't gonna be full tonight, so you can go on and take any cabin you want." He had to go into Lafayette that night to attend traffic school. He told me to keep an eye on things until he got back around ten. I decided to take Cabin 1.

Cabin 1 was decorated like a sea captain's quarters and had a door in the back of the room that opened to a deck that stretched out over the bayou. I took a nap in the most comfortable bed of my entire trip. Somehow I doubt that slave quarters had such cozy beds with good back support.

I woke up an hour and a half later, and went out on the deck and updated my journal. I sat in a folding chair under a yellow porch light that was a magnet for every moth in the area. Across the bayou about two-hundred yards away was a bar set back off the main road behind a large warehouse. I heard somebody repeatedly rev their car engine, and even through the darkness I could see the gray clouds of exhaust pouring from it. After the car was good and revved up, the driver started kicking up dust in the dirt parking lot by spinning the car around in a series of tight circles. The car would lunge forward with a burst of unleashed power and then immediately jump to a stop. I got up and walked over to the deck rail to get a closer look at just what this guy was doing. He

continued to do the same thing—revving, lunging, stopping, circle spinning—then he started speeding off toward the main road. Halfway to the
road, he lost control of his car and plowed into an air-conditioning unit
on the side of the building and then into the metal siding of the warehouse. He tried to get his car out, but the back wheels were spinning. He
repeatedly attempted to free his vehicle. By now the bar's customers had
come out to see what the commotion was all about. Somehow he was
able to free the car and it hobbled off slowly like a crippled animal. The
car made it to the main highway where it collapsed with a broken front
axle. Breaux Bridge's finest arrived, and I joined the other onlookers at
the scene. The man was already in the back of the police car by the time
I got there. An officer announced, "Did anyone here see the accident?"
A few other people besides myself said they had seen it.

"Okay, we'll need a statement from each of you," he said. He tore
off pieces of paper and gave one to each of us. He had only one pen in
the pocket of his uniform, so he asked the other officers on the scene for
theirs. The policeman separated us like a school teacher on test day. He
told us to write our name, address, birth date, and what we had seen,
and then to sign and date it at the bottom. I got about two sentences into
my witness statement when the pen I had been given ran dry. I asked for
another one, but none of the officers had another. One of them looked
through the suspect's car and found a pen over the visor. He handed it to
me and when I tilted it up to write, the black bathing suit of the woman
pictured on the side of the pen slowly slipped away, exposing her beautiful naked body. It was at that moment I had a terrible feeling. I was
helping put this guy in jail using his own naked-lady pen. I couldn't go
through with it. I turned the pen upside down, putting the bathing suit
back on the woman. Then I placed the pen on the hood of the car and
slipped away into the cover of night.

The next morning I told Charles what had happened while he made
me a "Cajun breakfast," complete with boudin, cracklin's, and hogs-
head cheese, although I couldn't tell you which was which. I didn't really
care for any of it, especially first thing in the morning.

There was a bus going to New Orleans in an hour and I decided I'd
take it. I had the same feeling as I'd had with Port's family. It's tough

leaving when you're comfortable with the setting and enjoy the people, but the job wasn't going to get finished from Breaux Bridge.

Charles handed me a bag of cracklin's, so at least I found out what they were—fried pork rinds. I walked to the bus station and had about twenty minutes before the bus left. The ticket cost me nine dollars, but I was doing okay with money due to my Granny Kitty's settlement in Beaumont. Plus I had the quarter I'd picked up for my efforts at Charles's. I killed the time in the bus station looking at the United States map on the wall and the bus routes that connected the cities. I counted the states I'd been in and where I still needed to go. The ash sprinkling total now stood at Haves thirty-eight, Needs ten, but the tallies would soon change when I scattered some of Dad's ashes in the Crescent City.

The bus pulled out on time and thirty minutes later we were in Baton Rouge. We stopped just long enough to drop off and pick up passengers. A middle-aged black woman got on and sat next to me. We didn't talk much because she was busy applying and painting press-on nails. It seemed to me she'd done this before because she had the timing down perfect. She finished the last fingernail just as we pulled into the New Orleans bus depot.

I asked a man in an information kiosk for directions to the French Quarter. It wasn't too far of a walk, just down Canal street a few blocks. I saw a small, brown street sign that read simply, and appropriately, "Bourbon." I turned left down the cobblestone street, which was home to nightclubs, strip bars, souvenir stands, and restaurants. I strolled down America's most notorious alcohol alley at a leisurely pace, trying to take in the sights and sounds as well as the smells of vomit, stale beer, and urine left behind by past revelers. I was approached by a thin, black man in a red T-shirt with white block letters reading "FIGHT BACK!"

"Hey, man, I bet I can tell you where you got those shoes."

"What?" I asked.

"Your shoes. I'll bet you five dollars I can tell you where you got your shoes."

I thought, *How would this guy ever know I bought these shoes at some no-name shoe store back home in Maryland?* It sounded like an easy five bucks so I said, "Okay."

"You got 'em on Bourbon Street, New Orleans, Louisiana," he stated proudly and then stuck out his hand to be paid.

"Hey, wait," I said, trying to reason with him. "You're just playing with words."

"Hey, I never said bought, I said got, and you got 'em on Bourbon Street."

I started to walk away and he followed me for a block and a half saying, "Come on, man, we bet. You owe me five bucks." As we walked further, he lowered his price, "Come on, man, I give you a break, four bucks." I continued walking. "Three bucks man, come on." I opened my wallet and gave the guy a dollar.

"A dollar?" he said. "I said three dollars. Come on, man. Two more and we'll call it even."

I opened my wallet one more time, pulled out another dollar and said, "That's all I'm giving you." He must have believed the sternness of my voice or figured that he had bigger fish to catch, because he took the other dollar and turned and walked away. I turned around to watch him and almost immediately he had another tourist thinking, "There's no way this guy could possibly know the no-name shoe store I bought these at back home."

I continued strolling down Bourbon Street and was constantly verbally assaulted by strip-club barkers in front of their shops screaming drink specials and other tempting offers. "Two-for-one kamikazes," one yelled.

"Topless, no cover."

"Live jazz," still another said.

"Boys will be girls," another barker said. "You'd never know these lovely ladies are all guys."

*Yeah, but now I do, which ruins it*, I thought, as I picked up the pace of my leisurely stroll.

I headed for Jackson Square, the heart of the French Quarter. There, between St. Louis Cathedral and the Mississippi River, in the center of a fenced-in sitting park, stood a statue of Andrew Jackson on a horse.

I sprinkled some of Dad's ashes in the flower bed at the base of the statue and picked out a piece of Uncle Spud's remains from the shoebox. Instead of placing the flat ceramic shard in the flower bed to be cleaned up and thrown away by the next maintenance crew, I decided to throw some of old man Uncle Spud into Old Man River. I stood on the river's berm looking over the slow-moving chocolate-brown water. Doing my best Opie Taylor impression, I skipped the fragment like a rock across the river's ripples. Content with my Louisiana drops, I searched out a restaurant for a celebratory meal.

I stopped at an open-air restaurant and had a bowl of gumbo. Halfway through, I discovered a used Band-Aid in my soup. When I told the waitress about my discovery, she offered me another bowl.

"Isn't it all from the same batch?"

"Yeah."

"Thanks anyway," I said.

"How 'bout we make you a Hurricane on the house?"

I agreed even though I didn't know what a Hurricane was, but I like just about anything that is followed by the words "on the house." She brought me a bright red drink in a curvy cocktail glass that contained impaled fruit on a small plastic spear. "Here you go, Sweetie, the official drink of New Orleans."

On the corner I could see four pre-teenage black boys tap dancing, using metal bottle caps attached to their tennis shoes. Their act attracted a small audience who flipped a few coins into the hat on the ground. This inspired me to take a crack at performing. I asked the waitress if I could buy three whole oranges. They appeared on my bill as "full-sized drink garnish, fifty cents each." I claimed the corner of Bourbon and Boudin as the stage for my New Orleans juggling premiere. I'd had just enough of the Hurricane to stimulate my confidence, but not so much that I'd lost any chance of catching the oranges on a frequent basis. I took my baseball hat off and put all my change and a one dollar bill in the hat as bait money and then I placed it on the ground in front of me. I started juggling the three oranges. Several minutes went by without anyone taking much notice. Then a kid stopped and started talking to me to see if I could do any tricks. I showed him a behind-the-back throw-and-catch followed by an under-one-leg throw-and-catch, which I dropped.

"You suck," the kid said. "My grandma can juggle better than that."

"Oh yeah?" I said. "I'd like to see her try."

The kid left and I continued to juggle, thinking our brief exchange was over, but he pulled over his grandmother, who was carrying plastic shopping bags filled with souvenirs, and said, "This is the guy, grandma. Show him how you juggle."

I gave her the oranges. She pulled the back part of her multicolored, tent-like muumuu between her legs and tucked it into her fanny-pack strap in front, so that she would be more maneuverable when she started juggling. I stood to the side as she threw the oranges high in the air, behind the back, under her leg, and around in a circle. Then she reversed the routine, never dropping an orange.

The tap-dancing black boys stopped their show and came across the street to watch. They started clapping and chanting, "Go Grandma! Go Grandma, Go, Go!" Others joined in and the noise drew such a crowd that cars were having trouble passing the mob. For her final trick, she threw an orange high into the air and attempted to catch it in her mouth. She got under it as the orange reached its apex, and as it started to fall, she opened her mouth wide to catch it. Instead, the orange hit her upper lip and shattered her top denture plate.

She screamed with pain and slowly the crowd dispersed. She sat on the curb and bit down on a Pat O'Brien's souvenir napkin she had in her purse to stop the bleeding.

"You'd think after all these years I'd learn I can't do that trick; my mouth's just too small," she said to herself.

I followed the lead of the woman's grandson and helped pick up the pieces of her shattered teeth. It looked like other souvenir hunters had beaten us to the bigger pieces, because all we found were shards of artificial teeth bits. I returned the handful of denture pieces I'd found, and she put the pieces into a light blue change purse. The purse reminded me of my tip hat. I quickly searched for it only to find that both my hat and the bait money had disappeared.

I decided at that point that I had had enough of the Big Easy. I exchanged juggling pleasantries with the bleeding-gum granny who'd stolen the show and started to walk back toward the bus station. On the walk back toward Canal street I heard someone yell at me from half-a-block away, "Hey, bro, I bet I could tell you where you got them shoes."

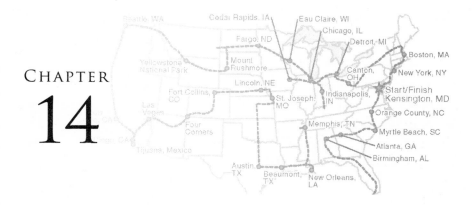

CHAPTER

# 14

I GOT TO THE BUS STATION just as a bus was loading for Memphis and quickly got in line to buy a ticket. It was the start of Mother's Day weekend and everybody seemed to have a "get out of town" attitude. The line wasn't moving, and I saw that the passengers boarding the bus were almost all on board. The swarthy man behind me kept wiping his brow with his handkerchief and saying, "Jesus Christ," in a disgusted tone. I knew I didn't have time to buy a ticket, so I walked over to the bus and got on. The driver asked me for my ticket, and I told him the situation and then tried to pay him, but he ordered me off the bus. The next bus to Memphis was in two hours, so I killed some time in the terminal updating my journal and people watching.

I watched with wonder as a homeless-looking man perused the terminal's ashtrays for cigarettes that hadn't been completely smoked to the filters. When he discovered a cigarette that was extinguished before its time, he'd pick it out of the ashtray and place it neatly in a Marlboro box for safekeeping. I had seen people recycle cans, bottles, and newspapers, but never cigarettes. As a Depression-era baby, my dad would have approved of the bum's efforts, I'm sure.

With ticket in hand, I boarded the next bus for Memphis on the last leg of Operation Doris Drop. We drove for about four hours before we got to Jackson, Mississippi. There was a Bojangles' Famous Chicken 'n Biscuits restaurant inside the terminal, so I ordered the wing-lover's special and sat at a table next to two robust black women fanning themselves with magazines.

"Lord iz hot in here," one said.

"Iz muggy and buggy all over," the other lady answered.

"Didn't seem this hot back in Nawlins."

"Shore do."

I took a stroll around the depot to stretch my legs before reboarding the bus. Near the entrance to the depot I spotted a red-brick wishing well with a small plastic sign affixed to the side that read "Proceeds benefit the Boys and Girls Club of Mississippi." I looked inside to see a few coins sparkling under the rusty metal grate just under the water level. A few Bojangles' drink cups and other bits of trash floated on top of the water, thrown by people that apparently thought the wishing well was a trashcan or that they could make a wish by donating trash.

I thought the wishing well would make an okay Mississippi drop, especially since my bus was leaving for Memphis in ten minutes. I took a quarter from my pocket, wet it in a nearby water fountain, then tossed it into the plastic bag containing Dad's ashes and gave the bag a shake. The ashes stuck to the quarter like bread crumbs on a veal cutlet. I walked back to the wishing well, carrying the quarter gently between my thumb and index finger, made a wish, and tossed the coin into the wishing well. It hit the water, creating a small cloud as the ashes separated from the quarter, then fluttered down to rest at the bottom. I'd like to tell you what I wished for, but then it wouldn't come true, would it?

The Jackson-to-Memphis leg of the trip was an uneventful five hours. We pulled into the bus terminal in downtown Memphis and I focused on my mission of dropping Doris at Graceland, getting my money, and getting on with the trip. Once I was through the terminal and out into the street, I asked a young black man wearing a red Trailways shirt how to get to Graceland. Without looking up he said, "Bus 27."

*He must get that question a lot*, I realized.

When the number twenty-seven bus pulled up, I asked the bus driver if this bus went to Graceland. "Shore do, but they closed up tighter than a drum now," he said, the hot setting sun gleaming off his upper-front gold tooth.

I checked into a nearby fleabag motel room for the night and caught the morning bus to Graceland. As it winded its way through the streets of Memphis, I could tell we were getting close to Graceland because Elvis-themed businesses appeared more frequently: Graceland Chrysler

Plymouth Auto Mall, Hound Dog Souvenirs, The Blue Suede Shoe Store, Jail House Rock Jewelry Store.

"There it is, boy," the driver said to me, pointing to his left. There were hordes of fans milling around the famous, white, wrought-iron gates affixed with guitars, musical notes, and an Elvis image. The fans were all taking pictures and scribbling graffiti messages on the brick wall in front of the dead King's compound.

Tickets had to be purchased across the street. There were several different tour options: the Graceland mansion, the Lisa Marie airplane, and the Elvis cars. I decided to go on just the regular Graceland tour, though I was tempted to see the inside of the plane that Elvis used to spontaneously fly to Denver for peanut butter–and-banana sandwiches.

I purchased a ticket but had an hour to kill until my tour group's departure, so I strolled up Elvis Presley Boulevard and stopped in at a Kentucky Fried Chicken for some greasy fried chicken and some buttery biscuits. Chicken and biscuits on back-to-back days; Elvis would have been proud.

I stopped at the souvenir shop next to where I'd purchased my tour ticket. The shelves were filled with every kind of Elvis-related souvenir conceivable: belt buckles, license-plate holders, key chains, shirts. Any item that could possibly bear the name or likeness of Elvis was for sale in this shop. Plenty of fans were eager to buy a piece of the King. The line at the checkout counter never fell to fewer than ten people during my browsing.

An announcement over the intercom stated that my tour was now boarding. Tour workers traded us our ticket stubs for audio tape players and headphones and loaded us into a small bus that drove us across Elvis Presley Boulevard, through the gates, and up the curvy driveway to the steps of the Graceland mansion.

The woman sitting next to me on the bus was slightly overweight, with long, stringy, dishwater-brown hair, the kind of hair that should be declared a fire hazard during the summer months. She was carrying a shopping bag full of Elvis souvenirs and wearing a pair of recently acquired official Elvis stick-on sideburns.

"Boy, is this exciting!" she said to me. "Can you believe in a few minutes we're actually going to be in the house where Elvis lived?"

I just gave her a slight smile. She rambled on. "Excuse me," I said, "I'm trying to listen to the tape."

"Oh, yeah, sorry," she said. "I bought one of the tapes in the shop. I'm going to listen to it later."

The tape was being narrated by Priscilla Presley and was to be started and stopped as the tour progressed. The tour group consisted of about twenty people, and I would have been surprised if the majority of them could read (the unshaven man with the marijuana-leaf tattoo on his shoulder naturally excluded from that sweeping generalization).

We walked through the front door and looked at Elvis's living room to our right and his dining room to our left. The house looked like the Brady Bunch would have lived there if Mike Brady had pulled in more green. Looking at the living room, it was easy to imagine Elvis lying there on the couch in his sequined jumpsuit, his cape wadded up into a makeshift pillow, yelling, "'Cilla, bring me s'more sweet tea."

The tour continued through the kitchen, then downstairs into the taxi-cab yellow, three-television lounge. The billiards room was dark red, with ruffled fabric hanging from the walls and ceiling. We went back upstairs to what is known as the "jungle room," complete with waterfalls, animal-skin furniture, and deep-shag carpeting. There was a red-velvet rope to keep the tourist groups from entering the room. For added security, they had a gum-chomping teenage girl standing on a piece of plastic strip in the center of the room. Someone from our group actually asked the girl, "Was that plastic carpet runner there when Elvis lived here?"

"No," she said. "We put it here to protect the original carpet."

"This is the original carpet?!" the girl with the stick-on sideburns asked excitedly.

"Yes, it dates from 1972."

The girl then handed me her camera and said, "Would you take a picture of me and the carpet?" I couldn't believe what I was hearing. I wondered if, in the history of spoken English those words had ever been strung together in a sentence. The girl kneeled down so her face was next to the carpet. Through the camera's view finder, I noticed a glimmering sparkle in the carpet. I took the photo and returned her camera to her, then dug into the shag carpet and pulled out a large, sharp toenail clipping. Just as I started to throw it back on the carpet with disgust, the girl with the stick-on sideburns screamed out, "It's the King's toenail!"

The security girl asked to see it so I put it in the palm of her hand. "It could very well be Elvis's toenail. We've heard he often trimmed his toenails in this room." She then handed it back to me with a hearty, "Congratulations!"

Our group walked outside toward Elvis's racquetball court. Everybody in the group wanted to hold the King's toenail. Several of them had their photo taken with the toenail. Most of them told me how lucky I was. The girl with the stick-on sideburns was relentless. She offered me twenty dollars for the toenail clipping. I refused and she kept raising the price. By the time we'd gone through his museum of old guitars, jumpsuits, and gold records, she was offering me eighty dollars for the object of her desire.

When we walked past the pool, I thought this would be a good spot, so I stepped over the small fence and sprinkled some of Dad's ashes into Elvis's pool. I stepped back over the fence and got in line to walk past the Presley family's graves.

The time had finally come to clock-in and complete the job I had accepted in Colorado. I handed the camera to the girl with the sideburns and told her to take as many pictures as she could while I sprinkled Doris's ashes over the grave of Elvis. We approached the King's grave. I reached into my backpack, grabbed Doris's urn, and began scattering her ashes over the brass gravestone, though most of them settled on the grave of Vernon Presley instead. Sideburns took several pictures of "Operation Doris Drop," and then I hurried back to the shuttle bus before being detected by members of the Memphis Mafia.

*That's the easiest five hundred dollars I'll ever make,* I remember thinking just before Sideburns said to me through her tears, "All I have left is ninety-five dollars. Please sell me the toenail. Please." Being the nice guy I am, I agreed to sell her the toenail. When she paid me, the last few dollars were in change, and I really think she was telling the truth that she had no more money. Since I lack a killer instinct when it comes to business, I gave her back a five-dollar bill and all her change. My net profit after paying for the tour ticket and returning some of her money was seventy-eight dollars, which isn't bad for a toenail. Years later, I read in *USA Today* that a collector on eBay bought an Elvis toenail clipping for $24,500 from an undisclosed seller, and I wondered if Sideburns had taken me to the cleaners.

I took the film to a one-hour photo shop and was discouraged to find that none of the Doris-drop photos showed adequate proof of a successful sprinkling. I needed a picture of me, the urn, the ashes, and the grave of Elvis, all in one picture. Instead I had several pictures of Sideburn's thumb, her damaged hair blowing in front of the camera lens, another tourist walking in front of me, and a clear photo of my shoes near the King's grave. There was no way I could send these pictures back to Double V and expect payment.

My only option was to restage the Doris drop. At the waiting area across the street from Graceland, I collected cigarette ashes and the sand from the stand-up metal ashtrays to simulate the worldly remains of Doris. I bought another ticket to the King's crib and another disposable camera and boarded the shuttle bus. I tried to bypass the home tour and go straight to the gravesite but was ordered to "stay with the group, sir," by some girl named Crissy. I again had to bide my time looking at knick-knacks from the lowest point in interior-decorating history until I could go to work in the graveyard.

Finally back at the job site, I asked an old man wearing a plaid tam-o' -shanter cap to take photos of the Doris-drop sequel. I told him the photo arrangement I was looking for and to keep taking pictures until they were all gone. He was able to take only about six pictures before a security guard ordered me to stop. With his large, hairy hand wrapped around my left bicep, Mr. Solcolm, Graceland security, personally escorted me to the shuttle bus.

The one-hour photo shop was about to close, and with the next day being Mother's Day, I couldn't get my pictures back for two days. Without much choice and with my newfound toenail wealth, I decided to stay in Memphis and check out the Beale Street nightlife. I checked into a motel called the Captain Ahab Motel Lodge. The connection between a fictional sea captain and a motor lodge just off of a southern interstate was beyond my grasp, but the place was cheap and it had on-site laundry, which I desperately needed.

That night I walked to Beale Street, passing the small clapboard house of W. C. Handy, the Father of the Blues. I ate at a barbecue place called "Mama's." Everyone sat at long, wooden picnic tables, and if you wore a tie, you'd soon find it cut off and hanging from the ceiling. The teenage waitress, who I can only assume wasn't "Mama," though I didn't catch her name, sat me between a family from Cincinnati and a guy with a spider-web tattoo on his elbow and his girlfriend, who reeked of patchouli oil. Afterward, I strolled down Beale Street, passing one club after another with music spilling out their open doors, entertaining the loiterers who were unwilling or unable to pay the cover charge.

A skinny white man about forty years old approached me with a hard-luck travel story about needing three more dollars to catch the bus home to some little nowhere town in Alabama. For his final sales pitch, he lifted up his shirt exposing a huge scar across his stomach. "I lost 80 percent of my stomach in the war," he told me. I'd learned on this trip that every scammer has a story to tug at your heart and open your wallet, but I particularly liked his. It wasn't just panhandling, it was more of a show-and-tell. I'd had a pretty good payday, so I gave him a dollar.

"God bless you, man," the man said.

"You too," I answered.

I went into B. B. King's blues bar, which was dark and packed with blues fans digging the tunes. When the band took a break, a few seats at the bar opened up. I had a Heineken and chatted with the guy next to me. He introduced himself as Benny, and nearly crushed my hand when he shook it. He was in his early sixties and made a clicking noise as he spoke. I realized after speaking with him for a few minutes that the clicking noise was from his upper denture plate sliding down and hitting his bottom teeth as he formed words. Benny was a real talker. All I had to say was "Really?" or "Is that right?" and it would send him on to another story. I didn't mind, though; in fact, I even bought him a drink. He ordered a ginger ale and went off on a story about giving up drinking.

"I used to be a mean sumbitch," he said. "I don't get messed up and do that no more. I don't like to get riled up. I don't want no problems with no one."

I asked him what he did for a living. He slumped down in his seat a bit and sheepishly admitted he was out of work. I could tell it was painful for him to say that, and he quickly added, "I've worked my whole life. I used to be a real hustler. I'd go up and down the alleys hoeing people's weeds or sellin' soap. Anything for a buck. I'm still out there hustlin', trimmin' trees, haulin' trash, what have you."

Benny was wearing a bright red tank top and thick, blue suspenders to keep his pants up to his pot belly. He had an old, faded shoulder tattoo that blended in with his brown skin to the point I couldn't even make out what it was or said. I asked him about it and he said, "Marcela," the name of his first wife.

"We was together for ten years, but she was drunk the last three of 'em."

He went on telling me the details of his sobriety and eventually I got around to asking him the obvious: "If you gave up drinking, why are you hanging out in a bar?"

"I date one of the busboys," he said matter-of-factly. "I'm just killin' time 'til she's off. We're goin' over to Arkansas to the dog races."

"How far is Arkansas?" I asked.

"Just over the bridge in East Memphis. You wanna go?"

"I wouldn't want to be a third wheel," I said.

"No, I gotta pickup," was his response.

In a little while, a short, stocky, middle-aged Mexican woman approached us with a white plastic apron over one shoulder and a crooked and tattered hairnet. She told Benny the boss needed her to stay late because one of the other busboys called in sick. This blew the dog races plan for the night, but Benny said they'd try again tomorrow night and if I was still in town I was welcome to go along.

The next morning I bought a *Memphis Commercial Appeal* from a sidewalk newspaper rack where someone had placed a "Kill Your Television" bumper sticker over the glass. I was served a big, fatty breakfast by an emaciated waitress named Norma in a mom-and-pop restaurant near my motel.

The top local story in the newspaper dealt with the rescue of a man who had locked himself out of his house and tried to enter it by going down the chimney, only to get stuck halfway down. I wondered if people who do stupid things that get in the paper buy an extra copy for their scrapbook, or call friends and family members to say, "Hey, did ya see me in the paper today? Front-page picture. Those were my legs comin' out of that chimney."

Norma refilled my coffee cup several times while I sat in the old, burnt-orange weathered booth for over an hour reading the newspaper cover to cover. A television in the corner was on, but I didn't pay much attention to it until I realized it was showing the Indianapolis 500. Millions of people were watching the race worldwide, and I felt a giddy sense of accomplishment every time they showed the lead car circle the track and cross over the white start/finish line that contained some of Dad's ashes.

After my protracted breakfast, I washed my clothes in the motel's on-site laundromat. By now, for lack of anything better to read, I was skimming the classifieds: garage sales, apartments for rent, lost dogs. I came across the ticket section in bold type and found this ad: "One-way ticket to Miami $100 O.B.O. Missy." This piqued my attention. I called and talked to Missy, who had a very sweet-sounding Southern drawl. I wanted to climb through the phone line and kiss her, but first I wanted to try to get her to cut her price. I told her that I could only afford to pay fifty dollars. She told me that the ad had only been running two days, but if she couldn't sell it by Friday, she'd sell it to me.

I rode the bus back to Graceland to pick up my photos. This time the photos came out great. Me, Doris's urn, my second-try make-believe ashes, and Elvis's grave were all in the same shot. It was the proof I needed, and I quickly enclosed all the photos and a letter to Double V and mailed it overnight express. I asked him to send the balance to me at the motel as soon as possible. Now all I'd have to do was wait.

That night I went back to the bar and again found Benny sitting on a barstool waiting for his girlfriend to finish work. Our conversation, one-sided though it was, resumed where we had left off the night before. I asked him if he had any kids and he said that he "ain't seen hide nor hair of 'em since their mother let 'em drop out of school."

"How long ago was that?"

"Oh, a couple years, I guess. It wasn't my fault. I used to work with those kids on their homework and tell 'em how important an education was, but they just up and pissed their shot away," he said, and then passionately interjected, "And they was smart too. They was in them spelling bees and would be one of the last kids standin'. Then they'd end up gettin' out on some apostrophe."

The blues band playing that night had a bass guitarist who smoked during the songs. Whenever he wasn't playing, he'd take a hit off the cigarette, then free his hands to play by wedging the cigarette between the guitar's shaft and the top string.

Benny's girlfriend got off at nine o'clock, so we all piled into the front seat of Benny's truck and drove on a bridge over the Mississippi River. We were welcomed into Arkansas by a sign that hung overhead in the middle of the bridge. We pulled into the parking lot of the Southland Greyhound Track. Benny slid a blue plastic handicap placard onto his dashboard and we drove right to the front. He said that he'd gotten the placard a few years ago when he'd had his foot operated on. "I jus' never gave it back," he stated proudly. "If the police ever say anything to me about it I'll jus' start limpin'."

It was only three dollars to get in, so I paid for all of us and Benny picked up a racing program. We walked through the grandstand with its smells of buttered popcorn, cigar smoke, and stale beer and heard the announcer state, "Three minutes to post."

It was the seventh race and I decided to put two dollars on Harriet Tubman, the number-three dog, to win. I waited in line at the betting window between a young woman who looked like she'd been "rode hard and put away wet," to use one of my dad's lines. She had a rose tattoo on her neck, with the stem continuing down her shoulders under-neath her exposed black bra strap and disappearing into her purple tube top. Behind me in line was an older man with a three-day growth of beard who bumped his lit cigarette into the back of my bare arm.

"Ouch," I said, jumping out of the way.

"Oops, did I get ya?" he answered slowly with a drunken slur.

"It's okay," I said.

"No, it's not. I burned you and I'm very, very sorry," he said. He then tried to hand me his cigarette saying, "Here, you can burn me. What's fair is fair."

"No, I'm not going to burn you," I told him. "It's all right, it was just an accident."

"Well, at least let me give you a smoke." He reached into the pocket of his plaid shirt, pulled out three filterless Camel cigarettes, and handed them to me. "There, now we're even," he said just as the bet-taking man said, "Next."

"Two dollars on the conductor of the Underground Railroad," I said, with a smirk on my face.

"What dog, what race?" he asked in a hostile tone.

"Harriet Tubman, in this race."

"Look, kid, I need numbers. This machine doesn't know any dog named Harriet Tubman. Give me a number."

The old drunk man behind me looked in his program and said, "She's number three in the seventh."

"Number three in the seventh," I told the man.

"How much?"

"Two dollars."

"Win, Place, or Show?"

"You mean I can bet whether the dog shows up for the race or not?"

"Show is third place."

"Well, why would I bet that she finishes third?"

"One minute. One minute to post," the announcer stated over the loudspeaker.

"Are you betting or not?" the man stated flatly.

"Yeah. Give me two dollars on number three in the seventh to show."

He took my money and gave me a little electronically printed ticket. As I turned to walk away, a kid maybe fifteen or sixteen in a red Arkansas Razorbacks T-shirt said, "Hey, man, can I bum a smoke from ya?"

I handed him all three cigarettes and said, "Enjoy."

"Have a lucky night," he said with a Christmas morning happiness about him.

I walked out of the grandstand down toward the finish line and sprinkled some of Dad's ashes on the dirt track. Benny and his girlfriend were leaning on the rail and I stood between them and two old black men tightly clutching their rolled-up programs.

"Here comes the bunny," said the public-address announcer as I heard the clickety-clack of the mechanical rabbit racing around the inside track on a metal pole affixed to its side. When it got in front of the metal holding cages at the starting line, the announcer shouted, "And they're off!" The greyhounds charged out to kill that unobtainable mechanical rabbit, and the roar of the crowd grew as the thin, muscular dogs sprinted around each turn and headed for home. Harriet Tubman was in the middle of the pack, but began falling back at the last turn.

The two black men next to me were yelling, "Go, bitch. Run, bitch. Run, bitch," increasing the volume and frequency the closer the dogs got to the finish line. Harriet Tubman was out of it by now, so I joined in with the "Go, bitch, run, bitch" cheer, and when their dog finished first and the crowd quieted down, I heard one tell the other, "Damn, that bitch run like the wind."

Benny hadn't bet on a dog in that race or the next one. He was waiting for his "sure fire, can't lose" pick in the ninth. I lost another two dollars in the eighth race on a dog named Barking Spider. In the ninth, I bet five dollars on Benny's dog, called Preachin' to the Choir. I saw Benny kiss his gold crucifix necklace when the track announcer shouted, "And they're off!"

Preachin' to the Choir was the number-four dog right in the middle of the pack. When the gates flew open, he and another dog bumped, which gave the others dogs an early advantage. Preachin' to the Choir was clearly the fastest dog in the race, but due to the bad start he was forced to take all the turns on the outside of the track. Down the stretch, Preachin' to the Choir charged for the finish line, bypassing all but two dogs. We all screamed our support as the three-dog race became a two-dog race with just twenty yards to go.

The announcer bounced back and forth with his call of, "It's Preachin' to the Choir and Receding Hairline. Receding Hairline and Preachin' to the Choir. They're neck and neck, and at the wire . . . it's a photo finish."

It took a few minutes for the judges to rule. There was a general hush among the crowd as we collectively waited for the results. The electronic scoreboard in the infield flashed "Photo Finish," and I saw Benny kiss his necklace again. The numbers on the scoreboard began to light up and rapidly change.

"We have the results from the ninth race. Dog number four, Preachin' to the Choir, was declared the winner of the photo finish."

The crowd was divided between cheers and moans. We were ecstatic, hugging each other and jumping up and down. We collected our winnings, and it was only then that I learned Benny had bet five-hundred dollars on the race. He rolled his wad of bills up, secured it with a rubberband, stuffed it into his front pocket, and off we drove back to Memphis.

On Friday I called Missy to see if she still had the ticket. She did and agreed to sell it to me for fifty dollars. I had to take several different city buses to get to her house out in the suburbs. It took me most of the day thanks in part to a few wrong transfers. She met me at the front door wearing a colorful print sundress and a lemon-yellow baseball hat with the word "Grits" on it. Closer examination revealed that Grits was an acronym for Girls Raised In The South. We sat in white Adirondack chairs on her front porch and conducted our business transaction.

"Well, I hope y'all have a better time in Miami than I would have had," she said. "I was supposed to be goin' on this trip with my boyfriend. That is 'til we broke up. You'll probably be sittin' by him unless he sold his ticket to someone else."

*Oh, great,* I thought, *two hours on a plane with a disgruntled exboyfriend who will see me using her ticket and only be more angry.*

When I returned to the motel I had a Federal Express package waiting for me. Inside was a check for $500 and a letter from Double V.

> Dear Roastbeef:
>
> Your letter and pictures arrived today, and I wanted to say thanks for a job well done. I know Doris is happy as a two-peckered goat to be layin' there with Elvis. Anytime I want ashes spread around the country, I'm callin' you!
>
> Thanks again,
> Double V

An eight o'clock flight on a Saturday morning is awful. I had to get up by five-thirty, check out, and hope I was on the right bus going to the airport, all the time with butterflies in my stomach knowing I was going to be checking in as Missy Adams and sitting next to Missy Adams's former boyfriend. I had my response all ready in case the ticket agent gave me any flack about checking in as Missy. "Missy had to run to the restroom real quick, she asked me to check in for her." I went over my line several times, trying to make it sound spontaneous and off the cuff.

"Next," the ticket agent at the end of the check-in counter hollered as she waved her arm. I walked down to her with a smile and a hearty "Good morning," which was my first attempt at buttering her up. I placed the ticket on the counter. She asked me the usual questions, "Are you checking any baggage this morning?"

"Nope."

"Gate five," she said, handing me my boarding ticket. I felt like I'd just cleared customs with forty pounds of hashish.

I took a seat near gate five and waited for the boarding call. I decided to board the plane when the line was at its biggest, feeling there's safety in numbers. The line went slower than usual because the attendant tearing the tickets only had one arm. He placed the boarding ticket in between the two metal claws that were his left hand, clamped down, then tore the ticket with his right. I heard the guy behind me quietly say to his wife, "How do you think that guy gets his arm through the metal detector?"

After a rip and a stroll down the long portable hallway, the Missy Adams impostor had one foot on the plane. I had a middle seat in aisle twenty, but I was hoping for an uncrowded flight so I could move. I could see aisle twenty from several feet away as the aisle got clogged. I was trapped behind several other passengers as we waited for very slow people to safely stow their carry-ons in the overhead compartment.

There was a woman sitting on the aisle seat of row twenty wearing a sad-looking, wilted-brown, travel-weary flower lei. When I asked to get by, it was immediately apparent she didn't speak English. I didn't know where she was from, but she had that European "I've been eating sausage and drinking whiskey" kind of smell seeping from her pores. At the window seat sat a guy about my age, who I assumed was Missy's boyfriend. He didn't take his eyes off his magazine as I situated myself.

Once we were in the air, he did say to me, "Did Missy sell you that ticket?" When I said she had, he just looked back down at his magazine, muttering something about what a bitch she was. I was able to strike up a bit of a conversation with the lei woman. She was from Vienna, Austria, and was going to Miami to visit friends after visiting her daughter in Hawaii. With her limited English and my complete lack of anything resembling German, the only assistance I could give her in understanding me was to talk loudly and slowly and gesture a lot. It took us all the way through the beverage service to communicate that much. Whenever she was confused by a word, she'd start thumbing through her pocket-sized English-German dictionary. She was nice and friendly, but speaking pidgin English and waiting twenty minutes for a response was a bit wearing. I watched as she thumbed through her dictionary looking for a word and couldn't help but notice the woman had a small white-headed pimple on the side of her nose. I thought to myself, *If the cabin of this plane loses pressure, that thing's going to explode all over my rewarmed cheese omelet.* Luckily it never did.

When we both agreed to give up on our conversation through the international language of frustration, I began browsing through the airline's in-flight magazine. I came to an advertisement from a rent-a-car dealership announcing they had used cars for sale. I had saved up a few hundred dollars, so I thought about buying a used car for the rest of the trip. When we landed in Miami, I stopped at a pay phone in the terminal to thumb through a dog-eared yellow pages with multiple pages missing. Most of the used-car dealers seemed to be centrally located in the Little Havana section of town. There was a quarter-page ad with red printing that read "Trust Jesus!" touting the honest dealings at Jesus Delgado's Previously Owned Autos. The ad stated they'd pick you up anywhere in Dade County, which was the selling point that hooked me, so after taking a family photo for some tourists who were proudly documenting they had successfully claimed their luggage in Miami, I called Jesus and asked him if he had any cars in my limited price range. The man assured me they had something for every price range and that a representative would pick me up within an hour. I waited outside in the humid Miami morning. Rental-car pick-up vans circled, travelers came and went, and there I sat for well over an hour. I noticed a guy in a blue station wagon stop and ask ladies waiting with their luggage, "Are you waiting for Jesus?" When I heard that comment, I started waving my hands. He sped over and laid on the brakes to the point where the tires chirped. "Are you waiting for Jesus?" I nodded and he jumped out and opened the back door for me to get in. He handed me a clipboard with a list of the cars Jesus had in stock that day. "Check 'em out," the driver said, "while we pick up another customer in Coral Gables."

There were about twenty cars on the list, and one was a Hyundai. I thought it would have been cool to finish the trip in the same make of car that I started the trip in, but it was out of my price range.

"Oh, those are just the asking price, Jesus will make you a deal. He's got a car for every buyer."

We picked up an old Cuban woman, and she and the driver spoke Spanish all the way to the used-car lot, where we pulled in and were greeted by Jesus himself.

"Welcome, amigo," he said with a warm smile and firm handshake. "Have you looked over our list of mobile opportunities?"

I again explained there was nothing in my price range. "How much were you looking to spend, my friend?"

"Five hundred dollars."

He explained I could have any car on the list with five-hundred dollars down and that they financed anyone.

Jesus showed me three cars: a 1972 Oldsmobile Delta Eighty-eight with a quarter-of-a-million miles on it, a 1975 orange Gremlin with passenger-side impact damage, and a 1986 Yugo that needed a new clutch and had a "Free Tibet" bumper sticker possibly holding the cracked plastic bumper together. I test drove all three and decided on the Gremlin. I put down $250 and financed $750 for one year with Liberdad Auto Finance of Miami.

Mobile but broke again, I decided to seek the aid of family. My cousin Tim, who I hadn't seen in about seven years, was running a motel down in Key West. Although he was probably my least favorite cousin, I figured he was good for a place to stay and a couple of free meals. He was eight years older than me and the cousin who liked to give me a hard time because I was the youngest and smallest. He was the kind of mean-spirited kid who would push me down in a pile of dog crap on the front lawn and laugh as I threw a tantrum, crying to my parents. At one Easter dinner, the cousins had a dirt-clod fight in the field behind Grandma's house, and he hit me square on the forehead with a dirt clod the size and hardness of a baseball, which ended up costing me six stitches. I spent most of the time at family parties screaming, "I'm gonna tell," so all the cousins started calling me "Jimmy-Spill-the-Beans" and "Jimmy-Cry-to-Mama."

I drove down Highway 1, stopping at a resort on one of the lesser-known islands just long enough to swim in their pool, catch a brief nap on their lounges, and stare at the women in thong bikinis with orange tropical fish tattooed on their asses. I called Tim at the motel to let him know I was coming. He wasn't there, so I left a message with his effeminate desk clerk and, since the car was running great, decided to keep on driving.

The mile markers decreased as I chugged along over bridges connecting the Keys and separating the Atlantic on my left from the gulf on my right. Fishers and sunbathers did their thing near the highway, and an impatient woman in a black Mercedes with Connecticut plates rode my tail for several miles until a passing lane appeared. When she passed, I could see she had closed the car door on part of her dress. The trapped dress flapped in the South Florida breeze and hopefully was a greasy, weather-beaten discard by the time she got her type-A personality to her vacation retreat.

At mile-marker zero I drove over the last bridge and arrived on the island of Key West. I stopped and called Tim again.

"Hey, it's Jimmy-the-Ash-Sprinkler," Tim said in a sarcastic tone. "Are you still on your crazy ash sprinklin' trip?" We talked a little, then he gave me directions to his motel.

Tim had had a lot of trouble growing up. He'd spent some time in juvenile hall, so his very wealthy father, who never married his mom, said he'd give him the motel if he could prove he could run it successfully for two years. His plan, he told me, was to "run the place for two years and one day sell it to some fat cat Conch and am-scray with a shitload of cash."

It didn't take me long to realize that Key West is a kooky town, full of gays, misfits, seasonal workers, drunks, trust fund kids, tourists, vagrants, and drifters, with several of those categories overlapping on a nightly basis.

I saw an old local man passed out drunk in a wheelchair wearing a "No Beer, No Work" cap down over his eyes, which seemed to be the general philosophy in that part of the world. We stopped at a ten-foot-tall concrete marker designating the area as the southernmost spot in the continental United States. The marker looked like a command module purchased at a NASA garage sale, then painted with red, black, and yellow stripes. Next to the marker was a brass plaque that had turned greenish-brown from constant exposure to the sea air. The plaque was in tribute to the Cubans who had lost their lives at sea trying to come to America. I sprinkled some of Dad's ashes onto the rocks by the sea's edge and tossed a piece of Uncle Spud's monkey fragments into the crystal-clear water.

"Enough of this," Tim said. "There's beer to be drunk."

We walked down Duval Street. The most famous bar in town is Sloppy Joe's. It's the place where Hemingway used to drink booze and brag about all the animals he'd killed. After a few hours and a half-dozen beers each, Tim insisted on showing me "the best strip bar in the Keys."

One of the dancers was standing out on the verandah having a smoke. She winked at us as we passed her on the way in. The swarthy, middle-aged Middle Eastern man at the front door took our ten dollars, which entitled us to four drink tickets.

We had hardly settled into our seats when a dancer came over and sat next to me. "Would you buy me a drink?" she asked.

"Sure," I said. I still had three tickets, what's the big deal about sharing one?

She sat down saying, "Hi, I'm Candi Cupcakes, what's your name?"

"Roastbeef."

"No, really," she asked.

"Hey, if you can be Candi Cupcakes, I can be Roastbeef."

"Fair enough," she relented.

The waitress came over and Candi, my new drinking buddy, ordered a seltzer water. She tried to make small talk with me, which was very awkward. When the waitress brought the drinks out, I ripped off a ticket to pay for her drink.

"Her drink is twenty dollars," the waitress said.

"Well, forget it," I said. I thought, *I'm trying to be a nice guy 'cause this dancer is thirsty and this is the thanks I get?* The waitress gave me my ticket back and Candi got up to find someone else to wet her whistle. I went back to tell Tim the twenty-dollar seltzer-water story and he laughed at my naiveté. As we left, he gave our leftover drink tickets to two guys in sailor suits sitting at the bar.

The next day I helped Tim work around the motel until noon. I was severely hungover and vomited outside one of the rooms at the base of a banyan tree. I decided right then that my body couldn't take another night in Key West, so I drove back to Miami.

I found a hotel a few blocks from the art deco section of Miami Beach. It was geared more toward long-term tenants. The room was more like an efficiency apartment, complete with refrigerator, stove, sink, and the occasional roach. I put my things in the room and went out to stroll on Ocean Boulevard, where all the young hot Hispanic studs mingle with wannabe supermodels. I ended up standing on the sidewalk talking to a cigar salesman about whether or not his cigars were Cubans. "All I'm going to say is this is the best cigar you're ever going to smoke," was his reply.

I stopped to listen to the reggae music coming from an open-air night-club that I couldn't get into because I was wearing thong sandals. A young black man approached me and said, "Don't spray me with nothin'. I'm a good guy. I'm just here for a donation for the United Negro Fried Chicken Association, and if it helps any, I don't have rhythm, either."

I laughed. I liked his refreshing angle to stereotypes, so I reached deep into my pocket and gave him thirty-seven cents. "Here you go," I said. "It's not much, just thirty-seven cents."

"It's a donation," he said, quite content with my contribution. Why couldn't all beggars be as witty, friendly, and satisfied as he was? A truly pleasant bum encounter it was.

I strolled Ocean Boulevard for a few more hours, taking in the sights, sounds, and smells of South Beach. I returned to the hotel at two o'clock in the morning, even though the nightlife was just getting into full swing. When I went to crawl into bed, I pulled back the bedspread and saw a big, nasty toenail clipping resting right in the middle of my sheet. There were also spaghetti sauce stains up near the head of the bed and a long, ugly, black hair. It was too late to do anything about it. The only hotel employee in sight was an old Cuban night-watchman who was sleeping in a chair in the lobby. I shook out the sheets and turned them over and went to sleep. Needless to say, I took a long soapy shower the next morning before checking out of the Dirty Sheets Inn.

I headed north on Interstate 95, passing one beach-city playground-of-the-rich-and-famous after another. Just north of St. Lucie, I got onto the Florida Turnpike that crisscrossed the state on a northeast diagonal. I needed some gas, so I pulled off and stopped at a Citgo station. I got out to pump the gas and heard the voice of a little old man. "Hold on there, young fella, I'll do that."

"Oh, you pump the gas, huh? Well, I sure don't want to take your job from ya," I said as I went to use their restroom. It was without a doubt the cleanest restroom I'd seen on the whole trip. No graffiti, no trash or foul smells, just an old-fashioned metal vending machine mounted on the wall dispensing three brands of cologne for twenty-five cents per spray. By now I'd learned that if given the opportunity to improve one's smell on the road, one should take full advantage. My choices were Aqua Velva Seabreeze, Aqua Velva Musk, or Aqua Velva. From this I could surmise that Floridians love Aqua Velva. I chose to mask my travel odor with a squirt of musk, even though most of my twenty-five-cent, odor-improving investment dripped through my fingers and down the side of my hand before I could apply it.

The old man had his squeegee resting on the hood of my car and was leaning over the windshield scraping something with a pocket knife.

"How's it goin'?" I asked.

"I'm havin' a bitch of a time gettin' that bug in the middle off."

"Yeah, he's been on there a while."

"This Florida sun bakes them dad-gum things on there. You'd think you're never gonna get 'em off."

"Well, I sure appreciate the effort," I said.

"Just part of the service," he said as he squeegeed over the windshield one more time. "Picked the musk, huh?"

"Yeah, I did. Is it that noticeable?"

"It's okay. I use the regular stuff so I can tell."

"How much do I owe you?"

"The gas came to $15.03. How 'bout we call it fifteen," he said. I gave him a ten and a five, thanked him, then awkwardly offered him another dollar for a tip. It felt strange tipping a man who was old enough to be my grandfather, but the man had no problem quickly snatching it out of my hand and tucking it into his shirt pocket covered by a sewn-on oval patch that read "Morrie." He gave a hearty, "Thank you, sir. 'Preciate ya."

I smiled and got into my car.

"You take'r easy now," the old man said. "And come see us again."

"Sure will," I said. "Thanks a lot, Morrie."

"Oh, I'm not Morrie. My name's Nate. Morrie quit three days after we ordered new shirts and I'll be damned if I'm just gonna flush twelve-fifty down the toilet."

I continued up Interstate 75 to Interstate 10, which took me west along the Florida panhandle. I decided to take a small country highway to Montgomery, Alabama. Large clusters of rural-route mailboxes occasionally lined the road, as well as hand-painted signs stating "Read Your Bible."

I stopped for gas in Dothan, Alabama, at an Amoco station. I unscrewed the gas cap, put it on the hood of my car, filled up, and drove off. As I drove back to the highway, three teenage girls in a chocolate-brown Ford Granada pulled alongside me, honking their horn and waving. *I guess it's true what they say about Southern hospitality*, I thought. *They must have seen my out-of-state plates.* I smiled and waved back at them. The girl in the passenger's seat had her hair braided into two ponytails. She made small circular movements with her hand, which is the international gesture for "roll down your window." I started thinking it was more than just hospitality and that these girls really liked me. I rolled down my window, and as the wind blew in I heard her yell, "You drove off with your gas cap on your roof. It fell into the street." They all smiled and laughed. I smiled and waved "thank you" and turned up the radio to squelch out the pffff sound of my deflating ego. I turned around and headed back toward the gas station and began the Easter egg hunt for my gas cap. I looked around for fifteen minutes through the knee-high grass blades along both sides of the road. I found plenty of cigarette butts and other debris, but no gas cap. I was almost to the point of joining that rare group of dysfunctional motorists who stuff a rag into their gas-tank opening, when I found it. I screwed the gas cap on tightly, listening for the click, click, click of a secured connection, and pulled out of Dothan feeling a little more humble than when I arrived.

I drove north on Interstate 65 to Birmingham. I saw a sign announcing the exit to Legion Field and decided to get off, see the stadium, and have some lunch. I drove through a depressed area filled with dilapidated homes with broken-down cars and assorted junk resting in the front yards.

I located the stadium and stopped to have a look around. I was greeted at the stadium's entrance by a large bronze statue of Bear Bryant, a man who could have run for Governor of Alabama against God and won in a landslide.

Maintenance workers had the gates open, so I was able to walk onto the synthetic grass of the field's south end zone. When no one yelled for me to get out, I ran around the field, breaking imaginary tackles, looking just like a Heisman trophy statue. I imagined hearing the roar of 80,000 cheering Crimson Tide faithful. I was quickly brought back to earth when one of the maintenance workers in the stands yelled out across the vast empty facility, "The powder-puff game's next week." I smiled and waved at the workers in an attempt to mask my embarrassment and sprinkled some of Dad's ashes in the corner of the south end zone as I left.

Across the street was a small roadside diner called Mom & Pop's Touchdown Cafe. I walked in to find I was the only customer in the restaurant. I sat down on a stool at the counter. The older man, who I assumed was Pop, gave me a menu and asked, "You one of those fellers workin' on the stadium?"

"No, I'm just passin' through," I said.

"Well, you picked the right place, cause we're the only white place around here."

I looked over the menu, which I noticed had several misspellings, including the first side dish listed as "Chesse & Frys." Written on a chalkboard was the daily special: PBR & PB&J $1.50.

"What's the special?" I asked, unable to decipher their war-like code.

"Pabst's Blue Ribbon and a peanut butter-and-jelly sandwich."

"Oh," I said. "I'll have that, and some of your cheese fries, too."

I talked to Pop while Mom made my sandwich. A little while later, a Miller beer delivery man named Shawn entered, pushing a dolly stacked high with twelve-packs. He wheeled them into the back room and then sat a few stools down from me at the counter and had a Dr Pepper while ruffling through his invoices.

"We were just talkin' a little football," Pop said, trying to bring Shawn up to speed.

"I don't follow it much. Back home, our game on Saturday night was finding a nigger and kicking the shit out of him."

I was stunned that he could be so outwardly racist in front of a total stranger. He went on with his white-supremacist monologue, talking about how he'd quit his last delivery job because the company always had him driving through areas that were heavily populated by blacks. He talked about blacks breaking into his truck and the sawed-off shotgun he had "no trouble" using.

"I don't have anything against blacks that worked for what they got, it's these niggers with the welfare and gold rings," he stated.

"Yeah," Pop chimed in. "My neighbors are colored . . . black," he said correcting himself "And they got it better than I do. At least they got whites for neighbors. I got niggers."

These people were so extreme I couldn't help but think that they were putting on the Southern White Racist Stereotype Show for the out-of-towner. I'll never know. I paid and headed east for Georgia.

THIRTY MILES SOUTH OF ATLANTA on Interstate 75, I pulled off into the drive-through at a Hardee's for a soda. After I ordered but before I reached the pick-up window, the car's engine sputtered and died. I tried starting the engine but it wouldn't turn over. The noise of a car engine that couldn't answer the bell piqued the interest of diners. I tried repeatedly to start the car and eventually the engine did start, but it followed with a loud, dying cough of white smoke and turned off again. Cars behind me in the drive-through couldn't pull forward to receive their food and new cars couldn't move up to place their orders, so what else could they do but honk? Hearing the commotion, two workers came out in their Hardee-issued brown-polyester uniforms and pushed the car as I steered to a vacant space in the parking lot. I slammed the door in frustration. "This damn, good-for-nothin', piece of crap!"

"Don't sweat it, son," one of the guys who looked younger than me said. "Pop the hood."

The three of us looked at the engine, trying to find the problem. The only way I was going to be able to locate the problem was if a red flag popped up saying, "Here's the problem!" And even after finding the problem, I wouldn't have known what to do with it.

The two guys didn't know what the problem was, but they knew what it wasn't. All I heard for the first five minutes they were looking at the engine was, "It ain't the belts" and "It ain't the hoses."

"Hey, I don't want to take anymore of your time. Maybe I should call a mechanic."

"Nah, it's cool. We'll find it."

"Don't you guys need to get back to work?"

"Nah, the manager's not here today and Jimmy, the assistant manager, don't care."

"Yeah, he's a car buff himself. He'd be out here right now but he's right in the middle of mixin' the secret sauce."

"Hey, boy, right there," he said, pointing toward something. "You gotta crack in your water pump you could drive a truck through."

The other worker followed his finger to the crack, "Dad-gum, he sure do."

"Is that very expensive to fix?"

"Not really. Seventy-five for the pump, and I'll put the sumbitch in for ya for fifty."

"Besides that, does it look okay?"

"As far as I can see."

"Well, when could you do it?"

"Probably not till Sunday. I got work every day and got my kids on Saturday."

I gave him seventy-five dollars for the part and agreed to pay him fifty when I picked up the car on Sunday. I took a bus into Atlanta. I'd been carrying Heidi Bright's brother's phone number since Nebraska, and the time had finally come to give him a call. I reached Kevin's answering machine on the first call, so I started explaining who I was and how I got his phone number and beep. The machine cut me off mid-sentence, making me sound like a fool, so I had to call back to tell him I'll call back later. I was in the downtown area between Interstate 10 and the State Capitol. A black guy walked up to me and said his car had run out of gas on the freeway and he was trying to get enough money together to drive back home to Alabama.

"If you can spare a couple bucks, I promise when I get home, I'll mail it right back to you." I knew there was a 95 percent chance I was being scammed, but people had been so nice to me on the road that I bet on the 5 percent and gave him two dollars. He had me write my name and address on a piece of crumpled up paper that he pulled out of a nearby trash can.

"Ah right," he said. "I'll be gettin' this right back at ya soon as I get home."

I took a stroll around the grounds of the Georgia State Capitol and sprinkled some of Dad's ashes near the bronze statue of a casually dressed Jimmy Carter sporting a decorative-fish belt buckle.

I walked back to the pay phone and tried Heidi's brother again. This time he answered, and to my surprise, he knew my situation and actually said, "Heidi told me about you. I was hoping you'd call."

He gave me directions to his apartment, which seemed confusing because almost every street in Atlanta is named Peachtree. "Take North Peachtree Road to East Peachtree Road and it'll eventually merge into South Peachtree. Make sure you stay on South Peachtree Road until it hits West Peachtree. If you pass Peachtree Place, you've gone too far. Turn around and get back on Peachtree. If you get lost, ask for directions at the Peachtree Center."

He lived in an apartment over an appliance store. I could hear some country music blaring as I walked up the stairs to his apartment. Once I was close enough, I determined the song was called "T-R-O-U-B-L-E" by Travis Tritt. Looking back now, I should have taken that as a sign, but I knocked on the door. He came out of a room across the hall. His apartment consisted of two rooms across the hall from each other with the bathroom and kitchen on one side and bedroom on the other. His apartment was a filthy mess. He kept his dirty dishes in the refrigerator to keep the roaches away. When all of his dishes were dirty and in the refrigerator, he'd either wash them, buy paper plates, or just go out for fast food.

"You got here on a good weekend," he told me. "There's a shitload of good weddings." He explained to me that he attends wedding receptions uninvited without knowing anyone for all the freebies. He showed me the wedding announcements in the newspapers and how he keeps records in a planner for months ahead of time.

"So you just show up at the reception without knowing anyone?" I asked.

"No, you gotta go to the church first to mingle with some of the old-lady guests. They're so happy that someone is talking to them, they tell you everything you need to know. Then you use that information on other guests. All you have to do is get in good with a few people, and you're in. You gotta remember all the bride's friends and family don't know the groom's friends and family, and, of course, the friends bring dates. And, remember, this is a sneak attack; I mean who would crash a wedding, right?

"Right. I guess."

"Hell, it's the easiest way of eatin' prime rib every week that I know of."

"Have you ever been caught?"

"When I first started, I got drunk and turned into Chatty Charlie and let it slip. I was escorted out of the reception by security, but I got the last laugh when I puked in the seat of the couple's horse-drawn carriage."

I asked him more about it and he gave me a three-by-five laminated index card with the ground rules that he gives anytime a rookie accompanies him. The card read:

1. Let them play their cards. If they know the bride, you know the groom and vice versa.

2. Don't draw attention to yourself.

3. Get bride/groom information from old people.

4. Get a take-home dinner box for your sick "Uncle Fred."

"Tomorrow will be a fun one," he said. "It's a rich Catholic wedding. Those are always the best. The food's good, the booze flows, and the bride's friends are usually weddin' horny."

"Wedding horny?" I asked.

"Yeah, you know—they get all emotional over the dress and cake and shit. They have some champagne, I tell them they look pretty, and next thing you know they're blowin' me in the alley behind the trash dumpster."

I laughed. "Has that happened?"

"Oh, yeah, all the time," he said with a smirk on his face. I couldn't tell whether to believe him or not. He had that friendly, outgoing, salesman-type personality that your gut feeling tells you not to trust.

The next day, true to his word, he started laying out his wedding clothes and tried to fix me up with something presentable. We were about the same size except his legs were longer, so he pulled out a roll of duct tape and did the bachelor version of tailoring slacks. This was the first time I'd been dressed up since I left home a year and four months ago, and I thought I looked pretty good.

The wedding was in a suburb just north of the city. The wedding started at noon, so we left at twelve-thirty because, he said, "Those Catholic ceremonies are so long and drawn out. It's nothin' but kneel, stand, kneel, stand; it's like Pope-aerobics."

"Do you know where the church is?"

"Yeah, I've been to this one a dozen times."

When we got there, the parking lot was nearly full and the ceremony wasn't over yet, so he strolled around looking at the cars. He had a hand-sized notebook in which he jotted down ideas for conversations with the wedding guests: NRA stickers, Pro-Life stickers, Georgia Tech license-plate holders. The church bells chimed.

"Time to go to work," he said. "Stay by me and keep your mouth shut until I get some information."

We stood in front of the church talking to each other as the guests started to exit the church. Kevin spotted an elderly woman standing by herself and he slowly worked his way over to her. After a few moments he smiled and said, "Beautiful ceremony, wasn't it?"

"Gorgeous, just gorgeous," the old lady said with her face lighting up with excitement, just the way Kevin had explained.

"Those were some of the prettiest flowers I think I've ever seen. Do you know who picked them out?"

"Well, Bob, of course."

"Who's Bob?"

"The bride's father," she said. "He owns seventeen florist shops all over the Southeast; I certainly think he's qualified."

"Oh, I didn't know he was a florist. We're friends of the groom." And on Kevin went, pumping this old lady for information as we made mental notes. When he felt he'd gotten all he could from her, he moved on. By the time the bride and groom came out of the church after taking pictures, I felt like I'd known them and their families for years.

*This is going to be easy*, I thought. My anxiety over the situation calmed and I actually started enjoying the process.

We had found out that Terry and Teri Lovejoy had met while working in the cafeteria at the Student Center at Georgia Tech University. He
was an engineer major, and she was a physical education major trying
to get her "MRS." degree. They lived in Atlanta with their cat Nixon.
Terry played softball on his company's team, and she worked at a day-
care center.

We followed the caravan of cars from the church to the reception hall
at the Peachtree Hotel. Kevin honked his car horn with glee all the way
from the church to the reception, just like the real invited guests. We
walked into the lobby with two of the bride's girlfriends who we had
befriended. I signed the guest book as Serge Vienna. Below me Kevin
scrawled, "Congratulations, Joe Stalin." Young skinny Mexicans in
poor-fitting tuxedos served us champagne in a waiting area just outside
of the banquet room where the Lovejoy reception would soon begin.

The two girls we walked in with were Ann and Heather. They were
good friends of the bride growing up, but had fallen out of touch in
recent years, which made it very easy talking to them. We started making up stories about "the Terries," which we were now calling the bride
and groom, and Ann and Heather never questioned our stories.

There was a beautiful table filled with rich, cheesy hors d'oeuvres,
vegetables trays, and jumbo shrimp the size of my thumb. The seven-tier
wedding cake was on display nearby, and I pointed out how the frosting roses on the cake looked like the radishes cut to look like roses on
the vegetable-tray table. Kevin grabbed a handful of radishes and, when
people weren't looking, randomly placed them on the cake. He wasn't
happy with just the handful, and even though I tried to get him to quit,
wouldn't stop until he had placed every radish on the cake.

When they opened the doors to the banquet room, Kevin could see
there was no assigned seating, which, he said, "always makes it easier."
He took a table near the dance floor, and Ann and Heather joined us
as well as three middle-aged lesbian friends of the groom's mother. The
lesbians all wore African-style print dresses and long, dangling, metal
necklaces. The woman sitting nearest to me was growing a menopause
mustache and was in dire need of an estrogen shot.

Kevin offered to go to the bar and get a drink for everyone, and I went
along to help him carry them back. "People like you if you give them

something, and it's a host bar, so it's no sweat off of my balls," he told me on the way over.

The disc jockey introduced the wedding party. They walked into the room to cheers and applause. Everyone stood when "the Terries" came through the doors smiling and waving, working the crowd like lifelong politicians.

A scared and nervous best man stumbled, stammered, and stuttered his way through a very lame alphabet-themed toast where, for example, he would say, "'A' is the aisle that you walked down in the abbey. 'B' is for the bouquet of beautiful blossoms." Kevin and I looked at each other with a "this guy can't be serious" curiosity. By the time he got to 'N,' I was praying that one of the NRA people would do us all a favor and deliver a head shot to the best man.

We ate prime rib and drank the bottles of wine standing on the table, and occasionally the revelers hit their utensils against the side of their wine glasses, which apparently is some sort of wedding code to get the bride and groom to kiss. We decided it meant we had to take a big gulp of booze instead.

They had disposable Kodak cameras on each table for the guests to take photos of themselves and to otherwise document the event. Kevin took the camera into the restroom, went into a stall where no one else could see, pulled down his pants, and holding the camera out in front of him, took a picture of his naked genitals. He brought the camera back to the table where no one was the wiser and the photos wouldn't be developed until "the Terries" had returned from their Cancun honeymoon.

Kevin went up to the disc jockey and asked to request a song. "Sure," said the goofy DJ with blond highlight streaks in his short, dark spiked hair.

"Would you play 'D-I-V-O-R-C-E' by Tammy Wynette?" The DJ just smiled and went back to selecting music. "I always request it, but I've never met one DJ with enough balls to play it," he told me.

They had the bouquet and garter tosses, followed by the cake cutting. The mother of the bride discovered the first radish on the cake and started freaking out like she'd been wronged by the world. She took the microphone from the DJ and began ranting to the crowd, "Who put radishes on my baby's wedding cake? I want an answer right now! We spent ten thousand dollars on my baby's big day and you thank us by putting radishes on the wedding cake." She was raising her voice more and more with each word, by the end reaching the point of hysteria.

"Mom, you're ruining the wedding," the bride said, nearly at the point of tears. The groom tried to calm his new bride down. Members of the wedding party began perusing the cake for radishes as if they were on an Easter egg hunt. They picked all the radishes from the cake, giving them to the little kids in attendance to lick off the frosting. One of the caterers, using a butter knife, attempted to fill in the frosting divots left by the radish removal. The young Mexican servers tried to hide their smiles and laughter by holding cloth napkins in front of their faces. Besides the staff, I think we were the only ones who saw the humor in the radish removal.

"This has been the easiest wedding I've ever done," Kevin told me as we bellied up to the bar for an after-dinner Cognac. When the bartender turned around to grab a bottle, Kevin helped himself to two dollars that were standing upright almost hanging out of the tip cup.

Later in the reception, the disc jockey announced they were having a dollar dance and anyone interested in dancing with the bride or groom could line up on each side of the dance floor. We lined up behind several portly old men to dance with the bride. Kevin gave me one dollar worth of dance money borrowed from the bartender. Kevin went first. He put the dollar into her pearl-beaded purse that dangled loosely around her wrist. The purse hadn't been cinched tightly and a fifty-dollar bill, folded in half lengthwise, stuck partway out. Kevin tried to pull it out with a distraction spin and dip. With all eyes in the room on the bride, it was a little like robbing a rock star at a concert, but he tried. He knocked the fifty out of the purse, then stepped on it and tried to walk off the dance floor, sliding his foot across the parquet floor.

"Hey, that guy's stealin' from the bride," someone yelled. Kevin froze. Seeing people approaching, he screamed out and pointed at me as I danced with the bride. "That guy put the radishes on the cake!" We both took off running out of the reception hall, through the lobby, and out the doors. "Split up," is the last thing I heard him say. He went right so I went left. I ran through a neighborhood, turning each corner that I could. I huffed and puffed until I couldn't run anymore. I jumped inside a trash dumpster behind an apartment complex and pulled the lid down over me. Although the trash had been emptied, the smell of the dumpster was sour, like spoiled milk had been in it. There were also armies of ants crawling around looking for a meal and thinking it might be me. When I caught my breath, I took off my jacket and tie and left them in the dumpster to alter my "Saturday afternoon you've just been to a wedding" look.

I walked through an alley and came up to a shopping center. I went into the Wal-Mart and bought a new shirt, short pants, tennis shoes, and a baseball cap. I changed clothes in their restroom and asked the greeter to cut the tags off. I browsed in the strip mall's other shops for several hours until I figured the wedding lynch mob had given up on finding me. I called Kevin's phone number but got no answer. I decided to cautiously stroll back to the Peachtree Hotel to see if his car was still in the parking lot. From across the street I could see people in tuxedos standing by their cars talking and decided it would be too risky to walk through. I went back to the shopping center and sat in Wal-Mart's snack area until they closed at ten o'clock. There was still no answer on Kevin's phone. I walked back to the hotel and found his car still in the parking lot. I could only guess they had caught him.

I walked back to Kevin's apartment, which took me four hours. I stopped occasionally to call to see if he'd made it home. He never answered. I spent the night sitting on his doormat with my back resting against his front door. He showed up the next morning with a black eye and a split upper lip, claiming he'd spent the night with Heather or Ann.

"I forget which is which," he said.

We went inside his apartment, drank orange juice, and listened to the half-dozen messages I had left for him.

"So tell me what happened to you?"

He lightly rubbed his eye, grimacing slightly, "Well, a couple of the Bubbas trapped me in the parking lot and proceeded to tap dance on my face. Luckily, Heather and Ann came out and cooled them down, which really saved me from a severe ass-kicking. Then the girls took me back to their apartment to treat my wounds. One thing led to another, we started drinking a little, and so I suggested we play strip poker. I'm sure you can fill in the blanks, but let's just say I came out the big winner."

I didn't believe Kevin any further than I could throw him. He was the embodiment of the cliché my dad used to say when politicians would speak: "If you can't dazzle 'em with brilliance, baffle 'em with bullshit."

Kevin drove me back up to the Wal-Mart so I could return my "escape clothes" for cash to pay for my car repair. I thanked Kevin for an interesting time and took the bus back to my car. I paid the Hardee workers/shade-tree mechanics my fifty dollars and headed north for South Carolina. I stopped in the capital city of Columbia with a carload of dirty clothes in need of a laundromat. The shopping center near the University of South Carolina had a place called Harlin's Gamecock Wash. I changed into my swimsuit, thongs, and sweater vest and took every other piece of clothing in to be washed. I needed to get some quarters for the machines, so I went up to the attendant sitting in a little wooden kiosk and reading a dog-eared paperback book by Zane Grey. Later, as I sat reading an abandoned copy of the *National Enquirer,* he came by with a broom and dustpan, sweeping lint and other refuse off the floor. He looked at me as I wiped the sweat from my brow and took a deep breath of thick humid air.

"It's a hot one today," he said. "And it ain't gettin' any cooler 'til Christmas."

I nodded. "You gotta coke machine?"

"No, I sure don't, but ya'nt some sweet tea?" he asked me with a slow Southern drawl. "Just made some fresh 'fore ya got here."

"That would be really nice, thank you."

When he brought it back to me he said, "I've been in the laundry b'ness thirty-six years and I've got a theory that no one doin' their laundry is ever wearin' any underclothes. And by the looks of you, I'd bet my theory would hold true."

"You got me pegged."

"Not just you, everyone. I reckon no matter where you go on God's green earth, folks doin' their warsh ain't wearin' no britches."

"That's why we're here," I said. "Man, that's some good tea."

"Help yourself to some more if ya'nto."

"Have you developed any other theories in your thirty-six years in the business?"

"Hundreds. But most of 'em aren't warsh related."

I asked for him to tell me some of his theories. He only had a few theories committed to memory, but as I was moving my "warsh" to the dryer, he returned with a tattered, yellowed notebook where he wrote his thoughts, ideas, observations, and theories. He set it down in my lap saying, "Just thumb through it. Some of 'em aren't bad." It was one of the most enjoyable reads of my life. His simplistic wisdom made me feel like I'd run into a modern-day laundromat Mark Twain.

"This is unbelievable," I told him.

"Not bad for an old fart that didn't get through eighth grade, huh?"

"I bet you could publish this stuff."

"Aw, come on, now. Who'd ever buy the thoughts of an old laundry-man?"

"I don't know, but they should."

I continued reading, sometimes laughing, sometimes touched. I don't know why this one stuck in my head but he wrote, "Life is like a buffet dinner. You can have whatever you want, but you have to get off your ass to get it."

He asked me if I was going to school at "S.C.," and since he'd opened his world up to me, I told him my story. As I talked of my travels and experiences, he continually reiterated, "Aw, that's great. Good fer you." When I finished, there was a long, contemplative pause.

"You gotta travel while yer young," he stated. "I've been on tours with senior citizens where they load yous in a bus and drive yous from one tourist attraction to another tourist attraction to take a photo. That's not travelin'. You mi's well stay home and subscribe to *National Geographic*. The fun of traveling is the things that go wrong, not the things that go right. Whenever ma kids, course they're older 'en you, whenever they remember our ol' family trips, it's always about the fights, the flat tires, the di'rhea from some roadside hot-dog stand."

Then he reached for his notebook to write down his new theory. "Traveling," he muttered to himself, "the things that go wrong."

I changed into my clean clothes and decided to try to beat the heat by driving along the coast. I arrived in Myrtle Beach around five o'clock without any golf clubs, which, given the number of golf courses, driving ranges, and miniature-golf centers in the area, could be construed as blasphemy. I ended up in North Myrtle Beach, essentially the bastard son of the more renowned resort to the south, which accepts the overflow tourist crowd and second-class riffraff. There were plenty of hotels and motels along Ocean Boulevard I resorted to my traveling tenet, that the worst-looking place would have the best price and best chance of vacancy. I noticed an old, wooden two-story building that looked like a boarding house. The peeling green paint on the house and crooked dark-brown shutters made the place look like a two-story scoop of mint-and-chip ice cream. I went up to the screen porch only to find the door locked. A note scotch-taped to the door read, "Charlie, we're at the Attic."

There was a convenience store next door so I went over to buy a drink. The counter girl was a redhead about my age, and I detected an accent when she told me the price. She was from Cork County, Ireland, and very friendly. I told her I was looking for a cheap place to stay. She said there was an old couple a few houses down the block that would rent out a room in their house for the night "if they like the way you look." She left her post, which didn't seem like a major violation since the whole time I'd been there not one other customer had made the front door chime, and walked me out to the parking lot to point down to a little white house set back from the street with a wishing well on the sprawling green lawn. "It's that place with the wishing well," she said, as she started back for the store, which two teenagers on skateboards had just entered.

I walked up to the door and saw an old lady sitting in an easy chair with her bare feet elevated on the footrest and watching a baseball game on television. Her swollen feet didn't look that bad until I noticed her thick yellow toenails, which could have cut glass. I lightly tapped on the glass door and smiled when she got up, hoping she'd like my look. She cracked the door a few inches, and the cool air-conditioned air rushed into my face. "I was wondering about a room for tonight?" I asked.

"For just you?" she asked suspiciously.

"Yep."

"Where are you from?"

"Kensington, Maryland," I said. "It's just outside of Washing—"

She cut me off. "Oh, you're from Kensington," she said, like it was some magical place. "My sister lives in Kensington. Estelle Walker. She lives on Crawford Circle." When she looked into my eyes and saw no recollection she continued on. "Oh, I've been to Kensington several times."

I figured this was the "in" I needed so we talked about how great Kensington is and her trips there visiting her sister. Eventually I asked how much the room was and she said, "We usually charge twenty a night, but I'll let you have it for ten. Just don't tell my husband. He's never liked my sister, and he hates when I lower the price."

She walked me around to the back of the house to a separate entrance. The room was the first one as we entered. There was no room number, just a bedroom door with a lock on it.

"This used to be my daughter's room," she told me as she opened the door. "Though that was years ago," she added. The room had a closed-off, stale-air, "grandma's house" smell to it. The walls were covered in pink-and-white striped wallpaper with frilly lace curtains. "I hope this room's not too feminine for you."

"No, this is great," I said. I couldn't wait for her to leave me alone so I could open up all the windows and throw the rose-print bedspread in the closet. Once she left, I got into my bathing suit and walked across the street to the beach. It was now six o'clock and most of the daytime tourists had gone back to their hotels. I swam in the warm, brown salty ocean waves among the shrimp and other tiny forms of sea life as a shrimp boat trolled just past the breakwater.

After sweltering in the southern heat for several days, this was a special treat. I got out, dripped dry on the sand, and looked out over the horizon in between updates in my journal. I noticed an older man with a gold cornucopia necklace talking and laughing and building a sand castle with his nubile daughter, who seemed to be about my age. After watching them for a while, I could see there was a little too much love there for him to be winning the Father-of-the-Year award.

I dug a small hole in the sand, sprinkled some of Dad's ashes inside, dropped in a piece of Uncle Spud's broken monkey, and covered it back

up. The list of "Need 'Ems" was now only two, and as I sat on the
beach, for the first time I felt real confidence that I was going to complete
my promise to Dad. I decided to celebrate another successful sprinkling
at a bar-and-grill on the sand's edge called the "Shag-n-Snack."

I strolled over to the epitome of a "Frankie & Annette" beach-style
snack shop, except for the flowing booze and the age of most of the
patrons. I found a place at the bar and ordered some half-priced, happy-
hour chicken wings, which came in three levels of spiciness: mild, hot,
and "Holy Jesus!"

The bar's shelves were fully stocked with every kind of hard liquor
imaginable, but the liquor was only available in the miniature airplane-
style bottles. A sign hanging over the bar said, "Tipping is not a city
in China." On the parquet dance floor, a teenage boy, with the look of
disdain for everything except his paycheck, tried to teach out-of-towners
the regional dance called "Shag." I watched the group of mostly senior
citizens try their luck at this dance, which looked to me like the comingling of a country line dance and a waltz. The dance instructor continually spoke into his static-ridden microphone, trying to get more men to
take part in the lessons. When a pair of Carolina cupcakes in T-shirts and
cut-off jeans with fraying strands dangling on their trim tan legs came in
from the patio to take part, I gulped down the last few sips of beer and
got in line beside them. It was quickly obvious as the high-school dance
instructor put us through our paces that the girls were quite familiar
with the dance. They followed the moves with a natural instinct as my
feet shuffled forward and back with indecisiveness. The girls talked and
giggled at each other.

"You're fast learners," I said quickly, so I wouldn't lose my concen-
tration.

"We were born shaggin'," said the one with the glossier lips.

"Then why are you taking lessons?"

"It beats hearing our boyfriends talk about football."

After ten minutes of learning the steps by ourselves, we were told
to "couple up." I stood there momentarily frozen, reminiscent of my

experiences at junior-high-school stag dances when a slow song was played. At that moment, you either had to muster up the courage to ask a girl to dance or retreat to a wall with the other dorks and talk about how lame the song is.

I turned to the nearest girl and said, "How 'bout it?"

"I gotta pee," she said with a giggle in her voice. "Bonnie'll dance with you."

I was well aware of the ol' pass-off strategy. I'd done it myself on past occasions. Bonnie didn't seem to mind that her friend had obligated her. I tried to perform the steps I had learned, but more often than not, I was going forward when she was going forward and I'd step on her sandal-wearing feet. "Sorry," I repeated over and over, like I was cornering the market on apologies.

"Relax," she said. "You're too tense. I can feel it in your shoulder."

"Sorry," I again said, wishing I had never gotten up off the barstool. She counted off the steps, whispering softly into my ear. I began feeling more comfortable with the dance, then she told me to twirl her around.

"When I say 'now,' give me a twirl." She again counted out the steps, then said, "now." I raised my hand to twirl her one way and she wanted to twirl the other. Our fingers got intertwined and we stood idly for a moment, waiting for a place in the song where we could start again. Bonnie's boyfriend walked in with his shoulders back and his chest sticking out of his Semper Fi T-shirt.

"What's going on?"

"I'm helping this guy learn to shag."

He looked me over without making eye contact and said to Bonnie, "I think you better come back to the table."

"Yeah, well, thanks a lot for the lesson," I said quickly, trying to avoid being punched by a jealous jarhead boyfriend. The instructor could see I was being abandoned on the dance floor and was all too willing to give me his dance partner. He shifted this blue-haired old lady wearing a woven palm-frond hat into my arms. Within seconds, I had gone from young and nubile to old and patchy. Doloris, from Michigan's upper peninsula, had white, wrinkled skin with red, sun-burned patches around her face and neck from a poor application of sunscreen.

I led her around the dance floor a couple times and decided to give her a spin. I raised my hand and twirled her through. "Weeeh," she said. She was a bit unstable as she turned around, and before I could grab her, her feet got crossed and down she went onto the floor. Crunch. It sounded like she'd sat on a bag of potato chips, but it was the noise of an eighty-year-old hip shattering into bite-sized pieces. She sat there on the floor with a matter-of-fact reaction.

"I broke my hip," she said, with one leg in front of her and the other pointed off at an angle no leg should ever point in.

CHAPTER

16

FRESH FROM MY ABUSE of the elderly, I decided to get out of the Palmetto State before a rogue mob of AARP members demanded justice for their fallen comrade and flogged me with their canes and walkers. I zigzagged on a variety of two-lane country back roads in a northeasterly direction, trying to get back to Interstate 95. The entrepreneurial spirit of America flourished along the grassy roadsides as black women set up shop in weather-beaten souvenir shacks. They all seemed to be selling a variety of the same thing: items woven from palmetto fronds.

The country road briefly became a town road as it wound through a one-stoplight town just over the North Carolina border. A slow-down-ahead notice was written in white paint on a blue car hood that had been removed and affixed to a tree. I liked the recycling spirit of these Carolina folk. Why throw your tree leaves away when you can make a hat out of them? Why throw away a perfectly good car hood when the town needs a speed-limit sign?

The one traffic light was green, so I passed through the town as quickly as they'd legally let me. On the outskirts of town, just about the place where motorists were allowed to resume speed, I noticed an old black man with snow-white hair standing on the side of the road. A young boy with a bright yellow Tonka dump truck played in the dirt at the man's feet. The boy didn't look up as I passed, but I briefly made eye contact with the man. He had deep, dark, sorrowful eyes and was hold-ing a cardboard sign with a big black triangle drawn in the center. He held the sign out for me to get a good look at it and stuck his thumb up with the other. I just didn't get it. Was this old man a Trekkie waiting at the mothership stop? Perhaps he was a symbol artist. Maybe he couldn't write the name of the place he wanted to go. No matter what the reason behind his sign, I drove by him and resumed speed at the resume-speed sign on the way out of town. About a mile out into the country, I began to experience the gut-gnawing feeling of guilt. I debated with myself about giving them a ride, and I hated the safe side of me that told me to keep going.

"Geez, if you can't give a ride to an old man and a little kid, who can you give a ride to anymore?" I said to myself as I turned the car around over the grassy median and headed back to offer them a ride. As I pulled up to them, the old man's face lit up with an Osmond-esque smile. He grabbed the boy's hand and leaned in toward the car as I rolled down the passenger-side window.

"Where you headed?"

"Anywhere near the Triangle would be right fine," he said.

"Where's the Triangle?" I asked.

"The Triangle? You ain't never heard of the Triangle? Where you from?"

"Maryland."

"Well, I sure ain't needin' to go that fur."

"Well, you're welcome to ride along if I'm going toward the Triangle," I said.

"As long as you be headin' up this there road, you be headin' toward the Triangle."

I said something about the boy, calling him his "grandson," and the man quickly corrected me as the boy crawled into the backseat.

"Oh, no, that ain't my grandson, that's my son. Just because there's some snow on the roof don't be thinkin' there's no fire in the fireplace."

I chuckled and he stuck out his hand and introduced himself as Clifton Cox. "But all my friends call me Curly, and since you be givin' me and my boy a ride, you can call me Curly."

Curly's son started driving his dump truck up and down the seats and across his lap, making revving engine sounds. He had a six-inch-tall plastic action figure that had been stripped of all of its clothes. The doll appeared to be either Rambo or Rocky, definitely some sort of Sylvester Stallone look-alike. The doll was being continually run over by the dump truck while the boy, speaking for the doll, would plead, "no, don't, stop, ouch," followed by the noise of bones crunching under the wheels.

Curly told me the Triangle is a term for the area around Raleigh, Durham, and Chapel Hill. He reached down into his pants pocket and pulled out a clear sandwich bag with some dark tobacco in it. "You mind if I have a chaw?" he asked. "I brought ma own spit cup."

"Sure, go ahead," I said.

He dug down into the bag and came up with a clump the size of a golf ball, shoving it inside his cheek like a squirrel storing nuts for the winter.

"Care for any?" he asked, adding, "Grew it myself."

"Really? You grew this?"

"From seed to lip, I did it all," he said proudly as he handed me the bag. I noticed his hands. There was no doubting they were the hands of a hardworking man. His old black fingers were dried, cracked, and wrinkled and looked like Tootsie Rolls that had been left outside for years to face the elements.

"You best take it easy, my stuff is puny strong," he said. I stuck my fingers into the bag and pinched off a clump of the moist, almost gooey tobacco, which was practically dripping with nicotine, and popped it in my mouth. He'd hold the spit cup as I drove and hand it to me when the juices in my mouth were starting to overflow. Within a few moments, I was feeling the first wave of an intense nicotine buzz, and a few minutes later I think I could have been arrested for driving under the influence. The fun quickly ceased as I started to feel nauseated. I spit out the tobacco, but the damage had been done.

"I seen dead people that looked better than you, boy," Curly said. I pulled over to the side of the road, got out of the car, and walked toward the tree line, but before I got there, up it came. I threw up like I'd never thrown up in my life. Everything inside my body demanded to exit with the violent expediency of rock fans at a festival seating concert. If it's possible, I believe I had just overdosed on nicotine. I was down on all fours vomiting into the grass, my nose running and tears streaming down my cheeks. Not one of the finer moments of my life. When I had nothing left to throw up, including bile, my body moved on to dry heaves.

"Yeah, it's a little harsh if you're not used to it," Curly explained.

By the time it was over, my sides hurt from the experience. All I had to wash my mouth out with was some Mountain Dew, one of the most caffeinated drinks known to man. I washed my mouth out but didn't swallow any.

After recovering at a nearby rest stop for the better part of an hour, I finally felt able to continue the drive. Since I had no real destination other than north, I offered to drive Curly all the way to his destination. He was going to his oldest daughter's house. He told me she had been born while he was stationed in Hawaii during the late 1950s.

"She was born six hours after Hawaii officially became a state. She was the third baby born in Hawaii. I found out later they were givin' money and scholarships to the first baby born after statehood. If'n I would have known that, I'da had the doctor take her cesarean."

His daughter's house was off a two-lane country road north of Durham in Orange County, North Carolina, though on my drive through it I saw no oranges. When I pulled into the gravel driveway, Curly insisted I go in and have something to eat. Unfortunately for me, no one was home. We sat around on her front porch for a while. Curly kept turning his head, looking up and down the road for an approaching car.

"I dunno where on earth they could be," he'd say. We were running out of small talk and Curly's son was starting to get cranky, so I lied and said I wasn't hungry anyway and needed to be someplace by a certain time. Curly profusely apologized about not being able to feed me.

"Well, you just gotta take somethin' with you, that's all," he said, disappearing into the house. He returned and handed me what was left of a bag of miniature marshmallows. "Here, this'll give you a li'l somethin' to snack on while ya drivin'."

Highway 57, the two-lane country road that led me back toward the interstate, passed in front of a race track with a lawn marquee sign touting a stock car race. "Qualifying races 5:30. First race 7:00," read a sandwich-board sign set out on the edge of the highway, with a black-and-white checkered flag protruding from the top.

*Cool,* I thought. *I would have never found this if I hadn't given Curly a ride.*

I was several hours early for the race, so I sat on the hood of my car and updated my journal and watched as the good ol' boys started to arrive. Pickup trucks with gun racks pulled into the grass-field parking

lot and out stepped race fans in denim overalls and Winston caps carrying coolers into the grandstands. The concession stands sold baloney
burgers and boiled peanuts, but not to me. The wooden grandstands
extended thirty or more rows from the track and were an excellent place
to pick up a splinter if you weren't careful. I took a seat next to two
guys, one wearing a Rusty Wallace T-shirt, the other wearing a shirt that
read "Been There. Whooped Ass."

Before the first race, the track's chaplain stood at the start/finish line.
The crowd hushed as he offered a prayer for the safety of the drivers
and thanked God for the generosity of their sponsors. He barely got
"Amen" across his lips before engines began revving with a deafening
roar. The drivers for the first race drove around the half-mile oval track,
slowly slithering in a small "S" pattern like snakes in the grass to warm
their tires. The volume of the car engines continued to intensify, to the
point that I was now envying those in the crowd wearing headsets.
Earlier I had thought they looked like dorks. I was sitting on the fourth
turn, and as the cars came out of the third turn and blazed toward us
in pyramid formation, the deafening hum of the engines resembled a
swarm of bees.

As certain cars passed, fans screamed encouragement. For some reason, the man in front of me flipped off the yellow number-four car every
time it circled the track. As the cars sped past, small bits of tire shreds
and other debris on the track would be kicked up against the metal-mesh
protective fencing. Some of the car drivers who were still looking for
sponsorship had painted "This fender could be yours" on their cars with
a local phone number below it. Others used the unsold door or fender to
spread the word: "Jesus, the way, the truth, the life."

There were ten races of different lengths scheduled for the evening,
and after each race the track announcer briefly interviewed the winning
driver. "I'd like to thank my sponsors for the new set a tars."

By the time the fourth race rolled around, my ears were ringing like
I'd been at a heavy-metal concert. I ripped the corner from a paper napkin and wadded it into two small balls just big enough to fit in my ears.
When that didn't seem to help much, I pushed them down a little farther
into my ear canals. When I wanted to take them out in between races, I

discovered that one was in too deep. I went into a stall in the restroom and tried to pry the napkin out with my car key, which only seemed to push it in even further. Before the napkin ball hit my brain, I thought I'd better find someone, preferably not wearing overalls, to help me get the thing out of my head. The first-aid station was on the infield part of the track. A security guard with a very bushy beard walked me through a tunnel that smelled of gasoline and urine. The tunnel emerged on the infield side, near the first-aid station, which was housed in a seventies-model motor home. The nurse was sitting in the driver's seat, trying to watch the race when I arrived.

"So, what've we got here?" she asked.

I sheepishly explained, hoping she wouldn't laugh at me. She led me to the back of the motor home where two examination tables stood side by side. She pulled down a sheet of white butcher paper over the table and told me to "grabba seat." It sounded to me like she said, "rabbit feet," which I was thinking might be a Southern good-luck expression when you're having a napkin taken out of your ear at a stock-car race.

Sitting on the examination table next to me was a shirtless, over-weight man who had electronic sensor pads hooked up to his chest. His chest was nearly completely covered by a large tattoo of a bald eagle. The bird's wings were fully extended over his saggy male breasts and the bald eagle's feet held a banner reading "God Bless America," the "o" in "God" being the man's navel. The man had an enormous scar that ran down the center of his chest, obviously from a past open-heart surgery. The scar split the eagle in half, making it appear more like a turkey on Thanksgiving. My animal-loving neighbor caught me looking at his tattoo. "Whatcha in for?"

"I got a little something in my ear," I said, trying to downplay it.

"What? A bug?"

"No, it's nothing. What are you in here for?" I asked, trying to divert attention away from my stupidity.

"Ah, it's just precautionary."

"What's precautionary?" I asked.

"Oh, my ticker's just a tad outta whack, it's no big thang."

"Looks like you've been through it before."

"Yep. I been in the zipper club 'bout twelve years now," he proudly stated.

"Yeah, and he's gonna join it again the way he keeps eatin'," said the nurse.

He looked at me and pleaded his case as if he was on the witness stand. "They want me to eat rabbit food and exercise all the dang time. To hell with that. I'm not gonna live my life tryin' to extend it. If I want a cheeseburger and a beer, good golly, I'm gonna have me one, and then when the good Lord calls me home, I'm gonna go."

"That's a good way to look at it," I said.

"My name's Doug, by the way. Should I get off my soapbox yet?"

I introduced myself and told him about my trip—that is, until the nurse returned with a shiny set of over-sized tweezers. "Just relax," she said.

That's the way it always is with doctors and dentists. They bring out the scariest-looking medieval-torture devices imaginable, and then tell you to relax.

"Turn your head to the left," she said and stuck the cold tweezers into my ear so far it felt like she was tapping Morse code on my spinal column. She prodded and pulled and twisted and turned the tips of the tweezers around in my ear until I yelled, "Stop!"

"You've got to relax," she scolded me. "You're too tense."

"Sorry," I said, "but it's not like this is the most natural thing I've ever done."

"Well, if you can't do it this way, we'll have to put you in a straight-jacket."

"What if we just left it in there? Wouldn't it eventually work its way out or disintegrate or something?"

"Well, yes, I guess eventually it would get out of there, but that could take years, which I guess would be okay because you'll probably be deaf and it would give you long enough to learn sign language and read lips."

"Okay, continue," I said, admitting defeat in the napkin-removal debate.

She again started digging into my ear, and I began to squirm.

"I'm gonna break your eardrum if you don't quit squirming around." She then asked for Doug's help, saying, "Tell him about the farworks show you boys are puttin' on tonight."

"Oh, we got a big show tonight. Twelve minutes, thirty-five skyrockets, it's gonna be a helluva good show, long as you unplug me from this damn machine so I can do my job."

"If you don't relax and take it easy, you're gonna end up in the hospital tonight."

"Ah, give me a nitroglycerin and turn me loose."

She slowly pulled on the napkin ball; it felt like she was moving furniture in my head. "I've got it!" She placed the napkin ball in my hand. "Here's your souvenir for a night at the races."

"Thanks," I said. "And thanks for not laughing when I came in. I felt really stupid telling you I had a napkin stuck in my ear."

"Oh, I've seen way stupider things than this," she said in a consoling voice.

"Do I owe you anything?"

"No, but just remember that the only thing you should put in your ears is your elbow."

I nodded and gave her a charity laugh. As I started to leave, Doug asked if I wanted to be "the master switchman."

"What do I have to do?"

"Just push a button. It's a ceremonial job we usually let someone in the crowd do."

"Sure," I said.

Doug was released about thirty minutes later when his blood pressure reached a normal level for someone of his size and condition. Together we walked out of the motor-home hospital to the race track's grassy infield, where his crew was setting up for the fireworks display.

There was a crew of six guys and one woman, who was dressed in camouflage-style military fatigues with her long black hair rolled up into Princess Leia buns on the sides of her head. Doug told the crew, "This guy's gonna be our master switchman."

"We already told this kid he could do it," said another member of the crew, pointing to a ten-year-old Cub Scout with his left arm set in a cast.

"Hey, instead, do you want to shoot some of your dad's ashes up on a skyrocket?" Doug asked with inspiration in his voice.

"That would be great," I said. Doug began looking through his tool-box for a small plastic bag to put some of the ashes in. When he couldn't locate any, he asked the crew if any of them had a sandwich bag, to no avail.

"Put it in this," said GI Princess Leia, as she flung an individually wrapped single condom at us.

"Perfect," said Doug.

"Perfect?" I questioned. "I'm not putting my dad's ashes in a condom."

"It'll be great. It'll explode with the rocket, sending the ashes every which way."

"What if I go back to first aid and see if the nurse has a small bag we can use?"

"There isn't time. We got to get these rockets in sequence and check the timers and ignitions. It's either the condom or nothing," Doug said.

I was stuck with the same feeling I'd had when Dad's ashes blew into that girl's cotton candy in Seattle. At what point does a noble act of respect and love turn disgusting and immoral? Certainly stuffing your father's worldly remains into the reservoir tip of a ribbed and lubricated, glow-in-the-dark condom has to come pretty close to that fine line. The more I thought about it, though, the more I thought Dad would get a laugh out of the situation.

Doug opened the condom wrapper and unfurled the thin latex to the end, and I started dropping pinch after pinch into the condom like I was adding spices to soup. When the condom was a third of the way full, Doug got all the air out of the condom, tied a knot near the top, and taped it to one of the sky rockets in the grand-finale sequence.

After the final race of the night, a collection of John Phillip Sousa patriotic marches began to play, and "boom"—off went the first rocket with a blast that made the noise from the race seem like a day at the library. If I have severe hearing loss as an old man, I'm sure I can trace its origins to this race course.

The rural North Carolina night was illuminated by the fireworks display. The fans "ooooed" and "ahhhed" for every amazing multicolored explosion and cheered loudly for the broken-condom finale as Dad's worldly remains showered the Tarheel crowd. I left the race course that night feeling the kind of complete joy and happiness one only experiences after being excused from jury duty.

The next morning, I headed north on Interstate 95 through Virginia, my last state of the trip. The last drop spot of the trip was an uneventful sprinkling in the bushes of a Stuckey's restaurant where I stopped for lunch in Colonial Heights, Virginia, a little town just north of Petersburg. The final drop seemed so anticlimactic after the fireworks explosion in North Carolina. The experience left me with a hollow feeling, like I was falling back into the "cut every corner" attitude I'd spent almost a year and a half trying to shake. I heard Dad's voice in my head encouraging me as he always had at the end of every school year: "Hit it hard, you're down to the short strokes."

"This is no way to end the trip," I told myself. I had to come up with some finale better than a Stuckey's planter. I stopped at a rest stop with a traveler's information center and perused through countless brochures on burgs: Williamsburg, Fredericksburg, Lynchburg. I read through a pamphlet on Charlottesville, the hometown of the University of Virginia as well as of Thomas Jefferson. I thought that it sounded promising and read on. When I read that James Monroe had had a plantation there called Ash Lawn-Highland, the final drop was set.

I drove on Interstate 64 toward the Blue Ridge Mountains. Thick green trees lined both sides of the highway. I managed to avoid running directly over a large pile of bloody fur and fleshy pulp in the middle of my lane. I couldn't help but think as I looked back in my rearview mirror of the baby birds back in the nest, wondering why Mom has been gone so long.

Just as Interstate 64 crossed over the Rivanna River for the second time, I came upon a beat-up gray Buick with cream-colored Bondo repair marks all over the driver's side door and fender. It looked like the car was being held together exclusively by the Bondo and gum. It had a bumper sticker that read "If you can read this, thank a teacher."

"Thank you, Mrs. Paulsen," I said out loud as I noticed the Charlottesville city-limits sign. A sign pointed me toward Monticello and Ash Lawn. Ten minutes of driving on a curvy country road put me at the home of James Monroe. The house was closed for restoration, but it didn't really matter to me anyway, because all I wanted to do was add some of Dad's ash to the lawn of Ash Lawn, which I did. Still not as exciting as the fireworks drop, but it was much better than a Stuckey's planter.

I could have made it home that night, but it was already late in the afternoon and I had nothing to get home to anyway, so I decided to stay in Charlottesville. The university was on its summer schedule, so the town was fairly quiet. I had dinner at a Cracker Barrel restaurant and a beer at a bar called Bottoms Up, where I sat next to a guy wearing a baseball cap with a picture of an American flag on it that read "These colors don't run."

I left Charlottesville the next morning, and by noon I could see the capitol dome in the hazy distance as I approached Washington, D.C.

I pulled off the beltway and crossed into my hometown of Kensington for the first time in just over fifteen months. Things seemed different. The trees seemed bigger, the town seemed smaller. There was a new Krispy Kreme donut shop in the business center where the pet shop used to be. *If only they would have put that in when Dad was still alive to enjoy it,* I thought.

Even with the changes, Kensington still seemed the same, only now there was a nostalgic quality I never remembered feeling before. Everywhere I looked held a memory: houses where friends had lived, the supermarket where I'd bagged groceries, the public pool where I'd slipped while running on the wet deck and got four stitches on my forehead. This town holds the memories of my youth.

I drove down Johnston Knoll, the sight of our childhood whiffle-ball and football games. The house at 1501 looked the same, only smaller. When I pulled into the driveway, I didn't know whom I'd find living there. I knocked on the door, which in itself is a weird experience—the first time you don't just throw open the door, charge into the house you've lived in for years, and shout, "I'm home!"

My youngest sister Karen had moved her family into our house. She had cleaned out my room, boxed up all of my possessions, and put them up in the garage rafters next to the Christmas decorations. She told me I was welcome to stay there until I found a place of my own. The downside of that invitation was that I'd have to share my former bedroom with my three-year-old nephew, Joey, who called me Uncka Beef.

The next day I started going through two shoeboxes full of mail from Jeff, Charlie Parker, Lonnie, Al, Double V, Greg, and Charles. I figured that by now, somebody was probably walking around downtown Tokyo in my jeans.

Curly Cox's son sent a misspelled note written in purple crayon saying, "Thanks for the ribe." There was an eighth-grade graduation announcement from Port and a wedding/birth announcement from Quincy and Kitty. A postcard with a picture of Big Sur on the front was signed, "Open up those golden gates. Your friend, Wally." A large overstuffed manila envelope came from Teec Nos Pos, Arizona, with an eight-by-ten Gargle-family reunion photo enclosed, with me in the lower-left corner grinning from ear-to-ear like any other Gargle.

There were three payment requests from Liberdad Auto Finance of Miami, the last one stamped "Urgento!" The biggest surprise came in a small, white envelope with a Huntsville, Alabama, postmark and no return address. The envelope was sealed and secured again with short strips of scotch tape on the flap. I opened the envelope to find a well-worn two dollar bill and a dime inside. There was no note, but I had a pretty good feeling that the Atlanta traveler-in-need had settled his debt . . . with interest! A lump came to my throat and my faith in humanity was elevated.

News of the trip spread by word-of-mouth and several people inquired about my services. Would I consider sprinkling their loved one's ashes somewhere, and if so, what were my fees? Since I hadn't finished college and didn't have anything else to do, I took them up on their offers. My company's name is Worldwide Resting Places, just in case you ever need my service.

I remember in high school we had to take a career-aptitude test to determine which career was best suited to our personality and talents. The test determined that my ideal career was as a sod farmer, so I'm pretty happy with the line of work I've fallen into.

In case you're wondering, yes, sprinkling human ashes without a permit is illegal in most places. I have to work "on the QT" as Dad would say. Most of my customers still come by word-of-mouth, and some of the assignments have been every bit as interesting as my trip around the United States.

Recently, an old lady offered me $5,000 plus expenses to sprinkle her husband's ashes into the Basque section of Spain from the summit of the Pyrenees mountains. The job nearly got me and my Portuguese guide killed due to a series of rock slides, inclement weather, and wild animals. I got about the same amount of money to scuba-dive the ashes of an old Navy man back inside the USS *Arizona* in Pearl Harbor to be with his 1,177 shipmates who didn't make it off the ship that infamous Sunday morning in 1941. Although I was successful, I had some explaining to do to the Navy officials who caught me. My latest customer was an eccentric blue-haired socialite from Baltimore who paid me $4,400 to sprinkle the ashes of her French poodle off the Eiffel Tour. I was arrested and sent to a modern day Bastille, and if you think that the French normally stink, try spending three days in lockup with Pepe and Jean-Jacques.

In all, I've sprinkled the ashes of more than fifty people or pets in twenty-eight different countries. Maybe someday I'll be able to write the story of these sprinklings, but right now, business is too good. It seems like nobody wants to be worm food anymore.

# ABOUT THE AUTHOR

In this, his first novel, David Jerome combines travel and comedy writing—two of his passions—into one warm and funny travel-adventure. *Roastbeef's Promise* is loosely based on the author's experiences while visiting the forty-eight contiguous states during the mid-1990s.

Prior to this effort, Jerome had written jokes for Jay Leno on *The Tonight Show*, and performed his own monologue on the ABC late night talk show *Into the Night with Rick Dees*. From 1994 to 1996 he wrote and published a comedy newspaper, *The Irreverent Times*. Under the pen name James E. Spamm Jr., he authored a collection of humorous fan letters to celebrities and other notables, called *I'm A Big Fan*. Mr. Jerome currently resides in Southern California where he is working on a sequel called, *Roastbeef Sprinkles*.

## Hungry for more Roastbeef?

There's more Roastbeef at these sites and pages.

» smackbooks.com

» Myspace/roastbeefspromise.com

» Facebook/roastbeefspromise.com

## Get a free Roastbeef T-shirt

» Blog about *Roastbeef's Promise*. Send us the link and we'll send you a free Roastbeef T-shirt.

» Take your picture holding up your copy of *Roastbeef's Promise* at one of the many locations in the story and send it to us, and we'll put it on our website and send you a free Roastbeef T-shirt.

» Make a YouTube-style video about *Roastbeef's Promise*. Send us the link and we'll send you a free Roastbeef T-shirt.

\* \* \* Send links and photos to: Roastbeef@smackbooks.com \* \* \*